THE SPHERES OF HEAVEN

CHARLES SHEFFIELD

THE SPHERES OF HEAVEN

This is a work of fiction. All the characters and events portrayed in this book are fictional, and any resemblance to real people or incidents is purely coincidental.

A Baen Books Original

Baen Publishing Enterprises
P.O. Box 1403
Riverdale, NY 10471
www.baen.com

ISBN: 0-671-31856-X

Cover art by Bob Eggleton

First paperback printing, January 2002

Library of Congress Cataloging-in-Publication Number 00-049427

Distributed by Simon & Schuster
1230 Avenue of the Americas
New York, NY 10020

Typeset by Brilliant Press
Printed in the United States of America

WEL[illegible]

"Oh my god, [illegible]
a human inside [illegible]

"Is anyone with him?" said Chrissie. "Is he a prisoner?"

"Doesn't look like it. He's coming this way. He's smiling—and he's *waving*. What do we do now?"

"We ought to turn and run. We were told, no risks."

"Hello there," the approaching man called. "Welcome to Limbo."

"You're hurt," Chrissie said. She could see streaks of dried blood running down from his temples and ears, and more blood on his left thigh.

"Oh, that's nothing." He was still grinning, and he dismissed his wounds with one wave of his hand. "I don't need help, and I feel great. This is a wonderful planet. Wonderful people on it, too. Come on, I'll introduce you."

"Wait a minute," Chrissie said. "These people. Are they *people*? Or aliens?"

"They're people, but not exactly like us. But that's all right, because they're better than humans. Far better."

"I don't like the sound of that," Tarbush said. "Did something happen to you, messing up your head? Your ears have been bleeding."

"I've never thought so well and so clearly. Come on. If you're lucky, The One will make you feel the same way."

Tarbush grabbed Chrissie's arm. "Let's get out of here. It was stupid to come this far." Two meters and they would reach the safety of the scrub.

He heard a faint popping from behind, then his brain was boiling. He heard Chrissie scream, and he began his own scream which was never completed. They were unconscious before they hit the ground. . . .

BAEN BOOKS by CHARLES SHEFFIELD:

My Brother's Keeper
The Compleat McAndrew
Convergent Series
Transvergence
The Mind Pool
The Spheres of Heaven
Proteus in the Underworld
Borderlands of Science
The Web Between the Worlds

To Hank and Angie

1

Recruiting on Madworld

Dawn was breaking on Earth, and it could seldom have been more beautiful. The eastern sky wore a gorgeous stippling of salmon-pink and light gray clouds, the perfume of opening blossoms scented an easterly breeze, and soft bird-song filled the air.

Dougal MacDougal stared around him and hated every bit of it.

"Come on, come on," he said to the short, scruffy man standing at his side. "I thought you said you knew the way? Get me out of this stink."

His nose, accustomed to the filtered air of the Ceres habitats, wrinkled in disgust. Every moment that they stood on the surface of Earth, spores and bacteria and unknown filth made their way into his delicate and unprotected lungs. His boots, which five minutes before as they stepped clear of the Link exit point had gleamed bone-white, already bore a thin layer of grime picked up from the ground—the ground, he reminded himself, composed entirely of *dirt* to an unknown depth.

"Yes, sir. Yes, *sir*." Kubo Flammarion did not move. It was a flaming lie; he had never told Dougal MacDougal that he knew the way. All he had admitted, back on Ceres, was that he had been to Earth a few times himself. But that had been twenty and more years ago, and the place had seemed like Madworld even back then. Earth had scared the life out of him, long before the quarantine of Sol had led to the general going-to-hell of everything in the solar system.

On the other hand, they couldn't stand here forever. Flammarion didn't mind dirt; as a man who had spent lonely years out on the Perimeter where personal hygiene was a matter of choice he kind of liked it. But the natives close to the Link exit point were watching them and a few of the shadier specimens were starting to shuffle in their direction. Flammarion knew the sales pitch—he'd once fallen for it himself; but Dougal MacDougal, lordly Ambassador to the Stellar Group, was unlikely to appreciate it.

"This way, sir." Kubo Flammarion hustled MacDougal toward a long covered ramp that led below ground. Behind them, the pitch had started. "Nippers, oughta see nippers. Hottest line on Earth" . . . "Need a Fropper, gentlemen? Get you one easy, real cheap" . . . "Trade crystals, highest rates and no questions asked" . . . "Wanna see an execution? Beheading, first-class Artefact, never know it from the real thing" . . . "Needler lab visit, squire? Top of the line products, won't see 'em any place else."

Flammarion tried to ignore them. With luck, Dougal MacDougal wouldn't be able to understand that confusing babble of poorly pronounced standard solar.

"Right along this way, sir." Flammarion was used to being the shortest person, man or woman, in staff meetings on Ceres. Here he was half a head taller than most people, while Dougal MacDougal, striding along with his nose in the air and a pained expression on his face, towered high above everyone.

The corridor widened steadily as they moved deeper underground. Flammarion scanned the people they passed, most of whom seemed to have nothing at all to do. They were dressed in bright purples, scarlets and pinks, in striking contrast to the pristine Ambassadorial white of Dougal MacDougal or the stark black of Flammarion's Solar Security uniform. They were not what Flammarion wanted. He sought one particular style of dress. He was beginning to wonder how much longer he could pretend that he knew what he was doing when he caught sight of a roly-poly little man with a round, smiling face and a patchwork jacket and trousers of green and gold, lounging against a steel support beam.

Flammarion changed direction and pushed his way through. "You're a busker, right?"

The chubby man grinned. "That I am, squire," he said, in very acceptable solar with only a touch of Earth dialect. "Earl Dexter, at your service. You'll be newcomers here, right?"

"Yes, we are. We need—"

But Dexter, automatically, had moved into his pitch. "So it's a hearty welcome to the Big Marble, sirs. Whatever you want, I can get. Love juice, tipsy pudding, Paradox, worm-diving. You name it. Tiger-hots—"

He stopped abruptly. Dougal MacDougal had reached down and placed one enormous hand on Earl Dexter's collarbone, his fingers curved toward the busker's throat.

"Thank you, Ambassador. That ought to help." Flammarion stepped close to the fat man.

"Slither, Velocil, starbane, jujy rolls," Dexter said half-heartedly.

"None of them. We need a person."

"Ah, a person. Well, I can do that. Only—" The busker hesitated. "Only, like, what are you wanting to *do* with the person? I got girls, see—and boys—who'll go along with most things, but if it's snakes or snuff you're talking about—"

"We need to find a particular man. And the Ambassador here wants to talk to him. And that's enough for you, you don't need to know any more."

"Sure, sure. *Talk* to him, right?" Earl Dexter craned his neck to one side and eased himself clear of Dougal MacDougal's grip. "Do you know where this man is?"

"We know he's on Earth. We know this is the closest Link exit point to where he lives. I know what he looks like, and we have an old address, down in the Gallimaufries—isn't that what you call the basement warrens? And we know his name."

"Then you're home free. If he's in the Gallimaufries and you give me the name, I can find him."

"And bring him here?"

"Don't know about that. But I can take *you* to *him*." Dexter took another step away from Dougal MacDougal. "Of course, a service like this, it's a little bit out of the ordinary. Won't come cheap." He paused, at a growl from Dougal MacDougal, and added weakly, "Extra expenses . . ."

"I'm sorry, sir. I know it's illegal on Ceres, but it's standard practice in these parts. Leave it to me, I'll take care of it." Flammarion had been addressing MacDougal. Now he turned away from the Ambassador and led Earl Dexter a few paces farther along the corridor. There was a muttered conversation and then the dull glow of a trade crystal changing hands, while Dougal MacDougal studiously looked the other way.

"Thank you, squire." Dexter instantly recovered his chirpiness. "And the moniker of the party, if you please, that you want me to find, and his address."

"His name is Chan Dalton," Flammarion began. "His address—"

He paused. Earl Dexter was staring at him, pop-eyed.

"Chan Dalton? You don't need to tell me *his* address. And you mean that you"—he turned toward MacDougal—"that you—your Lordship—your Worship—*you* want to talk to *Chan Dalton*?"

"You know Dalton?" MacDougal was reaching out again toward Dexter. "What about Dalton, why shouldn't I want to talk to him?"

"No reason." Earl Dexter had skipped out of the way, and now he turned and wriggled around a group of noisy newcomers hurrying along the broad corridor.

"No reason at all," he called over his shoulder. "Chan Dalton! Give me an hour to make sure he's there, then I'll be back to take you right to him." He laughed, a high giggling chortle of mirth as he scurried away through the crowd. "You can talk to him as long as you like, and good luck to you."

Kubo Flammarion didn't know what was going on; all he knew, with absolute gloom and certainty, was that so far as the Ambassador was concerned, whatever happened next was going to be Flammarion's fault.

There was no justice in the world. He had done exactly what he had been asked to do. He had guided Dougal MacDougal all the way from Ceres to the correct location on Earth; he had located a busker who knew how to find Chan Dalton; they were even now on their way to meet with the man.

And the reward? MacDougal was glaring at him, for the commission of his numerous sins. What sins? Flammarion had no idea, except that, over twenty years ago, he had met Chan Dalton. Earl Dexter, pressed for information upon his return from the Gallimaufries, might as well have taken a vow of silence. All he would say was that they would be with Chan Dalton soon enough, and they would then have answers to all their questions.

As one small consolation, the Ambassador had become too preoccupied with their upcoming meeting with Dalton to continue his endless complaints about being down on Earth; which was just as well, because Earl Dexter was leading them through a setting which combined every conceivable element of noise, dirt, confusion, and strangeness.

The first part of the journey was a long drop through the black depths of a vertical drop-shaft. Earl Dexter had particularly warned about it, not realizing that to Kubo Flammarion and Dougal MacDougal this would provide a few welcome seconds of comfortable free-fall.

But that was the end of comfort. They had emerged into a series of vaulted chambers of rock where everything felt wrong. Instead of curves, following the natural stress lines of a habitat, every wall was flat as a plate and straight up-and-down. The roof, by contrast, was all random lumps and dimples, broken at intervals by ugly, powerful, and inconstant lights that threw broken reflections onto the jumble of cables, tents, guy ropes, and partitions that cluttered the floor. Above them, ramshackle multilevel platforms hung tipsily between steel pylons, with rope ladders stretching from one to another or hanging down to the ground beneath.

And that floor! Not metal, or plastic, but black granular soil in which blossoming plants grew everywhere, sprouting along zigzag walkways while blood-red vines festooned every column. A flowery perfume filled the air, tainted with a hint of a less pleasant smell.

The human population of the Gallimaufries was as tight-packed as the flowers. There were no wheeled vehicles, and everyone went on foot or was carried on swaying sedan chairs with a bearer at each corner. On these lower levels, gaudy yellow and vermilion was favored in clothing, trimmed with sequins and piped with gold, silver, and chartreuse. The people rivaled the flowers for color. They also, Flammarion realized, made a lot more noise and they smelled less pleasant. Blame the quarantine for that, packing them in ten to a box—except that Earth had been this way, crowded and dirty, long before the big Q.

Dougal MacDougal was sniffing the air and glowering around him. "Inconceivable." He had to shout to be heard above the general racket. "Twenty-three years ago, Dalton returned a hero from the Stellar Group expedition to Travancore. He could pick anywhere in the solar system as his home. And he chooses to live *here*."

"It's where he started," Flammarion replied loudly. "He was born and raised in the Gallimaufries." Then he wished that he had kept his mouth shut. Earl Dexter's behavior suggested that there was much more mystery to Chan Dalton than his choice of residence, and Flammarion didn't want to get into that delicate subject with the Ambassador.

Instead he went on, "Are you sure we are looking for the right man?"

Dougal MacDougal had been conspicuously reticent about revealing to Flammarion just *why* it was so important to find the particular person of Chan Dalton; and as a fishing expedition for information, this latest effort also proved a failure. The Ambassador turned to favor Flammarion with another silent glare, then trudged on behind Earl Dexter. Kubo wheezed his way after them with his head down. Earth's thick air and gravity were killers, no wonder all the people down here were crazy. Much more of this, and he would need one of those sedan chairs himself.

Earl Dexter halted abruptly at a corridor that connected two chambers. "This is it, squire."

"This is *what*?" MacDougal, Flammarion was pleased to see, was wheezing even worse than he was. On Earth, being big and heavy had its drawbacks.

"This is where I leave you," Dexter said. He pointed. "Dalton's right ahead, sitting at the far end. You don't need me any more." He looked at Flammarion and held out his hand. "I did my bit, like I said. So if you wouldn't mind . . ."

"You get the rest when I'm sure it's Dalton, and not before." Flammarion squinted into the dimly lit chamber ahead. "Where is he? I can't see a bloody thing, and there's dozens of 'em."

"You'll know him easy enough. Soon as you get used to the light." Dexter tried to eel away, but Dougal MacDougal caught and held him. "Look, I don't need to go in there. I told him you were coming, I got no business with the Boz."

Kubo Flammarion took no notice. His eyes were adjusting, and he could see a long, darkened room. A score of men and women stood in a line that stretched to a tall, elevated dais at the far end. On the dais was one enormous and flower-bedecked seat, and on that throne sat one man in stiff robes of dark green. He was wearing a ridiculous yellow hat perched like a beehive on top of his head.

Kubo peered, swore, and peered again. One man was walking forward to go down on one knee before the seated figure. After a few seconds of conversation, inaudible to anyone but the two of them, he rose to his feet, bowed, and retreated. He walked right past Flammarion and his companions without even a glance.

The next person in line, a woman in a long dress of pale yellow, stepped forward toward the dais. Kubo pulled a little image cube from his pocket and stared at it.

"It's him!" he hissed. Half a dozen heads at the back of the line turned. Flammarion stared again, to make absolutely sure. The man in the chair was big, solid, and somehow menacing. "He's changed a hell of a lot, bigger and broader, and he looks funny with that hat on. But that man in the chair is Chan Dalton."

"Excellent." MacDougal's growl turned more heads, of everyone except the woman at the front of the line. "We've found him. Now I can do my part."

"I hope you can." Kubo flinched at the Ambassador's glare and went on, "It might not be so easy. See that hat? He's not just Chan Dalton any more. He's a top enforcer for the Duke of Bosny—boss-man of this whole shooting-match. Down here, he doesn't follow the rules. He makes them."

It was a miracle, at least from Flammarion's point of view: Dalton remembered him.

They had to wait until the whole line of supplicants had been attended to before they could approach Chan Dalton. But when they did get near, even before Kubo or Ambassador MacDougal could speak, the man in the chair removed his hat, grinned, and said, "Why, Captain Flammarion. It's been a while."

"It's been over twenty years!" Kubo recalled Chan Dalton as a young Adonis, lithe and slim and golden-haired. The man before him now was thick through the middle and had a scarred, weary face. Had Kubo himself changed as much? "Do you really remember me?"

"Of course I do. You were sent to see me when I was stuck on Horus, out in the Egyptian Cluster. Typical—you were the one they used to dump all the shit on, weren't you, when anything unpleasant had to be done? Things have changed, I hope."

"Well. Maybe." Kubo coughed and glanced uncertainly at Dougal MacDougal. "This is the human Ambassador to the Stellar Group."

"Oh yes?" Chan offered MacDougal a polite, distant stare.

"He has come all the way from Ceres to talk to you."

"That right?" Chan turned back to Flammarion. "He came with you?"

"Yes. No. I mean, I came with him."

"Why does it take two of you? You could have told me why you're here. I would have listened to one of you just as well, and I know you from the old days."

"It's nice to hear that. Very nice. But as a matter of fact . . ." Kubo wasn't sure how to say this. "As a matter of fact, I don't *know* why we're here."

Dougal MacDougal took over. "Captain Flammarion performed the invaluable service of locating you—"

"Not too difficult, I would have thought. I'm known through this whole sector."

"—and guided me here. Mr. Dalton, I cannot overemphasize the importance of this visit, and what I am about to say to you. When the other species of the Stellar Group imposed their quarantine on humans, restricting us to travel at most one lightyear from Sol, humanity began to stifle. Instead of being able to look outward to new frontiers, we have been forced to turn in on ourselves. We are beginning to choke and suffocate, to weaken our resolve, to lose our drive."

"You don't have to tell me that. Earth has felt the effects more than anybody."

"But Earth people are used to living in a static world, a sluggish backwater where opportunities are small and progress is minimal."

Kubo Flammarion avoided looking at Dalton. If the Ambassador were seeking favors, he was going about it the hard way.

MacDougal continued, "So when there is a chance, no matter how small a chance, of changing our status and removing the quarantine, nothing in the solar system can have a higher priority. Such a chance now exists! Next week, at their request, an Assembly of the Stellar Group is planned to take place in the Ceres Star Chamber. There will be representatives of the Tinkers of Mercantor, the Pipe-Rillas of Eta Cassiopeiae, and the Angels of Sellora. All the known intelligent species!"

"Except for humans. Are we being invited?"

"We are. The Stellar Group requires that our representative be present, otherwise the Assembly will not occur."

"That's you, isn't it? You are the human Ambassador to the Stellar Group."

"I am the Ambassador. That is quite true." Dougal MacDougal stood up straighter, but at the same time he seemed to Flammarion to have mysteriously shrunk a few inches. "However, this will be an exception to the usual rules for Assembly. Although I will be permitted to be present—as an observer—the Stellar Group insists that a different human be present as a participant. They inform us, very specifically, that Chan Dalton—you—have to be that human."

"Do they indeed." Dalton sat up higher in his raised chair and became very much a top advisor to the Duke of Bosny: cold and thoughtful, with an unreadable look in his eye. "The Stellar Group wants me to leave the Gallimaufries and travel out to Ceres. Very interesting. But pardon me, Ambassador, if I say I find that hard to believe. On the other hand, I can very easily believe that there are acquaintances of mine—I won't go so far as to call them enemies—who for a variety of reasons might want me away from Earth for a while."

MacDougal's face reddened. "I know nothing of such things, or such people. I am telling you only that the members of the Stellar Group demand your presence. And they have hinted that this might have some bearing on the present quarantine of humanity."

"Fine. So tell me this: *Why* do they want me, and only me? What do they want me *for*?"

"Well . . ." Dougal MacDougal stood woodenly to attention.

Looking up at that tall figure, Kubo Flammarion felt his first moment of sympathy for the man. There was a good reason why the Ambassador had not taken Flammarion into his confidence concerning the reason for bringing Chan Dalton to Ceres.

The Ambassador didn't *know* the reason, any more than Flammarion himself did. The need for Chan Dalton, and Chan Dalton alone, was apparently a mystery to every human.

2

An invitation from the Stellar Group

With the Link return to Ceres closing in an hour, Kubo Flammarion had time for only a few private minutes with Chan Dalton before he had to guide Dougal MacDougal back to the surface.

"You could fight it, you know." Kubo gestured around him. "I mean, with all this going for you and the Duke to help you, you could say no and I bet we'd never get you out of here. Why did you say yes?"

In the hours since they arrived at the Duke of Bosny's court in the depths of the Gallimaufries—that's what it felt like, a court, even if it wasn't called that—Kubo had been mightily impressed. The way Dalton gave orders, casually; the way everyone nodded and scurried off to obey; the way they all cringed and kowtowed and *groveled*; no one on Ceres, or anywhere away from Earth, had so much power and control.

The change, he suspected, was not in the inhabitants of the Gallimaufries. It was in Chan Dalton. Kubo remembered Chan as an innocent and compliant youth. Now he was a cool, calculating adult, whose battered face said he had seen everything and did only what he wanted to.

"I don't know why you agreed," Kubo went on, when Chan stared at him silently. "I mean, the aliens . . ."

"You don't like them, do you?"

"Forget the 'like' bit. They give me the willies. Especially the Angels. I mean, they're not just aliens. They're not even *animals*. Why did you agree to meet with 'em?"

Dalton, Flammarion was pleased to see, did not go into the old "I do it for the good of humanity" speech. He had an odd little frown on his scarred face, of mixed puzzlement and annoyance.

"Fair question, Captain," he said. "I don't think I have a choice, but that's not an acceptable answer. Or I could say it's curiosity, and it's certainly partly that. This will be the first Stellar Group Assembly with full human participation since the quarantine. It must mean the aliens want something from us. But what? Will they really end the quarantine if we help them? I'm as keen as the next person to find the answer. If I'm honest, though, there's a bigger and a worse reason: vanity. The aliens don't just want to meet with humans. They want to meet with *me*, Chan Dalton. I used to be nothing. How can a man resist that?"

Flammarion shivered. "I'll tell you one man who'd have no trouble resisting. Those creepy Angels, and the Tinkers aren't much better, crawling all over everything." He turned his head. Dougal MacDougal was calling from outside the chamber. "Got to go."

"Expect me tomorrow, Captain. I need tonight to wrap a few things up down here."

"Good luck. I don't expect I'll see you again before the Assembly."

When the Assembly convened in the Ceres Star Chamber, Kubo Flammarion wanted to be as far away as possible. A quick Link to the Dry Tortugas, maybe, out at the remote edge of the solar system and as distant from Sol as humans were allowed to go under the quarantine; that felt just about right.

So why, two days later, was he sitting here on Ceres, hidden away where he could see and hear whatever happened during the Stellar Group Assembly? Why had he cajoled and coaxed Milly, who handled the monitors that recorded for posterity every element of the meeting, into letting him sit next to her in the control booth?

Chan Dalton had put his finger on it: the same reason the monkey put his hand in the jar, the same reason the cat sniffed the high-voltage wire. It was curiosity, stupid curiosity. What *did* the aliens want? But now, with the Assembly just minutes away, Flammarion decided that he didn't much care. He could feel his insides curdling within him—even though he was a hundred meters from the Star Chamber, even though the aliens themselves would be no more than three-dimensional images, linked in from their homeworlds lightyears away.

"Milly," he whispered. "I don't feel so good . . ."

Milly Grant turned to give him the glare of a woman handling an important task. "I told you, if you want to be in here you have to keep quiet." She gestured to the blank monitors. "I've got work to do."

"I'm sorry. I was just wondering how long we have before it starts. I was thinking maybe I might go to the bathroom and—"

"It's starting now, you wasted imbecile. Are you blind as well as ignorant? Use your eyes!"

And now he could see it. The monitors provided a clear view of one hemisphere of the Star Chamber's central atrium. The front of the room was empty, except for Chan Dalton slumped black-clad and scowling in an easy chair. Dougal MacDougal sat far off to the rear, on the observers' bench. Now three oval patterns of light were flickering into existence close to Dalton. The lights gradually solidified to become three-dimensional images of the Stellar Group Ambassadors.

On the far left hung a shrouded, pulsing mass of dark purple. As the image steadied, the shape became the swarming aggregate of a Tinker Composite, imaging in from Mercantor in the Fomalhaut system. The Tinkers had clustered to form a symmetrical ovoid with appendages of roughly human proportions. Next to the Tinker Composite, still showing the margin of rainbow fringes that marked signal transients, hovered the lanky tubular assembly of a Pipe-Rilla. It was linking in from its home planet around Eta Cassiopeiae, a mere eighteen lightyears away. And far off to the right, beyond a vacant spot in the Assembly (but fifty-plus lightyears away in real space, halfway across the domain of the Stellar Group) loomed the dark green bulk of an Angel.

That was the one that made Flammarion shiver in his boots and wish he was somewhere else, as it acknowledged its arrival with a wave of the blue-green fronds at its top end. An Angel wasn't an animal, it wasn't a vegetable; it wasn't *anything* that Flammarion could relate to. It was some weird symbiotic life-form, discovered a century and a half earlier when the expanding wave-front of human exploration reached the star Capella and the planets around it. The visible part of the Angel was the Chassel-Rose, slow-moving, mindless, and wholly vegetable. Shielded within the bulbous central section lived the sentient crystalline Singer, relying upon the Chassel-Rose for habitat, movement, and communication with the external world. The Angels, depending on the situation, were either very stupid or super-smart in ways that humans could hardly comprehend.

MATTIN LINK NETWORK COMPLETE, said the voice of the computer at Milly Grant's side. THE CONFERENCE MAY NOW PROCEED.

"Present," the Pipe-Rilla said. It was a fourteen-foot nightmare rearing high on its stick-thin legs. The forelimbs clutched the tubular trunk, and the long antennas were waving.

"Present." The whistling voice of the Tinker Composite appeared from deep within it, accompanied by a flutter of purple wings of its thumb-sized components.

"Present," said Chan Dalton. "Ambassador MacDougal is also in the Star Chamber with me."

"As an observer," the Angel added firmly, "not as a participant. There can be only one participant from each member of the Stellar Group. Is that understood? *Too many cooks spoil the broth.*"

Flammarion grunted and said to Milly, "Still at it! Don't you *hate* it when they do that?"

The Angels had an annoying habit of using human cliches and proverbs at every opportunity. No one was sure if it was the symbiotes' sense of humor, or some perverse notion of species politeness.

In any case, Chan Dalton was used to it. He nodded. "We understand. I will be the only human participant."

"Then all are present," the Angel said. "We can proceed."

There was a silence, long enough for Flammarion to wonder if Milly had lost sound from the monitors. Finally the Pipe-Rilla writhed its limbs, produced a preliminary buzzing sound, and said, "Twenty of your years ago, the members of the Stellar Group were obliged to take an action that we much regretted. Humans, a known intelligent species, were denied access to all Link entry points except those close to your own sun. This quarantine was not imposed lightly, or for no good reason. It was done following more than thirty incidents in which ships with human crews undertook acts of piracy and aggression. Acts of trickery. Of treachery. Of *violence*."

On the final word, the voice of the Pipe-Rilla rose in pitch, while surface components rose from the Tinker Composite and flew in an agitated fashion around it.

The Pipe-Rilla's narrow thorax leaned forward. "Chan Dalton, we do not accuse you, personally, of such things. Your actions when you worked with our colleagues, so long ago on Travancore, showed you to be a simple, honorable being."

Flammarion glanced at Milly. "Twenty years ago, maybe. Look at him now."

Chan was nodding at the Pipe-Rilla. His weary and battered face wore an expression of cynical amusement. "Nice of you to say kind things like that."

The Pipe-Rilla went on, "However, a species must take responsibility for the actions of *all* of its members. When humans showed no inclination to deal with the problem, we—Pipe-Rillas, Tinkers, and Angels—were obliged to act for you. We closed the interstellar Link system to human access."

"Yeah. We noticed."

Sarcasm was lost on the Pipe-Rilla. She continued, "Of course, the Link closure was never intended to be permanent. We would continue to observe, and look for beneficial change in human behavior."

"And you've seen it?" Chan's face now showed genuine surprise.

"Regrettably, no. Such a modification has not, so far, occurred. However, a new factor has recently entered the picture. It could lead to the end of the quarantine. What do you know about the region of space known as the Geyser Swirl?"

"Not a thing. Never heard of it."

Dougal MacDougal sat upright on the observers' bench. "If I may say—"

"You may not." The Angel's deep voice cut him off. "Remain silent, or leave."

The Pipe-Rilla went on, uncertainly, "The Geyser Swirl is an ultradense gas cloud and associated embedded stars that lie on the Perimeter of the Angel section of the Stellar Group. Until recently, it was believed to be uninhabitable, unremarkable, and of no special interest. However, one year ago we discovered evidence of a Link entry point within the Swirl. This was surprising, and most puzzling. The Link is certainly not of our creation, nor is it under our control. Neither is it a Link of natural origin, which would have been discovered during the first survey of the Swirl.

"Our curiosity at such an anomaly was aroused. It has been our experience that the most valuable discoveries are often associated with the strangest events. We dispatched an exploration team of Tinkers and a Pipe-Rilla to the Swirl using the new Link, and we had no thought of danger. Why should we, since Link access has always been perfectly safe? When the team failed to return on schedule, we thought there had perhaps been an equipment failure. We sent a second team, this time with an Angel as captain and crew."

"And it didn't come back?" Chan Dalton had lost his slouch.

"That is correct. How did you know that? It did not return. Neither expedition has returned. A single equipment failure is unlikely but possible. Two such, in immediate succession, represent a vanishingly small p-probability." The Pipe-Rilla was beginning to stammer. "B-but what other options are there?"

"Something—or somebody—in the Geyser Swirl doesn't like company. They're knocking off your expeditions as fast as they arrive."

"That is our f-fear. B-but how do we d-determine if that is true?"

"Easy enough. You send a third team. If it doesn't come back, you'll know for sure."

"Regarding a third team—" began Dougal MacDougal, but he was drowned out by the Pipe-Rilla, screaming a reply.

"*Y-yes.* A third t-team. But that would m-mean s-s-sending s-s-s-someone t-to almost s-s-s-sure d-d-d-d-d." The Pipe-Rilla's speech degenerated into a series of sputtering noises. The Tinker Composite broke into a myriad small components that darted frantically around the imaging volume.

"It is difficult to speak of such things," the Angel said slowly. "Impossible for a Pipe-Rilla or a Tinker, and possible for me only because I am able for brief periods to operate in human simulation mode. You know the prime rule of the Stellar Group: *Intelligent life must be preserved. It cannot be destroyed—ever.* But we suspect that it is being destroyed in the Geyser Swirl. The Swirl is *dangerous.*"

"Sounds like it. But you won't be sure of that unless somebody goes there again and takes a look."

"Yes indeed. *It is a capital mistake to theorize before one has data*. Therefore let me, quickly, attempt to say the rest of this. We concur with your suggestion. We should send a third expedition, to learn the fate of the first two and if possible rescue them. But that might mean our sending intelligent life, knowingly, to its death in the Geyser Swirl."

"Can't be helped. That's what you have to do."

"But, Chan Dalton, that is what we are *unable* to do."

"Then you got problems."

"Problems indeed. And, as we see it, only one possible solution. Humans. You do not have the same attitude toward the preservation of life—even of your own lives—as other Stellar Group members. An expedition to the Geyser Swirl, headed by a human whom we already know and trust, a human who is willing to do whatever is necessary to learn the fate of the earlier teams, and if possible bring them home . . ."

The Tinker Composite had vanished from the Star Chamber. Its components, mindless as individuals, had dispersed and flown out of the imaging volume. The Pipe-Rilla was still present, but it had bent forward and curled its body until the narrow head was almost on the floor.

"Let's see if I have this right." Chan Dalton stood up. "You want me to leave the nice, cushy job I have back on Earth and fly a team out to the Geyser Swirl in the ass end of the known universe, where chances are I'll get knocked on the head the second I come out of the Link exit. I'm supposed to bring the other two teams back, dead or alive. Suppose I say yes—and I'm not saying that I will. What's in it for me?"

"If you undertake this task, we, the members of the Stellar Group, are ready to lift the quarantine on humans. Naturally, it will be for a trial period, while we again evaluate human behavior. But this time we will recognize, as we are recognizing now, that certain tasks cannot be performed without the assistance of humans."

"Very nice—for humans. You haven't said what's in it for *me*, but we'll worry about that later. So I go off to the Swirl, and when I'm there things get kind of nasty. I have to kill off a few aliens before there's any chance of coming home. Are you saying that will be all right?"

"No!" The blue-green fronds on the Angel's upper body were thrashing in agitation, while the recumbent Pipe-Rilla in the next imaging volume uttered a continuous spluttering moan. "You refer to the killing of other intelligent beings! Of course it is not all right! It is absolutely forbidden. *Violence is never the only solution*. The rules of conduct of civilized beings must not be violated."

The Angel turned slowly, from right to left. "It appears that the other representatives are no longer able to participate in this meeting. What is your decision?"

"No decision. I have to think about it."

"Then think about it well, Chan Dalton, and with all possible speed. We will return, one of your days from now, to learn your answer."

The Angel became a prismatic blur of colors. The Link was closing.

And that was probably just as well. Chan Dalton happened to be looking right at the monitor as he moved toward the front of the chamber, and his muttered words came through clearly to Flammarion and Milly Grant.

"Crazy. What do they think I am, some kind of human sacrifice putting my butt on the line for nothing? I'm out of here."

But he could not leave. Dougal MacDougal stood right in his path. "Ah, Chan Dalton." MacDougal took him by the arm, then released him when he saw Chan's glare. "That was most interesting, and most promising. They are ready to end the quarantine!"

"I agreed to nothing."

"Ah, but I know you will make the right decision—for the good of humanity. However, there are one or two points that we urgently need to discuss before the Stellar Group returns tomorrow."

The Ambassador had a most odd expression on his face. Flammarion would have said it was embarrassment, had he been able to think of any reason for such a look. He said urgently to Milly, "Don't turn off the monitor!"

"Of course I won't." She sniffed. "And don't you try to teach me my business, Flammarion. I've been doing this for years, and I know how to read MacDougal. When he gets that pie-faced look something peculiar is on the way. Sit tight, keep quiet, and maybe you'll learn something."

"Something to eat? Something to drink?"

The Ambassador was over by the Star Chamber's service machine, fiddling nervously with the controls.

"Nothing." Chan sat with arms folded and knees together. "Cut the crap, MacDougal. You knew, didn't you?"

"About the ending of the quarantine? I swear, it was a total surprise—"

"About the Geyser Swirl. I'd never heard of the place, but you had. I could see your face in the little monitor on my seat, and when they said that their expeditions hadn't come back, you nodded."

"I knew about their expeditions, but that wasn't what had me worried. It was what else I knew."

MacDougal moved to sit across from Chan. He had a gigantic drink in his left hand and placed another just as big on the table next to him. "Cheers." He raised the glass he was holding and took a long draft. "God, I needed that. I had no idea they were going to talk about the Swirl, and when they did I was more afraid of what they might *know* than what they might tell us. Look, Dalton, you've not been off Earth for a long time. You know they closed all the remote Links so we can't use them?"

"Of course I do. If it weren't for that I wouldn't be down on Earth. I'd be out where the action is—where it used to be, near the Perimeter."

"Then you should have some idea how frustrating it has been for me; Ambassador to the Stellar Group, and I can't even *visit* another star or a planet outside the solar system. It's been twenty years. We keep on testing, living in hopes that we might find a Link open. Nothing. The Stellar Group has some sort of general Link inhibitor that closes down everything for human ships. Or it did. About seven months ago, we picked up a signal from a new Link. You can guess where."

"In the Geyser Swirl."

"Right. The Swirl is at the edge of Angel territory, and we knew next to nothing about it. As the Angel said, it just seems like an uninteresting clot of dust, a few lightyears across, with no Sol-type stars. Why put a Link there? The answer was, nobody did. So humans never felt a reason to go there when we had Link access. When we picked up the signs of a new Link, we thought the Angels must have opened it. We did our usual tests, expecting the usual "denied access" message. But we didn't get that. The return signal said the Link was open to our ships."

"So why didn't you go there?"

"That's what I'm trying to tell you. We did! We sent the *Mood Indigo*, a small exploration vessel with a crew of three, through an outward Link near the Vulcan Nexus with destination the Geyser Swirl Link."

"And it never came back."

"Exactly. Of course, it could not be an *official* expedition. We hired a highly competent and experienced private team, whose members realized that we would deny any connection if the Stellar Group ever found out what had happened and started asking questions. But that meant we couldn't ask the Stellar Group for help if the *Mood Indigo* got into trouble. The ship is long overdue, and we assume that everyone on board is dead. So you see, there have actually been *three* test cases, the way that you wanted. And it's worse than you think. If the *Mood Indigo* had problems, it was equipped with a recorder that should have fired back through the Link automatically. Even if the rest of the ship were destroyed, the recorder ought to come home. It didn't. That means the ship must be a dead and derelict hulk, totally shattered. Somebody in the Geyser Swirl is catching Stellar Group ships and disintegrating them before they can return through the Link."

"Marvelous. And you think I'm keen to charge off to the Swirl, after hearing all that? One of us is crazy."

"You've had experience in other stellar systems. We would give you the toughest ship and the best crew that you could ask for. And it's obvious that this time the other Stellar Group members will do everything they can to help."

"Everything, except let us defend ourselves if some crazy alien comes screaming in to kill us. Then I guess we just lie down and roll over. Ambassador, it isn't just no. It's *no way*. Unless certain other conditions are met."

"There's more." MacDougal gestured to the other glass. "Here. Drink that. You're going to need it."

"Why? What else didn't you bother to tell me before the Star Chamber meeting?"

"Not a thing. I told you everything I knew then. But now that the meeting is over, I'll tell you one other thing." Dougal MacDougal leaned closer to Chan. "I'm an Ambassador. With only the two of us here, I'm willing to say I'm *just* an Ambassador. Lots of robes and uniforms and ceremonies, but I'm not one of the real power brokers in the solar system. Now, the Stellar Group is offering to *end the quarantine*. To open up the universe. Do you have any idea how much that means to groups like Unimine, or Foodlines, or Infotech?"

"I can guess."

"I don't think you can. The Stellar Group can't stand violence, but some of the corporate boys seem to thrive on it. You tell *them* you won't cooperate to end the quarantine. You tell *them* you want to go back to Earth. You'll go back to Earth all right—without a Link, and without a rocket. You'll do a solo reentry with or without a space suit and return home as a puff of dust."

Chan reached out and picked up the glass from the table. He drank long and deep, then said, "Now you're giving me the sort of logic I understand. I agree to go, or they skin me alive."

"If they're feeling in a kind mood. You're going, then?"

"I still need to think about it."

"Then you're not as smart as I thought you were."

"Or I'm smarter. There's something else. You sat in the meeting. Let me tell you something *you* didn't notice."

"I watched everything."

"But you didn't catch this, or you'd have said something about it already. You tell me the other Stellar Group members will do everything they can to help. But I'm not sure of that. They sent two expeditions to the Geyser Swirl, right?"

"That's what they told us."

"And I feel sure they were telling the truth. But why? Why *two* expeditions?"

"Obviously, because the first one didn't come back."

"That's obvious to you, and obvious to me. But you know the Pipe-Rillas and the Tinkers and the Angels. They're not risk takers. It must have been hard work persuading *one* team of theirs to head into unknown territory like the Geyser Swirl. And then they persuaded a second one to go?"

"Apparently they did. They do not lie."

"Think about that second ship. The Stellar Group members are born cowards. They wouldn't go for the love of exploration, or for scientific curiosity." Chan shook his head. "For that, they'd send unmanned probes. I don't have proof of this, but I'll tell you what I think. I think that the Stellar Group believes something enormously valuable may be hidden in the Geyser Swirl. So valuable, they were willing to send one expedition, and then another when that one didn't come back. Think of it, a whole new Link—think where it might take you, think what you might find there." Chan raised his glass and emptied it in one long swallow. "How keen are they to learn what happened in the Geyser Swirl? I don't know. But we'll get some idea—when we hear their response to my own conditions before I'll say yes."

3

Aboard the *Mood Indigo*

The Terran exploration ship *Mood Indigo* was not the dead, derelict hulk described by Dougal MacDougal. It carried a crew of three: owner and captain Friday Indigo, chief engineer and astrogator Bony Rombelle, and general factotum Liddy Morse.

They were certainly alive; but what they were, more than anything, was confused. They had entered a Link near the Vulcan Nexus, so close to Sol that the sun's flaming surface filled more than thirty degrees of the sky. Their destination was set as the Geyser Swirl. They expected to emerge in open space, at a location about as close to a star, planet or dust cloud as their departure Link was close to Sol. What should not happen—what the Link system should not *permit* to happen—was an arrival at a place where something was already there. The Link navigator would detect the presence of matter, and abort the transfer.

So much for theory.

Bony Rombelle stared out of the port at an expanse of cloudy green that faded off into the distance without discernible features. According to his instruments, the ship was in a weak gravity field and gently descending.

"Rombelle!" That was Friday Indigo's harsh voice, crackling through from the cabin. "I show us clear of the Link exit. Report our location and status."

Obviously, the captain was focused on the controls and not looking outside.

"All internal ship readings are normal, sir." Bony peered again through the port, looking downward. "However, sir, we appear to be under water."

"What! Liddy, keep an eye on things in here." Friday Indigo popped out of the interior cabin. He was mousy-looking and short, something he tried to hide with exotic, expensive clothes and elevator heels. He stared at the port with bulging eyes, beneath eyebrows that ran straight across with no break. "My God. How did we get here?"

"I have no idea. But we're descending, and I can't see the bottom." Bony glanced at his dials. "No problem so far, the hull can stand four or five atmospheres. We're not a submarine, though. If we sink too deep . . ."

"We'll be flattened. How about the drive?"

It sounded logical, but it made Bony shudder. His supposed training in science and engineering was mostly his own invention, but he knew he was smart and he did have a feel for what you could and could not do. Flying a spaceship underwater was definitely in the latter category.

"Not the fusion drive, sir, that's right out. I could probably fix the auxiliary ion thrusters to work in water—if it is water—but not without going outside to make a few changes."

"Then go outside. I assume you can?"

"Go outside, yes. And the suits will work there, no problem. It's coming back in that's the hard part. The airlock would be full of water, and we'd need to raise the air pressure high enough to force the water out."

Bony thought about it. "I believe we can do that, given time. But we don't have time. If we keep going down at the rate we are, we have only a few more minutes before the hull collapses."

Friday glared accusingly at Bony, as though the whole problem was the fault of his engineer. "Then hold tight. I'm going to start the drive, and the hell with it."

He headed for the control cabin, leaving Bony with a familiar sensation. *Out of the frying pan, into the—what?* Bony had signed on with Friday and the *Mood Indigo* near the solar hotspot known as the Vulcan Nexus. He had done that to escape a difficult situation back in the solar system. Now he was facing a worse one.

He stared warily at the cloudy green beyond the port. What happened if you tried to light a fusion torch under water? Bony's knowledge of nuclear physics was sketchy, but surely there was a good chance that you would initiate a fusion reaction within the water itself, annihilating everything in one giant explosion. *Was* it water out there? That seemed logical, but the Geyser Swirl was a very strange place and they didn't have proof. Given a few minutes, Bony could take a sample from outside, make a few tests, and prove that it was water. But he did not have a few minutes.

Loud cursing came from the inner cabin. "Rombelle! Get your fat ass in here right now. The fusion drive doesn't work!"

Thank God. Drowning, maybe, but no instant

incineration. Bony stood up to walk the few steps through to the control cabin. Then he paused. Looking down, he could see that outside the port there was no longer a featureless cloud. Below the ship was a forest of spears, their points stretching upward. The *Mood Indigo* was dropping straight down onto them.

"Hold tight! We're going to hit bottom." Bony followed his own advice and grabbed for the back of a seat, but the warning was a little too late. Amidst a crystalline tinkling sound like fairy bells—it came from right outside and underneath the ship—they smacked into the seabed.

Bony held his breath and waited. This might be *it*, the end of everything. A space pinnace like the *Mood Indigo* was designed to withstand certain stresses encountered during travel in space. It was not intended to bear the forces that came from contact with an array of sharp, up-pointed spears, at some unknown depth in some unknown ocean.

The hull flexed and groaned like an old man in pain. The cabin floor trembled and tilted. The port next to Bony, normally flat, bowed in a little under the pressure. And, from the control cabin, the voice of Friday Indigo came again. "Rombelle! You fat-ass idiot, what are you playing at out there? I've lost sensor readouts. Get in here!"

Business as usual. If Friday was yelling, they must still be alive.

Bony took the few steps through to the inner cabin. He couldn't say he hadn't been warned. *Never get involved in a venture with a man who inherited his money and didn't earn any himself. He'll assume he's smarter than you are, just because he's rich and you're not, and he'll expect you to bow down to his greatness because for all his life people have.* Bony had known Indigo for less than a week, but the man fitted the rich-man model to perfection. Friday Indigo; descendant of one of the original heirs to the Yang diamond; only son of a Kuiper Belt developer who was killed by a Persephone tunnel cave-in; self-proclaimed entrepreneur, space expert, and daring explorer.

And a bombastic, domineering little turd who never did a day's work in his life and blames other people for everything that ever goes wrong. Liddy, how can you share a bed with him?

Bony muttered that under his breath; then he popped his head into the control cabin. "Yes, Captain?"

Friday Indigo waved his hand at the display. "What have you done to those sensors?"

Bony glanced at the screen. "The ones you are pointing to are located at the rear of the ship. We came down tail-first, so I assume they were crushed when we hit the bottom of the sea."

"Well, do whatever needs doing to get them working again. I can't fly this ship when it's blind."

Or when you can see. You brought us here, wherever here is. "Yes, sir. It may take a while. First, I need to learn what the environment outside the ship is like."

"What are you talking about, what it's *like*. You can see it, can't you?"

"I need to know how deep we are. What the external pressure is. What the seabed is made of. If it's water out there, or something else."

"Of course it's water. What else could it be? Don't waste time on pointless tests. And you, my girl." Friday rounded on Liddy Morse. "Go with him, try to be useful for a change. Expand your repertoire, do something different from the usual."

He patted her rump in a proprietary way. Liddy gave Friday Indigo a look which to Bony's outraged eye combined equal parts of resignation and discomfort, but she followed Bony down a short ladder toward the rear part of the ship.

"And while you're at it," Friday called after them, "find out where we are."

That's right, Bony thought. Save the hardest question for last.

He moved downward carefully, measuring the pressure on his foot at each step. At the bottom he turned. "Try and estimate as you put your feet down, Liddy. How much would you say you weigh?"

He watched her descent and cursed his own cravings for food. Liddy was so slim and graceful, she made him feel as fat and clumsy as an elephant. She stepped easily all the way down and paused at the bottom for a moment to think.

"A lot less than on Earth. I was only on Mars once, but I think I weigh less than there, too. Maybe half of that—about the same as on the Moon or Ganymede."

"That's my guess, too. About one-sixth of Earth gravity."

"Does that tell you anything?"

"Nothing useful." He grinned at her, and was delighted when Liddy smiled back. She was a different person when she was not around Friday Indigo. He wondered, not for the first time, how a delicate and sensitive young woman like her came to be on board a dangerous expedition to nowhere.

And, thinking of nowhere . . . "I have no idea where we are, but the low gravity may be the reason we are alive. Water pressure at depth is a lot less here, so the ship's hull can stand the force. Let's see what else we can find out."

Time to show off in front of Liddy. And it wouldn't be easy. Everything about the *Mood Indigo*, inside and out, had been designed for a vacuum environment. Bony had to make things work on the ocean bed.

He went to the tailmost port on the ship and took another look outside. The array of spears had shattered under the impact and lay in pieces beyond the hull. Visual inspection suggested fragile, crystalline structures. Just as well, or the hull of the *Mood Indigo* might have been damaged by them.

If the liquid outside was water, they couldn't be too deep. Bony could make out no shadows, but he had a definite impression that he was seeing by light that streamed in from above.

Was it sunlight from some local star in the Geyser Swirl, diffusing down through the liquid and slowly being scattered and absorbed as it came to greater depths? Probably. But Friday Indigo would say, rightly, that guesswork was not proof. They needed to find a way to get outside and float up to the surface. But before that, they must have samples. Suppose it was acid out there, acid that was even now eating its way through the ship's hull?

Bringing a sample into the *Mood Indigo* was much easier than taking a person out of it. The liquid, whatever it was, would have filled the little cylinders of the fusion drive normally exposed to open space. He could isolate one of those and retract it without leaving the ship.

"Keep well back, Liddy. This may splash. I expect that it's water, but I'm not sure."

It was another test of a sort. When he opened one end of the cylinder's chamber to allow it to come into the ship, it would be forced in by whatever pressure existed at the other end. Bony placed his left palm in the way, preparing himself for the idea that the cylinder could possibly shoot out hard enough to break the bones of his hand.

Bony opened the valve. The cylinder, its flat end about two inches across, shot backward and smacked into his open palm. It didn't hurt. The pressure outside couldn't be much more than a standard atmosphere. That corresponded to a thirty-foot column of water, back on Earth; which meant that the liquid outside, assuming it *was* water under a sixth of a gravity, couldn't be more than a hundred and eighty feet deep. Once in suits and outside the ship, they could easily float up to the surface.

In spite of his warning, Liddy had stood too close. As the cylinder came backward, liquid splashed out of it onto her hand.

"Don't touch it!" Bony cried, but he was too late. Liddy had already bent her head and touched her tongue to the wet spot. Now she was standing absolutely still. Bony added, "Don't drink any," but she smiled at him.

"It's all right. I might as well be useful for something, even if Captain Indigo doesn't believe I can be." She licked her lips and frowned in concentration. "It's water. Not pure water, though. It tastes a little bit strange and salty. And it's *fizzy* on my tongue."

If she could risk it, so could he. Bony raised the cylinder and licked a few drops from the end. As Liddy had said, it was salty, but less salty than water from Earth's oceans. You could drink this if you had to. And it was carbonated, though the touch on his tongue was not quite the same as the carbon dioxide normally used in making fizzy water.

He poured more of the liquid from the cylinder into a triangular beaker and held it up to the light. It was quite clear; although of course, that didn't mean for a moment that the sample was free of microorganisms. Possibly he and Liddy had already allowed lethal alien bacteria into their bodies. The chances, though, were very much against it. Experience all through the Stellar Group showed that alien organisms were just *too* alien to find a human body an acceptable host.

Bony went across to the miscellaneous equipment cabinet and rummaged around inside. After a couple of minutes he found what he was looking for and pulled out a graduated measuring cylinder and a spring balance.

"What are those for?" Liddy said at last.

Bony smiled. He had been waiting for her to ask. "Tasting and guessing isn't the best way to do scientific testing. We *think* it's water—in fact, I'm almost sure it's water—but we have to do a real test. This tube holds fifty milliliters." He held up the measuring cylinder. "So first I weigh it on the spring balance. Then if I filled it with water and weighed it again, back on Earth that would weigh fifty grams more on the spring balance."

"But we're not on Earth."

"I know. So we don't know how much fifty milliliters of water weighs here. But we don't need to know that, to test that it's water. First, we weigh the empty measurer." He hung it on the spring balance and held it up to Liddy. "You note where the pointer is. Now we take some regular water, water that we brought with us." Bony went across to a small faucet set into the side wall and filled the measuring cylinder to the fifty-milliliter mark. He hung it on the spring balance and pointed to the new level of the pointer. "See, now we know how much ordinary water weighs here."

He looked for a place to pour the measure of water that he was holding, and after a moment tilted it up and drank it.

"All that's left to do," he went on, "is pour some of the water we collected from outside, and fill the measurer to the same level." Bony did that carefully, his eye on the marks on the side of the measuring cylinder. "And now, you see, because the balance is weighed down to the same place as it was with the water we brought with us, we know that . . ." His voice faded away.

"But it *isn't* at the same place on the balance," Liddy said. She gazed at him with dark, wide-open eyes. "It's pulled down quite a bit farther. That means it weighs more, doesn't it?"

"It weighs more." Bony was staring in disbelief at the balance. "Nearly fifteen percent more. It's a lot denser than water. And *that* means . . ." Bony went across to an access cover for the main drive and flopped down onto it. So much for his big show-off demonstration, the one that was supposed to impress Liddy Morse.

"Means what?" asked Liddy.

"It means it's not water. I don't know what the hell that stuff is out there." Bony waved his hand toward the expanse of silent green beyond the port. "But I know what it isn't. And it isn't water."

4

General Korin

The office suite of Dougal MacDougal was appropriate in size and splendor for someone with the exalted title of Solar High Ambassador to the Stellar Group. Lying within a huge and perfect dodecahedron, two hundred meters on a side, the suite sat deep beneath the surface of Ceres. In an architect's conceit, the other four Platonic regular solids were nested within it at a considerable loss in useful living space. A crystal tetrahedron formed the very center. By an ornate desk in that tetrahedron sat Chan Dalton. Awaiting MacDougal's return, he had been drinking steadily and popping fizz slugs. Now he felt wasted and was asking himself why he had done it.

The prospect of danger in the Geyser Swirl was not the problem. Danger was nothing new. Anyone who reached a position of power in the Gallimaufries faced danger every day. Chan had received—and given—his share of sudden and violent attacks. His facial scars spoke more of blood and guts than thrown floral bouquets.

Treachery was not the problem, either. You expected to be stabbed in the back, figuratively and literally, by everyone who wanted to get close to the Duke of Bosny. That was fair enough. Hadn't you done the same thing yourself?

Lies were not the problem. Of course you were lied to; you expected it and you discounted what you were told, no matter the source. Even when people were not trying to lie, their output was usually wrong because some rat-head had given it to them wrong. Over the years you had met a few men and women you could rely on, but no more than you could count on the fingers of one hand. Trying to reach them over the past few days, you learned—not surprisingly—that they were scattered all over. Quality was like a thin veneer on the unfinished rough-cut of the extended solar system.

Even uncertainty was not the problem. You didn't know where you would land when you passed through the Link Network to the Geyser Swirl, or what you would find there. But what else was new? The only certainties in life were unpleasant ones. Tomorrow was uncertain unless you were sentenced to die tonight. And even that was uncertain. You might be reprieved. You might escape. There might be a war or an earthquake.

Chan helped himself to one more fizz slug.

No. The problem today was not danger, treachery, lies, or uncertainty. Perhaps it was *impossibility*. The impossibility of things going so wrong, and the questions that raised.

Consider the evidence. Give them half a chance, and humans were likely to do stupid, rash things just for the hell of it, or to save themselves from dying of boredom. No other Stellar Group member was like that. The Tinkers, the Pipe-Rillas, and the Angels—*especially* the Angels—did not take risks. And they applied their safety-first approach to the Link Network. The system itself would not permit the violation of its three Golden Rules:

1. *Close is not good enough*. Travellers who missed the long, coded sequence of Link settings by a single digit might arrive as thin pink pancakes, or as long, braided ribbons of mangled flesh. Therefore, the settings must pass a multiply redundant checklist, so detailed and foolproof that every black hole in the universe would radiate itself away long before an incorrect sequence would be activated.

2. *Know your exit point*. Careless travellers who needed to breathe could arrive suitless in hard vacuum. An organism for whom high gravity was instantly fatal might land on the surface of Earth. To prevent those things, the Link checking system was supposed to match traveller life-support needs to destination and refuse to allow inappropriate transfer.

3. *Two into one won't go*. A Link arrival point had to be empty before a Link would be initiated. That lesson, too, humans had learned the hard way. A small high-temperature cloud of plasma in orbit near Jupiter marked the simultaneous arrival of two ships at a Sargasso Dump Link exit point.

The Stellar Group applied the safety rules scrupulously. They would have examined the Geyser Swirl Link point closely before sending their first exploration team. And before sending a *second* team? Chan couldn't begin to imagine the checking and the rechecking and the triple-checking that must have been done. Undoubtedly, their ships would also have been set up to return through the Network at the first sign of difficulty.

But even with all this, nothing had come back. Chan could imagine being more wily, cunning, and brave than a Stellar Group team. Hell, he wouldn't be here if that weren't true. What he couldn't imagine was being more *careful*. And that was a very bad omen.

The outer door of the office was sliding open. At last. Chan glanced at the clock built into the ornate surface of MacDougal's desk. As he suspected, the Ambassador had taken far too long. More problems.

"You couldn't get it?"

"Oh, I got it all right." MacDougal had a sour look on his face as he went to his desk. That was all right. Chan was in a foul mood, too. "The answer is not reassuring. It seems that we were provided with false information."

"Happens all the time. Our ship didn't go to the Geyser Swirl?"

"It went there all right. But I am no longer surprised that it failed to return. You see, this was very much a secret and undercover operation. We had to take many things on trust that would normally be checked through official channels. The 'highly competent and experienced private team' that I told you about? It doesn't look so good now. The crew captain, Friday Indigo, is a rich man, but it is all inherited wealth. He describes himself as an 'entrepreneur,' but he has never earned a penny in his life. And he is a 'space expert' who failed his space navigation examination three times and his engineering tests four times. Most upsetting."

"Not to me. It's more worrying when *competent* people don't come back." Chan studied the scowling image that MacDougal threw up on the display set into the surface of the desk. "That's Friday Indigo? He looks like he's got a pickle up his ass. What about the other crew members?"

"Two of them. The chief engineer and astrogator is a total mystery. We have been able to discover nothing at all about him. There is no name in the files, and we have no background. Not even a picture! He is described vaguely as a 'big, fat man.' Certainly he does *not* have official certification in either engineering or astrogation. But there is another mystery here. When we checked with Venus Equilateral, the *Mood Indigo*'s last stop before it departed for the Geyser Swirl, their senior engineering staff insisted that the ship carried an engineer who knew what he was doing."

"Self-taught, maybe. I am, pretty much."

"You are not claiming credentials that you do not have." MacDougal drummed his fingers nervously on the top of the desk. "Are you?"

"I'm not claiming anything. But if I thought I could get more out of this deal by lying about my credentials, I'd do it before you could spit. What about the third crew member, what do you know about him?"

"Not him. Her. The third crew member is a female, Liddy Morse. I am hoping you can help us."

Chan studied the image of a young woman with dark hair and curiously lustrous and liquid eyes. "Mm. How old?"

"Twenty-four. That's one of the few things we do know about her."

"She's a beauty. But I never heard of her, and I never saw her before."

"Maybe not. But she's from Earth, we think from the Gallimaufries."

"So are a hundred million others. Odd place to look for a space crew member. What are her qualifications?"

"For space work? None. She is described in the crew duty roster as a 'general worker with versatile personal skills.' But I think that is Friday Indigo's idea of a joke. Judging from her picture and the limited information that we do have about her, it looks rather as though Friday Indigo—" MacDougal paused. "Well, it seems as though he *bought* her a few months ago, when he was down on Earth. For purely sexual purposes. Is that possible?"

"If she's a Commoner, it's more than possible. Happens every day of the week and every week of the year. All he'd have to do is find out who owned her contract. Not me or the Boz, in this case. I would have remembered her."

"In this case? Are you admitting that you—"

"I'm not admitting a damn thing. I'm just telling you the way things run in the basement warrens. It's not all flowers and nectar down there, you know. If you don't like what you're hearing, stick it. Tell the boys in Unimine and Foodlines that I'm too immoral for you to work with, and the whole expedition is off. I'll be more than happy to go back home to the warrens."

"You know that is not an option. They would kill me."

"I doubt it. They know what the Stellar Group wants. They'd more likely come straight to me and put the screws on some other way. All right, what else do you have? You might as well get it over with—I can see you're fidgeting."

"Word from the Stellar Group members. I forwarded to them your requirement that the ship you take to the Geyser Swirl must have a Tinker Composite, a Pipe-Rilla, and an Angel on board."

"That wasn't a requirement. Call it more of a test shot. What did they say?"

"They say that they have absolute confidence in you, and that their presence would be quite unnecessary and even indicate a lack of trust. They will have no representatives on your ship."

"In other words, they're scared shitless. Don't blame 'em. That's one worry out of the way. Don't want them looking over my shoulder. Suppose I have to off somebody?"

"They still insist that there be no violence."

"Course not." Chan fumbled in his pocket and found nothing but empty fizz holders. Had he really taken that many? He shook his head and went on, "Violence. Think we'd tell 'em if there was? Good. No aliens. Makes things a lot simpler. Got a ship picked out yet?"

"The best one in the solar system. The *Hero's Return*, a former Class Five cruiser. An appropriate name, don't you think, considering the mission?"

"Depends whether or not we come back. It takes more than a nice name to make that happen."

"And you'll be under the command of a highly respected officer, General Dag Korin."

"Whoa there, Mr. Ambassador. What's this 'under the command of' crap?"

"The General is one of the system's great heroes."

"I'm sure he is. But if I'm going to a dangerous place I'd rather be led by one of the system's great cowards. And I'm not supposed to be led by anyone. I thought I was running this show."

"We need a person of known reputation in charge. With all due respect, that's not you."

"Then the expedition can go without me. You can stuff it. I won't have some general getting in the way when I want to do something a Pipe-Rilla might not approve of."

"I don't think you'll find it's that way with General Korin. His attitude to aliens is . . . different. At the very least, you ought to meet with him."

"All right." Chan swept his arm across the desktop. "Then bring him on. Bring 'em all on."

"Not just now, I think." MacDougal caught the glass as it skidded across and off the desk.

"Why not?"

"I don't think that you are in any condition to—I mean, I do not believe that the General can be available at such short notice. Let me arrange it for, let's say, tomorrow morning."

"Bright and early." Chan caught at the edge of another thought. "One more thing, Ambassador. I have to know when this ship—the *Return*—will leave. How much time do I have?"

"I will have that information for you. Tomorrow."

"Tomorrow *morning*. Bright *and* early."

"If you insist." Dougal MacDougal examined the way that Chan Dalton sat slumped in his chair, eyes half closed. Tomorrow morning, Chan Dalton's brain would feel like a boiled pudding.

A person ought to be careful what he asked for. He might get it.

Dag Korin. *General* Dag Korin. Chan was irritated by him already, and the man had hardly spoken a word.

It wasn't his age, though the General, hero of Capella's Drift, looked about a hundred and ninety-nine years old. It was his boots. Ceres gravity was so weak that you couldn't clatter or stamp on the floor. Chan had tried it, and reaction bounced him high into the air.

But Dag Korin could do it. He must have magnetic soles. He could march up and down on the hard floor of the Ambassador's main office, and every step produced a brain-piercing crash.

And now he was starting to talk, too. Not just talk, lecture, not in an old man's voice but in brazen and stentorian tones that resonated off the ceiling and the bare walls and right through Chan's fragile skull case.

"I share completely Mr. Dalton's dislike and utter distrust of the aliens." *Crash* went the boots, as the General made a sharp about-turn. "We do not want them with us in our expedition to the Geyser Swirl. What are they, after all? A Pipe-Rilla is no more than an oversized praying mantis, an ugly creature put together from lengths of leftover drain pipe. An *individual* member of a Tinker Composite has less brain than a horsefly. It takes ten thousand of them together to match a human in intelligence! As for the Angels, to my eye they have always looked as though they belong in a stewpot with other vegetables." *Crash, crash* went the boots. "And when it comes to the human virtues, of courage and nerve, what do we find? We find them wanting. The aliens—*all* the aliens—are the most craven, cowardly, fainthearted—if they even have hearts—pusillanimous, fearful, shivering, timorous beings imaginable. The idea that such objects should be able to limit human access to the universe via the Link Network is so totally outrageous that it takes my breath away."

Chan felt like saying, but I *worked* with those aliens on Travancore, and I *liked* them. I like them still. I just don't want them in the way if things get sticky in the Geyser Swirl and we have to protect ourselves.

He didn't have the strength to speak, and General Korin was just hitting his stride.

"However, we must not allow our natural disgust with these meddling beings to interfere with our primary goal. First, we will cooperate with them in our journey to the Geyser Swirl, so as to produce an end to the quarantine. Then we must assure our permanent access to the Link Network. We must learn how it was that they were able, twenty years ago, to place the embargo on us. I am told that will be much easier to do once we are again using the Link Network on a regular basis. And beyond that, we must pursue our long-term plan: to assert our dominance, to establish a *pax Solis* everywhere within the Perimeter—and then extend that perimeter."

No point in mentioning to the General that there was already peace everywhere within the Perimeter. Well, almost everywhere. Let's say, everywhere that humans were not in control. And Chan had no objection to increasing the human sphere of influence; he was in fact in favor of it, provided there was something in it for him. But did Korin have to be so *loud* about the matter, so early in the day? Chan took a drink of cold water.

How long would it take the expedition to reach and explore the Geyser Swirl? That started another thought. It wasn't just Dag Korin, it was also the other crew members of the *Hero's Return*. Who would they be, and what would they be like? Chan expected a battle regarding the composition of the crew. There would be room for far more people than the three apparent incompetents running the *Mood Indigo*. The General would surely propose some absurd collection of his military minions.

One of Korin's own candidates was in the room. She sat at the back, as far from the General as possible. She must have heard him speak before. She had been introduced by Dougal MacDougal at the beginning of the meeting, but Chan could not recall her full name. Dr. Elke Somebody. Some kind of scientist proposed by the General. She had shaken hands with Chan and stared down at him—she was very tall and blond and anorexic-looking—as though he was some kind of slime-mold at the bottom of a pond. Her last name had an 's' at the beginning, which she had spoken with a slight lisp. *Th-iry*, that's what it sounded like.

That was it: *Elke Siry*; a proposed crew member in need of a good square meal, but otherwise an unknown so far as Chan was concerned. Just as Dag Korin was a partial unknown. That was bad. One thing you learned, the hard way, was that before you went into a dangerous situation you needed to know your companions inside and out.

Not only that, if you had any sort of choice you didn't let other people decide your teammates. You picked them yourself. Your ass was going to be on the line, not Dougal MacDougal's or any other Ceres bureaucrat's.

Chan had recognized that from the start. He had sent the word out. But where were they? He had not heard back from a single one. So much for so-called old friends. They were as bad at keeping in touch as he was. On the other hand, could he be sure his messages had reached them?

Crash, crash. Loud, foghorn voice, rivets driving into his skull. " . . . If, indeed, the story of a new Link point in the Geyser Swirl, previously unknown to the Stellar Group and not created by them, is true. Suppose that we are being *lured* to the Geyser Swirl. Suppose that the aliens . . ."

Chan was as suspicious of motives as the next man, but he couldn't compete with this. Who could Dag Korin possibly be shouting at? Not Chan Dalton, who sat just a few feet away. Somebody on the far side of the Moon, judging from the volume of sound. *Crash crash*, turn, quick march back across the polished floor.

Chan couldn't stand any more. He lurched to his feet, almost overbalancing in the negligible gravity of Ceres. "Excuse me."

General Korin halted in mid-stride and mid-sentence. He stared at Chan with impatient eyes. "Do you have a question?"

"Yes. What makes you think that *anything* the aliens have told us about this is true?"

Korin stared. It must be a novelty, finding someone more paranoid than he was. "Are you suggesting—"

"Yes, I am. I think that every single thing we've been told by the aliens about events in the Geyser Swirl is a lie. When we go there, we must be prepared to deal with any form of chicanery and deception. I have not met the crew you are proposing for the *Return*, but do they include specialists in trickery and bluffing, or in the fine art of the double cross?"

Chan could read the look on the General's face. Surprise and suspicion, giving way to conviction and accusation as Korin turned to Dougal MacDougal.

"Dalton is quite right. We must be prepared for every form of misinformation from the aliens. As for our crew, Dalton, you are looking at it. I believe that this expedition will be best served by a minimal and flexible force. You. Me. And Dr. Siry. The ship runs itself. Are you suggesting that we need more military?"

"Of course not. So far as I know, solar military doesn't *have* specialists in deception and bluffing. I don't know where you would find people like that. But I know where I will." *At least, I know where I'll be looking for them.* "Give me one week—no, make that ten days—and permit me unlimited travel around the solar system. I will find the men and women we need."

"Civilian government workers?" Dag Korin's tone implied that he would rather work with a complement of toads.

"Not quite that."

"But they have experience operating in a highly structured and defined environment?"

"Oh, sure." Presumably time in prison counted. "Look, don't worry about these people. You carry on planning, but expect up to six more people on board the *Return*. I must go now."

Before I pass out. Chan didn't wait to hear the Ambassador and the General squabbling over personnel. He had ten days. Ten days to locate the members of the old team and contact them, wherever they were; ten days to persuade them—if he could—that there was still something in it for them after all these years, if only they would travel with Chan to the Geyser Swirl.

No need to discuss Dag Korin with them. They would have plenty of time to learn the General's little ways on the way to the Geyser Swirl.

[illegible]

Aboard the Moon Indigo

[illegible]

"I don't know. Moby said ... [illegible] It smells like water and it looks like water but it's fifteen percent denser than the standard [illegible] on board."

[illegible]

I have [illegible] ... he never did, giving details of his own background. ... [illegible] the Dead [illegible]

5

Aboard the *Mood Indigo*

"I don't believe you. You've made a mistake." Friday Indigo nodded toward the cup in Bony's hand. "That's water. What else could it be?"

"I don't know." Bony sniffed at the cup. "I agree, it smells like water and it looks like water. But it's fifteen percent denser than the drinking water we have on board."

"You're missing the obvious, Rombelle. As usual. Don't you see what this is? It's *brine*—salt water. If you had ever been on Earth, as I have, you would know."

"I have been on Earth." Bony cursed to himself. In his irritation with Friday Indigo he was doing what he never did: giving details of his own background.

"Then even you should have heard of the Dead Sea." Friday Indigo took the cup from Bony's hand. "The Dead Sea has so much salt in it, a person can't sink. If you step into it, you just bob around on the surface with your shoulders out of the water."

"I know that, sir." Bony made a decision. He might be self-taught, but he had a near-perfect memory and he had taught himself a *lot*. If they were all going to die in the Geyser Swirl, he wouldn't be talked down to any more by a nitwit like Indigo. "The Dead Sea is close to a quarter salts by weight. Mainly sodium chloride, magnesium chloride, and calcium chloride. Its density is twenty percent higher than ordinary water, even more than what we have here."

"So this is obviously somewhere between ordinary seawater on Earth, and the Dead Sea."

"No. The *taste* of water so full of salts is reported to be absolutely disgusting by anyone who has ever sampled it. This is a bit salty, but quite drinkable. Try it for yourself."

Friday Indigo did not seem keen on the idea, but he cautiously raised the cup and took a minute sip. "It tastes like water. Ordinary water, salt and carbonated."

"That's right. Although I'm not sure the dissolved gas is carbon dioxide."

"And still you say it isn't water? What that tells me, Rombelle, is that you don't know what you're talking about. And while you stand here and debate the mysterious properties of perfectly ordinary water, let me remind you that we remain stuck at the bottom of the sea. I don't want a discussion. I want to take the *Mood Indigo* back into space. So get to work." Indigo put his hand on Liddy Morse's arm as she seemed ready to follow Bony toward the lower level of the ship. "Not you, Liddy. It's been a tense few hours, and I think I've earned a little rest and recreation. Let's go."

Liddy, to Bony's annoyance, bowed her head

submissively. He descended the ladder alone, heading for the tiny room that served as his combined study and workshop. On the way he stopped at the galley and grabbed a double handful of candy bars. He wasn't sure that he would be able to work while Friday Indigo cavorted with Liddy above his head, but these might help.

In the study he stuffed a whole candy bar into his mouth and pulled up data on the airlocks of the *Mood Indigo*. There were three of them, one at the front end of the ship and two at the rear. All of them presented problems. The forward one faced vertically upward, while the other two might have been damaged on impact with the seabed. He would have to make an inspection, but before that he wanted to know if they could be used as sea-locks, even in principle.

He called up detailed schematics. It must be nice to be rich. Friday Indigo had bought a ship equipped with the best of everything, hardware and software. On the other hand, most of the test equipment had never been taken from its protective covers, and he could see from their access history that he was the first person to use these data routines.

Bony studied the airlock geometry and mechanics and gradually lost himself in his task. The first part would be easy. You put on an ordinary spacesuit and moved into an airlock. You closed the inner hatch, exactly as usual. Then you opened the outer hatch. Instead of air gushing out into vacuum, water came in. Depending on the airlock position and your own density, you either floated into the sea or you walked out onto the seabed.

And then did what? Bony examined the characteristics of the suits. The air supply and air circulation were self-contained and would operate exactly as in space. The main question was thermal balance. The suit had to lose the heat generated internally by its occupant. That ought to be easier in water than in space, because you could lose heat by conduction and convection as well as by radiation.

Easier in water. In spite of anything that Friday Indigo might say, it was not ordinary water. So what was it? Bony became aware of an idea that had been wandering around the fringes of his consciousness. He called for access to a completely different data base, and for on-line assistance. The next ten minutes flashed by as he and the ship's computer looked up basic physical constants and did calculations.

At the end of that time Bony smacked his hand on the desktop. Yes! He still had to perform a couple of tests, but the ship carried a small mass spectrograph for use in calibrating the fusion drive, and that should be all he needed.

He had been right; and so, oddly enough, had Friday Indigo. Bony decided he didn't want to think about Friday. He helped himself to another candy bar and forced himself back to his main task.

So you were in your suit, wandering around in the sea outside the ship. You were making engineering modifications designed to allow you to use the auxiliary thrustors underwater—another design task to be solved—but you couldn't stay outside too long. You had to come back in through the airlock to replenish your suit supplies. Normally, that was straightforward. You simply entered the lock, closed the outer hatch, and flooded the lock with air to replace the hard vacuum of space.

But it would not be a vacuum in the lock. It would be at least partly water, the water that entered when you opened the hatch to go outside. Therefore, you could not close the outer hatch when you flooded the lock with air. You had to leave the hatch *open*. The hatch could not be at the top of the lock, either, otherwise the air would just bubble up toward the surface and be lost. The hatch must be at the *bottom* of the lock, so new-pumped air would force water out. When all the water had gone, you could at last remove your suit, open the inner hatch, and enter the ship.

Bony turned to the lock configurations. Given the present orientation of the *Mood Indigo* . . . forward lock, outer hatch faced upward, no good . . . aft lock Number One, outer hatch facing upward, no good. Aft lock Number Two, outer hatch facing *downward*—and it was slightly higher, which ought to mean it was clear of the seabed.

Bony leaned back in triumph and was shocked to see Liddy Morse standing in front of him. He had been so engrossed in his work that he hadn't heard her come in.

If she was here, it meant that she and Indigo . . . "Liddy. Are you all right?"

"Of course I'm all right. Why wouldn't I be?"

"You and Indigo. I thought—did he—did the two of you—"

"He's asleep. Stop worrying. He's not my favorite person, but I owe him something. He did buy out my contract, you know. You're not from Earth, so you can't imagine what life is like in the Gallimaufries. Believe me, I've had to put up with a lot worse than Friday Indigo." She was studying him. "You don't like to hear about him, do you?"

"Not especially."

"Then let's not talk about him. Tell me what you were doing before you knew I was here. You looked so happy and pleased with yourself."

"I was working. Deciding how to get outside and come back inside. Liddy, I've figured out what's outside! What the liquid is."

"Who was right, you or Indigo?"

"Both of us."

"You can't *both* be right."

"We are. That's what's so strange. Do you know what hydrogen is?"

"Of course I do."

"But did you know that it can come in two forms? One of them is an atom where the nucleus is a proton, and there's one electron in orbit around it. That's the common form. But you can also have a form called *deuterium*, which has a nucleus, a *deuteron*, with one proton and one neutron. You still have one electron, so the chemical properties of deuterium are the same as hydrogen."

"So?"

"So you can make a molecule, a water molecule, with two atoms of hydrogen and one atom of oxygen. Or you can, just as well, make a kind of water molecule with two atoms of *deuterium* and one atom of oxygen. It's been known for centuries, it's called deuterium oxide, or *heavy water*—and it's about eleven percent more dense than ordinary water. It can be used just like ordinary water. You can bathe in it, you can cook with it. I'm pretty sure you can drink it, at least some, and not notice a difference. That's what we have outside the ship. We are sitting at the bottom of an ocean, but it's a heavy-water ocean."

"Are you sure of this?"

"Sure as I can be until I do the final tests of molecular weight. But assuming I'm right, it's good news. We can wander around outside in our suits and be quite safe. If we run low on water, we can even drink some. I suspect there are differences in diffusivity rates from ordinary water, and that could have long-term fatal effects, but . . ."

She was laughing at him. Bony stopped talking. "I'm sorry. I get carried away. I'm boring you, aren't I?"

"Of course you're not. I get such a kick out of watching you when an idea catches fire. You light up like a little kid."

"Sure. Thanks."

"Oh, stop that." Liddy pulled out the little chair on the other side of the desk and squeezed onto it. "Can't you recognize a compliment when you hear one? *Now* what are you doing?"

What Bony was doing, not very successfully, was crumpling up candy wrappers and trying to count them at the same time. He was amazed at their number. "I tend to eat when I'm working."

"Then you must have been absolutely slaving. And I interrupted you. I'll go away."

"No. You can help me. If you don't mind."

"I can't do that stuff to save my life." Liddy's wave took in the display of schematics, the computer dialog, and Bony's random notes on pressures and volumes.

"I don't mean calculations. I need practical help. Now we know what's out there, I'm ready to consider an EVA—a trip outside the ship. To do that, we have to make one of the airlocks work, underwater. I think I know how, but it's a two-person job. Are you free?"

"I think so." Liddy caught Bony's unconscious glance upward. "Don't worry, he'll snore for at least another hour. He always does afterwards."

"I don't believe it."

"Indigo sleeps a lot."

"I mean, I don't understand how he's able to sleep *now*. We're lost on the seabed of an unknown planet when we ought to be in open space. We're in a ship never designed for anything *but* space operations. We have no idea how we came here, or if we'll ever be able to get away. And he's asleep. How can anybody sleep at a time like this?"

"You really don't know, do you?" Liddy, head to one side, was studying Bony. "I can tell you've never been rich. Neither have I, but I've been around wealthy people. Things are different when you're rich. Indigo bought me, you know."

"That's terrible." Bony said the words automatically, but he was in some ways relieved. At least Liddy wasn't Friday Indigo's mate by choice.

"Being bought is much worse the first time it happens. But that's not my point. My point is, Indigo bought you, too."

"Never. I'm a free man."

"Then what are you doing, working while he's sleeping? What are you doing here at all, lost in the Geyser Swirl?"

Bony had a good answer to the last question, but he was not willing to give it. He stood up. "Come on. Let's go and work on the airlock while he's still asleep."

"You're trying to change the subject." Liddy followed him down the ladder. "Let me explain something to you. When you're born rich, like Friday Indigo, you don't *do* things. You *buy* things. And those things include more than material objects. You buy people. You buy services. You buy reassurance. Friday Indigo is using his money now to buy peace of mind. He bought your services, so he expects you to save the ship and him and find a way home. Why shouldn't he sleep easy?"

"He's crazy." Bony was in the airlock, moving to one side of the small compartment so that Liddy could join him. There was barely space for two people. "I don't even know if we can get outside this ship."

"Maybe he is crazy. But you know what?" Liddy stopped right in front of him, their faces six inches apart and eye to eye. "I agree with him. I expect you to save me, too."

Bony felt a curious heat and pressure in his belly, as though the inside was being cooked in a microwave oven at high setting. He stepped hurriedly backward, and a faucet for the delivery of air to the lock poked him hard in the small of his back. He exclaimed in pain.

Liddy laughed. "What are you doing? I'm not infectious."

"If Indigo comes down here, and sees us together like this . . ."

"Like what? You haven't touched me. And he was the one who told me to go with you and try to be useful for a change."

"He's an absolute bastard."

"Everything's relative. I saw a lot worse when I was growing up."

"Where was that?" Bony turned away, partly to study the hatch design and partly to escape Liddy's eyes. "I know you said you lived down on Earth."

"I did, but I'm not sure it would mean anything to you. Did you ever hear of a place called the Shambles?"

Bony couldn't help staring at her. "No."

"Yes, you did." She cocked her head to one side. "Your face gives you away. Why won't you tell me the truth?"

"I've heard bad things about the Shambles. It's supposed to be the worst of the Terran basement warrens."

"It's like most places, some parts better than others. I was lucky. I was educated at one of the better schools."

"Which one was that?" Bony knew more about the

Shambles than he was willing to admit, and schools were not what came first to mind.

"The Leah Rainbow Academy for the Daughters of Gentlefolk."

"My God." It didn't need his face to give him away this time, the words popped right out.

"Uh-oh." Liddy grimaced. "You've heard of that, too. Then I've said too much. I'm sorry."

"It's not your fault."

"I had no idea, not one in a million off-Earthers has heard of it."

"I have, because—" Bony was on the point of telling the truth, but he caught himself just in time "—because I've read a lot about Earth."

"That's even more peculiar. I didn't think anybody *wrote* about the Academy. Customers normally came through a personal recommendation."

"How did you come to be living there? At the Leah Rainbow Academy, I mean." Bony sank down on his knees, studying the geometry of the lock. The internal air pressure was the same as in the rest of the ship, one standard atmosphere. The hatch was facing almost directly downward. When they closed the inner hatch, sealing themselves off from the ship, and opened the outer hatch just a crack, one of two things would happen. If the outside water pressure was less than the internal air pressure, some air would bubble out. If the outside pressure was greater, water would enter until the pressures equalized.

Were there any other possibilities? Well, there was always the improbable case where the inside and outside pressures were exactly equal, but chances were strongly against that. And there was the case where Bony had forgotten to take account of some crucial variable, and as the hatch was cracked open something totally unforeseen happened.

He was willing to take that risk. But he didn't see why Liddy should be exposed to it, too. He stood up, suddenly aware that he had asked her a question whose answer he was very much interested in hearing; but he had no idea of how she had replied.

"I'm sorry. You were saying?"

"I wasn't. I can tell when somebody isn't listening." Liddy sounded more amused than annoyed. "I thought I was here to help? All I've done so far is stand around."

"You can help right now. You go back in the ship and stand next to the inner hatch. I'm going to stay here, close the inner hatch, and then open the outer one."

"Shouldn't you put a suit on? Suppose the fizziness in the water is something poisonous?"

"The tests say that's it's just oxygen, and lots of it. But I'm going to wear a suit anyway. And so are you."

"Why do I need a suit, if I'm going to stay in the ship?"

"In case you have to do a rescue operation. We will be in radio communication, and I will make sure I keep talking. If I stop, or if I start to sound or act peculiar, don't wait. Close the outer hatch most of the way—I'll show you how to do it from inside the ship—then pump air from the ship into the lock until the water is driven out. You may find there's still a little bit that won't leave, because the hatch isn't exactly horizontal. Don't worry about that. Close the outer hatch completely when it's as water-free as it will go. Then open the inner hatch, go into the lock in your suit, and drag me into the ship. Seal the inner hatch again. Until all that is done, don't waste a moment finding out what happened to me. Did you follow all that, and remember it?"

"Yes." Calm, quiet, and trusting. That made Bony feel good.

"Let's do it, then. Quickly, Liddy, so I don't have time to think of anything that might go wrong."

"Nothing will. I told you, you're going to save us all." Liddy didn't seem capable of a graceless movement. She stripped off her outer clothes and slipped into the suit as though it was something she did every day. Bony, aware that his extra pounds showed a lot more when he was undressed, did the same thing slowly and awkwardly.

Then he was standing in the lock, and Liddy was in the ship. The inner hatch, like the outer one, had a small, round port in it about six inches across. Bony closed the hatch and peered through. He could see Liddy, less than two feet away but with three layers of toughened transparent plastic between them. She raised her eyebrows at him in dumb show, then said over the radio, "All right?"

Bony nodded. "Everything is fine." He had promised to talk to her nonstop, but that might be more demanding than it sounded. What was there to say? He glanced down at the outer hatch, right beneath his feet. He had to be careful to avoid standing on it as the plate slid to one side to admit whatever it was that lay outside the *Mood Indigo*, but that was the only thing he had to do; the only thing he *could* do. When the hatch opened, the rest of it would be out of his hands.

Bony glanced again at the inner hatch. Liddy was still there. She pursed her lips in a kiss and said, "Good luck!"

Bony gave the signal and the outer hatch began to slide open. He watched closely, then said, "External liquid pressure seems to be more than pressure in the ship, but not much more. I think it won't rise much farther than my knees. So far, things are just the way I expected. When the hatch is fully open, if everything still seems all right I may try a short trip outside."

"That wasn't on your original plan." Liddy sounded alarmed.

"I know, but we can't stay inside the ship forever. We'll have to go outside sometime."

"Don't take chances, Bony."

"I won't." No one had ever worried on Bony's behalf before. He decided that he liked it—even if Liddy's concern was partly for herself. *I expect you to save me, too*. That was nice. Let's hope he could justify her confidence. "The outer hatch is fully open now. The liquid level has stopped rising."

All he had to do was take a step forward, and he would sink down. In another five seconds he could be standing on the seabed of—what?

This was a world with no name. Bony was nowhere, about to take a step into nothingness. Think of a name. *Swirlworld*. Not precise enough. *Heavy-water-world*. That was ugly. The world of the deuteron? That would be *Deuteronomy*—but at the moment he was more interested in *Exodus*.

"Are you all right?" said Liddy's anxious voice. "You've stopped talking."

"Sorry. Just playing around with stupid names for this place. Everything still looks good, so I'm going to take a look outside. Here goes."

Bony took a deep breath, added, "I hereby name this planet—*Limbo*," and stepped into the pale green unknown beyond the open hatch.

6

Recruiting on Mars

Ten days. Ten days, to find and recruit five people.

That was only one every two days. It didn't sound bad—until you realized that when last heard from the men and women you needed had been scattered all over the solar system, everywhere from the sun-skimming Hades of the Vulcan Nexus all the way to the Oort Harvester, rolling along in its multimillennial orbit half a lightyear from Sol.

So you might as well tackle an "easy" one first. Chan cleared the final Link exit point, sited conveniently on an island close to the geometrical center of Marslake, and stood for a couple of minutes adjusting to the changed air and gravity. He reflected that before the Link system, even this undemanding destination would have been a challenge. During the first centuries of space exploration, travel times and access to moons or planets were decided less by distance than by relative orbital velocities and the strength of gravity wells. Earth was a major challenge. The old space traveller's complaint, "If you wanted to explore the Universe, you wouldn't start from here," had been coined for Earth. Venus, almost as massive, was little better. While as for Jupiter, you might fly down into the roiling clouds and eternal hurricane winds, but it would be a one-way trip. The planet's vast gravitational pull would prevent you ever getting out.

Even now, fast journeys around the solar system or beyond it were not cheap. The Link would never be cheap. The power for a single trip between points of widely different gravity potential could eat up the savings of a lifetime. Linkage of materials from the Oort Cloud to the Inner System consumed the full energy of three kernels aboard the Oort Harvester. It was a measure of the importance of Chan's mission to the Geyser Swirl that no one had mentioned a budget when he said he needed to travel by Link in order to recruit.

Actually, he needed a good deal more than a *budget*. He needed an argument powerful enough to convince some of humanity's most talented but skeptical individuals that they would like to be on board the *Hero's Return* when it linked out to the Swirl.

What was the local time of day? Chan looked toward the Sun. Much of what you saw at Marslake was misleading. That blue sky above his head was an illusion, an artefact of the same anosmotic thermal field that held a hundred-meter layer of breathable air like a comfort blanket over the whole of Marslake and for forty kilometers beyond. That air was at a comfortable twenty degrees Celsius, while two hundred meters above Chan's head the near-vacuum hovered at a hundred below zero. The island on which he stood was real Mars soil, but it had been mined from ancient sedimentary layers far beneath the surface, where hid the once-and-future Martian life-forms. The serene blue lake itself was fifty kilometers across and listed as one of the Seven Wonders of the Solar System (low on the list, to be sure), but it was nowhere more than ten meters deep, and it held only a thousandth of the water of even the smallest of Earth's Great Lakes.

However, that bright Sun was no illusion. It stood high in the sky, as high as it would ever get at Mars latitude thirty degrees. That meant it was close to noon, much too early for Danny Casement to be in his office and fully awake. Dapper Dan, unless he had changed beyond recognition, put most nocturnal animals to shame.

Even a man in a hurry had to eat, and now was as good a time as any. Chan decided to have a meal before he went the rest of the way to Danny's office. He left Center Island and walked out along one of the many causeways that led in the right direction. The surface of Marslake was dotted with thousands of small islands, laid out on a regular grid and connected by roads wide enough for foot traffic or small wheeled vehicles.

The walking people were few and far between, and the only cars that Chan saw were slow and creaking. They, like the outside cafe that he came to at the end of the causeway, had seen better days. The cafe, Inn Paradise, could not even afford robot servers. Chan, the only customer, ordered his simple meal of bread and fruit jellies from a human. While he ate—Chan was not picky, but the food was dreadful—he heard the familiar tale of woe from the owner/waiter.

Marslake had been poised to take off as the solar system's greatest tourist attraction, ready to host multitudes of humans and Pipe-Rillas and Tinkers. Even the taciturn and mysterious Angels possessed plenty of negotiable materials, and they would be welcomed.

The quarantine had ended everything. Aliens had ceased to arrive. Humans from all around the solar system were affected by the general economic collapse and could not afford to come. And now . . . The owner waved his hand gloomily around. Old holo-images, with their advertisement of wondrous coming attractions, hung dim and translucent in the air, predictors of a false future that would never be. The only cheerful thing in sight was the Sun, which apparently knew no better.

"Where are you from?" The owner ended his mournful discourse and asked his first question as he gave Chan the credit slip.

"Earth."

"Ah. You're lucky. Not like here, I bet."

"No." Chan touched the payer ID unit and rose to leave. "Everything there is much, much worse."

Except, possibly, the food and waiters and restaurant owners. But Chan was already on the way out and he did not bother to say it.

He was able to pick out Danny's place long before he reached it. Unlike most other businesses scattered over the surface islands of Marslake, Danny felt a need for actual walls and a ceiling. Most enterprises found those to be unnecessary. With no wind and no weather, why waste time on structures? Only an occasional need for privacy demanded the use of enclosed space, and space for that could easily be rented.

Chan halted when he was still a couple of hundred meters away. He had come prepared. Dag Korin had made the portable Remote Observer available to Chan without question. Apparently the General found it quite natural that Chan would wish to spy on his own friends, which was something to bear in mind on the trip to the Geyser Swirl. Chan didn't think of the use of the R/O as spying or intrusive in this case. It was a way to save everyone's time if things were obviously not going to work out.

He took the R/O unit from his pocket and rested it on a railing at the side of the causeway. He adjusted the focus and inserted the tiny earphones. If this didn't produce the right result he would gain a working day but lose a team member.

Visual information was a more demanding technical problem than aural. The sound from inside a building was usually sharp and clear, while the image tended to be variable and slightly grainy. Chan also had the feeling that today the colors were a little off. It didn't matter. That, surely, was Danny Casement with his back to the viewing unit.

You could pick Danny out from his clothes alone. Today he was dressed, as in the old days, in a favorite combination of a high-necked shirt with fine green-and-white check and an ultraconservative business suit with a herringbone pattern of mixed brown and gray. As he turned, Chan made a confirmation. The R/O unit showed a small, neatly built man, with the brown face, wizened features, and wide mouth of a trustworthy ape. It was Danny all right, debonair as ever. He had a tall, elegant woman in his office with him, and he was shaking his head at her with a more-in-sorrow-than-in-anger expression on his face.

"It's a bad time to speculate?" Chan turned up the volume a fraction. "My dear, if your ex-husband says that, I must say I agree with Andrew."

"Arthur." The woman, hair piled high on top of her head, towered over Danny Casement.

"With Arthur. It's *always* a bad time to speculate.

What we are talking of here isn't speculation. It's *investment*."

"But Hyperion is an awful long way from Mars."

"And what does distance have to do with the value of an investment? We are talking of a proven resource that has already made thousands—tens of thousands—of people rich. Leonora, if distance is the only problem, I will personally take you there so you can see for yourself. Just the two of us." He touched her arm and quickly pulled back, as though he had acted on impulse.

The woman gave him a nervous smile. "That would be lovely. But Arthur says that the Yang diamond was completely worked out, years and years ago."

"As I already mentioned, this is not the original Yang diamond. It is a completely new formation, created by a different impact, which also happens to be on Hyperion. However, if your husband—"

"Not my husband. My *ex*-husband."

"My apologies. Your *ex*-husband. If Arthur is so reliable a source of information—"

"He's a jerk and a louse."

"Then perhaps his information—"

"But he's a smart louse. That's how he made so much money—not that he was willing to give me much. I can't afford to throw what I have away."

"Nor would I ask you to, or ever want you to." Danny reached out, and this time allowed his hand to stroke Leonora's forearm and remain there. "The final purchase price will be three hundred thousand, but I am certainly not proposing that you pay anything like that until we are absolutely sure that the return will be many times your investment. All that is necessary at the moment is that you make a small down payment, in order that your claim can be certified and your rights of ownership confirmed."

"How much?"

"Just twenty-five thousand. After that you will have a year of steady income from the mine before you need to pay out another penny."

"I don't know. I'd like to." Leonora placed her hand on top of Danny's. "But Mr. Casement—"

"Please call me Daniel."

"Daniel. It still sounds like an awful lot of money. Even the down payment. It isn't that I don't trust you, I do. But if I could just be *sure*."

"I know exactly how you feel." He removed his hand from hers, stood up, and turned around to give the whole room a thorough inspection, as though someone might be concealed within a desk drawer or one of the small cabinets. He dropped his voice to a whisper. "Leonora, I'm going to do something that I am not supposed to do. In fact, if the mine developers knew about it, I would be in very serious trouble."

"What's that?" Her voice fell in volume to match his. "What are you going to do?"

"This. And remember, if anyone ever asks you, it didn't happen." He reached into a vest pocket and pulled from it a small pouch of black velvet. "Hold out your hand. Palm up."

She reached her hand out in slow motion. He placed the square on her outstretched palm and carefully unfolded it, to reveal a tiny glittering stone that caught and refracted every light in the room.

"There it is." Danny Casement spoke in the reverent tones of a man in the presence of divinity. "That is a fragment of the Yang diamond. Just a little chip, of course—there are many tons more, free of all defects and waiting to be mined. I was shown this on my trip to Hyperion, when I made my own first investment. I asked to borrow it for a little while, just to marvel at its quality. Look at it closely, Leonora.

Let the light fall on it from all sides. You will see that this is diamond of the purest water. There is none finer in the whole solar system."

"It's—beautiful."

"You can be the owner of many more, like this and far larger. Or you can sell them, for many times your investment. But please do not tell anyone else that I showed it to you."

He reached out his hand to take the diamond. She pulled back, and he frowned. "What's wrong, Leonora?"

"Nothing is wrong." She closed her hand around the stone and the pouch of black velvet. "If only—if only I could just keep this for a day or two."

"I see." His tone was chilly.

"Oh, Daniel, it's not that. Please don't think that I don't trust you. I do. But if I could keep the stone a little while, it might help both of us. I could have it examined by a professional in gemstones. Neither of us is that."

"I have been told that my own expertise in this field is far from negligible. But I suppose I could be wrong. I am not infallible." His voice remained cold. "However, the decision is not mine to make. What do I tell the mine developers? If I say I do not have another investor—not even the down payment from an investor—they will certainly want the stone back."

"How much did you say it is again? The first payment?"

"Twenty-five thousand."

"Do you think they would possibly take twenty thousand? That is all I have available in liquid assets."

"It would be irregular, but I can probably prevail upon them to accept twenty thousand rather than twenty-five. I have already given them a glowing description of your character and reputation."

"Then let's do it. We'll make the transfer right now." Leonora held up her hand, fist still clenched around the velvet and the stone. "And then can I take the diamond away with me for a couple of days?"

"My dear Leonora." He lost his worried look and smiled. "How could I—how could anyone—resist a lady as charming as you? Take the stone with you. Have your tests done—nondestructive ones, if you please. You will find, I know, that you are holding a diamond of the finest quality. However, I must insist on one other condition of this transaction."

Leonora handed over a trade crystal, which disappeared at once into a small ivory box on top of the desk. "That will transfer twenty thousand. And I must be off, I'm already late. But what is your other condition?"

The simian face remained serious, but a twinkle lit the warm brown eyes. "Oh, nothing to worry you. But you and I must take a trip together, Leonora, and . . . examine our holdings. You show me yours, and I will show you mine."

"Mr. Casement! You are a wicked, wicked man."

"I said to call me Daniel."

"Oh. All right. Daniel." She giggled, gave him a quick kiss on the cheek, and hurried out of the building. She passed close to where Chan was standing. He had already put away the earphones and the remote-observing unit, and she didn't give him a second glance.

Chan waited five minutes, then strolled over to Danny Casement's building. He knocked gently on the solid paneled door, with its modest and tasteful inscription, *Daniel Walsingham Casement, Investment Counselor*.

"Just a second."

After a wait that was at least a couple of minutes, the door slid open. "Yes?" Danny Casement stood in the doorway with an inquiring expression on his face. Chan, peering past him, saw that the ivory box containing the trade crystal had vanished from the desktop.

"Yes?" Danny repeated.

"Yes, what?" Chan pushed past him into the room. "Dapper Dan Casement, that's no way to greet an old friend."

"Oh my God." Danny gave a howl of recognition. "Chan Dalton. You're the last person in the world I expected to walk in that door."

"It's been a long time."

"Nearly twenty years."

"But you haven't lost the touch, Dan. You're still the best in the system, and it's a pleasure to see you operate. Charm them, stroke them, scare them, soothe them, tempt them—and watch how they love you as they take the bait. Do you realize you told that lady that it was the Yang diamond you loaned her, and also that it was *not* the Yang diamond?"

"You've been spying on me." It was a simple statement of fact, not an accusation.

"Yes. I assume that wasn't a real diamond you showed her."

"Then you would be totally wrong. It was a genuine, first-class, defect-free natural diamond. When Leonora has it tested, as she surely will, she will learn that I told her the truth—and be suitably overcome with remorse for her lack of trust in me. The stone was even from the Hyperion mines, all one-quarter carat of it. A man has his operating expenses. But Chan, why would you do a thing like spying on an old friend?"

"Because, as you say, it's been close to twenty years.

People change. If you seemed different, in ways that matter, I would have saved your time and mine. I would have gone away and never knocked on your door. But you reeled that one in so smooth, it looked like anyone could do it."

"What do you mean, 'reeled in'? Leonora Coslett is a business associate."

"And I saw you giving her the business."

"Not at all. I am truly fond of the lady. I have, let us say, aspirations."

"If she proves to be wealthy enough."

"Now that is an unfair accusation." Danny waved a hand. A chair folded out of one wall and a table from the top of the desk, while a tray of flasks and glasses appeared from one of the cabinets. "However, if you are done casting aspersions on my honesty and reputation, take a seat. This isn't just social, from the look of it, but we can have a drink while you talk the talk."

"Provided your drink isn't like the food at the Inn Paradise."

"Better known locally as Ptomaine Central. You ate there? I could have warned you. It accounts for your surly countenance." Danny filled two glasses. "This will make up for it. Genuine imported Santory single-malt scotch, aged thirty days, from the Hokkaido deep cellars. Burn the hair right off your ass. Cheers!"

After a long pause, Danny went on in a strangled voice, "But what are you doing out here? Last word I got through the grapevine, you were Lord High Muckymuck to the Duke of Bosny."

"I was. Good job, but I had an offer I couldn't refuse. That's why I'm here."

Chan described his meeting with the Stellar Group, the appearance of the new Link point in the Geyser Swirl, the lost Stellar Group ships, and the upcoming human expedition. Danny Casement watched with shrewd brown eyes and listened intently. He did not speak until Chan, giving details of the expedition, added, "a big, powerful ship, but with your typical crew: military people and scientists."

Danny snorted. "And you thought, what will anybody get out of a dim bunch like that? Nothing. So why not give the old brigade, hand-picked and perfectly matched, a chance to do what we once planned? It's been twenty years, but if we can find the team and get it together, we have it made. It's even better than last time, because we don't have to scrape around to pay for a ship and crew. The government will provide us with a ship and a bunch of goons and gofers, for free."

"As usual, you're ahead of me. How does it sound?"

"Interesting. Another shot at the universe, the whole candy-bag, that sounds fine. Of course, compared with *this*"—Danny's wide-flung arms encompassed and dismissed the whole of Mars, quietly fading into futility as the once-open road to the stars remained blocked—"*anything* tends to look better than this. So it's tempting to close your eyes and risk your ass and hat. But I see a couple of big catches. First, your Stellar Group buddies say, no violence. That's all right when you're dealing with them, they don't *do* violence. But anyone else you meet might not agree. What are we supposed to do if some nasty comes at us with a meat-axe? Smile and get chopped?"

"That's probably what the earlier Stellar Group teams did. But they've made it very clear that they don't intend to go with us on this one. What they don't know about won't hurt them."

"Fine. They certainly won't hear it from me. All right, second problem. I don't see any fun in going all the way to this Geyser Swirl place, just to be wiped out when we arrive. And everybody who has been there so far, near as I can tell, got themselves knocked off. Why will we be any different?"

"For one thing, we'll defend ourselves, which the Tinkers and Pipe-Rillas and Angels wouldn't do. And as far as the human team goes, we're smarter. From everything that I've been able to find out, the man who led the human team was a rich idiot who couldn't find his ass with both hands."

"But the aliens aren't fools. And they're cautious."

"We will be cautious, too. And we will have new information. After the two ships disappeared with Tinkers, Pipe-Rillas, and Angels on board, the Angels did a survey—remotely, of course—of the whole Geyser Swirl. We will have that survey, every last image and data byte, so we'll know exactly where every star and planet and gas cloud is and what the possible dangers are. But look, before we get into details like that, I have to know. Are you in or are you out?"

"You ask me that, after seeing what it's like here?" Danny's thin eyebrows rose high on his wrinkled forehead. "After the big Q, the quarantine, everything on Mars headed straight down the toilet. Of course I'm in. I'm so far in you'd not get me out with forceps and a bucket of cold water. But you'll need more than just me."

"Sure. We need the whole team, or as close to it as we can get. We don't have much time, either—the *Hero's Return* leaves in less than two weeks. I've already started looking, but what do you hear about the gang?"

"Old news, mostly. Let's see." Danny leaned back on the rickety chair, closed his lips tight and puffed air behind them so that he looked even more like a chimpanzee, and held up his left hand, fist closed. After a few moments he lifted the index finger and went on, "Number one: Chrissie Winger. She's your best bet, even though it's a long journey. I saw a publicity release about Chrissie less than a year ago. She has her own magic show, big success, touring the Oort and making 'em gasp."

"One of us will have to make the trip out and talk her into coming. What else?"

"Number two: Tully O'Toole. I heard from him maybe five years back. He was on Europa doing God-knows-what. As much the dreamer and the wild man as ever, but Tully the Rhymer still picks up a new language as easy as I pick up a glass."

"Or a woman."

"I told you, Leonora Coslett is a business associate."

"I won't argue. Who else?"

"Well, there's Deb Bisson." Danny glanced uncertainly at Chan Dalton. "She's on Europa, too, easy enough to find. If you're willing to risk it. I mean, you and she . . ."

"We'll be fine. She and I got over that a long time ago." Chan grimaced. "I hope."

"Still a weapons master, is she?"

"That's not the sort of thing you advertise. But could you imagine a Deb who wasn't?"

"I could not. But I'll tell you one thing, I'll not be the one who visits her to find out."

"I know, I guess I'm stuck with it. All right, four and five. What do you hear about Tarbush and the Bun?"

"I can only help with one of them. Nothing on thc Bun. Tarbush Hanson still does his strongman stunts and his talking-to-animals act, and last I heard, three or four years ago, he was out in the Oort, too."

Chan nodded. "He was. I'm a bit ahead of you on this. Tarbush and Chrissie Winger teamed up a few years ago and there's a good chance they're still touring the Oort Cloud together. Did you ever figure out how Tarbush does it?"

"No. So far as I'm concerned the easiest answer is the one he gives people: Tarbush can talk to animals. We never had the chance to find out if he can talk to aliens, too, the way he claims."

"Maybe we'll find out in the Swirl—if we get him that far. As for the Bun, I'm like you. I've drawn a total blank. I know he was at the Vulcan Nexus for a while, and that's not a place you can easily hide a man. But I sent a trace, and it came back *name and identification unknown*."

Danny sniffed and a frown grew on the wrinkled and tanned forehead. "Did you try his real name? I know he hates it, but he may be using it."

"Bonifant Rombelle? Yeah, I tried that. I also tried the Bun, and Bunnyfat Ramble."

"How about Señor Bonifant and Buddy Rose? I've seen him sign that way."

"I tried those too. Tried everything I could think of. All the old ones, plus a few variations. Nothing. The common view on the Vulcan Nexus was that the Bun went outside with inadequate thermal protection and frizzled. Half an hour at those solar flux levels would bake you down to the bones. All you'd find in the suit would be a mess of blood and liquid fat."

"Do you mind? I'd like to eat breakfast in a few hours, but I won't if you talk like that."

"Sorry. Anyway, I said that's the *common* view. I didn't say it's what I think."

"You have another theory?"

"Yes. There's one other detail you need to know. At the time that the Bun vanished he was close to big trouble. Someone had cracked the Nexus code for solar activity prediction, and been caught doing it. Does that sound like the Bun, or doesn't it?"

"Does indeed. Only man I ever heard of could make a working laser out of a dog collar, a grandfather clock, and the lower set of your Grandpa's dentures. He could fix *anything*. Be worrying, working without the Bun." Danny stood up. "I always thought someone like him was an essential part of our team—and there *was* no one like the Bun."

Chan stared at him. "You thinking of backing out?"

"Hell, no. You know what they say: *There's nobody indispensable but thee and me; and I'm not too sure of thee*. If we have to manage without the Bunnyman, we'll do it. But you were talking tight time schedules, and it seems to me we have to start lining up our other team members right now."

Chan nodded. "We do. So where do you think you're going?"

Danny Casement was moving toward the door. "To say my sorrowful good-byes."

"To Leonora Coslett?"

"Her, and one or two others of my investors. Make that three or four."

"And return their money?"

"Please! Let's be reasonable. Ask yourself, what could they possibly buy with their money as valuable as what I provide? Go ahead, make the travel plans." Danny sighed. "I can leave tomorrow, but don't look for me till then. This is going to be one long day. And night."

Chan nodded without sympathy. "You can sleep all you want—once we're on the way to the Geyser Swirl."

7

The Oceans of Limbo

Bony was no deep-sea diver; still less was he a bold explorer. As he took that first, possibly fatal step, he paused and looked down.

The base of Airlock Number Two sat about three meters from the bulbous rounded end of the *Mood Indigo.* That base was where the drive unit was housed, and as the heaviest part of the ship it had hit the seabed first when the vessel drifted down through the water. Bony could see, directly beneath him, a broken array of sharp-pointed gold-and-green shafts, two meters long and scattered like toothpicks by the impact.

He held the side of the hatch and lowered himself slowly through the opening. When he was in water up to his waist, he hesitated. He had stated, very confidently, that the chemical properties of deuterium oxide were the same as those of ordinary water. But was that true? Was heavy water just like regular water for all normal purposes, except for its greater density? Bony thought so, but he was no more a trained chemist than he was a trained engineer. Also, he could not tell how strong those pike-like stems beneath him were. He had to be sure that he didn't impale himself on one that still stood upright.

"Are you all right?" said Liddy's voice in his helmet.

"Yes. Just being cautious." Bony had another thought. "I've realized something: radio signals designed for space or air use won't travel through water. Once I'm immersed we won't be able to talk to each other. Don't worry, though, I'll be all right."

I hope. Bony lowered himself farther. Mid-chest. Shoulders. Chin-level, nose-level, eye-level. He was fully immersed, staring into limpid depths. Was this what the oceans on Earth or Europa looked like? He had never been totally under water before, so he had nothing with which to compare. The water had a bluer tinge than he had expected. All the old talk about "the deep blue sea," and it really was. After hanging for a few seconds, he released his hold on the side of the hatch.

He was ready for a sudden drop. Instead, nothing seemed to happen. Another disturbing thought crept into Bony's head. Heavy water was quite a bit denser—eleven percent denser—than ordinary water. Suppose that he, in his suit, was *lighter* than the salty heavy water that he displaced? Then instead of falling to the seabed he would rise toward the surface. He did not know if he could use his suit's thrustors under water. If he went up, he might have no way to return to the ship.

And then he realized that he was in fact drifting downward, so slowly that he had time to tap on the lowest port of the *Mood Indigo* when he reached it, and still be there to wave reassuringly to Liddy when she hurried over to look out. She mouthed at him, he was not sure what. "Be careful," that seemed clear enough. But the rest of it? "Don't something-or-other."

Whatever it was, he would try not to. Bony turned his attention downward. He was just a meter above the surface, and there was no way that he could avoid landing on the flattened pikes. He was lucky to be so close to the ship, because a couple of meters farther out the thicket of spears still jutted upright.

The final impact was feather-soft. Even so, as his boots touched the spikes they crumbled to a cloud of dust that rose up all around him. They seemed like crystals, infinitely delicate and fragile. Bony realized that he had never been in a moment's danger.

Danger from the spears, that is. Bony stared along the gentle slope of the seabed, and as he did so the light around him dimmed. Just as quickly, it brightened back to its earlier level. Bony looked up. Far above him he saw a vague tri-lobed outline, moving away. Something huge, in the water or above its surface, had passed over his head.

Bony shivered. The smart thing to do was to return at once to the *Mood Indigo*. He had made his point. He had proved that they could leave the ship and make necessary modifications to the auxiliary drive, enough to allow them to leave Limbo's ocean floor. But Bony could see better now, as the dust from shattered pikes settled in the still water. The ship had landed in the lowest part of what seemed to be an underwater valley, right where the standing spears grew thickest. Forty meters away, the world of the seabed faded and merged into a sea of uniform green; but just before that, the array of spears ended. Bony could make out the faint outline of rounder shapes on the slope.

He stood still and checked the condition of his suit. He had air enough for eight hours, ample drinking water if he needed it, and good thermal balance. He felt neither too hot nor too cold. The light around him seemed a fraction brighter than when he first emerged. Assuming that they were on the seabed of a planet somewhere in the Geyser Swirl; that the planet rotated on its axis with a period to give it a day comparable in length with an Earth day; and that the planet moved in orbit around a star—lots of assumptions, but each of them reasonable—then the brighter light indicated that it was still morning on Limbo. The only thing at all abnormal was the tendency of his faceplate to become covered with small bubbles. That must be a side effect of the superaerated sea, and it ought to decrease as the suit visor became the same temperature as the water. Bony could go quite a bit farther, without a danger of being caught by darkness. And if he went back now, Liddy would wonder why.

He moved carefully forward, passing across the broken shafts until he came to the array of upright ones. Each standing spear was a couple of centimeters across and rose taller than his head. Close up, he could see a brighter line running up the middle of each. He reached out to take one between finger and thumb, and at once it shattered. He tried again, with the same result. No matter how delicate his touch, the shafts fell in two. As they broke he heard a faint chime like a crystal bell, and the bright line faded within seconds.

If he wished to know what lay farther up the side of the drowned valley, he had to cross the field of spears. Feeling like a ruffian, too ham-handed to touch anything on this planet, Bony pushed his way through. He left behind him an avenue of destruction.

If everything on Limbo was like this, the planet should be off limits to humans. It was far too delicate to withstand human contact.

At the edge of the field of spears, Bony halted and turned to look back at the *Mood Indigo*. The ship had faded to an outline of dark gray. Its dumbbell shape, the rounded bulbous lower part of drive and cargo hold topped by the slightly smaller ovoid of crew quarters, had an oddly out-of-place quality. Here on Limbo it was the Terran vessel, and Bony himself, who were the aliens.

He waved, wondering if Liddy would be able to see him from so far away. He fixed in his mind the contours of the underwater valley, so that even when the ship was out of sight he would have no trouble returning to it. Finally, he turned and began the slow, buoyant walk that would take him up the slope and onto the undersea ridge that marked the end of the valley.

He was almost floating, but in order to make forward progress up the steep incline he still had to put his feet down and exert pressure on the seabed. A carpet of spheres of dull orange-red had replaced the standing pikes, and he could not avoid treading on some of them. They flattened, even under his sea-supported weight of what could not be more than a few pounds; but at least they did not shatter and crumble to dust. Instead they produced an odd wheezing sound, like a chesty old man's sigh of complaint. When he had passed by, they slowly and silently resumed their original shapes.

Life-forms? Bony was not sure, but his guess was yes. Experience throughout the Stellar Group showed that life popped up everywhere you thought it possibly could, and in a lot of places where you felt sure that it couldn't possibly. There was life in the sulfur volcanoes of Io, life in the ammonia clouds of Uranus, life on fifty-kilometer fragments of radioactive ice in the far reaches of the Oort Cloud, even viral life of a sort coating arid rock shards of the Dry Tortugas. And this was all within the limits of the extended solar system. When you included the domain of the whole Stellar Group, the variety of life-forms, life-tolerances, and life-locations seemed endless. The idea of life on Limbo seemed very reasonable.

Intelligent life on this planet was another matter. Bony was ready to bet high odds against it. Thousands of worlds lay within the two-hundred-lightyear sphere bounded by the Perimeter, and they had so far produced only four intelligent species: humans, Pipe-Rillas, Tinker Composites, and Angels. There was a debatable fifth form on the far-off planet Travancore, in the form of a giant caterpillar-like creature known as a Coromar. The Coromar was capable of speech, which would normally argue for intelligence; unfortunately its entire vocabulary and interests were confined to finding food and eating it. Bony was as fond of his food as the next man—probably a good deal fonder than the next man—but as far as he was concerned the Coromar failed to make the cut.

And then there were dangerous life-forms. To be dangerous, life did not have to be smart. It merely had to be hungry, poisonous, bad-tempered, territorial, frightened, or accidentally lethal. Bony, as an Earth form, was almost certainly useless as food for any indigenous form on Limbo or any other alien planet. Unfortunately, that was the sort of discovery a creature made only after an attempt at eating had begun.

Occupied by such disturbing thoughts, Bony came to the top of the ridge. He guessed that he had walked maybe two or three hundred meters and risen twenty meters above the ship's location at the bottom of the valley. Everything was noticeably brighter. He raised his head and stared straight up, wondering how far he was from the surface. When they first arrived, he had guessed at maybe a sixty-meter depth for the *Mood Indigo* based upon the pressure outside the ship. But that estimate, he now realized, had ignored the air pressure of the atmosphere above the surface of the water. He might be within ten or fifteen meters of air—whatever air on Limbo might be. It must have a high oxygen content, because the waters of Limbo literally fizzed with dissolved oxygen.

The far side of the ridge descended in a shallower slope that seemed to lead to another valley. The seabed structures changed again. Now they formed clumps of long green strands with thick purple fingers at the end of each. Bony decided that he had come far enough for one day. He would, if the ship was still here tomorrow, take a closer look then. He was all ready to turn and head back when he noticed something about the green clumps. Although their height and degree of growth varied so that they covered almost the whole seabed apparently at random, the positions of their centers were not at all haphazard. They lay along a precise triangular grid, each one about half a meter from its three nearest neighbors.

It could happen naturally. For all that Bony knew, the separation was governed by some precise biological demand for light or nutrients. If, on the other hand, it was *not* natural, but a farm . . .

Bony sank down on his haunches to examine the nearest clump of plants. He reached out and tugged at one of the purple fingers. It came away easily and split open like a ripe pod, revealing a group of pea-sized objects within. A puff of gas came at the same time, bubbling up into the water. He lifted the pod to the visor of his suit helmet for a closer view of the dimpled seeds. They looked like a food crop, ripely edible—though probably not to humans. One of those might be enough to kill Bony. As he peered at the cluster his peripheral vision caught a movement far away.

They were on the floor of the valley, close to the limit of visibility. Three of them. At that distance, in the diffuse watery gloom, he had no way of judging size. Each one was rounded and iridescent, like an object blown from a collection of different-sized soap bubbles or a figure made by children from balloons, come to life and in its movements oddly ominous. Bony saw—or imagined—a round bubble head supporting bubble eyes that nodded on long thin stalks; a spherical multicolored body; string-of-bubble limbs or tentacles, that carried the creatures across the seabed as though they were floating ghosts.

Carried them *this way*. By accident, or by intention? Bony did not care to find out which. He had enjoyed as much novelty as he could stand, and his stomach felt knotted with tension. He stooped, to provide as small a visible target as possible, turned, and started back toward the *Mood Indigo.* He told himself that there were multiple good reasons for going back. Liddy would be worrying about him. He wanted to see her. He was hungry and thirsty. His bladder was uncomfortably full, and although the suit would accommodate such things he preferred the ship's facilities. Even the uncertain pleasures of Friday Indigo's company seemed desirable, compared with that of the creatures—Limbo-ers? Limbics?—slithering toward him across the alien corn of the underwater valley.

Only one thing preserved the dignity of Bony's retreat: it was physically impossible to run underwater.

As soon as the ship came into sight he turned to look back. He was glad to find that he left no telltale track of suspended seabed mud, nor could he see any sign of the bubble creatures.

Even so, the relief when he reached the protective bulk of the *Mood Indigo* and stood once more below the open airlock was considerable. He didn't feel hungry any more, and the urge to pee had mysteriously vanished. He crouched, leaped, and was able to grab the edge of the hatch on the first try. His head came above the surface of the water, and with another upward heave he was sprawled on the bottom of the lock. He stood up and splashed through knee-deep water to the port on the inner hatch. As he had hoped, Liddy was there. He gave her a thumbs-up and started the process of pumping air that would clear the lock of water. The air pressure in the lock was only thirty percent higher than inside the ship, and the water level dropped as he watched.

He removed his helmet as the outer hatch closed. By the time that Liddy matched air pressures and opened the inner hatch he had his suit halfway off. She interfered with that by coming up behind and giving him a hug.

"I wondered where you'd gone. You disappeared completely."

"I thought that since I was outside and the suit worked fine, I'd take a little look around." Bony tried to be casual. "Where is Friday Indigo?"

"Sleeping, I guess. I haven't heard a sound from up there."

"Still? But he's been asleep for—" Bony saw the clock. "That can't be right. I was gone for hours."

"Thirty-seven minutes, from the time you dropped out of the hatch to the time I saw you coming back. What did you find?"

"Lots of things."

Before Bony could say more, a voice from overhead grumbled, "You sure make a hell of a lot of noise down there. Have we sprung a leak or something? I heard a pump."

Friday Indigo came down the ladder. His dark hair was a tousled mess, but he seemed in a surprisingly good mood.

"An air pump," Bony said. "I've been outside, and when I came back in I had to pump water out of the lock. Captain, I think we ought to try to make drive modifications, raise the ship off the bottom, and get out of here as soon as possible."

"What's the hurry all of a sudden?" Indigo wandered into the galley and came out carrying a can of juice. He gulped from it noisily. "We have air, we have food, and the ship isn't about to cave in. I didn't come all this way so we could turn right around and leave."

Bony wondered if it was bravery or stupidity. Did Indigo have any idea of their situation? "I see several reasons to leave, sir. First, we have no idea where we are. As I understand the Link Network, it is impossible to make a Link to a place where matter is present. Even a Link into air requires special procedures. But we arrived in *water*."

"All that proves is that you don't understand the Link Network. Nor do I, and nor I suspect does anyone else. But I'm not in a sweat because of it. What else?"

"We've landed in a place like none I've ever heard of. The sea here isn't ordinary water, it's deuterium oxide—heavy water."

Friday Indigo said to Liddy, "Remember I told him it was water?" And then to Bony, "So it's heavy water. I've heard of that. How dangerous is it?"

"Not dangerous at all. I think. But it's—well, *unnatural* for an ocean to be heavy water. In Earth's oceans, heavy water is only one part in six thousand."

"Precisely why we came. For strangeness." Indigo tossed the empty can into a trash-squeeze and rubbed his hands together. "This is terrific. We've found a whole new world, one nobody has explored before. That information alone is enough to make this expedition famous. And when we get some idea of what sort of things might be here . . ."

"I already have some idea, sir." Bony gestured toward a port. "Things I discovered when I was outside the ship."

Friday Indigo stared at him. "You sound afraid. You're not scared, are you?"

"No, sir." But Bony had been.

"You don't have to be frightened, you know. Not with Friday Indigo as your pilot."

"Yes, sir. Of course." Bony knew that Liddy's eyes were on him, and he felt like a spineless groveler. He and Liddy had agreed that a ship with Indigo flying it was worse than a ship with no pilot at all. "Let me tell you what I saw, sir."

He summarized his findings while he had been outside. When it was told, rather than experienced with elevated pulse rate and nervous stomach, everything sounded flat and unremarkable. When he came to his description of the bubble shapes, Friday Indigo went over to the port.

"Where?"

Bony came to his side and looked at the peaceful forest of green-gold pikes, with beyond them a seascape fading into blue-green haze.

"You can't see them from here. They were over on the other side of that ridge."

"Are you sure you didn't imagine them?"

"Quite positive." But he could see that even Liddy was a little skeptical. "They were there."

"Good. Then tomorrow we'll go and take a look at them."

Bony had to swallow before he could speak. "Our weapons won't work underwater. Suppose that they're dangerous?"

"We'll be in suits. That should be protection against anything like teeth or poison. Your bubble-men won't have anything more than that." Indigo saw Bony's mouth twitch. "They won't, man. Use your brain. If you're worried about lasers or explosives or projectile weapons, forget it. These are sea-creatures. It's a well-known fact that creatures who develop in water, even if they are intelligent creatures, will never discover fire and never be able to develop technology."

Bony wanted to say, "It's not a well-known fact, it's a well-known *theory*." But it wasn't worth getting into an argument. Even though Indigo was wrong, the captain would ride right over him. Instead Bony said, "Don't you think it's less important to learn about the bubble-creatures than to get the *Mood Indigo* working again?"

"How? You were the one who insisted that the fusion drive could never operate underwater."

"It won't. But what reason do we have for thinking that Limbo—"

"That what?"

"Limbo. This planet. It's the way I've been thinking of the place. We entered a Link entry point back in our solar system, and now we're in the middle of nowhere. In limbo."

"Nonsense. We know that we're in the Geyser Swirl. If only we could get a look at the stars . . ."

"That's my point, sir. We're in water at the moment, but we have no reason to think that the whole of Limbo is ocean. There could be land just a few kilometers away. If we could move the *Mood Indigo* onto land, we could see the stars *and* we could use the fusion drive to get off the planet."

"Are you suggesting that we ask your froth-men the way to the nearest land?"

"No, sir!" Bony wanted nothing to do with those floating assemblies of bubbles. "I noticed that when I was outside and high on the underwater slope, the light seemed a lot brighter. It makes me think we're not perhaps all that deep, maybe as little as thirty meters. The buoyancy of the heavy water is greater than ordinary water, because of its greater density. We might be able to float the ship to the surface more easily than we think."

"Not a bad idea." Indigo smiled at Bony. "Good work, Rombelle. Of course, before we do anything with the ship we have to be sure what we'll find up at the surface. Are you volunteering to go out again and take a look?"

Bony was proposing no such thing. He had seen enough of deep-sea diving in modified space-suits for one day.

Before he could reply, Liddy said, "Let me do it. I'm no use fixing things inside the ship, but I'm sure I can put on a suit as well as anyone and go up to the surface."

"Do it soon," Indigo said, "before we have to worry about it getting dark." And, as Bony tried to hide his surprise, "Did you think I was doing nothing, while you two were playing your games with airlocks and romping around outside? I adapted one of our light-meters and I've been monitoring the ambient light level for the ship since the time we arrived. This planet has a twenty-nine-hour day, and we're more than halfway through the cycle. That means we have maybe five more hours before darkness."

"I'll get ready right now," said Liddy. Bony was still staring at Friday Indigo. He had written the man off completely, and now here came common sense and a talent for improvisation. Maybe you didn't have to be an idiot just because you were rich.

Indigo was nodding at Liddy. "Carry on, as soon as you're ready. Be sure to carry extra weights and inflate your suit extra hard when you go up. That way, when you bleed away the excess air you'll sink straight back down to the ship. The trip up to the surface will be useful even if you can't see land. We can go again after it gets dark and try for a fix on the stars. That will answer one other important question: where are we in the Geyser Swirl."

More sound sense from Friday Indigo. But Bony recalled the shape that had flown over him as he stood on the seabed, a form like a great three-leaf clover. Was that at the surface, or above it? He found himself saying, against his better judgment, "There may be other things up there. Don't you think I should go with Liddy, as a backup if things go wrong? And shouldn't we take a line with us, so that we can pull ourselves back if we get into trouble? And if we attach an insulated wire, we can have continuous two-way communication with the ship even though the radios don't work in water."

Indigo laughed. "My God, that's four ideas from you in one day. You're less of a fool than you look."

A dubious compliment, at best. But Indigo was continuing, "Now here's an idea for you. You said you intended to see if the suit control thrustors would still work under water, but you didn't do it when you were outside. So why don't you try it now? You can cruise around a bit on the way up or on the way down. Maybe you'll see your mysterious froth-men, and find out what they are up to."

It was phrased as a cheerful invitation, but Bony was under no illusions. He had to go outside again and face the horrible bubble creatures.

He turned to Liddy. "I'll come and help you to operate the airlock. Just give me a half a minute, then I'll be with you."

Bony's urge to go to the bathroom had returned. This time he felt sure that it would not vanish by itself.

8

Recruiting at the Vulcan Nexus

Salamander Row sits on the sunward side of the Vulcan Nexus. Shielded by four hundred million square kilometers of solar collectors, there is no visible evidence on the Row that the flaming disk of the Sun's photosphere lies less than two million kilometers away. Other than the Salamanders, the residents of the Row need never see the Sun and can remain oblivious of the solar presence.

The Salamanders themselves are a different matter. As monitors and custodians of the great array they ride their refrigerated spacecraft hair-raisingly close to the solar furnace, skimming low above vast hydrogen flares and across the Earth-sized whirlpools of sunspots. Occasionally a cooling unit fails. Vehicle recovery is performed—always—but never the bodies of the crew members. Those are burned, what remains of them, out in space by their Salamander brethren. On Salamander Row, by convention, the names of the dead are recorded but they are not talked about. The Salamanders refuse to admit the power of King Sun. Other residents of the Row often seem determined to deny his existence.

That is their privilege. It is, however, a privilege denied to the occasional visitor. Before an arriving ship can reach the Nexus and the Row, it must first drive inward until the eye of the Sun fills half the sky. Although the temperature inside the ship never rises past a comfort level, the psychological heat mounts by the minute.

Danny Casement had shed his jacket before they crossed the orbit of Mercury. Now he mopped at his wrinkled forehead, stared at the port where the photoglass turned the solar disk to an opaque circle of dark gray, and wondered how many more minutes to Nexus rendezvous.

And he, believe it or not, had *chosen* this. Chan Dalton, worried about schedule, had offered him a choice: did he want Europa, or the Vulcan Nexus?

"You out of your mind?" Danny, packing the things he would need on the *Hero's Return* and sending everything else to sealed storage, stared at Chan. "If you think I'm going to invite Deb Bisson on a trip with you as leader, you can think again. Anyone says your name to her, he'd better be ready to go home with teeth marks in his ass. You dumped her. *You* go to Europa."

It made sense at the time. Chan would go to Europa, find Tully O'Toole, and face Deb; but there was a trade-off: Danny had to go to Salamander Row and look for the Bun.

The ship was smart enough to fly itself and the only other person on board was a woman. Expensively dressed, clearly a lady, striking in appearance although no longer young, Alice Tannenbaum was big-bosomed and strongly built. Casement prime choice, under normal circumstances. She had also shown interest in Danny. Almost as soon as they had introduced themselves, Alice was saying, "If you have never been to the Vulcan Nexus before, I would love to serve as your personal tour guide." A little smile and a sideways glance. "The Nexus offers pastimes that most visitors never see."

"Ah—er—well." Danny did his own sideways glance, to where the occluded disk of the Sun loomed ever larger. Soon it would fill the whole port. "I—er—I—um." After a few replies of that caliber, she apparently decided that she was dealing with a half-wit and retreated to the rear of the passenger cabin.

Well, maybe she was. If the known dangers of the Vulcan Nexus gave you fits, how would you manage the unknown ones of the Geyser Swirl? You wouldn't, unless you took a better hold of yourself. And if she knew the Nexus, she might be able to save him some time.

Danny made a mighty effort, stood up from his seat, and wandered toward the back of the cabin. He smiled at his fellow passenger.

"I'm sorry I was rude a few minutes ago. This is quite an overwhelming experience, flying so close to the Sun."

"That's understandable. You'll get used to it after a while." She moved along the seat, making room for him. "Where are you from, Jack?"

He had assumed a false name and identity for this journey as a matter of course, without ever expecting it to come in useful. Danny, who for the moment was Jack Eckart and had better not forget it, made a more detailed inspection of Alice Tannenbaum. She had to be close to his age, but she was far better preserved. The skin of her face and hands was smooth and unlined. And she must be rich. Those epidermal rebuilders cost real money.

"I'd say that I'm from pretty much all over." He sat down next to her. "Born out among the Saturnian moons, spent a while on Mars, a while on Earth, a while on Ganymede. If it hadn't been for the quarantine, I might be somewhere out among the stars by now."

"That's so exciting." She turned as though to glance out of the port, but actually to display her profile, which she must know showed her to advantage. "You make me feel like I've been nowhere and done nothing. Never to Mars or Ceres, never to the Jovian moons. I wanted to, but my family wouldn't allow it."

"But you've been to the Vulcan Nexus before."

"A hundred times. That's different. Coming here is a family tradition. We were one of the Nexus first families, involved from day one."

The Vulcan Nexus was a major supplier of power for the whole system, drinking in solar energy through the giant arrays and sending it out to destinations as far away as Persephone in tightly collimated microwave beams. Abundant energy—at a price. Anyone with a piece of the Vulcan Nexus revenue stream had money to throw away.

Danny was here to see if he could find the Bun, not to pursue personal business interests. But the urge to play the game a little was irresistible, particularly when the target was as tempting as Alice Tannenbaum. He justified his next words with the thought that he would need help if he was to explore the Nexus in a day or less. He said casually, "I suppose I've been a user of your service and never realized it. The past few years I've been on one of the Saturnian moons, and we have a big receiver for energy from the Vulcan Nexus."

"Really." She turned to stare at him with wide hazel eyes. "What were you doing out there, Jack?"

"My family's business." Danny glanced carefully around the cabin, though the nearest human other than Alice Tannenbaum was a million kilometers away. "I was on Hyperion, busy with diamond mining operations."

He watched closely. Her reaction would decide what came next. Everyone in the system knew about Raxon Yang and his five-centuries-old discovery on Hyperion. Early explorers of the solar system had more or less ignored the lumpy, uneven hunk of rock that formed the seventh major satellite of Saturn. Old Yang, with nothing better to do, had landed on Hyperion and followed a surface fissure down and down and down. Seven kilometers below the surface he came to the upper face of the Yang diamond.

Even after the claim was filed, it took a while to learn exactly what he had. The Yang diamond had the shape of a forty-legged octopus. Its head, seven kilometers below the surface, was almost spherical and fourteen kilometers across. The legs ran out and down, each one half a kilometer wide and thirty to forty kilometers long.

Mining the Yang diamond had created the Vault of Hyperion, home to a polyglot melange of industries. Now no diamond was exported—because there was none left to export.

The first question was, did Alice Tannenbaum know that?

She did. She was frowning at Danny. "But Jack, I thought that the diamond was all—"

Danny was ahead of her. "Not the *original* one, of course. That's long gone. But a few years ago we had seismic hints that there might be another one. We organized a private offering, formed a new stable of investors, and began prospecting. The exploration was very difficult. We were about ready to give up when a month ago we struck lucky. Actually, that's why I've come to the Vulcan Nexus. We have been unable to reach one of our larger investors, and I've been sent to find him. If you are a regular visitor to the Nexus, maybe you've run across him. His name is Bonifant Rombelle. Some people know him as Señor Bonifant, others as Bunnyfat Ramble; but his close friends call him Bun or the Bun."

"I never heard of him." Alice's face showed her utter lack of interest in hearing more about the lost investor. "You say you 'struck lucky.' Do you mean you found another Yang Diamond?"

"Oh, nothing nearly so big. The new one is smaller, and much deeper. On the other hand, this diamond seems wonderfully pure and without flaws. So yes, it's a very significant find. It will make many people very rich."

If Alice Tannenbaum owned part of the Vulcan Nexus power stream, she was already very rich. But one thing that Danny had learned, early in life, was this: people, no matter how much money they had, never felt that it was enough.

Sure enough, Alice was leaning toward him. "I suppose that your original private offering was fully subscribed."

"It was indeed."

"Oh, phooey. How long will it be before you know for sure the quality of the new stones?"

"Oh, we know that already. The new mine will be every bit as good as the original Yang diamond, possibly even better. As a matter of fact . . . excuse me for just a moment."

Danny went forward, retrieved his jacket, and returned to Alice. He reached into one of the pockets and took out a black pouch. "A small sample, something I intended to leave with Bonifant Rombelle when I find him. But it will give you some idea . . ."

Twelve hours later, Danny was beginning to change his mind about a number of things. First, the Nexus itself was not a well-lit or a hot place. The collector array sucked in every last erg of solar power so that, nestled in behind and sheltered by it, Salamander Row was one of the coldest places of the system, as dark and chilly as interstellar space. Danny was comfortable with that. He didn't find space at all terrifying. Second, this was, as Alice Tannenbaum had suggested, a place where with the right companion you could have a whooping good time. The residents of the Row didn't seem to believe in moderation in anything. Finally, there were hints that Alice herself, in spite of her regal appearance, might be anything but a lady.

For one thing, she seemed to know every low-life pit stop in the five-kilometer sprawl of tunnels and chambers that made up Salamander Row, and she apparently had it in mind to dance in all of them before she considered sleeping. She had incredible energy, and when Danny pleaded fatigue and unfamiliarity with zero-gee dance technique she was quite ready to cavort alone, or with anyone else in the place. Danny was happy to go along with that. While Alice enjoyed herself he could have a quiet word with the regulars. There was no better way of making discreet enquiries about Bunnyfat Ramble.

On the other hand, with all his questions he was getting nowhere fast. No one had heard of the Bun, under that or any other of his preferred names. It wasn't until the sixth port of call that Danny had even a sniff of something promising.

"I never heard of your friend." The speaker was a tall black man with a face almost invisible behind a tangled beard. He was swaying on his feet and within minutes of final collapse. The cloud of secondhand intoxicants diffusing from him was enough to make Danny dizzy himself. The man stood frowning, as if making a mighty effort to think. At last he said, "D'you say he was good at making gadgets?"

"The best."

"Then you ought to go find Fireside Elsie. I heard talk of a fancy data tap with a top gadgeteer involved. It came through Fireside Elsie, but I don't think it was her game. If it was, you can be sure she didn't do the work herself."

"Why?"

"Why? Because she's a bleeding Salamander, that's why. No Sally would do gadgeting, it's beneath them."

"Can you tell me how to find her?"

"I could, but I'm not going to." The man sat down suddenly. "I'm going to sit here and pass out. Get your friend Leaping Lizzy to take you. She'll take you all right! Just look at her."

Danny turned to find Alice beckoning him from the tiny dance area. Her face was aglow, the top fastening of her dress was undone, and her body swayed and undulated to some inaudible rhythm.

The things you did for your friends. *I ought to have gone to Europa and let Chan come here*. But Danny waved back to her and moved forward. As he crossed the threshold of the dance area the music and the thumping rhythm, focused on the dance floor and inaudible everywhere else, filled his ears.

If you could use the word music for such a cacophony. Danny's tastes went back to a far earlier era of minuets and waltzes. He came up to Alice, was grabbed, swung around like a feather, and pulled close. He shouted into her ear, "Do you know how to find Fireside Elsie?"

"Now why would you be interested in a Sally woman?" Alice put her arms around his waist and squeezed him until he couldn't breathe. "Looking for something hot. Too cool for you, am I?"

"The investor I was telling you about. Fireside Elsie may know him."

"Phooey. You told me I could keep that diamond."

"You can." God, she was strong. It was Danny's misfortune to find physical strength highly attractive in a woman. He struggled to take a breath and gasped, "But I need to talk to her."

"Next stop but one you'll see Fireside Elsie—provided you treat me nice, I'll show you where. Come on, Jack, let yourself go. Have some fun."

Her breasts pushed into his chest. Her perfume filled his nostrils. As Danny put his arms around her, he thought, *What the hell, you only die once. It might as well be tonight.*

An hour later that prospect no longer seemed so fanciful.

Danny had heard the usual rumors about the Salamanders. They were said to be Artefacts, a prize creation of the Needler lab run by the late Margrave of Fujitsu. The DNA mix in a Salamander was unknown. What was known was that they bred true, unlike any other Artefact, and the body of a dead Salamander was always burned to ashes. Self-immolation was the standard act for any Salamander threatened with capture and inspection.

Danny knew all this, and he had seen pictures; but the real thing was a different matter.

Alice had dropped him off at a dark and airless cavern with a casual, "Here you are. This is the Fireside. I'll collect you in half an hour. Will that be enough time?"

"Should be. But what are you going to do?"

"Make sure we have a place to sleep."

"I already made a reservation at the Crystal Gate."

"Forget it. That's for old people."

Keep this up, and that'll be me. "But Alice, don't you think you ought to come in with me? I don't know anyone in there."

"Phooey. You've got a tongue." She stuck hers out at Danny. "One like this. Use it."

And she skipped away.

Danny stepped forward into the gloom. There were lights, he realized, but they were down close to the floor. They were also weak, red, and flickering. They couldn't possibly be actual fires, flames wouldn't burn right without a bigger gravity gradient to encourage convection; but they were highly plausible imitations.

A woman was approaching out of the shadows. Not a woman, a something. No, he had been right the first time. It was a woman.

"Sallies only in the Fireside," she said in a husky, musical voice. She was close to naked, wearing nothing but wisps of black cloth across her chest and hips. They emphasized her powerful build and the ribbed muscles of her abdomen, but that was not the thing that puzzled Danny.

It was her skin. It displayed a granular texture, like a layer of silver paint over a pattern of fine scales. Nobody had skin like that. "Sallies only," she said again when he did not move or speak. "Out."

"I don't want service. My name is Jack Eckart. I'm looking for Fireside Elsie."

"You found her. This is my place." She held out

a hand. Her grip was strong but the fingers were ice-cold, like the hand of a corpse. She went on, "Who gave you my name?"

"I don't know. He was a tall black man, back at the Golden Goose. He seemed about ready to pass out."

"Louie Lucas. Why'd he tell you about me?"

"I'm looking for a friend of mine, Bunnyfat Ramble. He was an expert in . . . certain kinds of equipment. Last time we heard from Bun he was on the Vulcan Nexus. Louie Lucas thought you might be able to help me."

They examined each other closely. Her face had a thin, prominent nose and a near-lipless mouth. Danny could see her eyes now. They were black and lifeless.

At last she said, "Can you pay for information?"

"Some. I have trade crystals. How much do you want?"

"Not for me. You make your own deal. Come this way."

She led him into the smoky interior of the Fireside, along an aisle bordered by a dozen small tables at which silver-skinned Salamanders sat cross-legged. The air held a curious aroma, like burning cinnamon and sulfur.

At the far end a little cubicle sat tucked away out of sight of the main room. The light was much brighter inside. She gestured to one of the cubicle's benches with an arm that bent and flexed as though it had no bone within, and said, "You wait right there. You can't get service, so don't ask."

"Where are you going?"

"Nowhere. But I have to make a call."

She walked away with an oddly sinuous grace. Danny thought of a snake, then changed his mind.

The Salamanders were more complicated than a simple human/snake splice. For one thing, the eyes were wrong. The limbs also had that curious flexibility, as though the skeleton was not bone but cartilage.

Could it be a human/snake/shark triplet? The Margrave had been a genius, and Danny had heard of stranger combinations.

Fireside Elsie was coming back, weaving her way past the tables. She was holding two tall beakers of black volcanic glass.

"He's on the way," she said. "Don't ask his name. And here's a Fireside special. You can't ask for service and get it, but I can give it."

She handed him one of the beakers and drank deeply from the other. Danny could not see what was inside, but as he took a first sip he comforted himself with the thought that she had no particular reason to poison him. He needed that thought, because the thick liquid coursed down his throat like a train of fire. He could feel it as the drink reached each separate inch of his oesophagus. His eyes began to water. He saw a blurred image of Fireside Elsie as she turned and walked away.

He wiped at the tears with the sleeve of his jacket. A Salamander who found it necessary to undertake self-immolation wouldn't need rehearsals, not with drinks like this available as practice.

But he was no Salamander. Danny placed the beaker carefully on the low table in front of him. He peered into the dimlit room, wondering when Anonymous would arrive and where he was coming from. After ten minutes he was considering taking a second sip from the beaker out of sheer boredom when a bulky figure appeared from the shadows and slid onto the bench opposite.

"You looking for somebody?"

Apparently they would dispense with introductions. That was fine with Danny. He said, "A friend of mine, Bunnyfat Ramble. Do you know him?"

Dead eyes stared into Danny's. Fireside Elsie was a model of geniality compared with the newcomer. "Depends. You say you're a friend of his. Who are you?"

"My name's Jack Eckart."

"Never heard of you." The Salamander rose and was leaving the cubicle in one lithe movement.

"Wait a minute." Danny had to make an instant decision. "I'm using that name at the moment, but it's not the one he knew me by. If he talked of me at all, it would be as Dapper Dan, or Danny Casement."

The Salamander had turned and was back in the cubicle. "I've heard of Dan Casement. But anybody could say that was his name. Give me proof."

"What kind of proof? I don't have any identification on me."

The wide, thin-lipped mouth opened, to show a multiple array of sharp triangular teeth. "If you're really Diamond Dan Casement, you have something else. Show me a sample."

Alice Tannenbaum had laid claim to the last wrapped stone, but Danny always allowed for emergencies. He removed his jacket. It took a couple of minutes to work the quarter-carat specimen out from the lining of his coat. He didn't want to touch the Salamander, so he laid the stone on the table in front of them. "There you are. Take a look. It's genuine."

"I don't care if it's genuine or not. The fact that you have it with you is the important thing. What's your question?"

"What was Bun doing, and what happened to him?"

"I can answer the first, but not the second. You ever hear of Flare-out?"

"Never."

"It's one of the big games on Salamander Row—there's a betting board right here at the Fireside. Solar flares can happen any time, so the managers of the Nexus run a pool on flare times and sizes. Now, computer models can't make a perfect prediction, but they can increase the odds. Of course, they rely on good inputs. You follow?"

"I do." Danny had run his own gambling operations; he knew the importance of inside information.

"Now, the managers don't want anybody beating the odds. So they make a law. The law says, it's all right to have any computer model you like, but the input data stays locked up. A gambling group didn't think that was fair—to them."

"Who were they?"

"You don't want to know. Do you?"

Danny looked into those deep-set, lifeless eyes. "You're right. I don't want to know. *Definitely* I don't want to know."

"So this group wanted to put a tap on the input data in a way that would never be noticed. People here tried and tried, and they couldn't do it. Not until somebody you and I both know came along, and he was smart enough to crack all the ciphers. The inputs rolled in smooth and regular and everything was fine. Until somebody talked. You don't need to know who he was, either"—Danny noted the past tense—"but one day the group was in big legal trouble. And so was your friend. Bun could have stayed and maybe bluffed it through and been all right, but although he was smart he was nervous.

"He ran. Borrowed a ship, left the Nexus, dropped into a low skimmer orbit intending to ride past and off to the outer system. But he never made it. The drive misfired and he went right into the Sun. Sent messages once he realized what was happening. Said good-bye to everybody. Salamander's finish. End of story."

Danny recalled the outsized solar disk, flaming outside the port. It was an awful prospect and a terrible way to die; but something was missing.

"You said you could answer one of my questions and not the other. But now you're saying he's dead."

"Smart Danny." The Sally gave a dry laugh like a chesty wheeze. "Logically, our friend is dead. But Bun was smart, too. I've wondered for the past few months. Suppose he wasn't on that ship? If anyone could rig a skimmer's communication system so it seemed he was there when he wasn't, the Bun was the man for that."

It was wishful thinking, playing the wrong side of the odds. The Sally didn't seem to realize what was involved. There would have had to be more than the faking of a death. There would have to be an escape plan, a total disappearance, an opportunity elsewhere.

"If he's not dead, then where do you think he might be?"

"I can't begin to guess." The Salamander was standing up. "But I know he's nowhere on the Nexus."

Danny stood up, too. "As far as paying you is concerned, I'll be glad—"

"Forget it. And forget we talked. I'm not doing this for you, and I'm not doing it for me. I'm doing it for him. I liked Bun, as much as you can like a human. If he's not dead, and if you ever do see him again, say hello from me."

"I don't know your name."

"You're right." The silver countenance was split by another sword-toothed smile. "You don't know my name. You also don't need to know it, and you don't want to know it. You'll have to go with a description.

Now get out of here. Do you want the rest of that drink?"

Danny shook his head. As the Sally lifted the black beaker and downed the contents in one long gulp, Danny turned and walked the length of the room. He could see little after the brightly lit cubicle, but he felt sure that the faces were all turned his way. Fireside Elsie nodded at him when he was close to the exit. She did not speak. Alice—how long had she been waiting?—stood just outside.

"Oh, dear." She took his arm and the smile faded from her face. "It's bad news, I can tell just by looking at you."

"It seems that way."

"Then it's my job to do what I can to cheer you up. You found out about your friend. Is he here?"

Danny shook his head. Bun was not here, he was dead, a puff of incandescent gases on the surface of the Sun.

"So what do you want to do, Jack?"

He had done what he came to do, all that he could do. Now he wanted to collapse into bed with Alice. But he could not suggest that.

"I'd like to go some place where I can get a cold drink. I don't think I was actually poisoned in there, but somebody wandered down my throat holding a lighted torch."

"You were permitted to drink in the Fireside? Then you were honored. It's for Sallies only. But I know just the place for us. Come on."

Alice did indeed know just the place, cool and intimate and soothing. It had been a very long day. Sitting across from her, watching her bright eyes and the pink tongue that licked sugar from the side of her glass, Danny felt himself beginning to relax. If only he could get Bun out of his mind . . . they had not seen each other for years, but the idea of Bun diving to his death in the Sun . . . He felt Alice's hand on his cheek. "Don't think about it, whatever it is. There's nothing you could have done. Unwind, Jack."

Unwind. He was trying.

He peered at Alice, across the table from him, with weary eyes. Quite a woman. A fine woman, rich and classy *and* sexy. He felt almost sorry that he had set her up with a phony mining investment.

The second place she took him to was dark, close to free-fall, and so ringing with Colchester brass that speech was impossible. He didn't recall ordering anything, but a bright blue potion mysteriously appeared in front of him. He and Alice sat in companionable silence, swaying together to the music.

Unwind.

There must have been a third place. He did not remember going to it, but suddenly it was darker yet. There was again a gravity field. He and Alice leaned close, speaking in whispers. And then they were sitting side by side, not talking at all but with Alice's thigh pressed against his.

Unwind.

Was he unwound? Yes, he thought so. Now he could suggest what he had wanted to suggest to Alice in the first place.

Danny did not so much wake as wander slowly up toward consciousness through pink clouds of bliss. He was lying naked on soft cushions in a low-gravity setting, and never in his life had he felt so rested and full of well-being.

How wrong he had been to think badly of the Vulcan Nexus. It was one of the most delightful spots in the solar system. Ten more minutes of quiet peace, and Alice could perhaps go about ordering something to eat. But then, regrettably, after breakfast Jack Eckart would bid her a fond farewell and Danny would leave the Vulcan Nexus for a rendezvous with Chan Dalton.

Eyes still closed, he reached out to where Alice lay in the bed. His left hand wandered around over the downy surface and found nothing.

So she was up already. Maybe taking a shower, maybe in the other room making a breakfast selection. Danny yawned, stretched luxuriously, and opened his eyes. The bedchamber was large, with a high, vaulted ceiling. Alice was nowhere to be seen. He stood up slowly, with wobbly legs—it had been quite an evening, and quite a night—and wandered through to the living room. There was no sign of Alice.

He walked back to the bedroom and through into the bathroom. She was not there, either. As he relieved himself, he realized that he could see no sign of the clutter of toiletries with which his female companions ordinarily decorated the premises. Alice was indeed an unusual woman.

Still naked, he stepped back out into the bedroom. He found his underwear where he had abandoned it, on the floor along with his shoes. His suit? He looked around. He had dropped that on the floor, too, but it wasn't there now. Alice must have hung it up in the closet. Good for her. In Danny's experience, rich women seldom made good housewives.

He walked over to the closet, opened it, and peered inside.

No suit. Then where was it?

He walked back to the dimly lit living room. Still no suit, but a piece of paper sitting on the low table next to the couch.

A note. Danny turned on a light and picked it up.

Dear Jack (or may I call you Danny?),

What a wonderful evening, and a wonderful night! I will remember it always, but unfortunately I must now be on my way.

In picking up your suit from the floor, where in our delicious haste we had abandoned it, I noticed in two hidden compartments a substantial number of trade crystals. The lining also held several samples of "Yang diamond," which I trust are genuine. I was obliged to take the crystals, samples, and the money that I found in your wallet, in order to defray certain incidental expenses of my own.

I also took the liberty of removing the suit itself. The color does not favor your complexion, and the cut makes you look much older than you are (or than you act!). Naturally, I needed the use of your travel bag in order to transport the suit, trade crystals, and wallet.

This suite is yours until midday. Unfortunately I was not able to make payment for it, or for my meal and a few other trifles that I purchased and charged this morning, so I leave you to settle the tab.

I do not think that we will meet again, Danny, so let me express once more my appreciation for a fabulous twenty-four hours. Believe me, had it been possible for me to stay longer I would have done so.

Yours in gratitude, Alice Tannenbaum.

P.S. In case you should feel an inclination to try to find me, I would not recommend it. It would surely be a waste of time. I feel confident that I left none of my possessions in the suite; also, as you may by this time have guessed, my name is not Alice Tannenbaum.

Danny read the note. Then he sat down on the couch and read it again. He had his underwear and his shoes. He lacked money, trade crystals, diamond samples, and outer garments. He owed whatever was the cost of this suite and Alice's "few other trifles." Considerable, he felt sure. Alice settled for nothing but the best.

Danny went back to the bedroom. He put on his underwear and shoes and looked at himself in the full-length mirror. It was no way to face the management, or anyone else in the known universe. He picked up the bed's outer coverlet from the floor, wrapped it around himself, and sat down at the suite's communications center.

He needed to do three things. Two of them could be done at once: arrange for a transfer of credit from Chan Dalton, to cover the bill here; and contact a local clothing outlet and have a suit delivered.

The third thing would have to wait until they returned from the Geyser Swirl. Then he would tackle the difficult problem of tracking down "Alice Tannenbaum."

Suppose that it took a long time, and involved a considerable effort. Would he still do it?

Danny, already calling Chan Dalton's personal ID, nodded to himself. He certainly would. A woman like Alice came along once in a lifetime, and any man would be insane to let her go.

9

Exploring Limbo

The ocean of Limbo seemed as peaceful as ever, but Bony made a careful survey of his surroundings as he drifted out of the airlock.

No sign of bubble creatures. Small purple objects like floating umbrellas opened and closed to jet rapidly away from him, but they seemed more afraid of Bony than he was of them. He waved to Liddy, peering from the airlock, to join him. While she was doing it he made sure that the line connecting him to the *Mood Indigo* was clear, then cracked open the suit's internal pressure valve. His buoyancy became slightly greater, enough to begin a slow rise through limpid water.

He looked down. Liddy was following him upward, her slim figure hidden within the bloat of her over-inflated suit. One of the annoyances of the situation was that radios meant for space use were no good under water. Although Bony could talk to Friday Indigo at long distance via the wire connection to the ship, underwater he could speak to Liddy only when they were close enough for sound waves to move directly between them. That meant they could not afford to get too far apart. He brushed his glove across his faceplate to rid it of the annoying layer of tiny bubbles that coated it after a minute or two in the superaerated ocean. High oxygen content must help the native sea-creatures, but to humans in suits it was a nuisance—like moving inside a gigantic bottle of soda water.

The light level was steadily growing brighter, just as it had when he ascended the undersea ridge. In the cumbersome suit it was difficult to bend his head to look upward. He craned back for a quick look and fancied that he could make out moving variations in intensity above him. Wave patterns, travelling across the surface? That would mean the ship could not be more than thirty meters down.

Before he could confirm that guess, his head burst through into dazzling sunlight. The photoreceptors in his helmet recorded an overdose of ultraviolet and modified the faceplate at once to screen out most of it. As he floated at the surface, chest-deep and feet-down, Liddy's suit bobbed up a few meters away. A long, sluggish wave gently lifted them and then lowered them as they paddled toward each other.

Bony tried the radio circuit. "Liddy?"

"I hear you. My suit shows a really high light level. Does yours?"

"Yes. It's real. There's the culprit." He raised an arm and pointed at the sun. "It's a blue giant type. That's really strange."

"You mean it *looks* strange. That's not surprising."

"No. I mean it *is* strange. For a planet around a

blue giant star, every astronomer will tell you that there should be no life-forms. A star can't stay in a blue giant stage long enough for anything alive to develop on its planets."

"Tell that to those funny little umbrella things down near the seabed. They don't seem to know much astronomy. Bony, can Friday hear us?"

"Only when I have something we want to transmit. Do you need to talk to him? The circuit is off at the moment."

"No. I was thinking I might feel like saying things I wouldn't want him to hear. We're really away from him for the first time, just the two of us. Isn't it great?"

Bony had mixed feelings about that. Sure, it was great not to have Friday ordering him around or using Liddy as a personal sex toy. But out of the frying pan . . .

As another wave lifted them he stared all around, seeking any sign of the winged mystery that had cast the tri-lobed underwater shadow on his first trip outside. He saw nothing like it, but far off to his left he caught a glimpse of a long horizontal line across the face of the sea. Land? Or clouds? Before he could confirm anything they were dropping back into the trough.

"Liddy, look that way when we hit the crest of another wave." He pointed. "I thought I saw something on the skyline. Could be clouds—if this planet has clouds."

While they waited he opened the circuit to the *Mood Indigo*. "We're at the surface, and in a little while I'm going to try the suit thrustors. They ought to move us about up here even if they have problems lower down. If I have to release our connecting line to give us more mobility, I will. We won't lose the line. The buoy stays on the surface and the beacon will let us find it easily enough from any distance."

A grunt from Friday Indigo, and that was all.

One more device that Bony had made from nothing and his boss took for granted. Apparently that's what it was like when you had enough money to buy anything, including people's brains and bodies. Bony broke the circuit to the ship before the captain could veto his proposal, and made sure that he could unhook the line and beacon easily from his suit. He was still busy with that when he heard Liddy's excited voice.

"It's not just clouds, Bony. It's clouds and *land*."

He stared, but too late. They were again dropping into a trough. "Are you sure?"

"Sure as I can be without going over and standing on it. See for yourself. Wait for the next crest and you can watch waves breaking on the shore."

If there was land, it was their best hope of escape. The planet's gravity field was weak, and the ship's drive should certainly function in an atmosphere.

But which atmosphere? The water samples he had analyzed back on the ship showed a high level of dissolved oxygen. That was encouraging—the only place it could come from was the air at the surface.

Bony glanced at his suit monitors. They were designed to warn if anything in the ambient environment was dangerous to humans. No red lights blinked. That didn't mean you could breathe whatever was outside. An excess of carbon dioxide would not show as dangerous, but try to breathe *that* for long and you would be in trouble.

"See?" It was Liddy's cry. "It *is* land."

He had missed it again. He paddled over until he was again right next to her. "Liddy, I'm going to do two things. I want you to watch, but I don't want you too close. If anything goes wrong, follow the line and go back down."

He unhooked the buoy and beacon from his suit, as she said nervously, "Bony, you mustn't do anything silly. I won't allow it."

"I'll try not to. The first thing I want to do is pretty straightforward. If we're to get anywhere at all on the surface in a reasonable time, we won't manage it by paddling. We must try our drives. So I'm going to use my suit thrustors to make sure they work and don't fizzle or blow up or do something else weird. I want you to stay right where you are. Don't follow me."

He swam slowly away until there were thirty or forty meters between them. He used his arms to turn in the water so that he was facing Liddy, and tried to sound more confident than he felt. "All right. Here I come."

He turned on the rear suit thrustors, keeping the setting to a medium level. That was just as well. Even on medium impulse he went racing through the water at a slight downward angle. The level rose on either side of his helmet and suddenly he was submerged and could see nothing but blue-green bubbles. He cut the thrust at once. When he bobbed up to the surface he was face-to-face with Liddy and only inches away from her. The expression of surprise and relief showing through her visor should have been comical. It wasn't. It was merely reasonable, because Bony felt the same way himself.

He said, he hoped calmly, "I guess that's a success. Be careful when you use yours, and keep it to a low or medium thrust level. Now for a trickier one. I'm going to let some outside air into my suit."

"Bony, that's dangerous. Suppose it's a poisonous gas?"

"I don't see how it can be. We know that the gas dissolved in the sea is mostly oxygen, and there must be a balance between what's in the water and what's in the air above it. The big question is, how much oxygen? It won't kill me, but too little or too much and I'll pant and pass out. Keep an eye on me and be ready to seal my suit."

"Bony, please don't."

"We must. I don't know how long we may have to stay on Limbo, and we don't want to have to live in space-suits indefinitely."

Bony made sure that the neck seal was tight, so that the rest of the suit would remain inflated even when the helmet was cracked open. The air pressure inside most of the suit had to remain higher than outside. Otherwise he would sink like a stone when the helmet pressure equalized.

He found himself holding his breath as air hissed from the suit. That was ridiculous, about as sensible as a man being hanged trying to delay execution by jumping up into the air a moment before the trap-door opened. The whole point was to get this over as fast as possible.

His ears were popping. As the air escaped he sank a few inches deeper into the water. Now air was entering his helmet. The smell of an alien sea was in his nostrils. Bony opened his mouth wide and gulped in the air of Limbo.

He felt a moment of dizziness and panic. He was panting, his vision blurred, and something was catching in his throat and burning at his lungs. He thought of Liddy's worries about poisonous gases. Then he realized that the strange sensation was almost surely the effects of a high ozone level. That made logical sense. The blue giant sun delivered a sleet of ultra-violet light to Limbo, and UV had the effect of ionizing oxygen to form the triatomic molecule of ozone.

The act of rational thought had its own steadying effect. His breathing slowed. His vision cleared and he saw Liddy reaching up to seal his helmet.

"No." He took her hands in his. "It's all right. I can breathe. The air pressure is a bit lower but the oxygen content is higher. I'm not sure what the long-term effects might be, but provided we always go back and sleep in the ship I think we'll be all right."

Liddy said suddenly, "Fine. It's my turn. I'm going to open my helmet and breathe it, too."

"Wait a minute." Another big wave was arriving. Lifted high, Bony for the first time was looking in the right direction at the right time. He saw a black mass bulging up from the sea, with a narrow band of sparkling white in front of it.

Land, and a line of breakers, no more than a few kilometers away.

"Hold off for the moment, Liddy. If we're going ashore we won't want open helmets while we're doing it. I'm going to close mine, then I'll show you how to use the thrustors."

It took a couple of false starts. The first time, Liddy set the wrong thrust angle. She was driven under water and popped up forty meters away like the bloated corpse of some sea-monster. The second time Bony used too high a thrust setting. He skated helplessly across the surface at speed and was buffeted hard by waves. Over the suit radio he could hear Liddy laughing at him.

The seabed's ascent as it approached the land formed a gentle incline. Waves began to break two hundred meters offshore, and with a hundred meters still to go Bony and Liddy could touch bottom.

The shore itself was a bleak shingle of black and

brown stones. Bony waded the final ten meters and sank to his knees.

Liddy moved anxiously to his side. "Are you all right?"

"I'm fine. Just looking for something. If you want to open your suit now it ought to be all right. I suggest you sit down before you do it—I felt dizzy for a few moments."

She flopped down at his side. Bony heard the hiss of escaping air, followed by Liddy's calm voice, "You said looking. Looking for what?"

Apparently his own discomfort had mostly been nervousness. He would never make a hero. Bony said, "Looking for signs of life. Little crabs, shrimp, sand fleas, barnacles, stuff like that." He turned over handfuls of pebbles. "I don't see anything alive. Not even plants. Do you?"

"Nothing. But you saw all sorts on the seabed, didn't you? Plants *and* animals. What does it mean?"

Bony stood up and gazed farther inland, to where black rocks rose to a jagged skyline. "If it's the same up there, and it's my guess it is, then regardless of what we find in the sea we won't have to worry about danger on land. Remember I was saying that you ought not to find life on a planet around a blue giant star, because it wouldn't have had enough time to develop?"

"And I pointed out that the theory is obviously wrong. There is life on Limbo."

"But I think the astronomers are half right. Back on Earth, there was life in the sea for billions of years before it emerged onto the land. That's what we have here on Limbo. Lots of plants and animals in the sea, nothing above the surface." Bony leaned his head back and squinted up into the dazzling sky. "I wonder if there's a moon? We might find out if we could stay here until dark, but long before that we'd better be back on the ship."

"A *moon*. I thought you said it was the type of *sun* that makes the difference?"

"A moon causes tides. Plants and animals that live in shallow water close to the shore get stranded by the tides, and over time they evolve so that they can live on land or in water. At least, that's the theory."

"Do you know *every* useless piece of information in the universe?"

She was teasing him. Bony didn't mind at all. They were on an alien world, in the middle of some God-knows-where mystery region known as the Geyser Swirl. They had no idea how, when, or if they would return home—or even if they would get back safely to the *Mood Indigo* before dark. It ought to be quite impossible to relax. Yet here he was, ridiculously cheerful and gratified by the sight of Liddy laughing at his side.

"Not every useless thing, no." He stood up, turning to gaze out beyond the breakers. "But when you're alone a lot, learning helps to take your mind off it."

She stood up, too. "Were you alone?"

"All the time, when I was a kid." Bony had been searching the horizon for any sign of the great cloverleaf shape that had swept overhead when he was down on the seabed. Suddenly he realized the total lack of logic in his action. If life had yet to move out of the sea on Limbo, no winged creature could have taken to the air. Whatever he had seen was a sea-creature. "Come on," he said. "Let's take a look farther inland."

"Why were you alone?" Liddy fell into step beside him. "And *where* were you alone?"

"You don't really want to know."

"I'll decide that—after you tell me. Come on, Bony. I'd tell you anything."

"I warn you, it's not very interesting." How much was he going to tell her, after so many hidden years? Well, the first part was safe enough. "You seemed surprised because I'd heard of the Leah Rainbow Academy for the Daughters of Gentlefolk. You shouldn't have been. I was born on Earth. I was a Gallimaufries kid like you."

"You didn't tell me that! You said you'd just *read* about Earth and the Leah Rainbow Academy."

"I know. It was a reasonable statement; almost everything else I know came through reading. I wasn't like you. To get picked out and taken into the Academy, even back then you must have already been absolutely gorgeous. You know, people say about the Academy—at the Academy, did you—I mean, did they teach you how to—"

"None of your business. You may find out one day, but it won't be through asking about it." Liddy hooked her arm through his. "So we have lots in common. Both from Earth, both born as Gallimaufry kids."

"I didn't say that." Bony wished they weren't wearing suits. He couldn't even feel Liddy's grip on his arm. "I wasn't *born* in the Gallimaufries, the way you were. And you must have been slim and beautiful. I was already fat and clumsy."

"Lots of kids are. No big problem."

"It was for me. My last name is Rombelle now; but when I was born it was Mirambelle."

She stopped dead, her boots grating loud on the barren basaltic rock of the slope. "You're a Mirambelle?"

"I was. Though you would never have known it." Bony knew the image that was in Liddy's mind. The Miraculous Mirambelles, poised and confident, aerialist builders with a grace and sense of balance that would shame a cat or a squirrel, directing the robot spinners in their monofilament spans three thousand meters above the ground. In seven generations, no Mirambelle had ever suffered a fall.

Bony felt that he could not breathe, his lungs were as starved as if the air of Limbo had suddenly lost all oxygen. He went on, "Naturally, my parents didn't want me anywhere near ultrahigh construction. Not on the ground, either. Too hard on me, they said. Also, of course, I would ruin the Mirambelle legend. Better to have me deep down below the surface, where no one would expect to find a Mirambelle. Better to have me hidden in the Gallimaufries."

"But you didn't stay there. You got out."

"I did. No thanks to the Mirambelle clan, though." This was the place to stop. This was where he ought to say no more. Bony went on. "I got out because of something else. When I was thirteen years old I became interested in remote viewing, and I heard about something that the Duke of Bosny had been doing. I wanted to take a look."

"What was it?"

"I'd rather not say." There was a long silence, then Bony continued, "He was, well, you know, fooling around in unusual ways. Doing things I wasn't sure were even physically possible. So I figured out how to make the equipment, and I built it, and I did the remote viewing. I wanted to see. I mean, I was only thirteen."

Now she was staring at him in a peculiar way. His instinct had been right, he should have stopped with the Mirambelles.

Liddy said, "Bony, you don't have to tell me if you don't want to. And you probably don't need to. Anything you've seen or heard about, I probably *did*. Oh dear. Now I've shocked you."

"No, no. I've—been around."

"I *was* at the Leah Rainbow Academy, you know."

"Yes. Yes. The Leah Rainbow Academy. The Academy."

"Bony, stop gibbering. Forget the Academy. I lived through it, so can you. You did the remote viewing. Tell me what happened next."

"I got caught. I wasn't as smart as I thought I was, and I had no idea how many levels of security there were around the Duke of Bosny. A man called Chan Dalton came to see me."

"Chan Dalton! He's a big wheel. He's the Duke's chief enforcer."

"He is now. But this was twenty years ago. He had some connection with the Duke that he didn't specify, and he had all kinds of weapons in his belt. I felt sure he'd come to kill me. He told me he wanted to know how I'd broken in, because the Duke's experts told him that remote viewing access to the inner court was impossible. He made me do it again, with him actually present, to prove that I could."

"And *then* he killed you."

"No. Then he recruited me. Not to the Duke of Bosny's service, but for a project of his own. He told me he was putting a specialized team together to go to the stars. He believed that the other freelance expeditions were doing everything wrong, and he knew better. His team was almost assembled, and an inventor and tinkerer like me was the final component. If I could learn what was needed, I was in. Otherwise, it would be back to Earth and the Gallimaufries. He sent me away to a little planetoid called Horus, and tried to give me a proper education. It didn't work out too well. Turned out I had to learn things my own way, or not at all."

"But you must have learned. You didn't go back to Earth."

"There were other reasons for that. Just before I finished on Horus and found out whether I was in or out, news came back from Mercantor about the Guljee Expedition, with all the killings. The other Stellar Group members decided it was the final proof that humans were too bloody-minded to wander free around the stars. Right after that they put the quarantine in place. Chan Dalton had to disband the team. We all went our separate ways. He gave me my freedom, and enough money to start another life. I kept in touch with the other team members for a long time, but when the quarantine went on and on we drifted apart and lost contact. With the road to the stars closed, there was no point in thinking of ourselves as a team. It was a depressing period for everybody. But you're too young to remember it."

"No I'm not. One of my first memories was the big news that none of the Link access points were working."

"Not quite that. We could go anywhere within the extended solar system. But nothing beyond a lightyear."

"Surely the Geyser Swirl is more than that. We're a lot more than a lightyear from the Sun."

"More than a hundred lightyears. That's one of the mysteries we came here to solve: Why is there a Link access point open to humans? Well, we're here, and no closer to finding out." Bony waved his arm around at their barren surroundings. They had been walking steadily as they talked, and had reached the top of a sharp-edged ridge. The black rock showed signs of weathering by wind and rain, but nowhere in all the expanse of hills and valleys ahead could the eye find any sign of a living thing. The sun was lower in the sky, and soon it would be time to turn back.

"In fact," Bony went on, "we have other mysteries.

How could we come through a Link and arrive in the middle of the sea? Our mass detector is supposed to inhibit a Link transit when there's matter at the other end."

He was talking too much, and more to himself than to Liddy. He was surprised to hear her say, "And now there's one more mystery to explain."

"What's that?"

"Well, you said there was no life on land, and I assume that included birds." Liddy was pointing off to the left. "But isn't *that* a bird?"

Bony followed her arm and at first could see nothing. Then he caught the dark moving point in the sky. A bird.

So there *were* birds, or at least some kind of flying animal. He had been wrong about that, and he must be just as wrong about life on land. Surely a flying form couldn't evolve directly from a sea-creature without a land form in between.

The moving dot was larger, drifting across the sky on a slanting course that would cross their own path far ahead of them. Bony stared hard, trying to make out details of the flying shape.

"I see a tail behind the main lobes," Liddy said. Her eyes must be sharper than his. "And a line of little dots on the side of the body. I think—yes, it's turning. There *are* wings. But—"

Bony could see them, too. The moving shape was banking. As it did so, the profile as seen from below was revealed. It was the same triple-lobe winged form that had cast its shadow on Bony when he was on the seabed. And something else. The sun was at their back, and the sunlight catching the underside of the object turned it to a silvery gleam.

"That's reflection from metal," Liddy said excitedly. "It's a ship!"

"It is. And it's *big*. Those 'little dots' you see on the side are ports. But how can it fly, with a shape like that? It seems to just hang in the air." Bony grabbed Liddy's arm. "Come on. It will be getting dark in another hour or two and we don't want to find ourselves wandering around the sea at night. We have to get back to the *Mood Indigo* and tell Friday what we've learned."

Liddy gave him a questioning look, but she turned at once and allowed him to lead her back the way that they had come. She didn't say anything, but Bony suspected that she knew the real reason he wanted to return to their ship. It had nothing to do with their responsibility to report everything they found to the official leader of the expedition, Friday Indigo. It was the fact that the outline of the ship they had just seen did not resemble any design in use by humans or other species of the Stellar Group. It was not the product of Tinkers, Pipe-Rillas, or Angels. The ship they had seen wasn't just alien, it was *alien* alien.

Bony had a sudden suspicion that the land surface of Limbo might offer greater dangers than the depths of its oceans.

10

Recruiting on Europa

Chan Dalton, his arrival at Europa less than two hours ahead, was still trying to make up his mind.

It was the classic question; you had two tasks to perform and one promised to be much harder and more unpleasant than the other. Did you tackle the tough one first and get it out of the way? Or did you postpone, and hope that before you came to the hard part you might be struck by a meteorite, or that a solar flare would wipe out life in the solar system?

The angry weapons master first, or the cheerful dreamer? Deb Bisson, or Tully O'Toole?

Chan made up his mind—after a fashion. Whoever was closer to his arrival point, that's the one he would call on first. And let's hope that it was Tully the Rhymer, the disheveled dreamer.

The message unit was nagging for attention. Probably to give the ship its final docking instructions.

Chan casually flipped the switch, then sat up straighter as the imaging region filled with a three-dimensional whirlpool of colors.

A shape gradually coalesced, a bulky green mass with waving upper fronds. A computer-generated voice said, "Chan Dalton?"

"You're an Angel."

"No. We are *the* Angel. The Angel who was with you on Travancore, the Angel with whom you once mind-pooled. Such pooling is now permanently forbidden, but are you that same Chan Dalton?"

"Of course I am. Can't you tell?"

"All humans, unfortunately, look much the same to us. We can now proceed. We are linking in from the home-world of Sellora."

"That's impossible. This ship doesn't have equipment for direct interstellar linkage."

"Not impossible, merely improbable. *When you have eliminated the impossible, whatever remains, however improbable, must be the truth.* We assure you, we are linking to your ship. Chan Dalton, we must talk. We have heard that you are in the process of assembling a team of humans; in fact, the same team of humans who many of your years ago submitted a plan for travel to unknown parts of the Perimeter."

"That's—" Chan had been about to say again that it was impossible for anyone except himself to know such a thing. He restrained himself. It would merely encourage the Angel to offer another human platitude or quotation. "How do you know what I'm doing?"

"An Angel has the potential to simulate the thought processes of any particular human, provided that there has been enough prior contact. You had a most intimate contact with us. We know how you think."

"Then you're ahead of me. I don't know how I know what I'm thinking. I don't know where I'm going when I land on Europa. I don't know if I can put a team together. I'm not even sure I can *find* some of the members, let alone persuade them."

"Let us assume that you achieve those goals. Then we wish to warn you. Without the tempering influence of Angels, Tinkers, and Pipe-Rillas, your team contains the seeds of instability and violence. Murder cannot be permitted. No matter what you find in the Geyser Swirl, no matter what violence you may encounter, you must not destroy intelligent beings to solve your problems."

"You told me that already, in the Star Chamber meeting."

"That was before we learned one other item of information. After the Star Chamber meeting, we employed a piece of equipment able to search for and locate any living Angel within large volumes of space at arbitrarily large distances. We applied that instrument to the Geyser Swirl. And we found—nothing." The blue-green fronds waved in an agitated manner. "Nothing. The Angel who went to the Geyser Swirl is dead."

"How could that happen?" Chan was genuinely amazed. The Angels offered a combination of guile, caution, and resilience that made them practically indestructible.

"We do not know. It is beyond our comprehension. There was no sign even of the Singer's crystal, which withstands huge force and high temperatures. Therefore we know only this: something in the Geyser Swirl provides great danger and offers potential for violence." The upper fronds were waving wildly. "We are unable to speak more. We wish only to warn you, and to say you must not seek to match violence with violence—" The fronds suddenly closed to cover the top of the bulbous upper part, and a chromatic flicker of colors moved across the image. The Link connection was beginning to break down. "Take care, take care," said the fading computer voice. "Remember this: *There are more things in the Geyser Swirl, Chan Dalton, than are dreamed of in your philosophy.*"

Thanks, Angel. That's just the sort of encouragement I could have done without. Chan did not bother to speak the words. He was staring at an empty image area.

Europa is only a fourth the size of Terra, but its ice-covered ocean has an average depth of more than fifty kilometers. The volume of water contained there is as much as in all of Earth's oceans. The world-spanning sea of Europa is deep and dark and the seabed beneath is a treasure trove of metals, delivered over billions of years by meteorite impact and melting slowly through and down. The waters themselves are clear and potable; they are also uncharted, and unpatrolled. They form, not surprisingly, a haven for some of the system's most desperate criminals.

Chan's task, to find and recruit Tully O'Toole and Deb Bisson in a couple of days, should have been impossible. He had hope, for one reason only: since neither Tully nor Deb was in hiding, the chances were good that he would find them on Europa's single land area. He had examined the image on the screen ahead during final approach, and felt encouraged. Mount Ararat was not much to look at. Europa's single "continent" consisted of four connected peaks, stretching in a knobby line over a dozen kilometers of surface. Even the tallest hill was no more than a black pile of igneous rock in an endless frozen plain. The encroaching ice pinched low points of the sawtooth ridge, almost dividing the knolls into separate islands. The total land area was just a few square kilometers, and like all of Europa it was subjected to a continuous hail of protons, accelerated by Jupiter's powerful magnetic field. No sane person would try to live there, and no one did. The population was beneath, in an interconnected labyrinth of chambers and corridors tunneled from the rock.

Chan studied the layout, and decided it should not be hard to find anyone on Mount Ararat who was not actively trying to hide. So now he had to answer the question that he had been avoiding: Who first?

As the transit vessel dropped in toward Mount Ararat's primitive spaceport, he entered the two names and requested information on their last-known locations. Answers came back at once, pinpointed on a map of the underground city. One glance, and Chan cursed. He might have known it. Tully O'Toole was at the edge of Mount Ararat's northern hill, as far from the port point as you could get. Deb Bisson was an easy five-minute underground walk from the ship's landing point. The issue was settled.

What time of day was it here? As it landed, the ship's display adjusted to local time. As Chan recalled it, Europa and the other Jovian moons used some crazy decimal system, dividing each day into ten hours of a hundred minutes. What did one-ninety correspond to? Late, well after midnight, but how late? He made up his mind. He was in a hurry. Night or day, he must go at once to Deb and talk to her.

Chan went through the landing procedures in a haze of anticipation, answering the machine's questions impatiently and with half his brain. Expected duration of stay? One or two days, maximum. Import/export materials? None—unless you counted a couple of humans. Purpose of visit? Chan paused for a moment. Discussions? Let's hope he was right about that.

And then he was inside, through the lock and hurrying along a wide poorly lit corridor designed more for automated vehicles than for people. His surroundings were as bare and forbidding as the naked rock through which the tunnel was carved. He could not imagine Deb living here. No prison on Earth was as bleak.

But then, beyond the first chamber and bulkhead, everything changed. Even Chan, hurried as he was, had to pause and look around him.

Anyone who believed that all residents of Europa lived simple, primitive lives should come here and take a look. The rough-cut walls of black rock had been transformed to smooth white surfaces, covered with murals depicting native Europan life-forms. The beauty of paintings showing the tube worms and crystalline arrays that flourished at the seabed vents was a matter of taste—Chan thought they were hideous—but they were original, expensive artwork. And there was no doubt about the cost of the deep, living rug across which he walked. The organisms of the carpet were tailor-made to thrive in Europa's individual gravity and atmosphere. So, too, were those in the ceiling of the corridor. The soft, bioluminescent glow that they provided verified that locally it was late at night.

Chan trod softly, almost tiptoeing as he came to the next corridor of residential suites. He was in an area that would qualify as high-class dwelling space anywhere in the solar system. Deb, whatever she was doing, was not living in poverty.

He came to a wide, solid door. The small plate attached to it read *D. Bisson* in discreet cursive script. A communication grille sat in the wall at the left-hand side. Chan hesitated. The logical—and polite—thing to do was to signal, identify himself, and request permission to enter.

But suppose that she told him to go to hell, turned off the communicator, and would not let him in? He had come a long way to leave without an audience. And he had been the one, back on Mars, who told Danny Casement that team recruiting must be done face-to-face. It was more true for Deb Bisson than for anyone.

He gently tried the door. As expected, it was locked. But this was a normal domestic lock, not one of the infinitely variable smart ciphers. For a man who had spent the past two decades in Earth's Gallimaufries, that was almost an invitation.

Chan had not seen a living soul since he landed on Europa, but he walked carefully up and down the corridor before returning to Deb Bisson's door. Everything seemed peaceful. He bent down to study the lock.

It took longer than expected, but within five minutes he was delicately turning the final cylinder and easing the door open. The inside of the apartment was even darker than the corridor. He stood on the threshold for a few moments to study his surroundings. He was in a big rectangular room, at least ten meters long. Judging from the equipment, with its beams and pulleys and weights, this was some kind of exercise area. The surface gravity of Europa was even less than on the Moon, and if you stayed here for a long time it was essential to work out regularly. Otherwise you lost muscle tone and bone mass. The higher gravity worlds like Earth and Venus would close to you permanently.

The far end of the room held three doors. The leftmost two were open, and by the faint light within them he could make out a hint of comfortable furniture in one and wall cabinets in the other. He guessed at living room and kitchen, or possibly living room and workroom. The third door was open just a crack. It was presumably the bedroom, and it was totally dark.

Chan tiptoed toward it. He didn't want to wake Deb up suddenly. In the old days, even at the best of times, that guaranteed a bad mood. The best way would be to stand at her bedside and speak in a soft voice, so that she would wake slowly and naturally.

He pushed the door wide and stood staring into the room. He thought he could make out the shape of a big bed, with what might be a sleeping body lying toward the right side of it.

He took another step forward. As he did so he was grabbed from behind and flipped end over end. He was caught in midair and both arms were twisted behind his back. Something that felt like a band of steel whipped across his throat, choking him.

A voice hissed in his ear, "All right, smart boy. Struggle and you're dead." The steel band tightened. "Don't even try."

It was an easy command to obey. It took Chan's best efforts just to breathe. He felt himself being frisked for weapons and heard a grunt of surprise. Suddenly he was thrown across the room and landed on the bed. He hit on top of something that yelped, and as he rolled over and tried to sit up a light went on.

Chan saw everything in one quick flash. He had been thrown onto a bed covered with a mess of tangled sheets. Deb Bisson crouched about three meters away. She was naked, her body damp with sweat and her dark hair in a wild cloud about her intent face. Her white limbs were deceptively smooth and feminine. In one hand she held a steel chain, and the tendons in that forearm flexed and stood out like cables. Next to Chan was the man whom he had landed on. He was big, blond, muscle-bound, also nude, and his mouth gaped open.

Chan saw the expression on Deb's face change from murderous intent to question to total shock.

"You!" she said. "I don't believe it. What are you doing here—in my apartment—in my bedroom—in the middle of the night—when I was—you bastard, what the devil are you doing here *at all*?"

"I need to talk to you." Chan held his hands up in self-defense, because Deb's face had darkened and she was raising the steel chain.

"I don't need to talk to you. Ever." The chain whipped from one hand to the other so fast that Chan heard it but didn't see it. "You get out of here before I slash your guts out and stuff them down your lying throat."

Chan had no doubt that she could do it, with her bare hands if she had to. He eased off the bed and stood up, very slowly and carefully. He knew better than to smile.

"Deb, I know you hate me. I understand why, and I can explain what happened."

"I'm not interested in your explanations."

"I know. And that's not why I came here. For years, I haven't called you or tried to contact you—"

"Do you think I don't know that?"

"—and I wouldn't be here now, if I didn't think you would want to hear what I have to say. All I'm asking is ten minutes."

"In the middle of the night? After breaking into my home, disturbing my privacy, without even a call to tell me you're coming."

"If I had called ahead, would you have agreed to see me?"

She did not answer. The chain whistled through the air. One end passed close to Chan's neck. Three inches more, and it would have severed his windpipe.

Call that encouraging. She could have killed him, and she'd decided not to.

"You wouldn't have spoken to me, Deb. I think you would have regretted it later when you learned what you missed, but you'd have hung up on me. What I need to tell you isn't personal. But it is private."

The flicker of his eyes toward Deb's naked companion would have been imperceptible to most people. Deb shrugged and tossed the chain casually to one side. She knew, and she knew Chan knew, that she could take him apart without any more weapons than her hands.

"Olaf, if you don't mind." She nodded to the man on the bed, who had wriggled back under a sheet. "I need to talk to this scumbag."

Olaf stood up, turned his back to Chan, and pulled on his pants with as much dignity as he could manage. "Are you sure you'll be safe?" he said over his shoulder. "I realize you know him, but if you would like me to stay and make sure you are all right . . ."

Deb's smile was at Chan, and it was not friendly. "Thanks, Olaf, but I can manage. I wish he *would* start something, just to give me an excuse to snap his rotten neck."

"Should I come back later, then?"

"We'll see. I'll call you."

As Olaf left, Chan began, "If I had known that you had a regular partner these days, I wouldn't—"

"Stuff it, Chan Dalton. You'll have to lie better than that to fool me."

"Was I lying?"

"You certainly were. Partner!" She spat the word at Chan like a curse. "I don't have partners any more.

How well do you think Olaf knows me, if he doesn't realize I'm a weapons master who can look after herself better than anyone on Europa? He's not my partner, he's a pick-up—and a lot better lover than you ever were. So cut the crap. Tell me what you want." She was reaching down to lift a white robe from the floor, and she saw Chan's look. "And you can stop staring at my ass. You had your chance, and you blew it."

"I was just marveling at how little you've changed. Your body doesn't look a day older."

"That's nice. What am I supposed to do, curtsey and say thank you, sir? I'll tell you one thing, I'm a thousand years older inside. So get on with it. What's so important that you have to track me down and stick your nose into my life?"

Chan sat down on the bed. "It's a long story."

"You said you needed ten minutes."

"If I had said I needed an hour, would you have agreed to listen to me?"

"Of course not." Deb tucked her robe around her legs and sank easily to the floor. "You have ten minutes to prove I should waste an hour with you, and if you can't you'll be out on your ass. Nine minutes now—you've wasted one. Better get started."

"We have a chance to put the old team together and take a ship to the stars."

"Bullshit." She glared up at him with angry brown eyes. "The Link network hasn't worked for twenty years and it doesn't work now. Are you trying to tell me that the Stellar Group is lifting the quarantine on us?"

"No. I'm telling you that they are allowing one ship with a human crew to use the network with their blessing. You can be on that ship, Deb."

"I'd love to. Provided that you aren't."

"Sorry. It doesn't work like that. The Stellar Group insists that I be there, because I worked with them before and they trust me."

"More fool them."

"They didn't insist on anybody else. It was my idea to put the old team together. You, me, Dan Casement, Tully, the Bun, Tarb, Chrissie Winger . . . the way we planned it. Remember, Deb? The perfect team, with just the mix we needed. The idea wasn't wrong, it's as good now as it was then. It was the quarantine that stopped us."

"The quarantine had nothing to do with what *you* did, you son of a bitch."

"Maybe it did, Deb. Maybe it had a lot to do with it. But you said you didn't want to talk about you and me, and I respect that. The new expedition isn't about you and me. It's about a chance to do what we once wanted to do, all of us, and never had the opportunity. It's about a chance to end the quarantine and open the road to the stars. Forget that I'll be on the ship. You won't even have to talk to me if you don't want to. Think of working with the others again. You and Tully the Rhymer always got on great with each other—the Tarbush, too."

The angry twist to her mouth was less tight. She stood up, came across to where Chan was sitting on the bed, and stared down at him.

"You're a wily bastard, Chan Dalton. You're still trying to push my buttons. Do you really have the others lined up—all of them, Danny and the Tarbush and the Bun and everyone?"

Chan cursed his decision to visit Deb first. He could see the look in her eyes. It was the old starlust, the way it had been twenty years ago. She was turning his way. If he could have just told her that Dan Casement and Tully were already definite, and

Danny was even now on the Vulcan Nexus, chasing down the Bun . . .

"I don't have everyone, Deb. I wish I did."

"Who do you have?"

"Well, there's me. And Danny Casement. And, I hope, you."

"And that's *it*? You absolute *asshole*, you don't have any team. You haven't changed, not one little bit. You make promises, and when it's time to deliver you just slip out from under. Get out of my sight."

She crouched slightly and stood with her arms bent. Chan came to his feet in an eye-blink. You didn't mess with Deb Bisson when she looked like that.

"Deb, I'm leaving. But if I could—"

"Out this minute, or I throw you out."

Chan said rapidly, "Just ten seconds, for one more thing."

"Nothing you can say will make any difference."

"Maybe not, but let me say it. I'll be going on this expedition with or without any others from the old team. I have to. But it won't be the same, and it won't be as safe. I came to you first, because if you come on board, I know for sure that Tully will, and the Tarbush will, and Chrissie will. They may not think much of me, but they worship you."

"That is the worst crap I ever heard. I haven't seen any of them for years. I don't know where they are, what they're doing, if they're alive."

"Now who's the one who's lying? Tully O'Toole lives right here on Europa, in the Mount Ararat settlement. You have to know that, Deb, this place isn't big enough to hide somebody like Tully the Rhymer."

"So what?"

"So come with me to see him. See how *he* reacts. If he says yes, it will be that much easier to talk to Chrissie and Tarbush."

"Why should I make things easier for you?"

"It will only take one hour of your time."

"One hour like your ten minutes?"

"If he says no, I'll accept that I can't get the old team together. I'll be out of here."

She stripped off the robe, turned, and walked across to a drawer set in the wall. "Do you know where Tully lives?" She was pulling out black pants and a tank top.

"I have a locator output."

"And that's all? I can do better than that. Tully's on the northern knoll, and I know exactly where."

"Are you proposing that we go there now? It's the middle of the night."

"That didn't worry you when you broke in on me. Of course I want to go now. What's the option? Sit here and listen to you talk about the old times, and why you did what you did? No thanks." She pulled a black hooded cloak over her skintight clothes and walked toward the door, smiling as if at some bitter joke. "You surprised me, it's time you had a surprise yourself. We'll go and see Tully. Then I think you'll agree that the 'old team' idea is a load of garbage. You'll be out of here. And I can forget that you ever came."

11

The Arrival of the Bubble People

Bony wanted to hurry without seeming to. The strange triple-winged craft had not reappeared, but it might at any moment and they were very visible out on the open rock. He didn't want to frighten Liddy by telling her of possible danger that might never materialize, and the only other reason for haste that he could offer was the blue sun, sinking fast toward the horizon as they came within sight of the sea.

He pointed ahead. "See the way it seems to be dropping straight down toward the water? Dusk won't last long here. We must have landed close to the equator of Limbo. Better hurry."

He did not mention the other thing that puzzled him. The surface gravity of Limbo was low. That should mean that the planet was small, about the size of Earth's Moon. But then the horizon should be close, as the planet curved away from them.

It wasn't. His guess was that the horizon was as far away here as on Earth. What did it mean, if you had a planet the size of Earth with a gravity like that of the Moon? The obvious answer was that the density was small. How small? Bony couldn't do the calculation in his head, but he vowed to pass it on to the ship's computer when they got back on board.

His attention was on the setting sun, the sky which had turned from violet-blue to green, and the far-off horizon. It was Liddy, hurrying down the pebbled shore, who stopped abruptly and said, "What's *that*?"

She was pointing to their right, at ninety degrees to the sun. The arc of a dark circle loomed over the horizon. Bony felt the satisfaction of a question answered.

"It's a moon. So Limbo has one—at least one." Bony held his hand out at arm's length, measuring the arc between his fingers. Everything looked big close to the horizon, but Bony estimated that if the full circle were visible it would stretch five degrees across the sky. Earth's Moon was only a tenth of that. "It's huge," he went on, "or else it's very close."

They had stopped walking and stood about twenty meters from the placid sea. Bony felt divided urges—to watch the moon rise and study it, or to get safely back to the *Mood Indigo*.

While he was trying to make up his mind, Liddy spoke again. "If that's a moon, shouldn't it either be rising or setting? It's not doing either. And it doesn't look like a moon to me. I can see a funny sort of pattern on it. Can't you?"

Now that it was pointed out to him, he could. The circular arc displayed a slow dilation and contraction, like the pupil of a vast eye. He could see moving color patterns, fringes of green and orange and yellow and blue. And Liddy was absolutely right; the object, whatever it was, was not moving relative to the horizon. But surely, if it had been there when first they left the ship and rose to the surface, they would have noticed it.

"Look *below* the water," Liddy cried. "You can see it there, too."

The circle didn't end at the waterline. The same pattern of expansion and contraction, much fainter, showed underneath. As the sun dipped toward the horizon and the light became less intense, you could pick out part of the circle even under water. It seemed to have its own source of illumination. And right between the two, at the surface, a narrow band of steam or white smoke created a line of brightness. The line rippled and shimmered as though it was the site of intense turbulence, a furious mixing and blurring of air and water.

"What is it?" Liddy asked. And Bony—Mister Know-it-all himself, who prided himself on having answers for everything—couldn't even offer a guess.

"I don't know." He made a decision. Despite its apparently peaceful appearance, Limbo had more potential dangers than he could imagine. "We can talk about what we've seen when we're back inside the ship. Come on, Liddy. Suits closed."

He led the way into the water, over-inflating the suit as he went to make sure that it would float. The unfamiliar cramped feeling around his belly and chest was proof that the pressure was increasing. He turned to Liddy, now an overstuffed roly-poly figure who nodded to him behind her visor. He turned on his suit thrustors at a low level, and side by side they coasted out to where the beacon still emitted its steady call.

As they went he became increasingly pleased that they had left the shore when they did. From this angle the sun was even lower in the sky. The sea was calm, but submerged in water up to his neck he found visibility increasingly difficult because of reflected glints on the surface. Without the directional radio feed from the beacon they would never make visual contact.

And then there was a new worry. Although the sea was calm he could feel the pull of a current. It was urging them in the direction of the rainbow eye.

"Can you feel that?"

"The current. Bony, it's getting stronger."

"I know. Angle your thrustors and give them higher power. Let air out of your suit. Don't worry if we lose radio contact when we go under. We should be close enough now to see the ship. Look down as you go."

No point in mentioning his own worry, that with the sun setting its light would no longer penetrate all the way to the seabed. Bony released excess air, switched the thrust of his suit to high level, and drove down into blue-green water. He could sense the pull of the current, weaker now, and he could make out the shape of Liddy's suit a few meters ahead of him. He could not see any sign of the *Mood Indigo*.

Unexpectedly, Liddy veered off to the right. Her eyes were exceptionally sharp, he knew that. Maybe she had caught sight of the ship and was heading in that direction. In any case, he didn't want to lose contact. Bony changed the angle of his own drive thrustors and dived to catch up.

He was looking for the ship, but what he finally saw was a faint blur of light. He swore at his own stupidity. Of course that's what they would see, the ship's internal lights shining out of the ports. Friday Indigo wouldn't be sitting in darkness. The light became steadily brighter, and finally Bony could make out its source, the bulbous, bottom-heavy shape sitting quietly on the sea floor. He had never in his life expected to be so pleased at the prospect of Friday Indigo's company. He came up behind Liddy and watched as she went under the airlock and up to its open hatch. He took half a minute more, reeling in the surface beacon and its connecting line. He had already worried that it might have been noticed by whatever or whoever flew that strange tri-lobe aircraft through the air of Limbo. Then he joined Liddy, heaved himself into the lock, and sat panting on the edge of the hatch. It was good to be there, but he wouldn't feel fully safe until the lock had cycled and he was once more inside the ship with both outer and inner hatches closed.

Friday Indigo was waiting for them as they emerged into the cabin of the ship—but he didn't wait long. Bony could tell that the captain was angry or nervous because his mouth was twitching. Bony hardly had his helmet open before Friday Indigo was in his face, shouting, "For God's sake, Rombelle, do you realize how long you've been gone? Hours and hours, without one damned signal back to me. You'd better have an explanation. And it had better be a lot more than you were just farting around on the surface up there."

"It was." Bony felt energy going out of him, like the extra air bleeding out of his suit. With his helmet still on his head and the body unit of his suit unopened he flopped down onto a drive housing. "I'm going to tell you what we saw. I'm not going to try to explain it."

"You'll do what I tell you to do. I don't pay you to be a robot or a parrot."

"I don't trust my own judgment, sir, that's why I don't want to guess at explanations. I've been wrong about so many things about this planet. I'll give you an example. We found land."

"That's great!"

"I thought so—at first. It's just a few kilometers from here, bare black rock with no sign of life. So I concluded there must be no land life, that plants and animals hadn't emerged from the sea yet. Then we saw something flying, and I decided that I'd been wrong. I couldn't imagine a flying form emerging directly from a sea-life form."

"Then you weren't thinking straight. Haven't you heard of flying fish?"

"I thought of that—later. But it didn't matter, because this was nothing like a fish, and we realized that it wasn't a bird or an animal, either. It was some kind of aircraft. But it was like nothing I've ever seen before."

"God *damn* it!" Indigo's dark brows lowered into a frown and he thumped the cabin wall with his open palm. "That's terrible news. It means we don't have this place to ourselves. We've been beaten to it. One of the Stellar Group expeditions came through alive."

"I'd love to think you're right, sir, but I don't believe you are. The flying machine wasn't like any aircraft or spacecraft in the solar system, but it also wasn't like anything else I ever saw or heard of. Like nothing inside the whole Perimeter."

To Bony, that was bad news. Friday Indigo obviously didn't agree. He was grinning hugely. "If you're right, we've got it made. Can't you see it? A new planet, a new intelligent species, new technology like nothing you've ever seen. And nobody but us knows a thing about it! We'll go up there, talk to whoever runs the flying machine—this ship has the best universal translator that you can buy—and go home with a negotiation position you wouldn't believe."

"If we can get home. That's another thing. There may be a way. As we were coming back, Liddy and I saw something that we feel sure wasn't there when we left the sea to take a look ashore."

As Bony stripped off his suit he described the rainbow-hued arc. It was difficult to find words for something so unfamiliar, the partial circle with its darker and poorly defined extension under the water.

"When we saw it," he said, "I couldn't think what it might be. But as I sat puffing and panting on the lock hatch, I had an idea The thing looks like a circle, but actually it must be a spherical region. I believe that it's a Link access point—the same one we came through to get here."

"Nonsense." Friday Indigo glared at Bony. "You can't possibly have a Link access point in water."

"We've never seen one before, I know that. But we did get here somehow, and we have no other candidates. If this is one, it isn't open always. It wasn't there earlier today. But if it's a Link access point and we can get the *Mood* into the right place at the right time, we can go home."

"Go home?!" Indigo was infuriated. "You talk of going home—when we haven't done a single thing that we came here to do. I want to find out all about this planet! I want to know everything here that's valuable! You saw just a tiny bit, as much as you could walk to in a couple of hours, and already you talk of leaving! Well, forget that idea. It's too late tonight, but tomorrow when it's light we'll head outside again and make another trip to land. This time we'll be better organized, and we'll take plenty of instruments. And before we're done with this damned place, I'll know it inside out. I'm going to find that flying vehicle you saw. I'm going to take a close-up look at it. Maybe I'll even take it back with me." Indigo was stamping up and down the cabin. "Rombelle, you're a fool. You just don't get it. This place, Limbo or whatever you want to call it, is *opportunity*."

Bony stared at the captain. It was the recklessness of ignorance, the confidence of a man who had always been able to buy himself out of trouble. How did you persuade a rich idiot like Friday Indigo that the biggest opportunity a new world offered was often the chance to be killed in unpleasant ways?

"It's not just the land area," Liddy said quietly, before Bony could find a tactful way of phrasing what was on his mind.

It was the first time she had spoken since she and Bony had entered the ship, and Indigo at once made a dismissive gesture of his hand. "Keep out of this. You weren't brought along on this trip to think, so shut up."

"I feel sure you'll want to hear this, Friday."

"It had better be good, girl, or you're in real trouble."

"I don't know if it's good or not; but it's important." Liddy turned to Bony. "When we left the surface and dived underwater to look for the ship, did you see anything unusual?"

Bony had seen very little. The swirl of blue-green past his visor, a stream of air bubbles from Liddy's suit. He shook his head.

"Well, I did." She paused, and this time Friday Indigo waited. "We were diving, but I wasn't sure where the *Mood* might be, so I was trying to keep an eye open in all directions. Then I saw a light under the water. For a moment I felt sure that it came from this ship—I mean, what else could it be?—and I was ready to turn in that direction. But it didn't look right. It wasn't just a light or two, like our lights shining through the ports. It was more like a column of lights, strung out in a straight line. It seemed like they pointed at something. I followed the line of them with my eye. I saw the lights of the *Mood Indigo*, and then the ship itself sitting on the seabed. And I turned to head in this direction, and Bony and I came aboard."

Indigo was silent for a moment, then he said to Bony, "Rombelle, did *you* see any of this?"

"Nothing." And, at Friday Indigo's contemptuous snort, "But I don't see nearly as well as Liddy, under water or above it."

"Yeah, yeah," Indigo said grudgingly. "She's got great eyesight, I'll grant you that. But a line of lights, under water? Give me a break."

Bony turned again to Liddy. "Can you tell us where the thing you saw was, relative to where we are now?"

"I think it was in that direction." She pointed to one side of the cabin. The three of them went to the port and crowded around it.

"Do you see anything?" Indigo asked. "I don't."

"Nor do I." Bony turned to Liddy. "How about you?"

"Nothing."

"So you imagined things," Friday Indigo said. "I warned you not to waste our time. Don't try thinking, Liddy, it doesn't suit you. I brought you along for your body, not your brains."

"Now you wait a minute." Bony felt his head ready to explode. He was going to hit Indigo unless he could find a distraction. "There might be something there. It's difficult to see outside when the cabin lights are on. Suppose we turn them off."

"Suppose we do. We'll still see nothing." But Indigo went across to the console, and a moment later the cabin lights dimmed.

"Just as I expected," Indigo said in the darkness. "Pure imagination. You and your damn lights, Liddy. You didn't see . . ." His voice faded.

The sun had set, and its light no longer diffused down from above. The *Mood Indigo* sat in a silent, stygian gloom. But far away, so faint that one moment it seemed to be there and in the next the eye had lost it, a tiny splinter of light shone wanly through the green water.

"There it is," Bony said breathlessly. "Liddy, you said you saw a *column* of lights."

"That's what it looked like from above. But they were all pointing in this direction, so from here they line up. I can still make out about a dozen of them, only not so clearly."

They were silent for a long time, peering into darkness, until Liddy added, "I can't be sure. But I think they're moving. Yes, they are."

Bony stared until his eyes felt ready to pop out of his skull. It was no good. To him, it was still a single blur of light. Indigo must have been in the same situation, because he said quietly and without skepticism, "Moving how, Liddy?"

"Moving this way. Look, can't you see that one of them is slightly ahead of the others?"

Liddy must have eyes like an eagle. Bony couldn't see any such thing. But then, suddenly, he could. The single line of light resolved itself into separate points. He tried to count them, but lost track when he reached ten. The splinter of light had at first been blue-green, now its separate points shone with a yellower glow. And each point was slowly brightening. Was it his imagination, or were they also moving up and down?

"They're coming this way," said Liddy. Her voice was calm, but Bony felt her hand take his in the darkness and grip it hard. "I wasn't sure before, but now I am. They seemed to point toward the ship when I first saw them, because they were moving in single file. And they still are."

"You're right." Indigo sounded anything but calm. "I can see them, too. If they keep up that speed they'll be here in another few minutes. Thank God I installed weapons on the ship, just in case. Rombelle—"

"We're under water, sir. Fire weapons in our situation, and we'll be more likely to blow ourselves up than anything else."

"Well, we have to do something. If we're attacked we can't just sit here."

"I don't think we have to worry too much." Bony offered that reassurance more for Liddy's benefit than because he believed it. He went on, "Remember, these are sea-creatures. Even if they are intelligent, they won't know about fire or have the technology to develop explosives or projectile weapons."

Bony didn't fully believe what he said. Nor, judging from the grunt from the darkness, did Friday Indigo, but there was a certain perverse pleasure in quoting the other man's own words back to him.

"The lights are being carried," Liddy said suddenly. "They are some sort of oblong balls, all filled with light."

"Bioluminescent," Bony added. To him they were still shapeless blobs. "That's what you would expect in marine organisms, some form of phosphorescence or bioluminescence. You wouldn't expect ordinary combustion."

"Stuff your combustion." Indigo sounded frantic. "I don't want idiot science lectures. Carried by *what*, Liddy?"

"I can't tell yet. But in another minute or two we can get a closer look—"

"The scopes!" Bony shouted the words, while he groaned inside at his own mental inadequacy. He had been peering hopelessly and unthinkingly into the darkness like Neanderthal man trying to see outside his cave, while the *Mood's* sophisticated imaging sensors and image intensifiers sat unused beside him. He fumbled his way to the console, turned on an internal light, and pulled up a display connected to the scopes. A few of them would certainly not work—thermal infrared sensors relied on radiation, not physical contact with the sensors—but visible wavelengths should be fine.

Another half minute when he seemed to be all thumbs, and then he had it. The screen showed a patch of lights at its center. He zoomed in.

And there they were. He had half known it, even before he thought of using the scopes. Fourteen bubble creatures—now he could count them, easily—were drifting toward the ship along the seabed. Each one floated in front of it a giant light, pear-shaped but the size of a watermelon. With that illumination Bony could make out every detail of their bodies.

The ball-like heads sat on rounded iridescent trunks that quivered when the creatures moved, as though the whole animal was boneless and made of soft jelly. Nothing in the head resembled a nose or mouth, unless it was the wide horizontal slit that sat close to the top of the rounded body. Above the head, connected to it by a pair of delicate-looking fringed stalks or antennae, hovered two green spheres that were probably eyes. If so they were separately controlled, turning independently and apparently randomly to point in different directions. The watermelon-pear light was carried easily by four string-of-bubble arms or tentacles, and four more waving limbs attached to the bottom of the globular body carried it easily over the uneven ocean floor.

The whole added up to such an appearance of fragility and vulnerability that Bony felt reassured. The creatures shown by the scope seemed as soft and harmless as children's toys. But so, he reminded himself, did a Portuguese man-of-war, with its agonizing sting.

Liddy Morse and Friday Indigo had moved away from the port to stand next to Bony, staring at the display.

"Son of a bitch," Indigo said softly. "They're real. You didn't make them up after all."

"They're real all right." Bony had the computer hooked in to the scope circuit, analyzing the movement of the creatures on the display. He glanced at its output. "Real, heading right for us, and unless they decide to stop they'll be here in seven minutes."

"What do we do?"

Apparently Indigo had decided that Bony, science lectures and all, was not such an idiot. Bony thought for a moment. "If they're as soft as they look, there's no way that they can damage the hull. But I've been wrong so often today I wouldn't put money on it. I suppose we could all put space-suits on. But I doubt if it's worth it. If they can break into the hull, the suits won't hold them for a minute."

Indigo nodded. "No suits, then. So what do we do?"

The same question again, and a very reasonable one. But Bony was out of ideas. He had been exhausted, even before he and Liddy arrived back aboard the ship. Now he felt giddy with fatigue, and his brain had already gone on strike. "I guess"—he looked apologetically at the other two—"I guess we wait."

Seven minutes.

The sea-creatures steadily came closer. The tension in the cabin grew until it was thick enough to choke them. No one had anything to say.

Six and a half minutes.

Bony decided that seven minutes would hardly feel longer if you were being operated on without anesthetics by a sadistic torturer. Purely for something to do, he asked the ship's computer what a planet would be like if it had the same gravity as Earth's moon and was the size of Earth. It asked him a bunch of foolish questions about density distributions, none of which he could answer. He told it to make any default assumptions it liked, and stop bothering him.

The answer came quickly, but it was not very informative. If a world had the same size and internal mass distribution as the Earth, then if its surface gravity was equal to the Moon's mean surface gravity, its average density would be 0.91.

Less than one. According to the computer, the average density was less than that of ordinary water. But the whole ocean of Limbo was salty heavy water, with a density fifteen percent *more* than ordinary water. There was no way that Limbo ought to possess an ocean at all. At that planetary density, all liquid water should have sunk below the surface.

Bony stared at the offending number. Nothing about Limbo made sense. The ridiculously low density. The heavy-water sea. The blue giant star, too young to allow life to develop on a planet around it. The Link access point, in water where no Link access could be. And if there were such a Link point, how had they been able to transfer to it when the ship's automatic protection system forbade transfer with substantial matter present? Limbo simply became stranger and stranger with every passing hour.

But maybe it was about to get stranger yet. In the darkened cabin, Liddy said softly, "They're here."

It was not necessary to use the imaging sensors and the enhancers to know that. They could see light shining in through the ports. The ring of sensors on the *Mood Indigo* stood about four meters above the seabed, and they gave an excellent view of the scene below. Fourteen bubble-creatures, each with its light, had drifted to surround the ship in a rough circle. As Bony watched, one of them left the circle and floated in toward the base of the vessel, beyond the imaged area. A soft thump vibrated through the hull. It sounded more exploratory than violent, but Indigo said nervously, "They're attacking the ship. What do we do now?"

"That doesn't seem like an attack. No, don't!" Bony spoke to Liddy, who was about to go over to the port. "Stay here, where we can see them with the image system and they can't see us. I don't think they have good night vision, because they're carrying lights. But if you get close to the port they may see reflected light from your face. Keep your voice down, too. If they can't see or hear us they may go away."

"It's back in the circle," Indigo said. "The one who banged on the ship, I mean. They're all there now. Uh-oh. What are they doing?"

The giant glowing pear-shapes were dimmer, and the scene provided by the ship's imaging sensors was fading steadily to a uniform gray.

"I don't know how they're doing it, but the lights they're carrying are going out." Bony clicked the image sensitivity range to a different setting, and the scene outside again became visible, now in black and white. "Look at them. They seem to be settling down. I think the Limbics are going to sleep."

"The who?" Friday Indigo stared. "Where the hell did you get that from?"

"We need a name for them, and they live on Limbo. I think they're probably intelligent, seeing how they use portable lights to see at night."

The creatures no longer stood above the seabed on their bubble strings of tentacles. Instead, the rounded end of the body had settled comfortably down onto the sea floor, where the array of pikes had been crumbled to dust by the arrival of the *Mood Indigo*. At the upper end of the body, the antennae with their green sphere eyes drooped down to sit on each side of the soap-bubble head. Each had placed its light neatly on the sea floor, with the wide end of the pear facing down.

The humans in the cabin sat in frozen silence, watching and waiting for what felt like forever.

At last Liddy said, in a whisper, "If they're going to do nothing, why did they come?"

"I have no idea," Bony replied just as softly. "But I suspect we're not going to find out tonight. Maybe they think that *we're* asleep. Animals without technology follow the same schedule as the sun."

"Do you really believe they'll stay quiet until morning?" Indigo had sagged slowly back in his chair as the immediate danger seemed less.

"It looks like it. They're not moving."

"Then I'm going." Indigo came to his feet, quietly but with determination. "To my own cabin. No, Liddy"—she had been sitting with her head bowed, but lifted it as he stood up—"not tonight. It's been a tough day. Tonight I need peace and quiet, not company. You stay here with Rombelle and keep watch. And you, Rombelle, none of your damned banging and hammering. You won't wake me, because I'm putting a wave feedback unit on as soon as I get up there. But if those Limbic things of yours are asleep outside, let's keep it that way."

Indigo went across to the ladder, carrying with him the tiny portable light that now provided the only illumination for the cabin. In the final glimmer before

Indigo and the light disappeared, Liddy glared—not at Indigo, but at Bony. As soon as the captain was on the upper level and out of hearing, she whispered, "Why do you let him treat you like that?"

"Who?"

Bony realized it was not a very intelligent question, given that Indigo was probably the only human male within a hundred lightyears. But before he could say more, Liddy burst out, "You're much smarter than he is. You do all his work, and all his thinking."

"Not so loud!"

Her voice had been rising in pitch, and when she spoke again it was shriller than ever. "Who explored the seabed outside the ship, and the surface of the water, and the land? Who may have found the Link? Not Friday Indigo. *You* did it all. But he treats you like dirt—and you let him, with never a word of complaint. He tells you *he* had a hard day, *he* needs to rest—when he hasn't done a thing. And you don't utter one peep."

The injustice of it had Bony speechless—almost. "Me!" He heard his voice squeak with outrage. "You think he treats *me* badly? What about you? It burns me up, the way he talks to you. How do you feel when he says, 'I brought you along for your body, not your brains'? How dare he say that? The nerve of the man!"

"What's wrong with my body?"

"Nothing." Bony wished there were enough light to see her facial expression. Was that anger, or insecurity? "I think your body is perfect."

"So you're agreeing with what he did. He didn't buy me for my brains. He bought me for my body."

"That might be *true*, but it doesn't make it *right*. You have a beautiful face and body, but you have a *brain*, too, a good brain. You're a *person*, Liddy. More than just a body, more than just a b-brain. A whole person!" He was stammering in his excitement, and his voice grew louder. "How can you let him treat you like a b-b-*bimbo*?"

"And how can you let him order you to keep watch while he sleeps? Don't you need sleep, too? Does he think you're a machine, and not a human being? Do you know the only reason I didn't scream when he said that to you?" Liddy was close to screaming now. "It's because I wouldn't feel safe if *he* was on watch, he'd do something stupid. But I feel safe with you. Indigo and I know we can rely on you to do anything that's needed. Doesn't that mean he bought you even more than he bought me?"

"The arrogant little bastard." In his anger Bony brushed off her question. "He talks to you like you're a moron. He makes you share his bed and he forces his body on you. When I think of you screwing with that mouse-brained idiot—"

"Mind your own business, Bony." Liddy's voice turned icy.

"It *is* my business."

"Oh, is it? Since when? You think now *you* own me, instead of Friday Indigo? Well, let me tell you, he owns you a lot worse than he owns me. With me, it's only an hour or two every few days. I can stand that, I was trained for it. Can you say as much? It's twenty-four hours a day for you, every day, servant and slave. How do *you* stand it, Bony Rombelle?"

Any thought of whispering was long gone. Bony was drawing in his breath for another loud exchange when he stopped, frozen. He was facing Liddy, and over her shoulder at one of the ports he saw a faint, pale circle.

He reached forward and placed his hand over her

mouth. He dropped his voice back to a whisper. "Don't move. Don't make a noise. There's a Limbic behind you, right outside the ship."

One of the bubble people was floating high above the sea floor, its round head level with the port. Green globe eyes pressed to the thick transparent plastic.

"I don't think it can see us." As Bony placed his mouth next to Liddy's ear he could smell the faint fragrance of her hair. "There's just enough glow outside for us to see it, but I doubt it can see much in here. I certainly can't."

He felt her breath on his cheek, and she murmured softly, "It was the noise, all the shouting and screaming. My fault."

"No! Mine, I got carried away. When I think of Friday Indigo—"

"Shh!"

He felt her hand on his mouth, and her body shaking. Was she shivering? No. She was laughing.

As she took her hand away he muttered, "Aren't you frightened?"

"No. Should I be?"

"I don't know. With all this." He made a gesture toward the outside, which he realized she could not see. "Uncertainty is enough to scare most people."

"Are *you* scared?"

"I can't say. This is almost too interesting to let me be frightened at the same time."

"Well, Friday Indigo isn't frightened, either. He's sure you can handle anything that comes along. Do you want me to have less faith in you than he does?"

"He's a fool and you're not. He thinks if you have enough money, you can buy safety. He thinks you can buy anything. He thinks he owns you, and any time he wants to stick his—"

Her hand was on his mouth again. "I don't want to hear what he sticks, and I don't want to think about where." He felt rather than saw her move to his side on the padded bench seat. She whispered, "Do we really want to start on Friday Indigo all over again? If we're going to talk about anybody, shouldn't it be you and me? But not yet!"

The pale face was still at the port. They waited, now in silence, for whatever might come next. Bony, with Liddy's body warm against his, felt willing to wait forever. At last there was a stir outside the port, and the round head with its green bubble eyes sank away out of sight. Liddy said in his ear, "What now?"

"You sleep. I keep watch."

"Would you like to trust me as much as I trust you?"

"Of course I would."

"Right then." She slid farther along the bench and pulled Bony down so that his head was pillowed on her lap. "Trust me. You did most of the work today, and you've looked exhausted for hours. You need sleep more than I do. I keep watch."

"I can't let you do that."

"Because you own me, right, and you can order me around just like Friday Indigo does?"

"Of course not. But if he gets up and finds me asleep in this position, instead of being on watch—"

"You mean that you don't own me, but he owns you twenty-four hours a day? Bony, answer me one question. Is anything going to happen before morning?"

"I don't think so. I'd be very surprised if it does."

"So lie quiet, and go to sleep. Trust me."

He ought to sit up and argue, but Liddy was stroking his hair and cheek and he didn't want that to stop. He decided that he would enjoy a few minutes of relaxation, then switch with her. After that he would watch and she could sleep.

Bony thought of the Limbics in their circle outside the ship. It was odd, but they seemed less ominous now that he had seem them close up. There was a thought you had to resist. Often the most dangerous things looked the most innocuous. It was still a mystery, though: *Why* had they come? To destroy, to communicate, from sheer curiosity? Maybe an answer would be provided after the long night watch.

A short time later Liddy moved her position. Bony grunted and opened his eyes.

Impossibly, the cabin was filled with diffuse sunlight streaming in through the ports. He turned his head to ask Liddy what had happened, and found that a cushion had replaced her lap.

He sat up. Liddy was over at the other side of the cabin. She heard his movement and turned.

"Sleep well?"

"Great. But you were awake all night."

"Don't kid yourself. I lack your sense of dedication. I woke up just a couple of minutes ago when I heard knocking on the hull."

"The Limbics?"

"That seems a reasonable assumption." Liddy was standing by one of the ports. "I was going to rouse you and Indigo in two more seconds if you hadn't woken by yourselves. Come look at something."

Bony moved to her side, rubbing the sleep from his eyes.

"They must be early risers," she said. "They were all up and about, and they noticed me as soon as I went to the port. I'd like to know if you have my reaction. What do you think they're doing?"

Bony stared out of the port. Down on the seabed the Limbics had moved from their guarding circle. Now they stood in a group. Forty or more bubble arms waved in unison in the quiet water.

Bony took a deep breath. He waited one more moment to make sure, but there was really no doubt.

"They're signaling," he said. "Those waves of their arms mean, *Come outside. We want to meet you.*"

12

Recruiting Tully O'Toole

She knew something she was not willing to admit. Chan, walking the darkened tunnels beneath Mount Ararat at Deb's side, kept glancing at her profile. A mirthless half-smile was on her lips. He could not see her eyes, hidden within the depths of the black hood, but whenever she turned her head his way her forehead was furrowed and her eyebrows lowered to a frown.

He wondered what surprises lay within the cloak. It was sure to be packed with hidden pockets and secret sewn-in compartments. Chan had been around Weapons-master Deb Bisson long enough to be ready for anything that popped out from the cloak's inner recesses. He had seen tiny mutated snakes, smaller than a finger, spring from a cloak pocket on command and kill with a single drop of neurotoxic venom delivered from minute fangs. He had watched a thief, tracked by blue-green borer beetles released from a vial in the cloak and tuned to pheromones at the crime scene, run screaming to Deb and beg for mercy after the patient little insects found him, entered his body cavities as he slept, and slowly began to eat him away from inside. He had seen a monofilament thread, woven into the cloak's hem, become in Deb's hands first a defensive weapon that cut a swinging club in two, and then in the same continuing movement an edge so keen that the attacker was decapitated while he still believed that he was bludgeoning his helpless victim.

Deb had promised a surprise, but it was nothing in the cloak. Something new and extraordinary—and unpleasant—would be needed to astonish Chan. Deb knew that. No mere method of attack or defense would be enough. Even twenty years ago, responding to a joking challenge, she had listed eighty-two different poisons that resided within her cloak and could leave a victim dead, apparently of natural causes.

The tunnels under Mount Ararat were narrower as they went north. At first, Chan and Deb were able to walk side by side. Then it was one at a time, with Deb in front. Ten minutes later, the hood of her cloak brushed the ceiling and Chan had to crouch in order to avoid banging his head on the unfinished rock of the tunnel roof.

"Are you sure Tully lives out here?" he said, as the tunnel dwindled another five centimeters in height and width.

She turned, so that for the first time since they started out her angry brown eyes stared directly into his. "You think maybe you know better?" She moved back against the wall so that he could squeeze past her, and waved a hand along the tunnel. "Go ahead. Be my guest."

"No, that's all right." Chan wished that he had kept his mouth shut. "I just didn't expect Tully to be in a place like this. The greatest linguist I ever met—"

"The greatest anybody ever met. But what need has there been for linguists since the starways closed? The translating machines are enough for talk between humans."

"Even so, Tully could have found a better place to live. Why would he choose to be out here?"

"Thirty seconds more, and you'll find out. Just around the next corner."

The tunnel was no wider than Chan's shoulders, and he had to bend far forward or go down on his hands and knees. The light came from wan yellow tubes, nailed one every twenty meters or so on the rough-cut walls or ceiling. He swore as the tunnel made a sharp turn and he failed to stoop quite low enough. His head banged on one of the lights.

"Welcome to Europa, low-rent district," Deb's voice said from around the turn. "Are we having fun yet?"

"This is no worse than parts of the Gallimaufries. The difference is, the Gallimaufries used to be the worst place in the solar system. Earth set the standard for lousy living. But since the quarantine, everywhere is getting more and more like the worst parts of Earth."

There was a silence from ahead, then Deb's cold voice. "You don't stop pushing, do you? I know we need the quarantine to end. If I didn't, I wouldn't have walked a single step with you. So get off my back, and be ready to say hello to Tully O'Toole."

Chan squeezed his way along to where Deb was standing in front of a door about four feet high. In the gloom beyond it, Chan saw a steep descending stairway.

"Down there." Deb pointed. "You, not me."

Chan hesitated. He had the feeling that something awful was waiting for him at the bottom of the stairs. "Are you sure Tully will be there?"

"If he's not, I don't know where he is."

The stairs were so steep, the only safe way to go down was to turn and hold the steps above as though descending a ladder. Chan began to go down, counting as he went. By the eighth step, a curious smell hit his nostrils. Suddenly he knew the nature of Deb's unpleasant surprise. The aroma was quite unmistakable and dreadfully familiar. He paused, wanting to climb back up and run far away.

He couldn't do that. For Tully O'Toole's sake, for old times sake, for Chan's own sake, he had to learn how bad it was. He continued down. As he reached the bottom he took a deep breath and turned the corner leading into a more brightly lit room.

They were on the floor, about forty of them lying on thin mattresses. Each facial expression was different, from joyful bliss to dark, haunted agony. Their dress ranged from expensive and new to old, worn-out rags. A few were fat, most were skeletally thin. All had in common a dead gray tone to the skin and lines of tiny purple-black dots on bare arms and legs: the stigmata of Paradox, the milky alkaloid to which everyone in the room was a slave.

Chan was appalled, but he had seen too many Paradox dens to be shocked by the condition of the occupants. He scanned the rows of mattresses, seeking a familiar face. He had almost given up, ready to tell Deb Bisson back at the top of the stairs that they had made a wasted trip, when a tattered wreck right at his feet raised a hand and croaked, "Mercy me, what do I see? Do my eyes scan Chan the man?"

It was the singsong delivery of the words more than

the voice. Chan stepped forward and sank to his knees. "Tully? Tully the Rhymer?"

"Less of that than I was. But yes, you have it right. The man you see, that is he."

Chan reached out, gripped Tully O'Toole's outstretched hand, and gently lifted until the other man was sitting upright on the mattress. The hand that gripped Chan's was all bone, and the fingers felt fleshless. "How are you, Tully?"

It was an inane question, given O'Toole's condition, but Tully laughed. "Oh, never too bad and never too sad. I'm not the man I once was, Chan, but who of us is? Sometimes I'm up, sometimes I'm down. Nights get worse as they go on, the darkest hour before the dawn. We're about halfway."

At least Tully knew that it *was* night. Third-stage Paradox addiction robbed its victims of all sense of time and place. From the look of him, Tully O'Toole was coming off the high point for the night and heading downhill. By morning he would be running a fever and shivering. Before that he had better be safe in bed.

"Tully, I have something important to tell you. But you'll have to wait another minute or two before I can say it. Will you wait? I'll be right back."

"Where would I be going? Take your time. I'll sit tight, if it takes all night."

"It won't. Three minutes, no more."

Chan hurried back up the steep stairs. Deb stood at the top, still and silent as a statue in her cowled cloak. She said, "Well, now you've seen for yourself. Ready to give up and leave me alone?"

"Deb, Tully can't stay here like this. We have to get him away."

"Where were you, all these past years? Do you think I haven't tried? I love Tully. In the old days he was close to me as a brother. I've been here a dozen times, and I've begged and pleaded with him to take treatment. And got nowhere. He won't listen. He *can't* listen."

"You don't have to tell me that Paradox is hard to break. But there are ways to get through. I'm going back to talk to him."

"Oh, sure. You think you'll succeed where I failed."

"I don't think that. But I know how to try, better than most. Look, Deb, I want to ask a favor."

"Whatever it is, no. I don't owe you a favor—any favor."

"It's not a favor for me. It's for Tully. If I can persuade him to leave this place, I have to head out at once to look for Chrissie and the Tarbush in the Oort Cloud. I'll be gone only a few days, but Tully can't be left on his own. Will you look after him until I come back?"

"I'd do anything to help Tully. But you don't know what you're asking. He'd be with me for a few hours, then he'd want the drug. Unless I chained him down I couldn't stop him from getting it—and I'm not so sure that would work, either. He'd find a way."

"He would if he was here on Mount Ararat. But if we left Europa—if you took him to Ceres—"

"I see. I take him to Ceres, so you get *me* to Ceres." She flung the hood back from her head, and her eyes were blazing. "You bastard. You think you're being so sneaky, but I read you easy. All you care about is getting a team together for your damned assignment."

"That's not true, Deb. I care about Tully. And don't pretend *you* don't care about the stars. You might fool yourself, but you don't fool me. I'm going back to talk to Tully now. If I can get him to come with me and you're still here when we come back, fine. I'll ask you again. And if you won't give it, I'll find some other way to help him."

Chan turned and stumbled back down the stairs without looking at Deb or waiting to hear her reply. In the smoky room at the bottom, Tully O'Toole lay like a dead man on his mattress.

"Tully?" Chan spoke softly. "I'm back. Can we talk now?"

"Sure, sure." The answer was a weak whisper.

"Do you think you'll be able to understand me?"

"Sure I can, Chan the man. This time of night I'm sharp and bright." Tully struggled to sit up, and Chan bent and placed his arm around the other man's back. As he lifted he could feel the separate vertebrae in the spine.

"I'll get right to the point. Tully, we have a chance to lift the quarantine. Did you hear me? *We can lift the quarantine. We can go to the stars*. And I don't just mean that humans can do it. *We* can do it, you and me and the old team."

"Wha-what?" Tully's pale blue eyes clouded and his thin features took on a puzzled frown. "I think maybe I'm not hearing right."

"You're hearing right. You're not imagining. I know, it sounds too good to be true. But listen."

Chan spoke slowly and carefully, giving details of his meeting with the Stellar Group, watching Tully's face. Occasionally the thin man frowned or seemed to drift away, but after a few moments he would nod for Chan to go on. The final proof that he was following everything came when Chan said, "We need you, Tully. None of the translation machines can talk to aliens, they're programmed for human languages. But you can do it."

"I can't do anything."

"You'll learn. It takes a genuine madman like Tully

the Rhymer to talk to aliens. The rest of us wouldn't know where to start, but we'll be there to back you up. Me and Tarbush, and Deb and Chrissie, and Dapper Dan and the Bun. Together again."

"Together again. The old team, it's like a dream." Tully's blue eyes filled with tears. "Oh, God, Chan. If I could I would. But I'm no use any more. I can't go."

"You *can* go, Tully. But first you have to break the Paradox habit."

"Do you think I don't know that? I can't do it. I've tried and tried. I close the door and fix the locks, and even throw the key away. But still I get out every day—and drink the milk of Paradox."

He was bent over, weeping hopelessly. Chan patted the thin shoulder. "It will be different this time, Tully. You won't be alone. You'll have me to help you, and Deb and Danny Casement. And in a few more days, as soon as I can reach them, Chrissie and the Tarbush will be along, too."

"Dapper Dan. Oh, how I'd love to see him again." Tully was laughing and crying at the same time. "Him and his lady friends. Do you remember how he used to sell them pieces of the Yang diamond?"

"Tully, he's still at it. When you see him, he'll tell you about it. Come on now." Chan had his arm around O'Toole, lifting him. "We have to do this in stages. First, we go to Deb Bisson's place. Then you two go on to Ceres."

"What about you?" Tully stood up, swaying for balance. "Where will you be?"

"I told you, I have to find Tarbush and Chrissie Winger. Then we'll have the old team together, and be all set to go. We'll be on our way to the stars, Tully. Come on. Deb Bisson's waiting for us."

He led the way to the steep stair and the two of

them slowly climbed together, Chan providing extra lift when it was needed. He was afraid that Deb had left, until she stepped forward out of the shadows.

Tully O'Toole stumbled over to her and draped his tall, gaunt form around her.

"Deb, I don't know how to thank you and Chan. When I came here tonight I felt sure I was done, a little while longer and I would be gone. But now there's hope. We'll get away from here, and head for the stars. We said we would, we said we could—and now we'll do it."

Deb patted him on the shoulder. "We will, Tully. We will. We have to go to your place first, to get your things, before we go to mine. You lead the way."

As Tully started back along the corridor, feeling his way along the dark walls, she held Chan back for a moment and whispered, "While you're gloating, just remember one thing. I'm not going to Ceres or anywhere else for you. I'm doing it for *him*."

"I know that." Chan tried to pull free. "You hate my guts. You don't need to tell me again. As soon as I can make arrangements for you and Tully to go to Ceres, I'll leave you and head for the Oort Cloud. I have to find Chrissie and the Tarbush."

Deb still held him by the arm. "Good luck, then—for Tully's sake. What do you think your chances are?"

"With you?" Chan pulled himself away. "Zero. With Chrissie and the Tarbush, excellent. I'll find them, and I'll bring them to Ceres."

"Cocksure as ever."

"It's all relative, Deb. Compared with the past few hours, anything in the Oort Cloud has to be easy."

13

Learning from the Bubble People

Bony was fascinated by the array of waving bubble arms on the seabed outside. He was also frightened of them, as any rational person was afraid of the totally unknown. How long he might have stood staring was anyone's guess, but a sudden clatter and a shout of "Rombelle! Rombelle!" brought his attention back to the inside of the ship.

It was Friday Indigo, dropping from the upper level without using the ladder. He shouted, "Look outside!" and then, when it became obvious that's exactly what Bony and Liddy were doing, "Why didn't you dummies wake me up?"

"We only just noticed them. We were asleep."

It was a measure of Indigo's excitement that he didn't blister Bony for a failure to keep watch. Instead he crowded with them to the port.

"I woke up," he said, "and I noticed it was light, and I went to look outside. And there they were, standing on the sea floor! Waving! Rombelle, they want us to meet with them."

That was not news to Bony. He said carefully, "Do you think that would be a good idea, sir? We know nothing about these creatures."

"Well, of course we don't. How could we, this is first contact. You hear me? *First contact*. No human or alien in the Stellar Group ever encountered these beings before. Of course we have to go out and meet them."

Bony should have expected that answer. He sighed, and reluctantly started toward the airlock.

Friday Indigo said, "And just where the hell do you think you're going?"

"I was going for a suit—to wear outside."

"And who told you to do that?" Indigo moved to Bony's side. "You don't seem to understand, Rombelle. This is *first contact*. A historic event. Naturally, the leader of the party conducts the initial meeting. You can come with me—provided that you stay a few steps behind and don't open your mouth. All right?"

Without waiting for an answer Indigo took a suit and allowed it to enclose his body. Bony did not move. At last Indigo said impatiently, "Come on, man. First you're trying to get out of the ship ahead of me, then you've turned into a statue. Get that suit on."

"Yes, sir." Bony knew what he needed to say, but he was afraid that it would offend Liddy. "I was just thinking, if we have people outside the ship, wouldn't it be really important to have somebody back on board in case there's an emergency? Someone who knows all the ship's rescue systems inside and out."

He had tried to phrase it tactfully, but tact was an

unknown quantity to Friday Indigo. The captain looked at him, then at Liddy.

"Hm. You think she's a dumb female who doesn't know what she's doing?"

"Well, I didn't say—"

"I agree with you. Liddy has her uses, but handling emergencies isn't one of them. All right. Change of plan. Rombelle, you stay here. Liddy, you put a suit on and come with me."

"Does she need to go outside at all, sir? I mean, what would she do there?"

"She'll carry the translation equipment. You don't think I'm going to lug it around myself, do you, when I'm trying to establish contact with the bubble people? Remember, we'll be recording this for posterity."

If we *have* a posterity, thought Bony. But the choice was pretty clear: either Liddy stayed here, or he did. And if there was trouble, he had a better chance of saving her than she did of saving him.

"You'll need to be able to communicate with the ship, sir, if everything is to be recorded."

"Sure, sure. Make arrangements for that while Liddy puts her suit on. You can't expect me to do everything. And jump to it!"

Bony jumped to it—but not because Indigo had ordered him to. For Liddy's sake he wanted the best possible link between the ship and the outside party. The easiest way was to run a cable directly from the ship's external line tap to the portable translation unit. It would handle only voice communication, but Friday Indigo and Liddy didn't need to see what was happening to Bony, and he would be able to watch their every move using the ship's imaging systems.

As Bony worked he kept an eye on what was happening outside. The Limbics maintained their circle around the ship, but they had backed away and risen a couple of meters above the seabed. Apparently they had some invisible way of varying their buoyancy and could hover at any depth they chose. They had moved beyond the region flattened by the arrival of the *Mood Indigo*, to where the forest of spears still stood upright. One by one they drifted downward. Bubble arms stretched down, gripped, and broke off the sharp-tipped spikes. Bony watched in amazement as the long spears were lifted and then inserted, sharp end first, into the wide dark slit on the top of the globular body. It was the ultimate sword-swallowing act. Slowly and easily, centimeter after centimeter, the whole long shaft vanished.

Were they *eating* the pikes? What else could it possibly be? Bony recalled how the shafts had broken under his slightest touch. Like the strange ship that he and Liddy had seen on their trip to the ocean surface, the Limbics were not just alien, they were *alien* alien.

"Why the hell are you standing there gaping?" Friday Indigo's voice was loud in Bony's ears. "I'm all set to go. Do you have that communication connection ready?"

"Just a couple more minutes." Bony bent over the translation equipment and went back to work at maximum speed. He hated the idea of Liddy going out there among those creatures. They had a soft, jellyfish appearance, and they hadn't done anything threatening so far; but they also had had no opportunity to do so. It was his fault that Liddy was going. Why hadn't he kept his stupid mouth shut?

He adjusted a final setting and lifted the translator. It wasn't big, and it wasn't heavy. Friday Indigo could have carried it easily enough without any help from Liddy. She was waiting patiently at Bony's side with her suit helmet ready to close, and he handed the instrument to her. "Here, Liddy. Be careful. It looks safe enough out there, but it may not be. If you see anything you don't like, don't wait to find out what it is. Head straight back for the ship."

He had spoken softly, but not softly enough. Friday Indigo came over to him, his boots clanking on the deck plates. "How many captains can a ship have, Rombelle?"

"One, sir."

"And who's the captain of the *Mood Indigo*?"

"You are, sir."

"Quite right. Don't forget it. You don't give orders, I do. Come on, Liddy."

He led the way into the airlock. Liddy, carrying the translator, followed. As the inner hatch closed she gave Bony what seemed to him like a forlorn little wave. It was a long minute before he could see her again on the imaging display, dropping silently toward the seabed with Friday Indigo.

Their exit from the ship had been noticed elsewhere. The Limbics ceased their grazing on the seaspears and drifted back toward the *Mood Indigo*. They formed a compact group, about five meters away from the humans.

Indigo held up one hand and said loudly, "Greetings, people of this planet. I, Friday Indigo, captain of the Terran ship *Mood Indigo*, and representative of all Terrans and all species of the Stellar Group, come in peace to your world."

There was a silence, during which Bony wondered if the Limbics used sound at all as a means of communication. At last, a pair of slits opened in one of the bubble creature's rounded sides. After a preliminary few seconds in which the openings pulsed like a bellows, Bony heard a strange mixture of hoots, whistles, gurgles, and hiccups.

Friday Indigo said, "What the hell is all that? Rombelle, I thought this thing was supposed to be a translator."

"It is, sir. But with a language it has never heard before, the translator needs a sample before it can begin to translate."

"So what did it do with *my* message?"

"I don't know, sir. I don't think it did anything. It needs a sample of their speech first."

"How big a sample?"

"I don't know."

"That's no answer. Why didn't you warn me, before you let me come out here and make a fool of myself? I want to know about this planet, and all I get are a bunch of nonsense sounds."

"Just a moment, sir." Bony could see the slits on the side of the body opening and closing again. "I believe the Limbics don't use their mouths for speech."

"So what are they doing, farting at us?"

"No, sir. They use gill slits. One of them is going to talk again."

The translator produced another string of gurgles. This time it went on for almost a minute. Gradually the sounds modulated into something with the cadences of human speech.

"Can you understand that, Rombelle?"

"No, sir."

"Nor can I. Liddy, give me that thing." Indigo grabbed the translator from her and shook it violently. "Goddamn heap of junk. It's not working. If I could get my hands on the assholes who sold it to me, I'd gut and garrotte them. I paid a lot for this worthless piece of crap."

It occurred to Bony that if Indigo's speech was still being recorded, this was going to make an interesting entry in the annals of first-contact history.

"It *is* working, sir. The translator sounded more like human speech toward the end. Just keep talking."

"About what? I can't have a one-way conversation with these stupid blobs."

The translator, unexpectedly, whistled and said "*Globs of blobs.*"

"Hear that, sir? Greet them again."

"Right." Indigo returned the translator to Liddy, struck a pose, and said, "Greetings, people of Limbo—damn it, the bubble heads surely don't call their own planet *that*. It's your fault, Rombelle, giving this place such an asinine name and getting us all thinking of it like that—anyway, where was I? I, Friday Indigo, captain of the *Mood Indigo*, come in peace to your world, whatever you call it, and wish you well in the name of humans and whoever. There. That should do it."

The Limbics appeared to be listening attentively. Their spokesman's gill slits opened, and after a few moments of silence the translator gurgled and said, "*The second walking makes it new after four braces. Next water will open the lonely day for gold.*"

"Damn and set fire to it, I *told* you it was a piece of junk. Are you going to tell me that you could understand that?"

"No, sir."

"It was gibberish."

"Perhaps it needs a larger sample." But Bony was not convinced. He had seen translation machines perform successfully after unbelievably small samples of languages. Of course, that was for *human* languages. "Sir, I'm not sure this is going to work."

"Of course it's not working, you dummy. Didn't you hear what it said?"

"I mean the translator may never work, no matter how big a language sample we give it."

"It was sold to me as a general translator."

"Between pairs of *human* languages. Maybe it even works with Tinker and Pipe-Rilla talk. But no one has ever had to deal with an intelligent marine organism before. The concepts that the Limbics evolved to deal with may be just too strange to translate."

Unfortunately, Bony didn't believe that. The gill slits were moving, and the translator said, *"Is it Monday for the flower, or was it the one at the end?"* But at the same time, the Limbics as a group were steadily backing away while still facing Liddy and Indigo. The bubble arms were repeating the signal they had given earlier. *Come. We want you to come.*

"You're full of it, Rombelle. I tell you, it's this crappy machine." Friday Indigo took the translator from Liddy and dropped it to the seabed. "*Concepts too strange to translate*, my ass. Look at them. It's clear enough what they mean. They want us to follow them. Come on, Liddy. And Rombelle, you stay here and look after the ship."

"Sir, I don't think that going with them is a good idea."

"Did you hear me ask your opinion?"

"But we won't be able to communicate with each other when you're more than a few meters away."

"How awful. Do you think I can't manage without the benefit of your advice? You'll find out what we learn when we get back."

Liddy spoke for the first time since leaving the ship. "Don't worry about us, Bony. We'll be fine."

"Enough of the soft talk." Indigo went to Liddy's side and took hold of the arm of her suit. "Let's go. They're waiting for us."

The Limbics had formed into a circle around the two humans. They began a slow and steady movement across the seabed, ushering Liddy and Friday Indigo away toward the undersea ridge. The water was less clear today, and in just a couple of minutes the group of figures was merging into a cloudy blue-green haze.

Bony watched until they were invisible. He had stayed on board the ship in case an emergency affected the other two and he needed to perform a rescue. But Friday Indigo, coddled from birth, would not recognize an emergency if he saw one. To know danger for what it was, you first needed experience with fear. Bony had that, if he had anything. But how would he know if an emergency had arisen, with the others out of sight and the water preventing radio contact? He had to put himself in a position where he could save Liddy.

He gave the command to reel in the cable attached to the translator and tuck it away in a cargo hold, and turned the unit off.

It was time to try an experiment that he had been thinking about in every free moment of the past twenty-four hours. With the others out of harm's way, the only person he could hurt was himself.

Bony slipped on a suit, left the helmet open but in a position where he could snap it closed in a fraction of a second, and went across to the main control desk of the *Mood Indigo*. He already knew that the ship's fusion drive could not be used underwater. The auxiliary ion thrusters ought to work, though. They could provide thrust for very long periods, but they had low power. They were designed only for small adjustments to position in space, and they could never lift a ship into orbit.

They might, however, be enough for what Bony had in mind. He knew the total mass of the ship, and he had calculated how much water it displaced. From that he could estimate the average density of the *Mood Indigo* as about fifteen percent more than the density of water. On Earth, that would mean the auxiliary thrusters would have to lift a lot of weight. Here, however, the heavy-water ocean of Limbo provided considerable extra buoyancy.

He could have deduced that fact without calculation, from the sedate and gentle descent of the ship in their first arrival. The question remained, just how much extra lift did the denser water provide?

He had gone as far as calculation would permit. Now he had to make the practical test.

Bony keyed in the command to provide aft thrust at a minimal level. There was a slight vibration through the ship, the view outside the ports vanished in a cloud of gray silt stirred up from the sea floor, and nothing else happened. The ship's inertial navigation system showed that the *Mood Indigo* had not risen a centimeter.

A slightly higher setting produced a similar lack of result. Bony added thrust in slow increments, waiting each time to make sure that the situation had stabilized. On the fifth increase he felt a different tremor in the ship. A silt cloud still obscured the view outside the ports, but the inertial navigator indicated that the ship was rising, slowly and vertically.

He did not want to go all the way to the surface, though it was nice to know that he could. Bony carefully adjusted the power setting until the *Mood Indigo* was hovering at a constant depth. He knew the direction that Liddy, Friday Indigo and the group of Limbics had taken, but the imaging sensors showed nothing but the continuous blue-green of sea water.

Bony activated a pair of lateral thrustors at their lowest level, so that the ship began to crab slowly sideways through the water in the direction taken by the group of Limbics. If they had changed their minds before reaching the ridge, Bony would be out of luck.

He was a little lower in the water than he had realized, and became aware of the approaching ridge by the reappearance of the cloud of blown silt. He raised the ship another ten meters, waited until he reached the brow of the ridge, then hovered stationary while he inspected the displays provided by the imaging sensors.

He stared desperately at the seabed, seeking a group of figures. He had a problem. If he went too high, the amount of scattered sunlight filtering down around the ship made it hard to see detail below him. But if he went lower, silt raised by the exhaust of the thrustors obscured everything.

If he could not find them he had to return the *Mood Indigo* to its original position, so that Friday Indigo and Liddy could get back to it. As he reached that conclusion, he realized that although he saw no moving figures, either bubble people or humans, the view below was not totally featureless. He could make out a faint trail of suspended mud, a haziness where something appeared to have recently disturbed the bed of the sea.

It must mark the way that they had travelled. Just beyond the ridge it angled wide to the left. Continue on his original course, and he would have missed them completely.

Bony rose, to a height where he could still just see the ghostly arrow of blown silt, and directed the ship along the trail. He went slowly. He wanted to know what was going on with Friday Indigo and Liddy, without the captain being aware of it. Indigo's instruction had been explicit: stay in one place and look after the ship. He had already violated that, and if he got in the way of what Friday Indigo was trying to do it would make things worse.

No danger of getting in the way at the moment.

On the seabed the trail went on and on, but no matter what he did with the image intensifiers he could detect no sign of figures, human or otherwise.

Was he following an illusion, a path made by some other creature that lived on Limbo's tranquil seabed? In fact, wasn't there a hint, at the very limit of visibility, of a quite different shape out there? He fancied he could discern a long, low form, with some kind of conical shell on top. The sort of thing you would see if the ocean of Limbo was home to a gigantic sea-snail.

He allowed the *Mood Indigo* to drift forward, slower and slower. Now he could discern a bright line along the upper edge, as though the body of the great snail was edged with gold.

Nearer. And just a little nearer yet, though he remained ready at any moment to cut in an alternate set of thrustors and shoot away at maximum power. The snail lay silent and motionless on the bed of the ocean.

And then, in a moment, the image changed—not on the seabed, but inside Bony's mind. It was like one of those optical illusions, where a figure suddenly transforms as you look at it into a quite different one. The sea-snail was even bigger than he had thought, and it was no longer a snail. It was a ship, lying on its side.

And not just any ship. The outer hull was misshapen, all bulges and wens. Although he had never encountered a vessel like the one before him, Bony recognized those lines.

The object on the sea bed was a Pipe-Rilla ship, built by—and unique to—that alien member of the Stellar Group.

14

The Crew of the *Hero's Return*

The *Hero's Return* was close to three hundred meters long and massed in excess of eighty thousand tons. It had been designed for "peacekeeping," which meant that it had been fitted out from stem to stern with the most hideous weapons of war that the human mind could conceive. Nothing ought to warm better the heart of one of the solar system's most experienced military men. Yet General Dag Korin stood in the main docking area and shook his white-haired head in disgust.

"You see how it goes," he said. "You form some sort of halfassed union with a load of goggle-eyed sapsucker pipestem-legged aliens, and they dump their jackass craphead lily-livered ideas on you, and before you know it you've come to *this*."

He waved his arm to take in the whole of the loading bay, forty meters across and twenty high. Flammarion, standing at the General's side, stared around at the ribbed walls, the array of displays, and the warren of pipes and cables. Everything looked fine to him. Not only that, the Angels to his certain knowledge didn't have eyes to goggle, and he very much doubted that they, the Tinkers, or the Pipe-Rillas had livers.

"Filthy!" General Korin ran a gloved hand along a rail, and it came away smudged with dust and grease. "Filthy, and neglected, and stinking. A typical civilian vessel. Swallow all the soft-headed pacifist nonsense that the aliens preach, and in just a few years here's what you have. What I'd like to know is, where did good old-fashioned military discipline go, the thing that made humans great?"

Flammarion couldn't answer. But since the *Hero's Return* had been for at least ten years a civilian ship, it didn't seem reasonable to look for it here. The weapons, except for strictly defensive shields, had been stripped out, and the human crew replaced by robots low-level to the point of imbecility. On the other hand, the ship's computer had been upgraded to the very best that humanity could produce. This was an area where humans led the rest of the Stellar Group by a wide margin. If you've got it, flaunt it.

Dag Korin was glaring at Flammarion, who knew better than to offer answers or comments. He had a lot of respect for the aged general, and he realized that he was more of a convenient audience than anything else.

"And the crew that we're getting!" Korin regarded Flammarion with something close to approval. "Now you, you're a military man yourself. You know the value of organization and training. Did you see the description of what's going to be arriving on board in the next few hours?"

"Yes, sir." It would be more like the next few

minutes. According to the status display, a transit vehicle to the *Hero's Return* had docked three minutes ago and Flammarion could hear the locks in operation.

"The scum of the solar system," Korin went on. He waved the manifest that he was holding. "The two arriving on this ship are a fine example. Coming from the Oort Cloud, and so far as I can tell they've never done one useful thing in their whole lives. See this one. '*Tarboosh Hanson. Areas of expertise: talks to animals; strongman and stuntman.*' A fat lot of use he's going to be when we're fighting armed aliens in the Geyser Swirl. And here's the other one. '*Chrissie Winger. Areas of expertise: magic and deception.*' What's that mean? They may buy this sort of nonsense out in the Oort Cloud, but not here. Now this other man coming in later today looks a bit better. He's not military but at least he has a career. '*Daniel Casement. Areas of expertise: financial investment advice, precious stones.*' Hmm. Maybe I should deal with him myself."

"Sir, the first two will be here any second. That's the outer hatch cycling. What should we do?"

"Hold your water, and take your signals from me. These people have to know who they're dealing with. First impressions are important."

Dag Korin strode forward. He placed himself firmly, legs wide apart, in the middle of the passageway leading from the main lock to the interior of the *Hero's Return*. Anyone who wished to enter the ship from the transit vessel would first have to pass by him.

The inner hatch of the lock opened. After a few seconds, a fat little animal with thick brown fur and a bulging pointed head emerged. It trotted forward and paused in front of Dag Korin. As he bent creakily forward to grab for it, the creature scurried between his legs and vanished underneath a tangle of pipes.

Korin straightened up to glare at the man who came strolling out of the lock. "Is that beast yours?"

"As much as she belongs to anybody, and as much as she's a beast, yes." The newcomer was very black, very broad, and very tall. His height was enhanced by the bright red fez on top of his head.

"You can't bring a dog onto a navy ship."

"It isn't a navy ship."

"A *former* navy ship, then. You can't bring a dog aboard."

"It isn't a dog. It's a modded ferret. Her name's Scruffy." The man smiled amiably at Korin. "And mine is Hanson, Tarboosh Hanson. Reporting to Chan Dalton."

"Get that filthy animal off my ship."

"Sorry. Can't do that." Tarboosh Hanson felt in the pockets of his blue jacket and produced a slip of paper. He came closer and handed it over. As the general studied it, he said, "See. *Approved for accommodation aboard the* Hero's Return, *Tarboosh Hanson and job-related equipment, the latter not to exceed fifty kilos in mass*. Scruffy weighs a lot less than fifty, she's as smart as I am, and for me she's essential job-related equipment. If you're going to talk to animals, you have to keep in practice. Anyway, I'm supposed to report to Chan Dalton. Where do I find him?"

"He hasn't arrived yet. He's on the next transit vehicle."

"Good enough. I'll wait for him on board." Tarboosh Hanson nodded agreeably. He whistled to the ferret, who came promptly from its hiding place, and walked past Dag Korin. The General, turning and ready to explode, was diverted by something new. Another arrival had appeared from the lock and stood watching.

She was a short, trim woman in her early forties,

dressed in a white sleeveless blouse, white pants, and long white boots. She had blond hair and a smooth china-doll face. Normal enough, except for the white headband that held back her long hair and hid most of her forehead. Across it, in black letters that became steadily smaller, ran the words:

You are now close enough for me to steal your wallet.

As soon as she saw that she had been noticed, the woman walked toward Dag Korin. He squinted at the headband as she approached, until when she was still two feet away she threw up her right arm in a snappy military salute. Guileless blue eyes stared up into his.

"Chrissie Winger, reporting for duty to General Korin."

Seven decades of experience made the General's return of salute a reflex action. His hand was not yet back to his side when hers was lifting toward him.

"Here, sir. I feel sure that you will need this."

She was holding a slim black folder. Korin clapped his hand to the empty pocket at the back of his pants.

"That's mine. How the devil did you do that? You were never closer to me than half a meter."

"Professional secret." A small card appeared from nowhere next to the black folder. "It's my stock in trade. You can't expect a lady to give it away."

Kubo Flammarion, watching from a distance, expected Korin to explode again. Instead, the old General laughed and took both the wallet and the card.

"You've got a nerve, Chrissie Winger. I've always liked that in a woman. Magic and deception, eh? If we're not allowed violence in the Geyser Swirl, maybe they'll come in useful. I'll make you a trade. Tell me how you managed to get your hands on my wallet two seconds after leaving the transit vessel, without ever coming near me, and I'll guarantee you the best living quarters on this ship."

She put a finger to her chin, considering. "Include Tarboosh Hanson in the deal, and you're on. We've been together a long time and we're kind of used to sharing quarters."

"All right. Now tell me, how did you steal my wallet?"

"I didn't. The Tarbush took it when you turned around and threw it to me."

"Well damn my eyes." Korin shook his head. "I should have known. That sort of trick was old when I was a lad. But I didn't feel or see a thing."

"You're not supposed to. If you did, it wouldn't be much of an act, would it? Now, what about these fancy quarters you promised?"

"Later. The *Hero's Return* is scheduled for midnight departure to an Asteroid Belt Link entry point, and your group is still four members short. Including your team leader." Korin pointed to the status display. It indicated that another vessel was arriving, this one from Europa via Earth. "If that doesn't have Chan Dalton aboard, we're in trouble. You go ahead—Captain Flammarion will show you the layout of crew quarters—and I'll catch you later."

"Yes, sir." Chrissie Winger saluted again. She walked across to Flammarion, who took a couple of steps back and looked at her warily.

"You're not going to do any of your fancy wallet-stealing stuff with me, are you?"

"Not a chance." She beamed at him, in a way that made Flammarion feel that he was an immensely entertaining and interesting fellow. "Does a brewer give away beer? It's as I told General Korin, I don't do that sort of thing for free. But I wanted to impress him, so Tarb and I arranged that little stunt."

"He likes you, you know. If he didn't he'd have gutted you for pulling something like that."

"Well, I like him, too—what I've seen of him. I expected an old fossil, but he's not like that. There's still plenty of firepower in him."

"There is. And you don't want it directed your way." Flammarion, leading Chrissie down the ship's main corridor, noticed an odd tightness in his jacket. He opened it as he walked and felt a bulge in his undershirt. And inside *that*—

He reached in and pulled out a bottle. "This is impossible. My jacket was closed, my shirt is tight at the neck." He stopped dead and stared at the label. "Is it really beer?"

"I'm not a brewer, so I *can* give it away, and there are a few things I would never do. One of them is deceive a man with a gift of fake beer."

"But how did you get it there?"

"Ah, now as to that, I am willing to deceive. Or at least, not to reveal." Chrissie Winger had not been told where to go, and since she had not stopped walking Flammarion was now behind her; but she unhesitatingly made the turn to the unmarked corridor leading to the crew's quarters. "I wouldn't worry about it if I were you," she said over her shoulder. "A girl has to have her little secrets."

She walked confidently forward. Flammarion trailed along behind. He didn't know quite what kind of team was assembling for this expedition, but he was sure it was unlike anything he had met before.

Fifteen minutes ago, Chan Dalton had been relaxing for the first time in ten days. It had been a desperate, sleepless dash around the solar system, but against the odds he had done everything. Chrissie Winger and Tarboosh Hanson had jumped at the idea of a new stellar expedition, almost before he could tell them about it. Apparently life in the Oort Cloud was too dull and easy. They had taken the first available inbound ship and should already be on board the *Hero's Return*, waiting for him.

He had spoken with Deb Bisson two hours ago, and although she was as cold as ever she swore that she, too, would arrive before the deadline. She was bringing Tully O'Toole with her. He was shaky and feverish with Paradox withdrawal and occasionally hallucinating, but with guidance and encouragement he was somehow hanging on.

That left only Danny Casement and the Bun, and Chan had been more sure of them than anyone. Danny had enormous persuasive power, but he probably wouldn't even need it. In the old days the Bun had been keenest of all to go to the stars. Now they would fly out from the Vulcan Nexus and complete the old team.

And then reality intruded. Danny's message, chasing Chan around the solar system, finally caught up with him. It told of the Bun's disappearance and his almost certain death. The *Hero's Return* was looming up ahead but Chan didn't see it. He was turned inward, looking at the collapse of his plans. Deb Bisson had promised to go along only if he had the full team. With the Bun gone, Deb would back out. Without Deb, Tully would not make it. The dominoes would fall. No Bun, no Deb, no Tully . . .

No team.

The transit vessel docked. The hatch opened. Chan didn't have the energy to stand up and go through it. He sat, hands gripping the padded arms of his chair, until the robots came along and began to service the cabin around him. The gentle probing touch of one on his leg, as though asking *Do I clean this?*, roused him.

He stood up and passed through the first connection chamber, through the outer hatch, through the lock and through the inner hatch. He was finally in the true interior of the *Hero's Return*, but he had sat so long after docking that anyone waiting for a passenger on the transit vessel would surely be gone. He glanced over to the couch at the side of the chamber, expecting to see no one. General Dag Korin lay there at full length. His eyes were closed and his mouth was open. Somehow he gave the impression of a man sleeping at attention.

Chan hesitated to wake him. On the other hand, what was Korin doing here if not waiting to see Chan? And when you had bad news to present, one time was as good as another.

Chan leaned down and shook the General's shoulder. Korin came awake so smoothly and quickly that it was hard to believe he had been sleeping.

Frosty blue eyes fixed on Chan as the General slowly sat upright. "You're running damn close to the deadline, Dalton. Are you sure you'll have all your team on board by midnight?"

"I'm sure I won't. One of them is dead."

"You tell me that *now*, with just a few hours to go to departure?"

"I only found out myself a few minutes before we docked."

"Can you operate without him?"

"If we have to. But it's not that simple." Chan outlined Deb Bisson's position, and how the death of the Bun would affect her presence on the team.

"So you've got problems to solve." Korin stood up. "And so do I. The two of us have to talk."

"I don't know that I have much to say. Not until I've had a chance to think about all this."

"Understood. But if you can't talk, you can listen. Come on. This is important."

Korin led the way into the cavernous interior of the *Hero's Return*. In the old days the cruiser had carried a military crew of nine hundred men and women. The ship's exterior with its massive armor and reinforced hull was little changed from those glory days, but once inside you wandered through a ghost ship. Your voice echoed through bare-walled compartments, your footsteps rang along empty corridors. Chan found himself reluctant to speak, while Dag Korin apparently did not want any discussion until they had privacy. The two men drifted along in silence, past dark chambers that had once housed weapons able to turn whole asteroids to slag; past engines that could drive the eighty-thousand-ton mass at anything up to seven gees; past the chamber housing a computer as sophisticated as any ever built, able to control the vessel's sensors, make autonomous decisions, and do whatever was needed to assure the safety of ship and crew; past the deserted quarters of that crew, where almost a thousand men and women had once exercised, eaten, and slept.

Dag Korin, with the pick of the whole ship available to him, apparently preferred simplicity. He continued on, beyond the section that had once housed the captain and the senior officers, until they came to a set of smaller rooms tucked away beside the ship's main control room. And there, at the very end of a corridor, Chan saw a tall form in a powder-blue work suit, lounging against a door painted a bilious green.

He heard Dag Korin's surprised grunt, in the same moment as Chan recognized the blond hair and anorexic face of Elke Siry.

"I believe you already met my ward," Korin said to Chan. And then, to the woman, "What are you doing here, Elke? I thought you were getting us ready for Link transition."

My ward? Dag Korin had said nothing about that at their first meeting. But the woman was speaking. "I was." There was no mistaking the high-pitched, nervous voice, with its trace of a lisp. "But I have disturbing information, matters that I must discuss with you."

"You, too? Looks like it's bad news all round." Korin opened the door. "We'd better go inside."

The room they entered was simply furnished even by the standards of Earth's Gallimaufries. Console, disk-case, small couch, writing desk, bureau, and chair, all without decoration or added niceties. Chan squeezed onto the couch next to Elke Siry, and noticed how she jerked urgently away when his hip accidentally came into contact with hers. Dag Korin went across to the metal bureau in one corner and returned with a box housing a dozen plastic bottles, each the size and shape of a small pear.

"Calvados?" He sat down on a hard chair opposite them. "I can personally recommend it."

Chan hesitated, then shook his head. Elke took one of the bottles, opened the cap with her thumbnail, and sucked down the contents in one long gulp. She was reaching for another when Korin pulled the box away.

"Talk first. If it's as bad as you say, maybe we'll sit here and drink the lot together. Now, Elke, what's the problem?" Korin caught Elke Siry's rapid sideways glance at Chan. "Don't worry, my dear, he's in this as deep as we are. If I can hear it, so can he."

"All right." But Elke Siry's face suggested to Chan that she thought it was far from all right. She bit her lip, shook her head from side to side so that her long blond tresses swung about her thin face, and burst out, "It's the Link point. The one in the Geyser Swirl."

"What about it?"

"I've wondered about it ever since I heard it existed. I mean, how could there be a Link in the network that no one knew about before? A Link is a spacetime anomaly. It pops out at you on any connectivity survey in a way you can't miss."

"We missed this one."

"No. I don't think we did. I believe that it wasn't there to be observed on any previous survey."

"Hm." Korin raised grizzled eyebrows at Chan. "Did you ever hear of anything like that? A Link entry and exit point that comes and goes?"

"I didn't know such a thing was possible. Link points are permanent features. Aren't they?"

Chan thought that he had offered a mild and reasonable response. He was not ready for the way that Elke blushed bright red, or for her breathless outburst: "Then that just proves how much you don't know. Links can be created—and destroyed. How much scientific training have you had?"

"Very little."

"How much?"

"Well, none." Chan held up his hands defensively. "Dr. Siry, I wasn't arguing with you. I'm just telling you what I've been told."

It didn't seem to help. She was as nervous and intense as ever, the absolute opposite of Dag Korin, who gave the impression he had seen it all before and found it no more shocking this time around.

"But there's worse," Elke said abruptly. "We had word today from the Angels. They have some way of monitoring the existence of the Link point in the Geyser Swirl. That Link wasn't there a year ago, and it wasn't there yesterday. But it was there two months ago, and now it's there again. It comes and goes in a totally unpredictable way."

Chan decided that it was nothing personal. Elke Siry wasn't angry with him, she was angry with a universe that didn't behave as it was supposed to.

He asked, "Is that what happened to the other expeditions? They tried to go to a Link network point that wasn't there?"

"No. If a Link exit point isn't available, the jump won't take place. The same will be true of us. If the Link isn't there, our ship won't be able to make the transition."

"Then what does it mean, so far as we are concerned?"

Again a rapid flush of color came to her cheeks. "I'm not sure. But I think we may pass through when the Link is open, and then find ourselves unable to get back. We could become stranded, somewhere in the Geyser Swirl. Maybe that's what happened to the other expeditions. One thing's very clear. This Link is nothing like the ones that we are used to. Whoever made it isn't a member of the Stellar Group."

"Which means what we'll be doing is even more dangerous than it sounds," Dag Korin said quietly. "All right, Elke. That gives me my cue. I had my own conversation today with a consortium of Stellar Group members. Seems they're still worried that when we're where they can't keep an eye on us, in spite of what they've told us we'll behave like naughty boys and girls. They gave me another severe warning: no matter what happens, we must not kill any beings who may be intelligent. When in doubt, we are to err on the side of nonviolence. I said, suppose that the aliens try to kill us? I was told, do whatever you can to save yourselves, but your actions may not include the use of lethal force. If this command is not obeyed, you, Dag Korin, will be held personally responsible."

Chan said, "In other words, if we're attacked we're supposed to lie down and die?"

"Exactly." The General winked, so quickly it might have been no more than an accidental blink of one blue eye. "Now I'm just going to talk a little at the pair of you. Dalton, you've probably been wondering why an old fogy like me, long past retirement, was put in charge of such an important expedition. Oh, don't bother to deny it, I've seen the look on your face. Ancient, asleep half the time, doesn't know what's going on. Isn't that about it? And maybe you're right, and I'm past it. But I do know one or two things.

"One of them I learned a long time ago, at Capella's Drift. It's as true now as it was then: a military genius who's a lightyear away from the action is likely to make worse mistakes than the average joe or jill on the spot. Just to make it quite clear what I'm getting at, *we're* going to be on the spot when we get to the Geyser Swirl. Not the Pipe-Rillas. Not the Tinkers. Not those damned brainy cabbages that people call the Angels. *Us*.

"But don't let me get carried away on the subject of aliens, because there's one other thing I have to say that's even more important to me than cussing out the members of the Stellar Group. It's this: I hate to lose people. If there's any way on earth or heaven that it can be avoided, the members of my crew aren't going to die, no matter what alien garbage has to get killed along the way to prevent it.

"No Stellar Group members are going to be in the Geyser Swirl to keep an eye on what we get up to there. If anything is ever discovered, by some method I can't imagine, I propose to assume full personal responsibility for violence. I don't give a damn what aliens—or humans—do to me. You know what they say about old soldiers. Well, if I have to I won't fade away. I'd rather go down in flames and in disgrace than see our people killed."

Korin stood up. "Right. I've said my bit, and I don't propose to repeat it. We're going, and we're coming back, as many as possible, and damn all aliens. Now let's get the show on the road and prepare this rustbucket for Link transit."

Elke stood up, but Chan did not move. The General glared at him. "Didn't you hear me?"

"Yes, sir, I did." Chan wondered about Korin's short-term memory. "I thought we were going to discuss my problem."

"Your problem?"

Hadn't the General understood anything of what Chan had said earlier? "Yes. You know. The problem with Deb Bisson."

"Didn't she tell you that she would arrive on board before the deadline?"

"Yes. She may be here already."

"Then you don't have a problem. You tell her the arrangement with the rest of your team members went just the way that you planned it. When we have left Earth orbit and are on our way to the Link entry point, you can tell her the truth. By then it will be too late for her to leave." Korin saw the look on Chan's face, and smiled. "Come on, man. I thought you said she hated your guts?"

"Not just my guts. All of me."

"So she finds out you didn't exactly tell her the truth." Korin ushered them toward the door. "So what? She's on the way to the Swirl. Do you think Deb Bisson can hate you any more than she already does?"

The door closed, leaving the general inside and Chan and Elke Siry once more in the corridor. She seemed in no hurry to leave. She lounged against the wall, in the same pose as when Chan and Dag Korin had arrived, and stared at him speculatively. She said, "Why does this woman, Deb Bisson, hate you?"

An odd question, from someone billed as the project scientist. But they were all going to be working together on a dangerous mission, and the more they understood each other, the better. Chan, for the second time in as many hours, summarized the deal that he had made with Deb when he was on Europa. If she would come along, he had guaranteed the whole rest of the team.

When he was finished Elke Siry leaned on the wall and stared at nothing, until Chan wondered if he had become inaudible and invisible.

At last she said, "Your explanation is nonsense. You are omitting essential data. Why does she *really* hate you?"

"I don't know."

"Then tell me of the previous times that the pair of you met, before your recent encounter on Europa."

She had no right in the world to ask for such information, and Chan had no reason to provide it to her. But he found the words spilling out, recalling things that had happened many years before. When he finished, Elke Siry nodded slowly.

"I have never met your friend Deb Bisson. I have hardly met you. However." Elke's red lips parted, to reveal sharp white incisors and slightly pronounced canines. "However, if you had done to me what you did to her, I would tear out your throat the next time that we met.

"Deb Bisson is a kind, forgiving woman, ever to speak to you again."

15

A Helping Hand for Tinkers and Pipe-Rillas

It was difficult to keep the *Mood Indigo* exactly balanced on its thrustors, and the ship was almost imperceptibly descending. It was also drifting slowly closer to the Pipe-Rilla vessel sitting on the seabed.

The crew of that other ship had been less lucky than Bony and his companions. Their vessel was longer than the *Mood Indigo*, and less of its mass was at the rear end. Instead of settling down stern-first and remaining upright, it had toppled onto its side. Any occupants now had to deal with a ship where floors and walls had switched roles.

There was no doubt in Bony's mind that this was a vessel built by Pipe-Rillas. They followed the "decorated" school of ship design, their thought processes apparently dominated by "Hey, look, here's another place on the hull where we can attach a gadget." Close up, the ship's exterior was bumped and lumped and pocked and knotted, draped with grapplers and thrustors and sensors.

And clearly there were beings inside. Bony was now close enough to see the tableau on the sea floor. The fourteen bubble-creatures had formed a semi-circle around one side of the Pipe-Rilla ship. Two suited human figures, who must be Liddy Morse and Friday Indigo, stood close to the center of the half-circle, right next to the ship. They were facing what was presumably a port, and one of them was gesturing toward the rounded upper part of the hull.

Without exchanging a word with anyone, Bony could guess at the problem. The Pipe-Rilla ship, like the *Mood Indigo*, possessed airlocks. But those locks were useless if their outer hatches opened at the top. In space it made no difference, but here under water you needed a hatch at the bottom, so that all the air in the lock did not escape when the hatch was opened. And again, Friday Indigo's ship had been lucky. Of the three airlocks, one of them had been situated with the outer hatch at the bottom. The Pipe-Rilla vessel had been less fortunate. Bony could see four airlocks, but not one of them had the right position for the outer hatch. The hatches sat at the top of the locks. A Pipe-Rilla who used the lock to leave the ship would have great trouble getting back in. It was a fair guess that the crew had been stranded on board ever since they arrived on Limbo.

Bony was willing to make another bet. Even with the *Mood Indigo* hovering less than fifty meters away from them, neither Friday Indigo nor Liddy would be able to think of any way to help the stranded Pipe-Rillas.

But Bony could.

First, though, he needed to talk to them. Normally that would be trivial for two ships so close together, but here in Limbo's ocean the surrounding water damped electromagnetic signals. It had to be a direct cable connect, or something much more old-fashioned: talking in person.

Bony's arrival had not gone unnoticed. One of the suited human figures was waving, but whether in greeting or irritation Bony could not tell. The bubble people, showing more sense than the humans, had retreated to the other side of the Pipe-Rilla ship and were peeping cautiously around the hull. They had the right idea. Even with low thrust, the auxiliary drives would be dangerous if you got too close to the exhausts.

With that in mind, Bony took the *Mood Indigo* sideways, away from the other ship, until there was a clear two hundred meters between them. Then he killed all horizontal thrust and gradually decreased the vertical drive. The *Mood Indigo* made a smooth and sedate landing on the flat seabed. When Bony was sure that it stood in a stable position he cut all thrust.

He had not removed his suit since first lifting the ship away from the seabed. All he needed to do was snap the helmet into position and move to the airlock. The usual nervousness as he waited for the lock to cycle and lowered himself into the water was replaced by impatience.

The sea bottom was quite different here. The sharp but fragile spears that had surrounded the *Mood Indigo* at its original location were replaced by fleshy pink fingers that reached to waist height and beyond. Bony assumed at first that they were plants—except that as he moved they had the disconcerting habit of reaching toward him, touching his suit, then flinching away. He picked his way carefully through them, across a narrow level plain and then up and down a sudden and unexpected incline. The fingers touched him delicately, in unexpected places, but always quickly backed off.

Friday Indigo and Liddy Morse had turned away from the Pipe-Rilla ship and were waiting for him as he approached. Direct speech would serve when they were within a few feet of each other, and Indigo didn't waste time in getting down to business.

He bellowed, "I thought I told you to stay with the ship."

"I *did* stay with the ship. It's right there."

"But I meant—oh, what the hell. We couldn't get sense from the bubble-brains, but they led us to this." Indigo reached out to touch the hull of the Pipe-Rilla ship. At the same time, Liddy grabbed Bony's arm and gave it a welcoming squeeze.

"Are they alive?" Bony asked. He had taken a quick look through the port of the ship, and seen only an inexplicable whirlwind of movement within.

"Oh, they're alive all right." Indigo sounded more irritated than pleased. Bony could see why. Living Pipe-Rillas meant that the *Mood Indigo* was not the first Stellar Group to contact the Limbics. Therefore, Friday Indigo would have no unique position in the history books.

"How many are on board?"

"How many?" Indigo's face was hard to see through the suit visor, but his voice was puzzled. "How the hell should I know? I don't see how you could count them even if you wanted to. Thousands, I guess."

Bony, after his own moment of bewilderment, understood Indigo's answer. It was not just Pipe-Rillas. There must also be a Tinker Composite on board. Bony had never actually seen one, but he definitely wanted to because he had read about them for over thirty years.

More than ever, he was curious to see the inside of the Pipe-Rilla ship. But his bright idea for getting the aliens in and out needed review. Just how did a Tinker deal with an airlock? It had to be in terms of the whole Composite because individual components were not intelligent until they clustered. What sort of suit was right for a being with no stable shape?

He didn't have to be able to answer that question himself. All he had to do was arrange things so he could enter the ship. After that, the Tinkers themselves would tell him how they managed exit and entry.

He turned again to Friday Indigo. "I assume they can't get out."

"Of course they can't. Look at the position of their airlocks. Open the outer hatch, the air in it will go right up to the surface and the lock will fill with water."

"I can solve that problem."

"I know, I know. The Pipe-Rilla and the Tinker Composite must have already thought of it, and so did I. Roll the ship using lateral thrustors, until the outer hatches are on the bottom of the locks. Only I dare not try it. The hull of their ship probably isn't as strong as the *Mood Indigo*, and I don't think it could take a roll."

"That's all right. We don't need to move the ship. All we have to do is add an L-section beyond their outer hatch, a wide tube that makes an airtight seal with the hatch and then turns *downward* for a few meters. That way, air can't escape when they open the hatch, and the level in the vertical section of the tube will just fall or rise to equalize pressures."

"If that would work, wouldn't they have thought of it themselves?"

"Maybe they did. But there's no way they could do it from inside. And there's no way we could do it, either, without the machine shop and materials on board the *Mood Indigo*."

"You're just trying to justify disobeying orders and flying my ship over here."

"I thought it was the best thing to do. Anyway, should I try what I said and modify the lock on the alien ship?"

"Oh, go ahead." Friday Indigo waved a hand in dismissal. "Do what you like. I'm not interested in engineering details. I'm going back to my ship. I have other ideas that I need to explore."

"I'll let you know when I'm done, sir, and you can operate their airlock."

"Don't bother. When I told you I was going first, I meant to meet *new* aliens, not the pain-in-the-ass Pipe-Rillas and Tinkers sitting inside that garbage can."

Indigo plowed away across the seabed, stomping pink fingers underfoot and raising clouds of silt with every step.

Liddy stood close to Bony, waiting. When Indigo was safely out of range she said, "I'm really glad you came when you did. You should have heard him after the bubble people brought us here, and he realized that we weren't the first. He was so pissed he was like a crazy man. I was afraid he'd try something terrible."

"What could he do?"

"I don't know. But if there were a way to kill everyone in the Pipe-Rilla ship, I suspect he would have done it."

"Oh, I don't believe that."

"I'm sure you don't. You're too nice, Bony. But in my line of work I've tended to see men at their worst.

Let me offer you a warning. Don't ever get into a situation where being rid of you might be to Friday Indigo's advantage."

While they spoke, something had been happening at the port of the alien ship. Bony moved closer, and realized that he could no longer see the interior at all. The port was shrouded by a purple-black sheet. He pressed his face to the window and saw that the shroud was composed of a mosaic of wings, each about as long as his finger. It was components of the Tinker Composite, clustering.

Why would they do that?

To learn the answer, Bony would first have to find a way into the ship.

"He didn't give you any orders, Liddy. Would you help me?"

"Of course. But don't expect me to build anything."

"I don't. Just give me a hand bringing the L-section of tube over to this ship when it's finished, and help me put it into position."

"I can manage that. I'm stronger than I look. You should try me some time."

She grinned at Bony through her visor and flexed her arm muscles. Even within the bulky suit, she seemed slim and graceful. Bony turned away so that he wouldn't look like he was staring. Not sure what to say, he started back toward the *Mood Indigo*. Liddy came close behind, followed by the bubble people.

"Why are they following us?" she said. "And what made them lead us over to that ship? We still don't know."

"Because we can't talk to them. Maybe you could have another try with the translator, while I'm building the airlock adapter."

"I'm certainly willing. But the first try was a total failure."

"That was Indigo's fault. He was too impatient. The translator has a big learning component. When the languages are far apart, you need long samples of both before it can make sense of them."

They had reached the *Mood Indigo*. Liddy unhooked the translator from its temporary storage on the side of the ship, strapped it at her side, and turned to face the advancing bubble people. Bony, worried about her being outside alone, waited until the advancing group had peacefully settled down a few meters from Liddy. Then it was back into the lock for him—he felt he had been away weeks—and down to the lower level where spare materials were stored. Indigo was noticeably absent, hiding away in his upper-level private quarters. A definite blessing. Bony dragged what he needed through to the cargo hold. It wasn't the most convenient place to do the work, but what he had to build was so big that there was no other option. It would be a classic blunder, make something and then find you couldn't get it out of the ship.

The job itself was straightforward; almost too straightforward. At first Bony found it hard to keep his mind on it, and after a few minutes he went up a level so he could stare out of a port and make sure that Liddy was all right. She was talking, then listening intently to the output of the translator. The bubble-creatures had not moved, except that their spokesman had floated forward and now hovered near Liddy half a meter off the sea floor. The gill slits pumped and pulsed. Reassured, Bony went back to work.

His task took time and patience. What he had when he was finished formed a great curved tube of transparent plastic, an inverted L-shape over two meters across and seven meters long. The upper end was designed to fit around the outer hatch of the

Pipe-Rilla ship and seal to its hull—or to anything else in the known universe. For the moment, Bony was not going to worry about getting it off again. The adhesive, ironically, had been produced using a chemical process given to humans by the Pipe-Rillas. Maybe they also knew a solvent.

Bony lifted the tube. In the low gravity of Limbo it was not heavy, but it was so big and awkward that it was close to unmanageable. Getting it out of the cargo hold would be tricky. He dragged the L-tube to the edge of the cargo bay, sweating and swearing. When he was almost there, Friday Indigo appeared at the upper level and stared down at the struggling Bony. He did not offer to help, but asked, "Where's Liddy?"

For the past half hour Bony had not been thinking about Liddy at all. He felt a bit guilty as he said, "Outside. Trying to talk to the bubble people."

"Huh. Fat chance. She doesn't know a thing about translation units."

"I suppose not. Do you need her back in here?"

"No. I don't need either of you. As soon as you get that piece of junk out of the way I'm going to take the *Mood Indigo* up to the surface for a look round. I expect I'll be gone for a few hours, so try not to do anything too stupid."

"Are you interested in the thing that we thought might be a Link entry point?"

"Could be." That was apparently as much as Indigo intended to say about his exploration plans. He turned away and added, "Get that lump of garbage outside. I want to start the thrustors as soon as you're clear."

Bony thought of half a dozen rude answers, said nothing, and set to work to flood the cargo bay. Let Indigo worry about getting the water out again. He pushed the awkwardly shaped tube over the lip and allowed it to tumble to the sea floor. Peering after it, he saw Liddy still squatting calmly on the seabed surrounded by an attentive ring of bubble folk.

He went out after the tube, suddenly aware of his own fatigue. He wanted to take a brief rest, but Indigo's voice at once came crackling in his ear. "All right, Rombelle. Stop loafing. You have three minutes before I lift the ship."

Bony nodded wearily—Indigo was clearly watching him on an internal display—and stumbled across to Liddy. "We have to get out of the way. Bubble people, too."

Liddy was bending low, peering anxiously at him across the gulf of their two visors. "Is everything all right?"

Bony swore a royal internal oath. If they survived—if he could free her from servitude to Friday Indigo—if she *wanted* to go—he would take Liddy on a year-long holiday, just the two of them, to the ends of the solar system and beyond. Three "ifs" in one sentence. "Everything is fine, but Indigo is proposing to raise the ship. We have to be well clear when he does."

"Are *you* all right?"

"I'm fine. I'm awake. I'm ready to go." Three lies in three sentences. He was improving. "Just let's get everybody clear."

She didn't argue, but grabbed one end of the L-tube and helped him to carry it across to the seated group of bubble people. With gestures from her, the whole party moved off to a safe distance from the *Mood Indigo*, and watched as the ship lifted away from the surface with a great stirring of sediments.

Liddy was staring at him again. "You look really tired. Is it all right if we talk for a moment?"

"With Friday Indigo gone I feel better already. I'm awake. Talk away."

"Well, I know I'm not very bright; but you see, when I was outside by myself I had an idea. We don't really know anything about the bubble people, what sort of information they absorb, or how much, or how fast. So as well as talking to them myself, I set up a vocal data feed from the *Mood Indigo*'s general data base. People a whole lot smarter than me, talking about humans and human activities."

"Liddy, that was a great idea."

"I'm not so sure. You remember the sort of gibberish we got when Indigo tried, that 'Is it Monday for the flower' sort of thing?"

"Of course."

"Well, for the past few minutes I haven't been getting exactly that. I'm not sure it's much better than Indigo's try, but it is different. I recorded everything of course, but I've edited what you'll hear. Listen to this bit."

Bony heard a sequence of squeaks, as though a colony of mice had invaded his suit's headset; and then, quite clearly, a synthesized voice: " . . . *we go to the other ship before we go to the other ship. The other other ship sent us to the other ship, and then sent us to this in the wood of sharp.*"

Bony wondered if that was supposed to make sense. Maybe he was more tired than he realized. "Play it again."

"All right. But there's another piece I want you to hear."

The recorded translation was repeated, then went on: "*The one ship is not the other ship or the other other ship. The one ship is the ship of the angels. The angels of the one ship send us to the other ship and the other other ship.*"

Bony yawned. He had never expected to find the seabed of an alien planet relaxing, but here he was half ready to fall asleep. "It doesn't make any more sense than what was said to Friday Indigo."

"Oh."

"I'm not criticizing you, Liddy. You tried. What did you think it meant?"

"Well, I know I'm not good at thinking. I wasn't trained to use my mind. From the time I was ten years old I was trained to use my body. But I thought—I guess it doesn't matter what I thought."

"It does." God, was he humoring her? That would be as bad as Friday Indigo. "Liddy, what's your idea?"

"Well . . . I wondered at that word, *angel*. Of all the words the translator might pick, why that one? I suppose it could be random. But maybe the Limbic really *meant* Angel, like one of the aliens we call an Angel. I know, there isn't an Angel on board the ship that we were taken to. But if the *Mood Indigo* is *this* ship, and the Pipe-Rilla vessel is the *other* ship, then what's the *other* other ship?"

"There were supposedly two alien ships that came to the Geyser Swirl before we did. You think—"

"Isn't it possible? That one of them, the ship Indigo and I were taken to, has a crew of Pipe-Rillas and Tinkers. But the *other* ship, what the Limbics call the other other ship—"

"Has a crew of Angels. I hear you. Play it one more time."

Bony listened hard, concentrating to the limits of his tired brain. At the end he shook his head. "I can't tell. I see what you're getting at, that there's another ship here and it directed the Limbics to us and to the Pipe-Rilla vessel. But this is all guesswork. Even if you're right, what we have to do next is clear enough. Come on. Grab the tube again, and let's go."

The walk across the ocean floor was only a few hundred meters. Say that fast and it sounded easy, but Bony soon learned that forward progress was difficult verging on impossible. The L-shaped section of tube seemed to have a mind of its own, tilting and twisting in unexpected directions. The seafloor pink fingers insisted on inspecting the pipe and were sometimes reluctant to let go, providing extra resistance to movement. The mid-sea rise, hardly noticeable when you crossed it unencumbered, seemed to have become much steeper. Bony's face-plate began to steam up, reminding him that the suit was designed for space and not for work under the sea. He looked for Liddy, holding the other end of the tube, and saw only a foggy blur. Everything must be just as difficult for Liddy, but she was struggling on without complaint. If she could do it, he could. He trudged on, head down, exhausted and unable to see where he was going.

He was at the end of his tether and ready to call for a break when suddenly everything became easier. The tube seemed to weigh nothing and glided forward of its own volition. Startled, Bony released his hold and looked around him. Four of the bubble people had taken the sides of the tube and were carrying it easily through the water. Their strength was impressive. Just as well that they seemed a peaceful lot.

Did they have any idea where he and Liddy were going? Apparently so. The Pipe-Rilla ship lay straight ahead, encouragingly close. During the final hundred meters, his suit visor lost its fog and his fatigue lessened.

Ten meters from the sunken ship, Bony released his hold on the pipe section and gestured to the bubble folk to do the same. They ignored him. He went across to them and turned the thrustors of his suit on at a low level. He pointed to the exhaust and said, "Dangerous. Don't stay too close." They didn't seem to understand; they didn't move.

Liddy came across to stand next to him. She repeated, "Dangerous. Drop the tube. Don't stay too close. Move away."

After an odd gobbling sound, Bony heard the distorted words, "Not too close. Move away."

They came from the translator, which he now realized was strapped at Liddy's side. She had carried it all the way from the *Mood Indigo*, while still holding up her end of the tube. She had not lied—she *was* much stronger than she looked. And now the bubble men were drifting away, moving off to a safe distance.

He turned to Liddy, who said softly, "The translator has heard a lot more of me than it has of you. At the moment it's better at my voice than yours. That's all."

"But you thought to bring it with you—I didn't. I don't ever want to hear you say again that you're not smart. Don't tell that to me, and don't listen to Indigo when he says it. Because it's not true. You're not just beautiful, you're also intelligent and resourceful."

"I'll do what you ask under one condition. Don't *you* ever tell me again that you are fat and clumsy. Because that's not true. You're well-proportioned and attractive."

There could hardly be a worse place and time. Liddy had moved very close, but they were separated by the infinite distance of two space-suits. Anything that Bony might have done—if he had dared—would have to wait. He stepped away from Liddy and said, "We're not finished yet, and the tricky bit is still to come. We have to get this tube up there and sealed to the hull, and it will be just the two of us because I'm afraid our suit exhausts might damage the bubble people. Are you up for it?"

"I'll manage."

"Wait until I lift the other end."

Maybe it was easier to turn the tube than to carry it across the uneven seabed, or maybe experience made the difference. Whatever the reason, they maneuvered the tube without problems up the side of the Pipe-Rilla ship, using their suit jets to lift themselves and direct the L-section into position. The seal was still tricky work and Bony wished—for maybe half a second—that Friday Indigo was there to help. It was a long, tedious, three-quarters of an hour until the horizontal part of the L-section was snugly mated to the hull of the ship. The vertical portion curved down toward the seabed. Now there was one remaining problem. The aliens inside needed to operate the lock. Bony could see no way of doing it from the outside.

"Stay here." He left Liddy inside the vertical section of tube and descended once more to the seabed. He advanced to the ship's port, but as before the view within was hidden by the cloak of purple Tinker wings. He swore, raised the gauntlet of his suit, and hammered as hard as he dared on the port.

Nothing. But with a second series of bangs, the cluster of Tinker wings shivered, fluttered, and was suddenly gone. In their place, staring at Bony with big-eyed concentration, was a Pipe-Rilla, lowering her fourteen-foot body with a cantilevering of long, multijointed limbs until she was face-to-face with him at the port.

He gestured and shouted, hoping she could see his expressions inside his suit or hear his voice through the hull. "Up there. At the airlock." A frantic turning of his hands, as though working a screw. "It's safe to use, you can operate it. I"—finger pointing at himself—"will go up there"— pointing up again—"and enter as soon as it's open."

Did she have any idea what he was getting at? He had no experience with the aliens, no way of knowing how to read their body language. As for facial expressions, you could forget them. The Pipe-Rillas had rigid exoskeletons.

He pointed upward again. "I'm going there now. You operate the airlock." More turning of his hands. "And I will come in."

Had there been a movement of the narrow head, a tremble of understanding? Bony watched. At last, when the imagined movement was not repeated, he left the port and rejoined Liddy. She was still waiting by the airlock.

"Did they understand?"

He shook his head. "I don't know. We'll have to wait and see."

He probably sounded as discouraged as he felt. His talent, if he had any, was for improvising. A more logical man would have prepared the ground thoroughly in advance, making sure through written signals that the Pipe-Rilla inside knew what he had been doing. As it was, he and Liddy might be forced to wait here until their air was running out, then return to the safety of the *Mood Indigo* with nothing to show but failure.

From somewhere, near or far, came a strange, creaking rumble. Liddy grabbed his arm. "Bony."

"I don't know what it was. Wait a few seconds."

It took considerably more than that. Maybe two whole minutes passed before the grinding rumble came again. But this time Bony recognized it for what it was: A motor at work, irising open a sealed hatch. It was another few seconds before the gap was visible, but now the wait did not seem long. Soon they heard a hiss of air.

Half a minute more, and the hatch was fully open. The water level in the vertical part of the L-section dropped a meter, then steadied. Bony and Liddy stepped through the hatch, and waited until it closed.

Liddy reached out and gave Bony a nervous hug. The inner hatch still had to go through its cycle, but the hard work was over. They were, at last, about to enter a Pipe-Rilla vessel.

They were going to meet Stellar Group aliens.

16

Linking to the Geyser Swirl

The *Hero's Return* was no longer a military ship, yet Chan Dalton assumed its affairs would run with at least a semblance of military precision.

He had been watching the clock. The time for leaving Ceres orbit was set for midnight. As soon as that departure took place, Deb Bisson would be unable to leave the ship. She would be forced to travel to the Link entry point, and from there to the Geyser Swirl.

He had checked that Deb was aboard and in prime living quarters, but to avoid meeting her he had moved hundreds of meters away, hiding far forward in an empty region once occupied by a major weapons system. As soon as the ship was heading out he planned to go aft and find her.

But midnight had come and gone, and the *Hero's Return* floated in space as silent as a ghost ship. After ten frustrating minutes Chan started aft. Something had gone wrong, and he needed to find out what.

The first person he met was Elke Siry. She was heading forward, though he knew of nothing that lay in that direction. She would have moved past him had he not stood in her way.

He spread his arms wide to block the narrow passageway. "Do you know why departure has been delayed?"

She frowned at him, pale brows shadowing her icy blue eyes. "What are you talking about?"

"We were supposed to leave at midnight. It's almost twelve-fifteen, and we haven't moved. Why?"

Instead of answering his question, she ducked under his arm and eased past him in the corridor. "Come with me."

Chan, baffled, followed. In seventy meters they were at the extreme forward end of the ship. Elke led him on, through a narrow round hatch into a bubble of transparent plastic.

"This is where I was going anyway," she said. "It's the bow observation port. There's no better place to look at the stars, and see what's ahead of the ship."

She spoke as though her words provided some kind of explanation. Chan was about to voice his frustration when he followed her pointing finger.

"Ceres," she said. The biggest of all the asteroids loomed large to the right of the *Hero's Return*. It was sliding rapidly backward, as though its orbital motion took it in that direction. But its sunlit hemisphere was also to the rear. That implied Ceres was dropping directly toward the Sun.

Chan turned to Elke, and found her watching him with a superior expression. "No, Ceres isn't moving sunward," she said. "We're moving *away* from the Sun. We're heading for the Asteroid Belt's closest Link entry point, three and a half million kilometers farther out. The drive was turned on precisely at midnight."

"But I didn't feel a thing."

"Because the *Hero's Return* was designed as a military ship. The engines can produce acceleration bursts of up to twenty-five gees. That would kill the crew if you didn't do anything about it, so anywhere that the crew might be was equipped with inertia shedders. We'll never reach those levels of acceleration, of course, but even two gees would be uncomfortable. General Korin thought we might as well get the benefit of the shedders."

"I can't hear the drive. Surely we ought to, even this far forward."

"Do you know what engine noise signifies?" When Chan merely shrugged, she went on. "Engine noise—noise of any kind—is a warning flag for *inefficiency*. Noise doesn't help the drive to work. It doesn't provide useful information on engine status. It's not something a designer *aims* to produce. Quite the opposite. In a mechanical system, noise and excess heat tell you that you are wasting energy. In a military ship it is worse than that. Noise and heat can also announce the ship's presence to an enemy. Hence, the engines of this ship were made as efficient—and noise-free—as possible. If you do hear anything, it's a sure sign that something is going wrong."

Her manner was so loaded with condescension and cool contempt that the temptation to argue was almost irresistible. Was she *looking* for a fight? Or was this her normal way of dealing with mere mortals?

Just now, Chan did not have the time to find out. He had asked Danny Casement to say nothing until he, Chan, had the chance to talk to Deb Bisson. But silence became harder for Danny as time went on and other team members wondered why they had not yet seen the Bun on board.

"Thank you, Dr. Siry. I promise I'll come back later and take a better look." Chan managed a smile and hurried out of the observation chamber. At the hatch he turned to ask, "Do you know when we are scheduled for transition?"

"Of course." Raised eyebrows, at so elementary a question. "Link entry will take place seven and a half hours from now."

"Thank you." After the first show of gratitude, the next one came easier. Chan resisted the urge to say more and began the long trip aft. The trouble with Elke Siry's superiority complex was that it appeared to be justified. Chan had wondered after their last meeting if she might be some sort of ringer, planted on the team as a supposed scientist because of her relationship to General Korin. He had done a data download, and decided that if Elke were a plant the job had been done thoroughly. The records showed a full life story, from child prodigy in mathematics and music, to original discoveries in theoretical physics by the time she was seventeen. Now, at twenty-five, her list of important contributions spilled over into three digits.

What was so valuable a scientist doing on this high-risk expedition? Maybe Korin had talked her into it, but Chan doubted that. There were hints in the record not only of a formidable brain, but just as formidable a will. What Elke wanted, Elke got. She was here because she was interested in the Geyser Swirl, and the mystery of the new Link entry point.

Chan was coasting along the corridor that ran as a central axis for the full length of the *Hero's Return*. It was the main artery for personnel movement back and forth along the ship, and in the vessel's military past there must have been people bustling through the thoroughfare all the time. Today he heard nothing and saw no one. About the halfway point he came to the old fire control room that sat at the protected heart of the ship. It too was empty, and he passed it by. This was where the ship's navigation system would take care of all actions on the way to Link entry, swapping flight data with stations on Ceres and the Jovian moons; only the final choice would require a human decision: enter the Link, or decline to do so? It occurred to Chan that perhaps this was the choice that humans were least qualified to make. He recognized in himself the tendency to say, we've come so far, we can't possibly change our minds now. People following that philosophy died climbing mountains, they signed disastrous contracts, they flew into hurricanes, and they embarked on lifelong commitments to the wrong mates. Perhaps they headed to the stars for the same reason.

The width of the ship narrowed as he moved aft. It was down from a maximum of seventy meters in its central part to maybe forty. He was beyond the old captain's quarters, beyond Dag Korin's chosen suite, into the region which had in the old days been reserved for visiting VIPs. Korin himself had placed Chrissie Winger and Tarbush in suites there, and the other team members had asked to be close by. Team members. Let's hope you could still call them that after his meeting with Deb Bisson.

He slowed down and examined the glowing numbers that identified each corridor. It was well past midnight, and unless Tully O'Toole was suffering bad withdrawal symptoms Deb should be alone. She would probably be asleep, and if he had to he would wake her. He had to get this over with as soon as possible, or he himself would never sleep.

This side branch. This door. Not locked—it was even slightly open.

He hesitated. On Europa he had entered Deb's apartment without permission and she had almost broken his neck. If she had known who he was, she probably would have.

He was encouraged by a flicker of light from within. She was awake, and she was watching some sort of display. He gave a token knock, slid the door wide, and entered.

Deb was awake all right, dressed in a black skin-tight suit and black slippers and sitting quietly on her bed. Unfortunately she was not alone. It was not just Tully, suffering from night shivers. Chan did a quick head count. Danny—Tully—the Tarbush—and, on the other side of the bed, Chrissie. They were all absorbed in a display on the far wall, and no one had seen him enter. Chan glanced at the imaging volume, and stood staring.

It was the Geyser Swirl, in three dimensions and in more detail than he had ever seen it. Gas clouds, twisting like a rosy triple braid inside and outside a necklace of stars, orange and green and blue, showed how the Swirl had gotten its name. The image was striking enough, but it was the prerecorded voice accompanying the picture that really grabbed the attention.

"In the words of one of humankind, the Geyser Swirl is *a riddle wrapped in a mystery inside an enigma.*" It was the flat, computer-generated tones of an Angel. "We are certain, beyond doubt, that a Link network point exists within the Geyser Swirl. We are equally confident that no member of the Stellar Group placed it there. At that point, knowledge becomes speculation. A test probe reported that it was entering the Link, but there was no standard return signal to report a successful transit, nor did the probe itself return.

"Meanwhile, contrary to the evidence of the probe, a recent remote survey indicates no evidence of a Link point's existence within the Swirl. The survey did define the stellar types present in the Swirl, as follows: F-type stars predominate, and there are seven of them. There is one blue giant star, one A-type, one K-type cool giant, and one G-type dwarf of mass similar to Sol. Detailed spectra are available. Five of the stellar systems possess planetary retinues. However, of the twenty-three planets in these systems, none is able to support life of any form resembling a member of the Stellar Group. Nine are massive gas giants, five possess hydrogenous or methane atmospheres, while the remaining five lack volatiles and an atmosphere of any kind. Note that this distribution violates the widely accepted principle of homeostatic convergence, whereby worlds able to support life tend to a common limit of atmospheric pressure and composition, temperature, and humidity. In the Geyser Swirl, all surface temperatures lie in the lethal range. . . ."

Since entering, Chan had not moved or made a sound; but Deb Bisson possessed the heightened senses of a weapons master. Without warning she rolled off the bed and came to her feet poised ready to spring. Chan held his hands wide, to show that he was unarmed.

"Only me. I didn't say anything, because you were all watching." He nodded at the display. "Doesn't look good for the teams that went there already, does it? No habitable planets. At least we're forewarned."

He tried to sound relaxed and casual. It didn't work. The others glanced at him, then at once turned their eyes to the woman standing by the bed. Chrissie held out a restraining hand. Danny Casement said,

"Easy, Deb, easy." And then to Chan, "I'm sorry, but I told her. A few minutes ago. I had to, because we were on the way."

Chan nodded, but he did not take his eyes away from Deb. "I understand. Don't blame Danny for this, Deb. I asked him not to say anything until we left parking orbit."

"I don't blame Danny for anything." She was still in the fighting posture that made the hair stand up on the back of Chan's neck. "You think you're smart, Chan Dalton, tricking me into being part of the team. But you don't know a thing. I was going anyway, with or without the other team members."

"I'm glad. This team wouldn't be the same without you. And I'm very glad that when I came in you weren't carrying weapons."

"Oh, cut the crap. You just want to use me, the way you used me before. The way you use everybody. As for having no weapons, try this."

She hardly moved, just the flick of her left index finger. Chan saw nothing, and for about five seconds he felt nothing. Then there was a curious sensation of something crawling up his chest.

He looked down and saw that a round white patch about five centimeters across had appeared in the middle of his long-sleeved shirt. While he watched, it spread rapidly. He realized that the white patch was part of his undershirt, and the outer garment was simply vanishing. The torso went, then the neck and finally the sleeves, creeping down his arms to his wrists until he was standing in a sleeveless white top. An odd smell of acetone filled his nostrils.

"I used a fabric version." Deb's face was stony. "I'll give you thirty seconds to get out of my room. If you're not gone by then, we'll see how the skin version works."

"Deb." But he saw her eyes. "All right, I'm on my way. I'll say it again, I'm glad you're with us."

He left, carefully closing the door after him. There was a long silence, broken surprisingly by Tully O'Toole. He had been staring, mouth open, first at Deb and then at Chan.

"Well, there's a surprise." He rubbed at his arm, with its line of purple dots. "Now we know why he always wore long sleeves. And where he got the words for me. He *knows* it can be done, you see."

Deb glared at him. "What are you talking about?"

"Chan told me that you can break the Paradox habit. He knew, because he did it. Didn't you see his bare arms when your potion dissolved his shirt away?"

"Of course I did. We all did."

"But I was nearer than you. I saw the marks. He's a Paradox addict himself—or I should say, he used to be. The stigmata have faded to little white dots; but still they show, from long ago."

"Long ago," Danny Casement added. "Tully has it right. Not any more, though. Not for a long time. Chan's over it."

"*When?*" Deb's voice would cut glass.

"You mean, when was he on it? Oh, I'm not sure."

"I know." Tarboosh Hanson stirred from his cross-legged position on the floor. The head of Scruffy the ferret peered out from a gap between the fastenings of his shirt. "I was there when it happened. It was right after the beginning of the quarantine when Chan came by Lunar Farside. He had found out that we wouldn't be allowed to go to the stars and he was in despair. He said he had let everybody down, and he couldn't stand that. He swore he was going to do something about it. You must know all this, Deb. He was with you on Vesta right before he came to Lunar Farside."

"He was. But the two of us had just had a big fight. He never said anything like that to me when he left."

"The Tarbush is right, though." Danny Casement stood up. "Chan was feeling so low—I didn't know about your argument, so I assumed it was about the quarantine—that I wondered if he'd ever come back to normal. And I know what happened next, though I didn't hear it until a long time afterwards. Chan left Lunar Farside and went down to Earth. He was in contact with people there who said they had worked with aliens, and he thought he might be able to make a special deal. Isn't that right, Tarb?"

"It is. He had some tricky plan worked out, something involving Pipe-Rillas operating in the basement warrens that could made an end run around the quarantine. But somebody was trickier than he was. A pusher slipped him a dose of Paradox during dinner, and that was it. You know what they say, one shot and you're gone."

Deb Bisson sat down suddenly on the bed. "I thought it had to be injected."

"For maximum effect, it does. Regulars always take it that way. But most people get hooked orally, the way Chan did."

"The way I did," said Tully. He had closed his eyes. "Oh, yes. That's the way it's done. One shot in your cup, and you never come up. That would still be true for me if you and Chan hadn't taken me from Europa."

"What happened after that?"

At Deb's question the others looked at each other.

"To Chan?" Danny Casement said at last. "He never came back. You can buy Paradox most places now, but right after the quarantine all the suppliers were down on Earth. So he didn't leave."

"He *couldn't* leave." Tully sat rocking to and fro,

his eyes still closed and his arms folded across his chest. "You have no idea how good you feel when it hits, or how frightened you get when you don't know where the next shot is coming from. You want to follow your supplier twenty-four hours a day, just to make sure. Get a shot, you're red hot; miss a hit, you're in the pit."

"Stay here as long as you like and help yourselves to anything you want." Deb was suddenly on her feet again. "I'm leaving."

"Where are you going?" Chrissie took her by the arm.

"To talk to Chan."

"Where is he?"

"I don't know."

"Should I come with you?"

"*No!*" Deb shook herself free and was out of the door before anyone could move.

"Better go after her," Danny said. "When she finds him she'll kill him."

"No." Chrissie spoke firmly. "You stay here. Don't you people understand *anything*? If she does kill him, it'll only be because he deserves it."

She settled back down on the bed and stared at the display. The Geyser Swirl was still pictured, and the voice of the Angel droned on: "Mean estimated survival time for a suited individual on the surface of the planet Swirl Kappa Three, sixteen minutes. On Swirl Kappa Four, four minutes. On Swirl Kappa Five, nineteen minutes . . ."

"Oh, shut up," Danny said. "Tarb? Tully? Should we follow Deb?"

"I'll go with Chrissie's judgment. We'll be at the Link in a few more hours. And then, if it works, we'll be *there*." Tarbush Hanson nodded gloomily at the display of the Swirl. "Relax, Danny, and have a drink.

Get me one, too, while you're at it. It may be our last ever."

Deb had not been totally honest. She did know where Chan was—or at least, she knew where his rooms were, thirty meters along the corridor from hers.

Only he was not there. Glancing around—if he could enter private rooms without knocking, so could she—Deb found no sign that he had ever been inside. The bed had not been touched and a travel case sat unopened in the middle of the floor.

Where was he? The only thing she knew for certain was that he must be somewhere on board. She stood still long enough to slow her pulse to an even fifty beats a minute, then set out on a careful and deliberate search.

After half an hour she had found no trace of Chan, but she had gained an idea of just how much space there was inside an eighty-thousand-ton warship. The interior volume was close to a million cubic meters, divided into thousands of rooms and chambers interconnected through a maze of tunnels and corridors. At the rate she was going, long before she located Chan the *Hero's Return* would have reached the Link entry point and made its transition.

She needed help. That was not going to be easy to find, in a ship where the service robots were too dumb to answer even the simplest question.

Deb headed for the main control room. Surely there, if anywhere, she would find other people.

Make that *person* rather than *people*, and she would be right. The control room of the *Hero's Return* had originally also been the fire control zone. Row after row of weapons terminals, all unoccupied, formed a three-dimensional matrix. At the far end of the great cylindrical chamber, lolling at ease on a couch, Deb saw a solitary blonde.

The woman, lanky and starvation-thin, turned at Deb's approach and said, "If you're looking for Dag Korin, he's taking a nap. He said he'd be here when the time came to make the Link transition." She glanced at one of the displays. "That's less than five hours from now. I hope he wakes up in time."

"I don't want General Korin. I'm seeking Chan Dalton."

Deb expected a casual "sorry" or "never heard of him." But the woman nodded.

"I don't know where Dalton is now. But I know where he *was*, half an hour ago."

"Where?"

"Forward. I told him, the best place to see what's ahead of the ship is the bow observation port. When he left there he said he'd be back later."

"Thank you." Deb was already on the way.

"All the way forward," the skinny woman called after her. "Follow the central corridor as far as you can go."

Which, as Deb soon found, was very far indeed. She seemed to race for miles before the corridor ahead ended in a small ring hatch. It was open, and she dived through headfirst and emerged into a bubble-like observation chamber.

Chan was there, sitting in a swivel seat and staring out at the stars. She had made no plans as to what to do when she found him. She grabbed the back of his chair to slow herself and blurted, "You were a Paradox addict."

He turned slowly and said in a sleepwalker's voice, "Yes. I was a Paradox addict."

"Down on Earth."

"Yes."

"For how long?"

"Forever." He roused himself. "No, I guess that won't do as an answer. From my first hit to my last, it was three years, five months and fourteen days. I didn't know any of that at the time, of course. All the days blended into one."

"How were you able to stop?"

"The hardest way. I needed money. An addict will do anything to pay for the next shot. One day I robbed the wrong person. He was chief enforcer for the Duke of Bosny. Next thing I knew I was in a labor camp in the Gallimaufries where the drug of preference was Velocil. The guards ran the trade in it, but Paradox and Velocil clash. Take both and you die."

"What did you do?"

"I died. Or felt like I did. The guards knew I was hooked on Paradox, so they wouldn't give me Velocil. I guess I ought to have been grateful to them, but I wasn't. I screamed and howled and begged and prayed. No good. Four years later I was alive, out of the camp, and free of the habit. But you know what? In my dreams, I'm a Paradox addict still."

It wasn't the passion in his voice that made Deb shiver. It was the total lack of it.

"Out of the labor camp," he went on, "and out of a job, too. Who would want anything to do with a man with a Paradox record?"

"Why didn't you come to—" She checked herself. "What did you do?"

"I went to the man who caught me and put me in the camp. I told him, look, if it wasn't for you I'd be dead now. It's your fault that I'm alive, so you owe me a job. He said I had a hell of a nerve. But he seemed amused. He put me on his own staff and I became an enforcer for the Duke of Bosny. I was a good one, too. I knew every trick in the book, and a lot that weren't there. I'd used them all to support my own habit."

Deb had sunk to her knees at the side of the chair. "After you got out. Why didn't you contact me?"

"It had been nearly eight years. Eight years going on forever. Too long." Chan turned away to stare at the cold stars. Far ahead the rainbow beacon of the Link entry point was visible as a bright point, warning space vehicles to stay away. At last he said, "I did check with a couple of the old team. They told me you were living with someone else. That finished it. I had nothing to offer, and it wouldn't be fair to contact you. Anyway, it would have made no difference."

"*Wrong!* It would have made a difference to *me*."

The feeling that swept through Deb was like nothing she had known in her whole life, a bloodred rage that twisted and tore at her insides. She raised her hand. One blow would break his neck.

He did not see the movement, because he was still staring at nothing. He could not possibly have seen her raised hand. But he said, slowly and thoughtfully, "You know, when I was asked to lead an expedition to the Geyser Swirl, I knew instantly that I would accept. But I didn't know why. I told myself that it was the chance to do what we had all talked of doing, long ago. Since then I've had other thoughts. This mission is so dangerous it sounds like guaranteed suicide. Sane people don't commit suicide. And only monsters talk their oldest friends into going along to die with them. Have I been building a team? Or have I been luring you and Danny and Chrissie and the others to share my fate?"

He sounded like a zombie, and his tone of utter hopelessness broke Deb. The blood seemed to drain out of her, leaving her weak and faint. She brought her raised hand down on the back of Chan's head, not violently but gently, touching his hair. "How long before we reach Link entry?"

"About four and a half hours."

"Then that's when you'll find out if you're a monster. Are you going back to the control room?"

"I don't think so. The Link transition is the job of the ship's computer. It's supposed to be close to omniscient, and close to infallible."

"So why are we here? What can humans do that it can't?"

"We can risk human lives. That's Dag Korin's job now; mine when we get through the link."

"Mine too, then. I'll wait here—if that's all right with you?" She waited, but there was no word, no nod of acceptance. Finally she went on, "I can tell you one thing right now. No matter what happens when we go through the Link, you haven't *lured* anybody here. Not Chrissie, not Tarb, not Danny, not anybody. Every member of the old team, they would rather be here than anywhere else in the universe."

Still he said nothing.

She added, "And so would I."

Link network transitions: every one the same, every one different.

Similarities:

- Before a transition can be initiated, coordinates must be provided. One hundred and sixty-eight decimal digits are needed, enough to specify origin and destination to within one meter anywhere in the universe. No exceptions are permitted.
- The matter density within the destination volume must be no greater than that of a thin gas; otherwise, Link transition will not be initiated.

Link points on Earth's surface come very close to that limit.

- Adequate (which is to say, enormous) power must be available at the originating Link point. Travel to the stars will never be cheap. The power for a single interstellar trip eats up the savings of a lifetime. When a large mass is involved, such as that of the *Hero's Return*, no private groups can afford the expense. Such Link transitions are the prerogative of wealthy species governments.

Differences:

- Link entry positions are absolute, but Link entry velocities depend on mass. A small ship, such as the *Mood Indigo*, can enter a link with some latitude in velocity and emerge unscathed. A ship the size of the *Hero's Return* must hit the right entry velocity to within millimeters a second.
- Velocity error converts kinetic energy to heat energy upon Link emergence. Miss the entry speed by a few kilometers a second, and your ship will emerge red hot.
- There is no uniformity in Link destinations, and no warning given of their properties. A traveller must learn of any dangers—high temperature, intense gravity field—ahead of time.
- Small fluctuations, believed to be amplified quantum effects, add a random element to the direction of travel on emergence. In the worst possible case, the one-in-a-million shot that no one likes to talk about, emergence never takes place at all. In any event, a ship had better be prepared to make sudden course changes.

That encourages one other permitted variation: the prayers of the crew about to undergo transition can be anything you like. The contribution of prayer to

Link transitions is not established—but almost everyone does it.

Zero hour was approaching for the *Hero's Return*. The entry point gaped open, a hole in the fabric of spacetime. In the final seconds before transition, every person on board fell silent. Men and women, young or old, believers or atheists, alone or together, outwardly nervous or outwardly confident, vanished into their private worlds.

The final second ticked away. Deb Bisson gripped Chan Dalton's hand, hard enough to bruise. He felt the pain, and welcomed it.

Time ran out. The great bulk of the *Hero's Return*, slowly, sluggishly, as if reluctantly, slid forward to enter the dark eye of the Link.

17

Say Hello to an Angel

Bony had known about Tinker Composites since he was a small child. He had studied the aliens, watched educational programs, asked a thousand (unanswered) questions of other humans, and read everything that he could lay his hands on. The Tinkers fascinated him. Pipe-Rillas fascinated him. *All* the Stellar Group aliens fascinated him. That was one reason he had been so eager to go to the stars, ever since he was a child in the basement warrens of Earth. And now . . .

As the inner hatch swung open and he took the first step forward into the ship's interior, Bony found that he was trembling.

His first thought—I hope Liddy can't see how nervous I am—vanished as a carpet of dark purple rose from the floor in front of him. He heard a whirring of many wings and flinched as a cloud of purple-black components, all apparently identical and each about as big as his finger, buzzed around his head.

As Liddy gasped and clutched Bony's arm, the Tinker components flew to the other side of the cabin and settled around a tall pole. Fluttering their wings in a blur of motion they hovered by the column, then grasped it with small claws on the front of shiny leather-like wings. Thin, whip-like antennas reached out and connected heads to neighboring tails. Each body possessed a ring of pale green eyes, all of which seemed to be staring at Bony. That lasted only a few seconds. Then a second wave with its own myriad of eyes was settling on top of the first, and a third over that. It was no longer possible to make out individual components, and Bony could see no way to count them. He knew that a Tinker Composite could form at many different sizes, but he did not know if this one was big or small.

The Composite was taking on a particular shape, a crude approximation to a human form. Within two minutes the main body was complete, a rough "head" above it, while "legs" extended outward and downward to make contact with and derive support from the cabin floor. To Bony's surprise—this was something he had not seen mentioned in the Tinker descriptions—many of the individual components remained unattached. Of the total in the cabin, only about four-fifths were connected to form a compact mass; the others stood tail-first on the cabin floor or hung singly from walls and ceiling.

The mass of the Tinker Composite began to form a funnel-like opening in its head-like extremity. From that aperture came a hollow wheezing moan. "Ohhh-ahhh-ggghh. Hharr-ehh-looo," it said. Then, in a crude approximation to solar speech, "Har-e-loo. Hal-lo."

Bony, feeling like a fool, said tentatively, "Hello."

He was reassured when Liddy echoed him, "Hello," and added, "I am Liddy Morse."

She was still wearing the translator at her belt, although for Tinkers it should be unnecessary. That idea was confirmed when a whistling voice said, "Hello, Liddy Morse," and, after a pause, "You may call us, Eager Seeker."

Did you shake hands with a Tinker Composite? If so, with what? Bony said, "I am Bonifant Rombelle. You can call me Bony."

The other occupant of the cabin had been crouching in a corner, telescoping thin limbs and narrow body into a small space. Now the Pipe-Rilla unfolded, taller and taller, until she brushed against the four-meter cabin ceiling. Her rear legs were still partly bent.

"So it is true." The head bobbed in greeting. "Eager Seeker was right and I, Vow-of-Silence, was wrong. It is as the Sea-wanderers told us, there is a third ship."

"Sea-wanderers? Third ship?" Bony had so many questions he hardly knew where to begin. He opened his helmet. The air smelled of peppermint, overlain with a faint odor of ripe peaches, but it was perfectly breathable. He began to remove his suit.

"The natives of this planet," the Pipe-Rilla said. She and the Tinker Composite were watching with interest, as though the removal of Bony's suit represented some molting action unique to humans. "*Sea-wanderers* is what they call themselves, as you surely know."

"We didn't know. We have been calling this planet Limbo, and these natives, Limbics."

"Hm." Vow-of-Silence bent her head to one side. "Limbo. Not bad, not bad at all. I think we may adopt it also. But since you are here, you must have been talking to your Limbics."

"We have." Bony didn't want the aliens to think that humans were total fools, but honesty made him add, "We had trouble with the language at first."

"That is understandable. It is unusually high in liquid consonants." Vow-of-Silence tittered.

After an awkward moment—was it a joke, and was he supposed to laugh?—Bony went on. "In fact it was Liddy who made the language breakthrough."

The Pipe-Rilla followed his gesture. Liddy was removing her suit also, and Vow-of-Silence stared at her breasts with enormous interest.

"Why, you are a human female. This is wonderful. I have never before met one. I would very much like the opportunity of extended conversation with you."

"Sure. Although this isn't the best time for it. We have more questions." Liddy glanced at Bony. "Right?"

"We sure do. And we have some answers, too, that you may find useful. This is not just a water-world. There's land here, too—and there may be great dangers."

The Pipe-Rilla leaned far forward, looking not into Bony's face but into Liddy's. "Would you please inform your mate, with as much respect as I am capable of offering, that we came to this world well before he did, have done more exploration, had more conversations with the natives, and may be well aware of what he seeks to inform us. We will exchange information gladly, but we suggest it may save time if we speak first."

"Exploration." Bony seized that one word. "But until we built the extension to your airlock, you could not leave your ship."

"Not true. Certain of us *did* leave it. Now, the rest of us *choose* not to leave it." Vow-of-Silence crouched low in front of the two humans, her vestigial forelimbs clasped across her narrow chest in a misleading gesture of supplication. The pleasant peppermint odor strengthened. "Listen, please, to our tale. The crew of this ship, the *Finder*, originally comprised myself and an extra-large Tinker Composite, Eager Seeker. We entered a Link point located in the Fomalhaut system and expected to arrive in the region of empty space within the Geyser Swirl. Instead, we found our ship under water. However, we learned from the Sea-wanderers here that there exists a nearby land mass. We decided to explore it."

Bony, wanting to ask *how* you explored a place when you couldn't leave the ship; bit his tongue.

Vow-of-Silence went on: "My colleague, Eager Seeker, detached a sizeable collective, to whom we gave a temporary name, Blessed Union. The components of Blessed Union would leave this ship and travel to the surface, from which they would fly to the land. They did not need a suit. The waters of—Limbo, you call it?—are high in oxygen, enough for individual Tinker components to survive without artificial assistance. Preparations for the journey were made with great care. Blessed Union would re-assemble when ashore, except when a few components were needed to fly ahead as scouts. Is this clear?"

Bony nodded. His self-image as smart savior of the Pipe-Rilla ship was steadily declining. It nose-dived when Vow-of-Silence continued, "We had been told that this could be a perilous undertaking. We had spoken extensively to the Sea-wanderers, and they said that death had come recently to many of their companions near the shore. However, we were confident. We did not believe that we were in danger, since we have ways unknown to the Sea-wanderers to protect ourselves against attack from native life-forms.

"The new collective of Blessed Union left,

promising to return no later than nightfall. After components of the collective had departed we pumped the airlock dry, slowly and laboriously; and we waited. That was days ago. We are waiting still, though our time of hope is ending."

The Pipe-Rilla began to rock slowly up and down, half-extending her hind limbs. Finally Bony asked, "Do you think that Blessed Union has been killed?"

At the question, the Pipe-Rilla covered her eyes with her forelimbs. Bony wondered if he had committed some dreadful inter-species violation of protocol.

Finally Vow-of-Silence said, "This is a matter of some delicacy. It is possible, yes, that Blessed Union was destroyed. However, it is rather more likely that Blessed Union *swarmed*. You see"—the narrow head bowed low and the sibilant voice dropped in volume—"we knew at the outset that there was a risk. Eager Seeker was, by intention, an unusually abundant Composite. Once on land, the urge of Blessed Union to swarm and breed and form a second independent Composite may have been irresistible. This possibility is, of course, a matter of great potential embarrassment to Eager-Seeker. A Tinker never admits to such unsanctioned breeding. And still we do not know what lies ashore. The Sea-wanderers cannot tell us. Are you able to answer the question?"

"Not completely. But *how* do you talk to the Sea-wanderers, if you can't leave the ship?"

"Through the translator, of course, on the hull. Did you not see it?"

Bony hadn't. Among the thousand devices that festooned the outside of the *Finder*, it was easy to miss any particular one. But Bony also had the feeling that he had seen too little overall, and understood even less.

"We did go ashore," he said. "Once. But we found no sign of your companions. Of course, we were there for only a little while, and it would have been very easy to miss them."

He described his and Liddy's experience, including the brief glimpse of a great trifoliate flying vehicle. He offered his impression of what the land interior looked like. Finally he told of the foaming circle in the sea, a place that might form part of a Link entry point.

That grabbed the attention of his audience. Vow-of-Silence said at once, "Aha! Where was this anomaly located?"

"It's hard to describe in words. If only we had a map . . ."

"One moment." Vow-of-Silence picked up a flat plate and a marker and began to draw. She did it without looking, and her movements were so fast it seemed impossible for them to be accurate. In less than thirty seconds she was showing the result to Bony and Liddy. She said diffidently, "This is based on conversations with the Sea-wanderers and our own observations. It is, of course, no more than a tiny region of the whole of Limbo, but it represents our current knowledge. Here is where we are."

She touched the plate, where she had drawn a tiny but recognizable picture of the *Finder*. "And here is the shoreline. Now, where was the steaming circle in the water?"

"About here." Bony stabbed at the drawing with an index finger. "I think that's right. Liddy?"

She nodded. "I couldn't put it any closer. When we went ashore we travelled as far as *here*." She touched a point on the upper right of the plate, and Vow-of-Silence instantly added a notation there and a dotted line leading from the shore. Liddy nodded, frowned, and said, "But what's *this*?"

Bony had not noticed it when he examined the plate, but a small circle toward the top left contained another small and stylized drawing. He stared at it. His eyes were not acute enough to make out the fine detail.

"It looks like—" Liddy turned to Vow-of-Silence. "I've never seen one, but I've seen drawings of Angels that look like that."

"Of course." The narrow head bobbed. "When I said at the beginning of this meeting that there was a third ship, I was referring to *your* vessel. The *second* ship, the one that the Sea-wanderers told us about and which apparently arrived soon after we did, is an Angel ship. And there is—not surprisingly—an Angel on board."

The Angel ship sat about five kilometers away from the original position of the *Mood Indigo*, on a narrow part of the same off-shore shelf. Looking at the map drawn by Vow-of-Silence, Bony realized for the first time how lucky they had been. Only a couple of hundred yards seaward of where the *Mood Indigo* had landed, the map showed the seabed dropping off steeply to a region marked "Deep Water." Too deep, apparently, for the Sea-wanderers, and more than deep enough to cave in the hull of any ship unfortunate enough to descend there.

The Angel ship had been even luckier than the *Mood Indigo*. According to the drawing it sat on the very brink of the shelf, which was unusually narrow at that point. Twenty meters in one direction would plunge the ship into the abyss. Fifty meters the other way would bring it onto the rocky beach. Eager Seeker and Vow-of-Silence had been considering a visit to the Angel when Bony and Liddy arrived, but they were reluctant to leave the *Finder* while there was any chance at all that Blessed Union might return.

There had seemed no great urgency in a visit to the Angel ship. That idea changed as Vow-of-Silence was pointing out a river on the map, used in the past by the Sea-wanderers to penetrate a little way inland while remaining under water.

"Here is the farthest point of their progress." The Pipe-Rilla tapped it with a black claw. "They call it Bad Things Fork, and also Death Fork. Any Sea-wanderer who went beyond it never returned."

She was interrupted when a unit in the control desk of the *Finder* suddenly beeped for attention, and a bubbling voice that seemed to speak without consonants said, "It darkens. Violence comes in the above the world. We will feel it in the world. We go to seek safeness in down."

"The Sea-wanderers." Vow-of-Silence leaned across to the sound unit and said clearly, "We hear you, and we thank you for the warning."

Liddy added, "I hear them, but what do they mean?"

"It has happened before, probably before your arrival on this world." Vow-of-Silence bent to a remote viewer and called for a new display. "So far as these natives are concerned, the sea *is* the world. The atmosphere of the planet is the above-the-world. The Sea-wanderers can tell when a surface storm is on the way, and when that is the case they refuse to go near the shore. There are huge breakers, and strong currents. Look at the sky thirty kilometers west of here, and you will see what is coming our way."

If the ship could receive a distant view from above the surface, why had it not been able to learn the fate of the Tinkers who went ashore? Bony postponed the question. It was less important at the moment than what filled the display. The time was close to the middle of Limbo's day, but the blue sun's disk shone only intermittently. The clear sky had filled with clots and streaks of gray and black clouds, torn by wind and driving along furiously. The same force that propelled them across the sky lashed the sea surface into monstrous surges, broken at their peaks and flecked with white foam.

"Can it hurt us?" Liddy asked.

"Not us." Vow-of-Silence was reaching out at full length to pluck a set of linked tubes from a cabinet. "The *Finder* is safe at this depth and in this location. So is your ship, providing that it remains more than twenty meters down. I am sending a signal to it, warning of the storm. But the Angel ship will be in peril. It lies on the narrowest part of the shelf. When the storm arrives, shifts of sediment might send it over the edge into deep water. Waves could pick it up and smash it on the shore. The ship must be moved, or at the very least the Angel taken to safety. Let me see, three kilometers across the seabed, that would take . . ."

Bony wondered how Friday Indigo was doing, up there on the surface. Also *what* he was doing. The captain had been very secretive. The *Mood Indigo* could always descend again and sit the storm out safely on the bed of the sea—provided that Indigo had the sense to listen to the warning message, and act on it. On the other hand, this was a situation where the *Mood Indigo* would have been invaluable. The ship could fly three kilometers far quicker than anyone could walk.

Eager Seeker was already in motion, Tinker components rapidly removing themselves from the main body. The process appeared totally random. Bony began to put his suit back on, but he could not hide his curiosity.

While he was waiting for his suit to climb back up his body, he asked, "How does a Tinker Composite decide what *size* to be?"

The Pipe-Rilla said at once, "It is all a question of necessary function. If there are—"

"Vow-of-Silence, do you mind? After all, this is *our own self* that is being discussed." There was a definite testiness to Eager Seeker's tone. Bony, recalling that the Tinker Composite had not said one word after their initial greeting, decided that *Vow-of-Silence* might represent not so much a name as a desire on the part of others.

The blunt head-like upper part of the Composite turned toward Bony, even as components sped away from it. Eager Seeker was taking on a distinctly ragged appearance as the Tinker Composite went on, "A full answer would require much time. But there are certain simple rules. First, if we wish to we can join every component together. When we do so, we have increased thinking power. But we are also less nimble mentally. We are *slower*, with a longer integration time. Thus, we are not so quick to complete a thought or to reach a decision. The integration time grows very quickly—*exponentially*—with the number of components. When the problem is large, we combine all units. This, of course, is why we came here as a Composite of unusual size, with the expectation of problems of unusual difficulty. Normally, we choose a compromise between *speed* of thought and *depth* of thought. In a possible emergency—as now—smaller is better. And since we must soon leave the ship"—more and more dark-winged bodies flew away from the main bulk of the Composite—"we will take that action not as an entity, but as a non-entity. As individual components . . ."

The voice faded to nothing, the speaking funnel

closed, and a blizzard of purple-black swirled about the cabin before vanishing up a narrow tube in the ceiling.

"Eager Seeker leaves through an airlock too small for me or you." Vow-of-Silence was wriggling her body and legs into the odd array of tubes, which mysteriously transformed into a suit. "We will use the exit method you so kindly provided. Come now. The Angel's ship waits for us, but the storm declines to do so."

She led the way back out through the airlock. Bony and Liddy followed. Under the sea there was no sign of the coming storm, although all the bubble people had vanished. Eager Seeker, in the form of its thousands of separate parts, was already outside. The components seemed as much at home in water as in air, turning and tumbling around each other with easy flaps of tiny wings. And then, in a moment, all of them darted off at great speed in the same direction.

Vow-of-Silence set off after them, saying, "Of course, our presence may be quite unnecessary. Eager Seeker can probably ensure the Angel's safety without us." Her voice came, perfectly clear, into Bony's suit. So much for the opacity of water to radio waves. He wondered what other technical tricks the aliens had up their sleeves, also what strange physiology the Pipe-Rilla possessed. Vow-of-Silence appeared thin and fragile, and she was strolling along at what appeared to be a moderate pace, but no human could travel so fast in water. Bony and Liddy had to rise off the sea floor and use their thrustor jets to keep up.

They had gone only a short distance when the Tinker components came winging back. A group of them formed a tight cluster about Vow-of-Silence's suited figure, so that the Pipe-Rilla was obliged to stop moving and stand half-hidden on the seabed. After a few seconds the Tinker bodies lifted and again flew rapidly away.

Vow-of-Silence turned to Bony and Liddy. "Strange. Very strange. Eager Seeker went to the Angel ship, which is in exactly the position reported by the Sea-wanderers. It appears unharmed. However, the ship is open to the sea and the Angel is not on board."

Liddy said, "Does that mean the Angel is dead?"

"Not necessarily. The actions of Angels are often impenetrable, but self-preservation is high on their list of priorities. If you will excuse me . . ." Vow-of-Silence ducked her head and the Pipe-Rilla took off with gigantic strides, stepping easily across waving sea-grass two meters tall. Her rate of progress was enormous. Even with thrustors set to maximum, Bony and Liddy fell steadily behind. The undersea light was fading, though nightfall on Limbo was many hours away. Bony took a quick swoop up toward the surface, close enough to feel turbulence in the water. A few meters above his head, the full storm was arriving. He looked up and saw dark and light patterns rippling across the surface, synchronized to the movement of pressure waves across his body.

He dove back down, peering into underwater gloom and suddenly afraid that he might lose contact with both Liddy and Vow-of-Silence. The Pipe-Rilla had vanished but he saw Liddy plowing steadily on, just far enough above the seabed to avoid the clinging sea-grasses. He flew after her, across a sea valley, over a ridge, descending steadily and trying to will the suit thrustors to produce more than their maximum possible power. Was it imagination, or was Liddy slowing down?

Yes. Not just slowing. She had stopped. And then he could see Vow-of-Silence. And the clustered components of Eager Seeker. And then, in the middle of the group, a stout and unfamiliar form shaped like a giant artichoke.

When he came up to them, the Angel was speaking. Bony detected an unmistakable petulance in the computer-generated tones. "Naturally we left our ship. It was impossible to predict whether we would be swept into the ocean abyss, or carried onto the rocky shore. Neither outcome was acceptable. The Bard of Terra spoke truth: *Cowards die many times before their death*. However, the superior coward prefers not to die at all."

Vow-of-Silence said, "But are you all right, Angel? You seem helpless. Can you breathe under water?"

"You do not need to call us Angel. In Stellar Group company we answer to the name of Gressel. And we are certainly not helpless. In fact, we were heading for your ship when you found us. And although we cannot breathe under water, we can *not breathe* under water, which is what we are doing now."

As the Angel spoke it was creeping along the sea floor. The roots of the Chassel-Rose that formed the Angel's lower part retracted, pulled free of the bottom silt at a glacial rate, and quiveringly stretched forward to root themselves again. Bony's guess was that the three-kilometer journey to the *Finder* could well be all over in a matter of weeks.

Vow-of-Silence must have reached the same conclusion. The giant pipe-stem figure bent over the Angel, said, "With your permission, Gressel," and hoisted the bulky mass effortlessly up. "It is likely," the Pipe-Rilla went on, "that no effects of the storm will be observed at this depth, but we cannot be sure of that. We would rather be in our ship than outside it." Vow-of-Silence turned with the Angel in her arms and headed rapidly back the way that she had come.

"Perhaps you are right." After one moment of resistance, Gressel allowed itself to be carried. The Angel gloomily added, *"A long farewell to all our greatness.* We perforce accept assistance, and admit the maxim: *better safe than sorry."*

So far as Bony was concerned, *safe* was a debatable term. The deep sea remained calm enough, but something was happening above the surface. Dense clouds must have covered the blue sun, because the deeper waters had become so dark that Bony could no longer see the ocean floor. He grabbed Liddy by the hand and the two of them followed the faint suit lights of the Pipe-Rilla through abyssal gloom.

And then those suit lights, though not shrinking in size, began to fade in brightness. After a few baffled seconds Bony realized what was happening. The waves on the surface could not damage him at this depth, but they could stir bottom sediments. Their whole party was moving through a thickening cloud of gray silt.

In that moment of understanding, the scene ahead of Bony lit in brilliant blue-white. Everything—lank sea-grasses, Pipe-Rilla, Angel, darting Tinkers, and pale mud cloud—became etched in light. There was a moment of startling clarity, which was as suddenly gone.

A lightning bolt—a major one—had hit the surface of the sea. The thunder came at once, shatteringly loud. The strike must have been directly above them.

But now Bony, blinded by the flash, could see nothing at all. Holding on to Liddy he allowed himself to coast to a halt. He had lost all sense of direction. The only hope was to follow Vow-of-Silence and the other aliens back to the *Finder*. But he could not see them, unless another bolt of lightning came to his assistance.

How many people stood and waited, *hoping* for a close lightning strike? Bony felt Liddy's arms around him. Even through the suits he could feel her trembling.

Come on, lightning bolt. Do your thing. Hit!

The response after five more seconds was a weak, far-off flicker, the puny glow of a lightning bolt several miles away. By its brief light Bony saw Vow-of-Silence, standing motionless with the Angel cradled in her forearms. Every Tinker component had vanished, he hoped to safety.

Once more it was too dark to see anything. Bony and Liddy stayed where they were, hoping that Vow-of-Silence was doing the same. Bony had a new worry. Suppose that the storm continued into the night and true darkness came to Limbo? He and Liddy would run out of air in eight more hours. He didn't know how it would be for the Pipe-Rilla, but long before morning the humans had to be back on board a ship.

Another lightning bolt came, hardly brighter than the last one. But this time a curious afterglow replaced the return of stygian darkness. It continued and brightened, and by its light Bony could once more make out the figures of the Pipe-Rilla and the Angel. He was about to head toward them when he heard Liddy gasp, "Bony! Look there. Up to the right."

His attention had been on the way ahead. Now he tilted his head back and followed Liddy's pointing arm. At once he saw the source of the new light.

It came not from the syncopated stutter of lightning bolts, nor from the faded gleam of Limbo's sun. The source of illumination was a ship. All lights blazing, it surged over them, about a hundred meters to their right. It was below the surface of the sea, and it must be gigantic because the forward surge of its great blunt hull produced a bow wave powerful enough to throw Bony helplessly backward and turn him upside down.

But it was not the pressure wave that made Bony gasp, nor was it fear of a war vessel alien and dangerous. He blinked in disbelief because he thought he *knew* that outline. That was no dinky space yacht, like the *Mood Indigo*, nor an alien flying machine like the one that he and Liddy had spotted on their trip ashore. Unless his eyes were deceiving him, that was a Class Five cruiser—a *human* design, symbol of former human military might, powerful and close to impregnable—driving its three-hundred-meter, eighty-plus-thousand-ton, thousand-crew bulk through the alien seas of Limbo.

And then, almost before Bony could bring himself back to an upright position, the monstrous ship was cruising on and vanishing into the fog of silt. The vessel was on a descending path. If it continued unchecked, ten more minutes would bring it to a halt on the seabed. A cruiser would surely survive that impact, and the little group on the seabed would be safer there than anywhere on Limbo.

Unless . . .

Bony could imagine a worse possibility. Suppose that the new ship's course was to the south or west? The coastal shelf ended a few kilometers in that direction. The cruiser might then be destined for a different fate: a descent into an unknown and unplumbed ocean. At sufficient depth and pressure, even the cruiser's solid hull would collapse like an imploding soap bubble.

18

Friday Goes It Alone

Friday Indigo had said not a word to anyone, but he knew exactly what he must do. It had been obvious as soon as he learned that other Stellar Group members were present on Limbo.

The Tinkers and Pipe-Rillas, damn their alien guts, had met the Limbics before he had. They had ruined his chances for first contact with a new intelligent species.

But you didn't have to be a genius to draw a few other conclusions. First, no matter what that moron Rombelle might think, the Limbics were in a primitive, pre-technology stage of development. Second, the bubble-brain Limbics were *marine* creatures, who did not and could not occupy the land area of their planet. Third, on Rombelle and Liddy Morse's visit to the surface they had seen a working flying machine. Fourth, the Stellar Group members were stuck at the bottom of the sea. They had not explored the land.

Put it all together, and the answer stared you in the face: *another* intelligent species existed on Limbo. Its members lived not in the sea, but on dry land. They possessed technology, advanced enough to build an aircraft, and the plane's home base must be reasonably close since Rombelle had also reported seeing the shadow pass above him on his first excursion from the *Mood Indigo*. Finally, and most important, *no one from the Stellar Group had been in touch with the land-dwellers*. First contact with them would be a truly historic event—not a useless contact with some shapeless underwater objects who spoke in gobbledygook and were made of glop.

Hey, the presence of another Stellar Group ship on Limbo might even be a blessing. It meant that Friday could go off and look for the land-dwellers alone, without having to drag along the dead weight of Bony Rombelle and Liddy Morse. For the past few days he had regretted bringing them with him at all. Sure, the sex with Liddy was nice, but hardly worth the hassle of dealing with incompetents.

The *Mood Indigo* lifted easily from the seabed as Friday applied power to the auxiliary thrustors. Flying the ship underwater proved to be no harder than doing so in space—easier, in a way, because water resistance damped any slight over- or under-thrust. Friday raised the ship ten meters, then spent a few minutes trimming the balance and experimenting with lateral and vertical motion. As soon as he had the hang of it he would approach the shore. He was delighted to find that he could move the ship in any direction, at the same time rising or falling in the water exactly as he chose.

At first he headed due north, so that anyone

watching would assume he was taking the ship back to its original position on the seabed. Only when he was kilometers away from the stranded Pipe-Rilla ship and could not see it using any of his instruments did he curve his course east, in the direction of the land.

He maintained a leisurely pace, not because he was worried or cautious but because he was savoring the moment. Let's face it, you could win a hundred space-sailing regattas from the Vulcan Nexus to the Dry Tortugas, and what did it get you? A shelf of rinky-dink trophies and your name in tiny print in some never-looked-at record book. You could start out in life with all the money you were ever likely to need, triple or quadruple it, and still find twenty Indigo family members with more. So if you were Friday Indigo, the name of the game had to be fame, not wealth. A first contact like this would put your name up there with Timbers Rattigan, who came back with news of the Tinker civilization, or Marianna Slung, who discovered the Angels of Sellora. You would be somebody little kids were told about in reverent tones: Friday Indigo, first human to encounter the—the—the what?

He needed a good name. The bubble-brains could be the "Limbics." That was a lousy name and anyway Bony Rombelle had chosen it. What to call the land-dwellers?

That was a no-brainer. Friday smiled. He was on his way for first contact with the *Indigoans*.

The *Mood Indigo* drifted steadily east, twenty meters below the surface. The ship's sonar told Friday that the sea depth beneath him was slowly decreasing, just as he had expected. It was his intention to move the ship as close to the shore as possible. With luck that would lift the upper decks clear of the surface, allowing him to use the top airlock and wade ashore without needing a suit.

The first suggestion that things might not continue according to plan came from the sea-bottom sensors. Friday had set the auxiliary drive to a constant level of thrust, which ought to guarantee a steady rise or fall through the water. But the instruments in the control cabin insisted that the depth of water beneath the ship was changing in a cyclic way, increasing steadily by up to ten meters and then, half a minute later, decreasing by the same amount. Also—Friday ended his pleasant musing and became fully alert—the inertial positioning system insisted that although he had set the thrustors to take him due east, the direction of the *Mood Indigo* was in fact more like northeast.

Damn the instruments. Were they feeding him garbage? Had Rombelle somehow screwed them up, in his endless tinkering?

There was one easy way to find out, without depending on instruments: rise all the way to the surface, and take a look using the imaging sensors.

Friday fed more power to the thrustors. The result was immediate and disturbing. As the ship lifted higher it began to roll and pitch, rocking Friday from side to side at the controls. He swore, locked in the autopilot—God knows how well an autopilot developed for use in space would perform at sea—and called for a wraparound display from the bow imaging sensor.

Confusion. The seabed depth sonar was all over the place, and in any case there was no way to tell from its readings if the upper end of the *Mood Indigo* was above or below the surface. But the display ought to show one or the other, a view of air or a view of water. It provided neither. Friday saw a crazy patchwork pattern of bubbles and foam and dark streaks, plus an occasional glimpse of clouded sky. At the same moment he heard a sound. Something above his head was thumping on the highest part of the hull, loudly, imperatively, sending violent shivers through the whole ship.

The *Mood Indigo* was close to the surface—the bow must even be above it. That idea was confirmed when a flash of light filled the ship's whole interior and the hull rang like a giant gong.

Goddamit, they'd been struck by lightning! The top of the ship was a natural target, projecting above the surface. This was not the smooth seas and calm water that he had expected, but the broken chaos of a howling storm. Those streaks and that foam were breaking waves, and the regular booming came from their ferocious impact on the ship.

Well, the hell with this. He'd had enough, and fortunately there was an easy solution. What went up would go down. Deep water was calm.

Friday cut the drive completely. At once the sky view dwindled in the imaging sensors and the ship's roll became less pronounced. They were sinking. Another half-minute, and he and the *Mood Indigo* would enjoy the haven of the seabed.

Within seconds he learned that this plan would not work, either. The downward movement came to a jarring end. The bottom of the ship had hit the seabed. They had been approaching the shore for the past few minutes, and now they were in water too shallow for total submergence.

Friday cursed and threw everything into reverse—an act warned against in all the manuals. The whole vessel shuddered as the lateral thrustors switched polarity, urging the ship back the way it had come. For a moment it worked. The inertial positioning system showed them moving to open water; then a huge wave smashed into the exposed upper hull. The ship started to tilt. And tilt.

It was going over—all the way over. Friday managed one last desperate act, turning off the thrustors before he clutched at the arms of his seat. The ship pitched forward, farther and farther. He was not wearing a restraining harness. He lost his grip and fell toward what had been the front wall of the cabin.

It was a two-meter drop, but in the low gravity of Limbo he had plenty of time to brace himself before he hit the panelled wall. He looked straight up. The move from vertical to horizontal should have helped, because the *Mood Indigo* was longer than it was wide. And it had. The ports showed only water. The ship was totally submerged.

But not submerged enough. As Friday watched, the topmost port showed a white spume of foam, then a glimpse of dark cloudy sky. At the wave's trough, the water level dropped far enough to expose the upper part of the hull. A few seconds later, a new rising wave lifted and pushed. Friday heard a groaning, scraping sound, and the ship jerked a couple of meters forward.

He could guess what came next. The *Mood Indigo* would be driven inch by inch toward the rocky shore, more and more exposed, hit harder and harder by the waves. The hull had not been designed for hammer blows. It could not stand much more of this kind of beating. Already he heard the groan of stressed bulkheads and tortured joints, and a grinding moan as something on the outside hull—communications antennas? manipulator arms?—was torn free.

Put on his suit, and struggle to an airlock? Even if he succeeded, he would be worse off than inside the ship. The waves outside were monsters, they would lift him like flotsam and smash his body onto the bare rocks. He dare not leave the ship.

Was that it, then? Travel hundreds of lightyears, and die on a storm-swept shore like some peasant fisherman?

Never. Not Friday Indigo. He held on tight as the attack of another giant wave made the ship's structure groan in protest.

First, a suit. The hull might be breached at any moment, and even though a suit could not protect him from the rocks it could keep him from drowning.

But his suit, damn it, was on the next level up. Friday started to crawl along the curve of the wall toward the ship's bow. He had to pause and grab and hold tight as each new wave hit. Twice he slid back a few feet. But he kept trying, and he made progress. When he finally had the suit in his hands, putting it on was far from easy. He had to wait for a quiet moment, release his handholds, and slide the suit on as far as possible in the few seconds before he was again grabbing and clutching and swearing. The suit did its best to help, but it was slow, focused work. Almost a quarter of an hour passed before he was waiting for the next shock to subside so that he could set the helmet in position.

He waited, and became aware of something else. He had been so intent on what he was doing that the strength of the blows on the outside of the ship had not been on his mind. Now he thought—or imagined—that the last few waves had hit less hard. Could it be that the storm had passed its peak?

The imaging sensors were useless, a blur of foam and mist. Friday clamped his helmet into position and began to crawl up the sloping wall. His target was one of the ports, normally on the side of the hull but now, with the ship turned horizontal, it stood right above his head.

This climb was even harder. When he reached the halfway point the hull curved over his head, so that soon he was relying on his hands only while his feet swung free. The impact of the waves still tried to jar him loose from his handholds, but now the low gravity of Limbo helped. He was able to hold on and keep climbing, until finally his helmet was level with the port and he could peer out.

His view was toward the rear of the ship and—for the moment—above the surface. The sky was dark, riven by clouds, but in a few places he saw far-off flickers of lightning. Their random flashes illuminated a series of gigantic white-topped wave crests, rolling irresistibly in toward him. They seemed bigger than ever. The storm was in no way past its peak. So why did he feel that the sledgehammer blows on the ship were becoming less destructive?

He held on tight, staring hard at the nearest wave. It was changing shape as it approached. Its smooth profile was breaking, falling in on itself as he watched. The wave was certainly going to reach the *Mood Indigo*, and it might push the stranded vessel farther forward. But some of the breaker's forward momentum was lost with every meter that it travelled.

Why? How?

Friday ducked his head and gritted his teeth until the wave had hit and passed, then turned to stare to the left and to the right. He saw water, as expected—but beyond the water was land. A gray shoreline, and farther away black, rocky hills jutted up on either side.

That was the reason why the storm felt weaker. The *Mood Indigo* had been incredibly lucky. Instead of being thrown onto the stony shore, to be hammered until it broke apart, the ship had been driven by the storm into some kind of fjord or drowned river valley whose sides broke the force of the waves and protected anything within its harbor. Every meter that an extra-large wave forced the *Mood Indigo* only served to protect the vessel better from the next one.

The danger now was that the ship was not in a true fjord, but in a narrow strait between two islands. If that were the case, relief from the storm might be only temporary.

Friday turned to find out what lay ahead. A passing wave threw up a screen of foam and it was a few moments before he had a clear view. He peered, stared, and whooped aloud in triumph.

"You did it, Friday-man, you incredible genius son of a bitch. You did it!"

A few hundred meters in front of the ship the river valley narrowed farther. Waves still broke on its shores, but they gradually diminished to a rolling surf no more than a meter high. Friday saw through blown spray a line of columns amid the breakers, together with the hint of a black jetty. Beyond, clear and stark in the odd half-light of the storm, stood a pair of jet-black buildings. They were low-built and ugly, hugging the shore like a pair of beached whales, but to Friday's eyes they and the whole scene were beautiful. Because this was undoubtedly the work of intelligent beings—beings who could in no way be the bubble-brained bottom-feeding nonsense-gurgling morons that Bony Rombelle had named as Limbics.

Friday Indigo feasted his eyes and murmured, "First contact, here I come!"

He couldn't recall anything in his life as frustrating as the next four hours.

The waves had moved the *Mood Indigo* as far as they could, until the ship was firmly grounded halfway along the river valley. The ship was now in no danger, but unfortunately it had not been moved quite far enough. Friday had no way to leave it and survive, as long as the waves remained big enough to lift a suited man and smash him on the rocks.

He fidgeted and fretted, doing all the possibly useful and time-consuming things that he could think of. The airlock, if and when he finally got to use it, was positioned above the waterline. He made sure that it was ready to use as soon as the waves subsided enough. Supplies, he might need supplies. He packed enough concentrated food for a week into a small backpack. Water was available, there was even too much of it, but an empty bottle might come in handy. Yes, and he mustn't forget a translation unit—one that he hoped would perform a sight better than the piece of junk he had tried on the witless bubble-brains.

It was slow work, moving about in a ship that had been turned through ninety degrees so that walls became floor and floor became a wall. The occasional super-wave thumped and pummeled hard enough to be worrying. Even so, he had done everything that could be done in less than an hour. Then it was a long, infuriating wait, with another worry: Night was approaching on Limbo. He could certainly spend thirteen hours of darkness on board the *Mood Indigo*, but he just as certainly didn't want to. He had not been able to coax an enhanced picture out of the battered imaging equipment—that sort of thing was one of the fat oaf Rombelle's few talents—but by staring out of a port until his eyes ached he believed that he could make out minute black dots moving near the two buildings on the shore. Sizes at such a distance were deceptive, but he guessed at something maybe a meter high. Midgets, if they were built like people. But the dots that he saw seemed much longer than they were tall.

Three more hours and it would be dark. He couldn't bear to wait any longer. The waves seemed smaller, and once he got close to the buildings on the shore they would surely present no danger. He clambered awkwardly into the lock. Operating it when everything was turned through ninety degrees was not easy, but finally he had it open and could look sideways and down at the water below.

Smaller they might be, but the waves still hit the hull of the *Mood Indigo* with frightening force and speed. He guessed the peak-to-trough distance as three meters. Much bigger than he'd thought when staring out of a ship's port. But that was only here, near the ship. Ahead, by the buildings on the shore, the waves damped down to one-third the size.

A darker cloud across the already hidden sun made up his mind. He must go now, or give up the idea until tomorrow. He waited for a calm patch between two waves, then dropped easily into the water.

Within a few seconds he realized his mistake. He had gauged the suit's internal pressure correctly, so that he bobbed comfortably in the water with his head and suit helmet clear. But he had misjudged his direction of travel. The waves tended to carry him forward, along the river valley and toward the buildings, but at the same time a strong crosscurrent wanted to take him sideways. He used the suit's thrustors to compensate, and found himself rotating helplessly in a complicated interaction of waves, current, and thrustors. He was still moving sideways, toward a place where head-high breakers met the shore among a jumble of boulders.

It would be a terrible place to land. Friday increased the force of the suit thrustors, only to discover that pushed him off balance and drove him face-first into the waves. He switched the thrustors off completely. As he came upright again, he felt his feet touch bottom. He immediately released air from his suit. As his buoyancy decreased, his footing became more firm. He should be able to walk parallel to the shore, until he reached the small breakers and calmer water near the buildings and jetty.

Confident again, he let out more air and turned to pick out the place where he would land. He was unlucky in his timing. While he was still searching for a preferred landing point, a great mother wave came sweeping in silently from behind. It picked him up effortlessly, turned him in midair, and crashed him headfirst down on the stony bottom. His helmet took the impact, as it was designed to do, but it left his head ringing. As he staggered to his feet again, a sister wave hit.

This one finished the job. Friday was lifted, carried forward, and deposited in a crack between two boulders. The wave retreated and left him there, breathless.

He was ashore—but still in danger. Another wave could soon be on its way. He forced himself to wriggle forward, grabbing at rocks and thinking of nothing but the next few inches of pebbles and stone. He kept going, forward and upward, for what felt like hours. Finally he saw that the boulder in front of his face was bone-dry.

He was safe.

He rolled over and lay on his back, staring up at the sky. The clouds were racing, but they seemed less thick and ominous. The storm was definitely coming to an end. If he had waited another few hours . . .

But if he had waited, although the sea would be

calmer it would also be dark, and he would not have tried to make it ashore. And here he was. He took a deep breath, sat up, and looked to his right. From his point of view his arrival on the beach had been filled with noise and violence; however, during a storm the whole shore must be such a chaos of wind and breaking waves that the arrival there of one human could pass unnoticed.

The beings over by the buildings had apparently seen nothing, and most of them had gone inside or about other business. A couple were still standing outside. He could see them more clearly now that blown spray no longer obscured the picture. They were multi-legged, with long, flat, bodies. They seemed to possess some kind of blue-black shell, but he was still too far away to tell which end was which, or if they had such things as eyes and ears.

Well, that would change soon enough. Friday struggled to his feet and checked that his backpack and the translation unit at his waist were in position and intact. The translator was in a case. The case was supposed to be waterproof, but you never knew when some crooked supplier would sell you another piece of junk. He turned the unit on, and heard the beep that indicated it was ready to go to work.

Maybe this time the damn thing would perform as advertised. Friday was going to have a few bruises after his rough landing, but he smiled to himself as he opened the front of his helmet and headed off along the pebbled beach. Maybe it was time for a little bit of luck.

He waved. Still the creatures over by the buildings did not notice him. Well, they would become aware of Friday Indigo soon enough.

First contact, here we come.

✧ ✧ ✧

There is no training manual, "Ten things to remember in first contact with an alien species." Even had there been one, Friday Indigo would not have opened the data file. You learned things by hiring other people to sort out what was important and tell you what you needed to know and when you needed to know it. In any case, there was no big mystery about first contact.

Friday was making no attempt to walk quietly, but the wind was blowing hard and the surf still ran high. He came within ten meters of the two aliens and still they had not noticed him.

He had been studying them as he approached. They were like nothing he had ever seen or heard of. That was good. The worst thing after all his efforts would be to learn that they were already members of the Stellar Group.

Not these babies, though. They were low-slung, with a long, horizontal body and what seemed like an inordinate number of jointed legs. He counted five pairs, each with a carrying pouch on its outer side. That total didn't include four at the front end terminating in pincers like lobster claws and surrounded by bristly projections capable of independent movement. The blue-black, hard-cased body was about a meter and a half long, so the creatures would be at least as tall as humans if they ever reared up onto their hind legs—which so far they showed no signs of doing. The two just seemed to be talking to each other, making chittering, clicking sounds and waving long stalky antennas.

One of those antennas finally turned in Friday's direction. There was probably an eye at the end of it, because he could see a dark-blue gleam there—and the alien in charge of that particular antenna at once changed its clattering to a high-pitched squeak.

Apparently the squeak meant something to the second alien, because they both swung round instantly to face Friday.

This was it, the big moment.

He raised his hand in a formal gesture. "Greetings, alien strangers. I, Friday Indigo, captain of the Terran ship *Mood Indigo*, and the representative of all Terrans and all species of the Stellar Group, seek your friendship and am delighted to make your acquaintance."

Of course, they would not understand him. That was too much to hope for. The translating machine had to listen to a bit of chat from both sides before it did anything useful. But his words would be recorded, and that was what counted. That was what went into the historical archives.

He lowered his hand and waited for their response.

It came in unison, and with astonishing speed. Two claws moved to two leg pouches, dipped in, and came out holding short black canes. The canes pointed at Friday. He heard sharp popping sounds like the bursting of small party balloons.

He didn't see anything, but suddenly he felt as though his brain had turned to boiling liquid and was fountaining out of the top of his head. That was impossible—he had opened the faceplate of his helmet, but surely the rest of it was still in position. He tried to reach up to check, but before he could get his hand past shoulder height he was falling backwards.

As he fell he decided that he had been wrong. The worst thing that could happen was not that the aliens would prove to be members of the Stellar Group. The worst thing that could happen to him was what was happening right now.

19

The *Hero's Return* Arrives on Limbo

Chan Dalton knew within half a second that something had gone wrong. Subjective time inside a Link transition—the only time that had meaning there—was the single dizzying moment when your head turned inside out. After that you were back in the real world. In this case the real world was supposed to be the gauzy starlit splendor of the Geyser Swirl; that's not what he was seeing. The forward observation chamber of the *Hero's Return* revealed a murky green gloom, and hovering within its depths sat a gigantic alien spaceship.

The alien ship moved, jerking forward. Chan's eyes refocused. Suddenly he was looking not at a distant behemoth but at a small fish-like creature, inches away from the transparent wall of the observation chamber. As Chan watched, the little animal darted away and disappeared.

Half a second in human terms was an eternity to the ship's computer. While Chan was still peering after the vanished fish, the audio outlet in the observation chamber sounded an alert and continued with a message: WARNING. ANOMALOUS ENVIRONMENT. CURRENTLY CHANGING SENSOR OBSERVATION SUITE, RECALIBRATING INSTRUMENTS, TAKING READINGS. THIS SHIP IS ON EMERGENCY STATUS.

In the pause that followed, Deb Bisson gripped Chan's hand harder than ever. "What's happening? Where are we?"

All her previous Link experience had been within the solar system. She didn't know just how unusual this one was. Chan tried to speak with a confidence that he didn't feel. "We completed the transition. I assume that we're somewhere in the Geyser Swirl. But we're in a gravity field when we expected to be in free fall, and we're under water when we thought we would emerge into open space. We won't know more than that until the computer has taken and interpreted sensor readings."

He was still staring outside. There was no light inside the observation chamber itself, but light shining out from other ports of the *Hero's Return* illuminated the cloudy water for a few meters. The outside view was a uniform green, broken now and then by faint glints of silver.

Apparently the ship's sensors had the same problem as Chan at visible wavelengths. A calm voice said, SWITCHING TO ULTRASONICS AND ULTRA-LONG FREQUENCY ELECTROMAGNETIC RADIATION AS PRIMARY SENSING MODES. PERFORMING PHYSICAL AND CHEMICAL ANALYSIS OF SHIP STATUS AND OF IMMEDIATE ENVIRONMENT.

And then, after a pause too brief for any human analysis, THE FOLLOWING STATUS REPORT IS RANKED ACCORDING TO PERCEIVED HUMAN SURVIVAL PRIORITIES.

ITEM ONE: THE SHIP'S HULL REMAINS INTACT, ALL INTERIOR SYSTEMS ARE OPERATING NORMALLY, AND THERE IS NO IMMEDIATE DANGER TO PERSONNEL OR EQUIPMENT.

ITEM TWO: THE SHIP'S EXTERNAL ENVIRONMENT IS RADICALLY DIFFERENT FROM PRE-TRANSITION ESTIMATES. THIS MAY LEAD TO LONG-TERM PROBLEMS.

ITEM THREE: THE SHIP FLOATS IN A CLEAR LIQUID OF DENSITY 1.156. THE LIQUID'S REFRACTIVE INDEX, DENSITY, CONDUCTIVITY, AND GROSS CHEMICAL PROPERTIES ARE CONSISTENT WITH THOSE OF DEUTERIUM OXIDE CONTAINING A SMALL FRACTION OF MINERAL SOLVENTS.

ITEM FOUR: THE SHIP SITS IN A GRAVITATIONAL FIELD OF 0.154 GEES. THIS IS TOO SMALL TO BE CONSISTENT WITH THE VALUE OF SURFACE GRAVITY ON ANY KNOWN HABITABLE PLANET POSSESSING A LIQUID WATER SEA. ALSO, THE PLANETARY RADIUS AS INFERRED FROM LOCAL HORIZON SENSING IS TOO LARGE TO BE CONSISTENT WITH THE OBSERVED SURFACE GRAVITY. NO EXPLANATIONS ARE AVAILABLE FOR THESE ANOMALIES.

ITEM FIVE: THE SHIP'S ESTIMATED DEPTH BELOW THE WATER SURFACE IS 161 METERS. THE ESTIMATED WATER DEPTH BELOW THE SHIP IS 1.52 KILOMETERS. THE CURRENT RATE OF DESCENT IS 1.1 METERS A SECOND. *WARNING*. IF THE PRESENT RATE OF DESCENT WERE TO BE MAINTAINED, HULL STRESSES WOULD EXCEED TOLERABLE LEVELS IN 13.8 MINUTES. AUTOMATIC REMEDIAL ACTION WILL BE TAKEN IN 9.4 MINUTES UNLESS HUMAN OVERRIDE COMMANDS ARE PROVIDED.

"Remedial action?" Deb glanced at Chan.

"I don't know. But the computer knows what it's doing. It will keep us safe unless we tell it not to." He stood up. "We're getting just the summary over the address system. If we really want to know what's going on we have to be in the control room. Come on, let's go."

Progress through the interior of the *Hero's Return* was slow. Walkways and handholds had been designed for free fall or for uniform fore-to-aft acceleration. In its slow watery descent the ship was canted far away from the vertical. That tilt seemed to affect Deb Bisson very little. She floated from chamber to chamber without effort and with no wall contact other than an occasional foot or hand. Chan, lacking the balance and sense of body position that made Deb unbeatable in single combat, floundered along behind.

The ship's computer continued to offer its summary from every audio outlet. ITEM SIX: THE SHIP'S OVERALL LOCATION WITH RESPECT TO KNOWN MARKER STARS IS UNKNOWN. THE ANALYSIS OF AMBIENT SUNLIGHT SUGGESTS A NATURAL STELLAR ORIGIN, BUT THE RECONSTRUCTED STELLAR SPECTRUM MATCHES NO KNOWN STAR AND NO POSSIBLE STAR TYPE. THIS DISCREPANCY HAS NO EXPLANATION.

No possible *star type*, Chan thought, struggling vainly to catch up with Deb. *Not just lost,* way *lost. We're near a star of a type that can't exist.*

She had turned in midair and was resting with her back against a bulkhead. "What does it mean?" She was not even out of breath. "I thought this ship's computer knew everything. How can we be near a star with no stellar type?"

"I don't know." Chan was eager to reach the control room, but he could use the breather. "The Geyser Swirl is one big mess of stars and dust and gas. Maybe we're close to a star whose light is being filtered through the rest of it."

"But shouldn't the computer know that, too?"

It should. Chan shrugged. They started out again as the steady voice came once more over the audio system: ITEM SEVEN: ULF RETURNS INDICATE THE PRESENCE OF THREE OTHER SHIPS WITHIN TEN KILOMETERS OF OUR PRESENT LOCATION. EACH ONE HAS PROVIDED AN ID RESPONSE TO OUR CODED SIGNAL. THE SHIPS ARE:

ONE, THE *FINDER*, WITH A REPORTED CREW OF ONE PIPE-RILLA AND AN UNSTATED NUMBER OF TINKER COMPONENTS. *CAMERON'S DREAM* WAS ITS LAST PORT OF CALL, IT ENTERED THE FOMALHAUT FOUR LINK BOUND FOR THE GEYSER SWIRL LINK ON 79/03/07 STANDARD DATE, AND IT HAS NOT BEEN HEARD FROM SINCE. ITS SLANT RANGE DISTANCE FROM OUR CURRENT POSITION IS THREE KILOMETERS, AZIMUTH IS 81 DEGREES, AND IT SITS STATIONARY ON THE SEABED AT A DEPTH OF 110 METERS.

TWO, THE *MINISTER OF GRACE*, WITH A REPORTED CREW OF ONE OR MORE ANGELS OF SELLORA. *AMBROSIA* WAS ITS LAST PORT OF CALL, IT ENTERED THE SKYRILLAN LINK BOUND FOR THE GEYSER SWIRL LINK ON 79/05/11 STANDARD DATE AND HAS NOT BEEN HEARD FROM SINCE. ITS SLANT RANGE DISTANCE FROM OUR CURRENT POSITION IS EIGHT KILOMETERS, AZIMUTH IS 151 DEGREES, AND IT SITS STATIONARY ON THE SEABED AT A DEPTH OF 52 METERS.

THREE, THE *MOOD INDIGO*, WITH A REPORTED CREW OF THREE HUMANS. THIS SHIP WAS LAST OBSERVED IN THE VICINITY OF THE VULCAN NEXUS ON OR ABOUT 79/08/02. THIS SHIP IS IN MOTION, AND ITS SLANT RANGE DISTANCE FROM OUR CURRENT POSITION IS SEVEN KILOMETERS, AZIMUTH 37 DEGREES. THIS SHIP'S CURRENT DEPTH IS 29 METERS.

"Nothing about the *Mood Indigo* being sent here." Chan and Deb had reached the control room, but he paused on the threshold. "I wonder what idiot decided that the first expedition was so secret that the next ship going in couldn't be told. The *Hero's Return* computer is no different from the rest of us—it only knows what's fed to it. What else didn't they bother to mention?"

The control room of the *Hero's Return* was in keeping with the ship's size. In its heyday three dozen officers had occupied the banks of communications and fire control consoles. Now the weapons had been removed, but the array of desks remained. Just three of them were occupied. Tully O'Toole sat over in one corner, staring at the lanky figure of Elke Siry. Next to him the physicist was curled up in a too-small seat like a praying mantis, ignoring everything except a quartet of data displays in front of her. A lock of blond hair hung over her forehead and she was gnawing at her lower lip.

Dag Korin sat in front of the main control console, his head slumped forward on his chest. He had one gnarled forefinger poised over the button that opened the circuit for oral commands to the ship's computer.

"Hey, Dalton!" He had seen Deb and Chan at the threshold. "Got a question for you. Your team is supposed to come up with bright ideas once we're in the Geyser Swirl, but I'm damned if I know whether we're there or some place else. Anyhow, I figure you should have a say in this. Did you hear what the computer said about remedial action to stop us sinking?"

"I heard it." Chan came across to Korin, Deb Bisson following. "But I don't know what the computer is proposing to do."

"That display shows the plan." The General nodded to one of the screens. "Reduce the ship's mass so the average density of the ship becomes lower than the water density, and we start ascending. I like that—I just don't like the way the computer's proposing to lower the density. See the listing? A lot of our mass is in the external defensive shields. Every one of them would have to be dumped into the sea. Even with that it's touch and go, but without the shields I'll feel as naked as a soft-shell crab. Anyone who feels like taking a potshot at us can blow the *Hero's Return* to pieces."

"All the ships that the computer has located are Stellar Group members."

"I know. And isn't that bad news? You know the Angels, it will be more of their 'Violence is never the only alternative' line of bullshit."

"But we know they won't shoot at us."

"So what? I learned a long time ago that it's a bad habit to waste effort counting your friends. It's your enemies you need to look out for. We don't know who might be just over the horizon. Anyway, what do you think? Let the computer do what it wants and dump the shields, or override it?"

"What are our other options?"

"None that I can see." Korin nodded his head toward Elke Siry. "Unless our resident genius over there can suggest a different answer. She looks like she's got her teeth into something."

Chan could see it, too. Elke Siry's face glowed with excitement. She was spitting out oral commands to the terminal in front of her, while at the same time hammering out with her hands a series of requests and instructions to the ship's computer.

"Elke!" Dag Korin called across to her. "You have all the status reports. Do you see any alternative to allowing the ship's external shields to be released?"

Elke Siry raised her head. The show of teeth was not a smile but a vicious snarl. "You expect me to worry about shields, when I have *this* to analyze?" She waved a thin hand to take in the displays. "Don't you realize what we have here? Do what you like with the damned shields, it's of no interest to me—and stop interrupting my work."

The General glared. He said loudly to Chan, "You'd never know I was her legal guardian for five years, would you? But it's pointless trying to talk to her when she has that look on her face." He placed a finger on the button in front of him.

"You were the one who insisted on bringing her," Chan said.

"Because she is a genius. Every army and every navy needs one—and no more than one. Most generals and admirals think it's them, but usually it isn't. We'll find out what Elke's so excited about when she's finished her analysis." Korin finally pressed the button. "Computer, d'you hear me? This is Dag Korin speaking."

AUTHORITY RECOGNIZED.

"Good. And don't play the idiot with me this time. Go ahead, dump the shields and take us up to the surface."

OBJECTION TO THE LATTER COMMAND. THE SONAR REPORTS A ROUGH SEA STATE WITH SURFACE WAVES OF TWENTY METERS AND MORE.

"You mean after all that hassle we can't go up?"

WE SHOULD NOT GO ALL THE WAY TO THE SURFACE. WHILE THE ATMOSPHERIC DISTURBANCES REMAIN AT SUCH A HIGH LEVEL, THE SAFEST PLACE FOR THE SHIP IS THIRTY OR MORE METERS BELOW THE SURFACE. THE OFFSHORE SHELF SHOULD BE SAFE. THAT IS WHERE TWO OF THE OTHER STELLAR GROUP SHIPS ARE ALREADY WAITING OUT THE STORM. IT IS ASSUMED THAT YOU WILL WISH TO ESTABLISH CONTACT WITH THEM.

"Two ships? You said three. What about the other one?"

THE *MOOD INDIGO* IS PROCEEDING TOWARD A LAND MASS NINE KILOMETERS DISTANT FROM US. SUCH AN ACTION IS NOT RECOMMENDED FOR THIS SHIP FOR TWO REASONS. FIRST, THE *HERO'S RETURN* IS MUCH LARGER THAN THE *MOOD INDIGO*, AND OUR GREATER DRAFT MEANS THAT WE

CANNOT GO WHERE A SMALLER SHIP IS ABLE TO PROCEED. SECOND, THE COURSE FOLLOWED BY THE *MOOD INDIGO* PRESENTS SUBSTANTIAL RISK. OUR BEST MODEL ESTIMATES THE PROBABILITY OF THAT SHIP'S DESTRUCTION BY NATURAL FORCES AT THE LAND-SEA INTERFACE AS NO LESS THAN 0.40. WE HAVE BEEN TRYING TO COMMUNICATE THIS CONCLUSION TO THEM, SO FAR WITHOUT SUCCESS.

"All right, all right. I didn't ask for a lecture." Dag Korin raised bushy eyebrows at Chan. "Chatty devil, this one—always has been. So what do you think? Land on the off-shore shelf?"

"If we can. But how do we maneuver to get us there? We can't use our drive under water."

"We weren't told that was a problem, so I assume know-it-all has it figured out." Korin again pressed the button to transmit an oral command. "Computer? Go ahead, dump the goddamn shields."

THAT ACTION HAS ALREADY BEEN INITIATED FOLLOWING YOUR EARLIER APPROVAL.

"Then take us to where the Stellar Group ships are sitting out the storm. Put us down near one of them—not the Angel ship, though. I can't stand the sight of those bloody upstart artichokes."

THE WATER IS TOO SHALLOW FOR THIS SHIP AT THE LOCATION OF THE PIPE-RILLA VESSEL. WE CANNOT APPROACH CLOSER THAN NINE HUNDRED METERS TO THE SHORE. HOWEVER, BEING IN WATER ALSO HAS ADVANTAGES SINCE THE SHIP IS PROTECTED FROM WAVE ACTION. WHEN THE STORM SUBSIDES YOU MAY BE ABLE TO LAUNCH A TWO-PERSON AIR-BREATHING PINNACE FROM OUR UPPER LEVEL. WARNING: THE EXTENT OF POSSIBLE DAMAGE TO THE PINNACE IS UNKNOWN AT THIS TIME.

"Fine. Go ahead and set us down in the best place you can find. I want to launch a couple of unmanned orbiters, too, as soon as possible." The General turned back to Chan. "That computer talks too much, but in this case it has the right idea. Always keep your head down until you know the situation. Even if we had weapons and our shields in place we'd still be vulnerable. We're like a shark on land or a tiger under water—misplaced. Staying alive is about the best we can do. I need an airborne overview."

Chan nodded. "If the pinnace hasn't been too damaged we'll have plenty of volunteers to fly it as soon as the storm lets up. Who do you think, Deb?"

They had hardly spoken during the hours while they waited for the Link transition, but in those hours their relationship had changed. It seemed natural now to ask her for advice and assistance.

She thought for a few moments. "Chrissie and Tarbush? They've been working together for years, and they're the best observers we have."

"That was my thought, too. We should find them aft. All right, General?"

"Hell, they're your people, Dalton. Do what you need to do. I've got my hands full trying to make sense of this garbage. Computer, what sort of a halfassed picture do you call *that*?" Korin gestured at the main screen, which showed a bizarre undersea terrain etched in black and silver.

WHAT YOU ARE SEEING IS AN IMAGE CONSTRUCTED USING THE ULTRASOUND RETURN SIGNAL. THERE IS NO WAY TO GENERATE TRUE COLOR FROM SINGLE-FREQUENCY SOUND DATA. WOULD YOU LIKE FALSE COLOR TO BE ASSIGNED ON THE BASIS OF IMAGE LOCAL TEXTURE MEASURES?

"How the devil do I know, until I've seen it? Give me another minute to look at this one."

As Deb and Chan left the room, the view on the big screen began to change. The ship was beginning a slow rotation, heading east and then north toward the coastal shelf. Like a great crippled whale, the *Hero's Return* sought a haven on the seabed.

Chan took a final look back. Dag Korin was scowling again, hunched over his console and arguing with the ship's computer. Tully O'Toole stared open-mouthed at Elke Siry, in open admiration.

And Elke?

She alone of the people in the room—probably of all the people on the *Hero's Return*—seemed *happy*, her attention fixed on the torrent of data flowing across the screens. Her expression remained one of blissful exaltation.

Chan had been exactly right in his assessment of the ship's computer. It controlled almost every aspect of the *Hero's Return* operations, and it could do almost anything—except knowingly risk the lives of humans.

The shedding of the massive defensive shields was slow and systematic, accompanied at every step by calculations of the ship's new density distribution, center of mass, and barycenter. The curve toward shallower water was gentle, an arc many kilometers across, imposing minimal stresses on the ship's structure and auxiliary thrustors. Storm conditions at the surface were evaluated constantly, together with more analyses of the blue sun that now appeared occasionally through breaks in the cloud cover.

The humans on board knew nothing about any of this, nor did they need to. Life support and life protection involves a million functions, most of them as essential, automatic and unnoticed as the flow of blood through a crew member's arteries and veins.

The computer was also able to obtain readings from the air-breathing pinnace fixed to the outer hull. The little craft, as feared, had been fatally damaged in shedding the defensive shields, and would no longer fly. The computer began its countdown for the other requested action. Two unmanned orbiters were to be launched from the depths. Their mission: to monitor the surface and sky of the planet and return their findings to the ship. The General had placed no restriction on the timing of the action, except to say it should be done as soon as the storm eased sufficiently. He knew that the computer was better able than any human on board to decide appropriate values for "sufficiently."

Three hours later, the *Hero's Return* sprawled its cumbersome mass along the seabed, a little less than six hundred meters away from the *Finder*. The storm still raged, but on the seabed all was peaceful. Darkness was approaching, above and in the depths. The computer again checked the status of all onboard systems, then it switched to rest-period protocols.

The recreation center on the *Hero's Return* had been designed on a large scale. Three hundred crew members could play there, with robot opponents if no humans were available, at everything from chess to table tennis to sumo wrestling.

The group around Chan Dalton had tucked itself away into one dimly lit corner. Business was over. The situation on the ship had been reviewed and reviewed again. Only one thing seemed clear: weather permitting, Chrissie Winger and Tarbush Hanson—to their delight and Danny Casement's mild irritation—would take an air-breathing pinnace up and out at first light.

Danny's half-hearted "I didn't come all this way just to sit around" had been countered by Deb Bisson's "All which way? We don't know where we are yet—and we won't, until someone can take a look at the star patterns."

"It's only a two-person craft, Danny," Chrissie added. "Don't worry, there'll be plenty of work for everyone once we get out of this steel can. We have a whole planet to explore. When we started out we didn't know if humans could live anyplace in the Geyser Swirl."

"The pinnace could hold three. They often do."

Danny was standing up. Chrissie went across to him, looped one arm in his and the other in Tarbush Hanson's, and led them toward the door. "Say it all again, Danny. Maybe you can talk the Tarb and me into your coming with us."

When they were outside the recreation hall Danny Casement stopped and stared at Chrissie with suspicion. "Why do you want to talk out here? Chan and Deb need to hear anything we agree to. Do you really mean there's a chance I can convince you?"

"Not in a million years. Sorry, Danny, but it will be just the Tarb and me in the pinnace." Chrissie took his hand in hers. "You're a big success with women, I know that. But sometimes I wonder how, because you can be as dense as Pipe-Rilla shielding."

"I don't understand."

"I know you don't. Don't feel too bad, though, because Tarb is no better." Chrissie nodded her head toward the closed door of the recreation hall. "Back there, couldn't you tell that Chan and Deb were just itching for us to leave? Couldn't you see that things have changed between them?"

"She wasn't trying to kill him, if that's what you mean. But look, we had to discuss where we are and what comes next."

"We finished with all that half an hour ago. Those two want to talk—but not about here and now. And not with us."

Danny Casement and Tarbush Hanson stared at each other. Tarbush, who had said not a word for the past three hours, slowly nodded and spoke. "I think she's right, man. They got serious catching up to do. Twenty years of it."

Danny walked across the room to one of the observation ports that studded the side of the *Hero's Return*. He stared out. The sea lacked the abyssal black of ocean depths, and an eye adjusted to the darkness could make out an occasional glint of phosphorescence.

"Twenty years," he said at last. "I guess it really has been that long. It is going to take a while."

Somewhere above them, far along the ship's side, a glare of orange fire threw the sea and the seabed into sharp relief. The three at the port saw startled sea-creatures darting away and felt the plates of the *Hero's Return* shudder beneath their feet. They heard a roar like a wounded sea-monster. In seconds the fiery light came from above, rapidly dimming. Within half a minute the darkness returned.

"Rocket launch," Danny said into a new and uneasy silence. "One of the orbitals is on the way. It must be getting calmer up on the surface." He turned away from the port. "You're right, Tarb, catching up is going to take a while. Let's hope they—and we—live long enough to see it happen."

20

Meet the Malacostracans

Friday Indigo could not move a muscle.

Not even eye muscles. He was lying on his left side on some kind of iron-hard table, low and sloping, and he could see only in one direction. Out-of-focus black objects moved jerkily in front of him against a dull gray background. He could not gauge their size, but the fuzzy outlines had the shape of the creatures who had gunned him down on the shore.

Gunned him down; paralyzed him; but not taken away the capacity to feel pain. He *hurt*. His head ached, a knife blade was in his left knee, and the side that he was lying on sent jolts of agony up and down his body each time he took a breath.

At least he *could* breathe. How was that possible, when no amount of effort would move arms, legs, and head a millimeter?

He could also hear. The clicking and chattering was

still going on, louder than before and with new sounds added to it. Suddenly he realized that the extra noises were coming from the translation unit attached to his own belt.

He concentrated on that. It was gibberish, hoots and whistles and obscene gurgles. But then the occasional word started to emerge. "*Water.* Bubble, burble, splutter, click. *Air.*" A sequence of fizzing sounds, like gas escaping from a bottle. "*Live—a-live—alive—alive.*" And then, after a suite of musical buzzes from the unit, "*Mala-costra-cans.*"

The translator was a piece of junk, just like the other one. If ever he got back to the solar system he was going to sauté the liver of the crooked swine who had sold it to him.

The unit babbled on. He had to stop listening, because suddenly his tongue and throat had a column of fire ants walking up and down on them.

He coughed, swallowed, and almost fainted with pain. A voice from the translation unit said, "*Malacostracans.*" Then, "*Air—breath. Wake. It live.*"

"You rotten bastards." He could speak! But what he had said wouldn't do him much good, even if the translator did work. "Greetings, alien strangers." Every word was agony. Keep it short. "I—Friday Indigo—captain of the *Mood Indigo*—come in friendship."

The muscles that controlled the lenses of his eyes were coming back to life. His eyeballs were on fire, but he could focus. He counted half a dozen creatures over by the wall. There was some variation in size, but the basic body plan was constant: a broad, blue-black carapace, held close to horizontal; ten supporting legs, each one with a pouch attached to its upper end; at what he assumed was the front, two pairs of formidable front claws surrounded by mobile bristles like thin fingers; stalked eyes positioned high on the body, above a trio of fringed slits. "Ugly" didn't even begin to describe them.

The translator hummed and said, *It live. It wake.*

Were they deaf, or just plain stupid? "Did you hear me? My name is Friday Indigo, and I am the owner and captain of the space-going yacht, *Mood Indigo*. I come to you in friendship."

"*Fridayindigo. Fridayindigo. It live. S-s-speak. Us—*" a pause and a fart-like groan from the translator "*—us Malacostracans.*"

What was it with the "malacostracans" bit? That was the third time the machine had said the same nonsense word.

Maybe the key to getting something sensible was to talk more, and to make the Indigoans talk back. "Hello. My name is Friday Indigo, and I have come here from another star system. I am the captain of a starship, the *Mood Indigo*. I am the representative of all humans, and of all other intelligent species who are members of the Stellar Group. I am a new arrival to your world, and I would like to compare your civilization with ours."

While Friday spoke he was taking a first hard look at his surroundings. Perhaps "civilization" was the wrong word. By any standards, the place he had been brought to was a dump.

He was lying on the sloping table with his head slightly lower than his feet, at the upper end of a chamber that was also sloping. Maybe twenty meters long and half that across, it was lit by cylindrical wall lamps of a sickly yellow-green. It was, in fact, not so much a room as a pool or tank. The creatures nearest to Friday stood in water only a few inches deep, but down at the far end he saw four more of them, all half-submerged and sloshing around. With its hundred-percent humidity, deadly chill, dank walls and ceiling of muddy gray, this wasn't a place where anyone in his right mind would stay for more than a minute.

Friday lifted his head, realizing as he did so that part of his discomfort came from the fact that he was still in his suit with his cheek resting on the hard edge of the open helmet. He worked his jaw from side to side and said, "Is the translator getting anything I've said across to you? It's doing a lousy job sending stuff this way—all I've received so far is about five words. Can you hear me? Do you understand me?"

The translator was certainly doing *something*. As Friday spoke, it produced a simultaneous string of stuttering clicks and squawks. Two of the Indigoans splashed their way closer to the table and leaned over it with waving eyestalks. Their interest seemed to be not in Friday, but in the translator unit at his waist.

"Hell-o!" He lifted his right arm and waved feebly. "You down there. I'm up here—that's just a machine that you're staring at. Can you hear me? Can you understand me?"

One of the creatures slowly turned to face him. The topmost of the three fringed slits began to move.

"*It speak. This the it speak?*"

"If you mean, am I the one who's talking to you and being translated by the machine there, then yes. I am the *it* who's speaking."

"*It breath air. It live air.*"

"That's quite right. I live in air, and I breathe air. I am"— was it worth the effort? Well, try it one more time—"I am Friday Indigo. I am a human, and so far as I know this is the first contact between your people and mine. This is a very significant meeting. Is there any chance that we could go someplace else if we're going to keep talking? This underwater dungeon gives me the willies."

"We you same. Live air, live water. Hu-mans you. Malacostracans we."

"Oh. I get it. Malacostracans. It's your *name*—what you call yourselves. It's the strangest name I ever heard, I must say, but I'll blame that on the translation unit." Friday tapped his chest with one gloved hand. "I'm Friday Indigo. I'm going to call you *Indigoans*, for our records. The name of our whole species is *humans*. My own *personal* name is Friday Indigo. What's yours?"

Apparently that was too much, either for the Malacostracan or the translator. Friday heard only a sullen hum.

"All right, let's leave it for later." He sat up and swung his legs over onto the floor. That produced violent pins and needles from his hips to his toes. He had to sit quiet for a while, cursing horribly and wondering if that too was being translated. He felt for his backpack of supplies, and was relieved to find it there and untouched. If he didn't feel better in a minute he'd take a painkiller. No point in suffering any more.

"*We you go.*" The Malacostracan waved a vicious-looking pincer in Friday's face. "*We you see one big one we.*"

"I think I get that. You're just gofers of some kind, so now I'm awake you'll take me to your leader, right? Fine with me. That's the way it should be, because I'm the leader for the humans and I don't want to talk to underlings. Uh-oh. Wait a minute. If you're going out *that* way, I may need to close my suit."

The creature had turned away and was scuttling down the incline toward deeper water. When it realized that Friday was not following it paused. The eyestalks reared up over the carapace to stare back at him as he closed the visor of his helmet.

The translation unit said, *"Take shell off, put shell on? Not we."*

"You're dealing with humans now, my friend. There's lots of things that we can do and others can't."

That was the way to do it, give the aliens an idea of human superiority right at the beginning. But the Indigoan merely waited until Friday was finished, then led the way into deeper water. When it came to a point where the bottom of its carapace was level with the surface, the creature ducked forward and submerged. That confirmed Friday's idea that the Indigoans were equally at home on land or in the sea. But where had they evolved? The bubble men hadn't mentioned them.

There would be plenty of time for answers to questions like that. First, the translation unit must finish its learning process.

Friday followed the Indigoan into a narrow tunnel with a semicircular arched ceiling. It was a tight squeeze, but by crouching slightly he could keep his head in the two-foot gap between the surface of the water and the low roof. The lights were all in the main chamber, and he plowed on through increasing gloom. The tunnel was so narrow that there was no possibility of mistaking the way.

He heard a sound ahead, a faint moaning cry that grew steadily louder. The unit at his waist made no attempt at translation. At the same time the water level went down. He walked a rising incline that led up into deeper darkness. Friday raised his arm above his head, and found that he could no longer touch the ceiling. Also—he spread his arms wide—he could not reach the sides of the corridor. The wailing had become louder and more unearthly. A strong, gusty wind pushed against his chest.

Confused and unable to see, he paused with water

up to his knees. After a few seconds, a light appeared ahead of him. The creature that led the way was holding an oblong lantern high in one of its fore-pincers, while the stalked eyes stared back to make sure that Friday was still there.

"It's all right." He waved at it. "I'm with you. You can keep going."

"We go. You follow."

Friday wondered if the translation unit couldn't work while the Indigoan was under water. A moment later he had other things on his mind. He had a sudden suspicion that they were not inside a room any more, but moving out onto exposed land surface. That wailing sound was from the same wind that pushed at his suited figure. As they came completely out of the water he could feel it swirling about his body. It was the tail end of the storm, raking the night surface of Limbo. From somewhere behind he heard another sound, the distant roar of surf on the shore-line.

He wondered how far they had carried him. How long had he been unconscious? How long until dawn? And had the *Mood Indigo* survived its battering by wind and water?

Well, for every question he had, they must have one about him. The trick was to make sure you got more information than you gave.

He was still walking, and now there seemed rather more light than the lamp provided. He stopped, leaned back his head, and stared straight up.

The heavy overcast of the storm had gone, to leave a cloudless night. He opened his visor for the clearest possible view, aware that he would be the first human ever to observe the night sky of Limbo.

The pre-mission briefings he had received before leaving the solar system had been sketchy, but they had told him pretty much what to expect. The Geyser Swirl was a compact mass of dust and gas in which stars lay strewn at random. The thick dust would scatter starlight, producing a sky in which an overall glow like an aurora was broken by the veils and dark bands of denser absorbing dust.

Well, so much for what he had been told. He might have guessed it, the briefers were like all briefers: screwed up. The sky here was no gauzy, aurora-like veil. The heavens were filled with glowing globes, many of them so faint that you had to look slightly away to see them at all. They were of different sizes, from faint sky-pearls to swollen balls seemingly close enough to reach out and touch. Even the brighter ones were too dim to possess definite colors, but he imagined that he saw a hint of green in one to the left, a touch of pink in the globe next to it. The sky was *full*, more globes than dark regions between them.

Friday heard the clicking of claws and brought his gaze back to ground level. The Indigoan was moving on ahead, up a rocky incline that threw back points of glitter in the light of the lamp. The creature was finding it hard going, scrabbling its way forward and up. Friday bent low and saw a surface so smooth and bare that it seemed to have been scraped clean. What was it Rombelle had said? That there was no life on the surface of the planet. Well, the idiot had been wrong about animal life, but he seemed to be right about the plants. There was no sign of them. What did the Indigoans eat? From the look of them they were more at home in water than on land. Maybe they found their nourishment in the sea. Apparently they thought he was like them, amphibious, if that "we you same, live air, live water" had been translated correctly by the unit.

The lamp lit a circle only four or five meters across, and the star-globe light was too faint to provide illumination. Everything on the ground beyond the lamp's circle apparently didn't exist. Friday had no choice but to trudge on after the Indigoan and hope the other knew where it was going. The pain of returning circulation was less in his legs, but they felt wobbly and with the continuing uphill walk his lungs were aching.

"How much farther?" he said at last. "I've got to stop and take a rest if it's going to be much farther. It's easy for you, you're not the one who got shot and knocked unconscious and just woke up."

That used up what little breath he had left. He paused and panted. He couldn't tell if the Indigoan had understood what came out of the translator, but it too halted and turned. In the lamplight, the creature with its cruel pincers, stalk eyes, and multiple mouth slots seemed like a gigantic and deformed crab.

The eyestalks waved. "*Soon top, top flat like water flat, place you we end.*"

That wasn't exactly a model of clarity. "You mean, when we get to the top of this rise, we come to a place that's flat in the same way that the surface of water is flat? And when we get to it, we'll be where we want to be?"

"*We think you speak back we say. Top flat like water flat, place for you and we.*"

The trouble with the translator was that it had to work both ways to be of any use. He didn't know if the Indigoan's speech had been garbled, and he also didn't know if what he had said in reply was just as garbled in translation. If it was, then no matter what the Indigoan replied he couldn't be sure of the meaning.

He nodded and took a couple of paces up the hill.

"All right. I've had my break, and with any luck I'll find out soon enough where we're heading. And if we don't get there soon, I'll have to take another rest. My legs don't feel right. I'll need a drink too." The creature said nothing. Friday groaned. "All right, then, let's go."

Actually, he had another piece of evidence that despite all the uncertainties the two of them were somehow communicating. With the light of the Indigoan's lamp no longer in his eyes, some way ahead he could sense more than see a horizontal line, a boundary curve separating black rock from a slightly paler region above. It was too bright to be star-sphere light. Rather, it was just how you would expect things to look if the area beyond the crest of the hill was lit by more of the yellow-green lamps.

The Indigoan overtook him with a frenzied clatter of claws on smooth rock and led the way up the final slope. Quite sharply, that incline ended on a broad shelf so flat and uniform that it did not appear natural. Friday stopped again, but this time it was not because of shortage of breath.

What lay ahead had all the markers of a military camp. Maybe thirty meters in front of him stood a tall metal lattice at least three meters high. Bright lamps placed every twenty meters along the top of it threw blue-white searchlights onto the ground inside and out, and the lattice fence ran all the way around a rectangular area maybe two hundred meters long and eighty wide. More significant still, an Indigoan was stationed like a sentry guard at the only two places where Friday could see anything like a gate. It made him wonder, what was being protected, and who was it being protected from?

Inside the guarded enclosure he counted six buildings. From the outside each one was identical, a twenty-meter cylinder cut in two along its axis and placed flat side down on the ground. The buildings were windowless and featureless, and they shone a uniform dull yellow in the light of the lamps. Every one had a new and unfinished appearance, fitting with the idea that this was more like a temporary camp than a place for permanent living.

Beyond the buildings lay a narrow airstrip. Evidence that it *was* an airstrip came from the sight of two tri-lobed winged vehicles, one sitting at each end. Friday saw them and thought, jackpot! Not just civilization, but *technological* civilization. Weapons and lamps suggested it, but aircraft like those were a final proof. He had never seen anything remotely like them. With those peculiar shapes it seemed improbable that they could ever leave the ground, but apparently they did. Alien technology was *different*. Alien technology could be the key to unimaginable personal wealth and power.

He was so excited by the thought that he reached an entry point to the compound before he noticed that the sentry guard held a black cane in one pincer, exactly like the one that had knocked him out on the shore. He stopped in his tracks. Suddenly it felt less like first contact, more like he was being taken prisoner.

"*You go. We not go. You talk, she talk.*" The Indigoan who had brought him held a weapon in its pincer, too. Had the creature been holding it ever since they left the watery chamber? It was waving it now, urging him forward.

"I'm willing to talk, more than willing. But who will I be talking to? Does your leader have a name?"

"*You go. You talk, and*"—there was a pause, while the translation unit buzzed to itself—"*you listen big little one—leader?—talk. You go.*"

Clear as mud. But the black cane was pointing at his head, and if Friday recalled little after it was used before, he did have the strong and unpleasant memory of his brain seeming to spout gray matter out from the top of his head. It was not an experience that he wished to repeat.

He allowed himself to be led through the gate and on into the compound. The sentry remained at his post, but at a high-pitched squeak from his companion, that the unit translated mysteriously as "*Call high servers*," three more Indigoans came scuttling out of one of the buildings. At the sight of Friday, a chorus of clucks and chirps came all at once. The unit at his belt was confused or overloaded. It produced only a squawk of its own. More weapons came out of side pouches.

Think of it as an honor guard. And don't do or say anything that might annoy or be misinterpreted. They lined up, two on either side of him, and Friday walked cautiously forward. Maybe he didn't want these brutish creatures named for him after all. If they preferred to be called Malacostracans, which was what the translator kept offering, he wouldn't argue.

They led him to a low arched doorway in the flat semi-circular end of one of the buildings, lined up outside, and urged him through with gestures of the black canes.

He said to the Indigoan who had brought him from the shore, "What about you? Won't you be coming in, too, to help translate? We're beginning to understand each other."

The Indigoan pointed with the black cane toward the doorway. The translator said, "*To the big little, go. You, one, in. We stay.*"

"Will the big little"—my God, they had him doing it now—"I hope that your leader sounds exactly the same as you do. Otherwise, the translator will have a hell of a time and may have to start from scratch."

"You to the big little. Go now. Talk, listen."

The black cane waved ominously, suggesting no room for discussion.

"All right, I'm going. See? I'm on my way."

Friday walked forward, down an unlighted ramp and away from the bright beams of the searchlights. At once he found himself splashing along in a foot of water. He paused to close the visor of his suit—for all he knew his next step would drop him in over his head—and realized as he did so that this building was even worse than the one where he had awakened. It not only had standing water, it had no lights at all.

He stepped gingerly forward, stumbled on a down step, and almost fell.

He stood still. "This is ridiculous. I know you gooks understand about lights, so why the hell don't you use them? It's black as a witch's ass in here."

He was talking to himself, and he certainly didn't expect an answer. But the room lightened as orange-red tubes lit up all along the side walls. Trills and chirps came from in front of him, and the translator said, *"Light is provided. Say what is enough."*

"That's fine." Friday glanced at the bright lighting on the walls and at the structures like huge easels that stood beneath them, but most of his attention was focused on the small table a few meters in front of him. It was low, no more than knee-high, only a third the size of the one on which he had awakened. That seemed appropriate, because the Indigoan who sprawled on top of it was also a miniature version of the ones outside. He realized that the table, like the one in the chamber near the shore, was designed to accommodate Indigoan body structure. Five pairs of walking legs draped over the side, while the flat lower body sat comfortably on the hard table beneath. The small body, unlike those of the other Indigoans, wore clothing. The blue-black carapace was dressed in a glittering wraparound of orange-red, while the double pairs of pincers emerged from mitten-like sheaths of the same color.

It was a dumb question, but he had to ask it. He splashed forward until he was within a meter of the table. "Was it you who turned on the lights, and asked me what was enough?"

Miniature eyestalks waved up at him, and the topmost mouth opened. The translator said, *"Who but I? No one else is here."*

"I don't get it. I understand you, but the one who brought me here hardly made sense at all. I know that the translator improves as it hears more of a language, but it shouldn't be this fast."

A pincer claw pointed to the unit at Friday's waist. *"Is that the 'translator'?"*

"Sure. Do you also have such things?"

"We have . . . other ways. Better ways for translation, ways that do not allow mistakes. I think that we communicate, but I am not sure. As for understanding the one who brought you here, it cannot be expected."

"Does it speak a different language?"

"It speaks no language, no true language. It is not a leader. It is a lower, a Level Three."

"You mean, a sort of moron?"

"It is Level Three. A patroller, a guard, a worker."

"I get it. I had the same sort of problem on my ship, workers who couldn't grasp the big picture. I'm a leader, too." He had missed with his earlier tries at first contact, but this looked like the right time for it. "Let me explain who I am, and why I am here.

My name is Friday Indigo, and I have come to this world from another star system. I am the captain of a starship, the *Mood Indigo*, which is stranded near the shore not far from here. I am also the representative of all humans, and of all other intelligent species who are members of the Stellar Group. I would welcome the chance to compare your civilization with ours, and if possible to exchange elements of our technology."

Even as he spoke, Friday wondered if he was being a trifle optimistic. The translator was working now—of course it hadn't worked when he was talking to a half-wit minion, how could it?—but he was throwing at it some pretty high-level concepts.

For a few seconds he was afraid that he was right, and his speech had been too much for the translator. The little Indigoan in front of him—funny, when you saw a pint-sized one it looked like a cross between an Earth crab and a lobster—was waving its eyestalks in an excited way and whistling loudly. The translator whistled in sympathy, and finally said, *"I question what was said to me. Repeat who you are, and what you are."*

"Sure. Let me try to keep it really simple. My name is Friday Indigo. I have come here from another star. I want to learn your technology, in exchange for giving you some of ours."

It was hard to say it clearer than that, but the Indigoan leader seemed as agitated as ever.

"You are not from this world? You are not the dominant life-form and intelligence of this world?"

"I'm dominant and intelligent, sure I am. But you got it right, I'm not from this world. I came here from a world that orbits another star." The oddity of the question finally got through to Friday. Why would somebody who was part of the dominant intelligent form of Limbo ask Friday if *he* was of the dominant form here? "Are you telling me that you're not the leading life-form here, yourself?"

"Not from here, you are not from here. Where, if not from here?" The Indigoan was standing up, lifting itself from the table. It seemed awfully excited. *"You will say all or die, as those died. You will say all, or you will join them."*

One pincer was now holding a small version of the familiar black cane, but that was not what gave Friday the chills. The cane was not pointing at him. It was directed toward the big wall panels that stood on each side of the room.

He wondered why he had not noticed them as he came in, then realized that once the lights came on he had been totally focused on the Indigoan leader. If he had observed on entry what he saw now, he would have run back outside and taken his chances with the line of guards.

On the easels hung four objects. They seemed oddly two-dimensional, but that was because they had been dried, carefully opened and dissected, and pinned flat.

Friday was staring at the desiccated remains of four bubble people.

21

Reunion

Bony had been very young when the quarantine was imposed, and in his childhood he had absorbed the widespread human bias against other members of the Stellar Group. Pipe-Rillas were hopeless cowards. Tinkers were unstable. Angels were enormously intelligent, but they were also obstinate, complaining, and inscrutable. It was an outrage that such flawed and inferior beings should control access to the stars, while denying it by quarantine to superior humans.

Perhaps; but when you were stranded on the seabed of an alien world with a major storm raging overhead, a limited air supply, and no idea what to do next, you became aware of other alien qualities.

Vow-of-Silence was crouching in the silt-filled water with the Angel cradled in two of her fore-limbs and an amorphous mass of Tinkers heaped by her side. As Bony and Liddy came up to her, the

Pipe-Rilla bobbed her head toward the humans and said, "There is a slight difficulty. Although the *Finder* is no more than two or three kilometers away, the storm has so filled the water around us with suspended sediments that earlier sea-markers are invisible. Also, night approaches. We do not know in which direction we should proceed to reach our ship. Do you?"

For a coward the Pipe-Rilla sounded remarkably calm—much calmer than Bony felt. He looked at Liddy. She shrugged, and said to Vow-of-Silence, "I'm afraid we don't."

Bony felt like an idiot—setting a beacon for your return path should be second nature to anyone who claimed technical competence. The Angel said, " *'Full fathom five, thy Finder lies,'* " which didn't seem to help at all.

Vow-of-Silence said, "Very good. Eager Seeker, I'm sorry to trouble you. If you wouldn't mind?"

Eager Seeker offered no reply, but the whole heap of the Tinker Composite disassembled, rose, and circled briefly like an underwater tornado. Then the components streaked away in all directions.

Bony said, "What?" but Liddy's nudge saved him from making a bigger fool of himself. After a couple of minutes the Angel added, " *'They also serve who only stand and wait.'* " Five minutes later the Tinker components came streaming back. They merged to make a tall column, held there for maybe ten seconds, then reformed to create a horizontal line that snaked away into the murk.

"Thank you, Eager Seeker." Vow-of-Silence gestured to Bony and Liddy with one of her fore-limbs. "After you."

"How could the Tinker understand that?" Liddy asked Bony, as they followed the strung-out line of components. "I thought they had no intelligence unless they were formed into a Composite."

She spoke softly, but Vow-of-Silence heard her. "Indeed they do not." The Pipe-Rilla with her Angel burden was close behind. As she moved to Bony's side, the individual components in the line of Tinkers behind her coalesced into a rough sphere.

"My reply was formal politeness," Vow-of-Silence went on, "and no more than that. I will repeat our expression of gratitude when we reach the ship, and Eager Seeker is once more fully assembled into a higher consciousness."

The Angel said nothing. The blue-green fronds were furled about the upper body, and to Bony's eye the resemblance to a large vegetable became complete.

The little party trudged on across the seafloor as twilight edged toward night. Flickers of lightning, faint and far-off, picked out the guiding column of Tinkers. It seemed far more than three kilometers when the rococo outline of the toppled *Finder* at last appeared.

Bony was too tired to do more than struggle aboard, remove his suit, and find a place to lie down on a cluttered floor that was actually a wall. After a few seconds Liddy came to curl up beside him. She snuggled close but said not a word. Bony was left to reflect that this was an adolescent's dream. He was spending the night with a woman who had been trained in the Leah Rainbow Academy for the Daughters of Gentlefolk, a woman who had been trained to please men in a hundred different ways. A woman, moreover, who seemed to like him and had told him that he was attractive.

Bony sighed. If Liddy knew a hundred ways to delight, Life knew a thousand ways to disappoint. Nothing was going to happen tonight.

He put a protective arm over her. In the few moments before he went to sleep he decided that human judgment was wrong. Pipe-Rillas were brave, not cowardly. Tinkers were not unstable, but steady and reliable. Only the Angels appeared to match their reputation. His final memory was of a synthesizer voice, grumbling from a dark corner: "Standing without the touch of soil, bare-rooted and bereft of light. '*How are the mighty fallen!*' "

Hunger woke Bony. He lay in darkness and could not recall when he had last eaten. His stomach was growling like a wild beast.

He reached out and found Liddy gone. He opened his eyes, and the Angel's corner stood empty. Over to his right, the port showed the first faintest glint of dawn. Off to his left, toward the ship's bow, he saw a brighter light and heard the sound of voices.

He rubbed tired eyes, stood up, and headed to the adjoining chamber. They were all there. The Angel stood directly beneath a glowing tube, its lower part in a container filled with dark liquid. Eager Seeker had assembled its components into a fat ring around the Angel's bulky middle section. As Bony came in, Liddy—wonderful mind-reader Liddy—handed him a white half-moon with a crumbly texture and said, "I don't know what it is, but it's not bad and it's supposed to be suited to a human digestion."

Bony took a big bite, nodded his thanks, and joined the others in staring at the Pipe-Rilla. Vow-of-Silence was crouched by the main control desk of the *Finder*, and she was shaking her narrow head. "We have a status report on the condition of this ship, which is not good. We also have other surprising news. I have called for an oral summary." Vow-of-Silence bowed to Bony and Liddy. "Recognizing your limitations, it will be provided in your form of speech."

In spite of the polite gesture the final comment was, at the very least, a dig at humans. Pipe-Rillas and Tinker Composites had no difficulty picking up in a few weeks everything from Swahili to Sioux, while less than a hundred human interpreters had mastered the alien languages. As for the native tongue of the tongueless Angels, even the Tinkers and Pipe-Rillas said it was next to impossible.

Even so, Bony wondered if this was going to work. The onboard computer of the *Finder* was probably as good as the Pipe-Rillas could make, but in this area of technology nothing in the Stellar Group came close to human products. Sure enough, the voice that came from the cabin address system had a labored, mechanical quality, with odd breaks between words.

THERE HAS BEEN A CONTINUED STEADY DETERIORATION IN THIS SHIP'S ENERGY SUPPLY AND STORAGE SYSTEMS. ONE STORAGE ELEMENT SUFFERED MAJOR DAMAGE UPON EMERGING FROM THE LINK INTO WATER, AND IT CANNOT BE USED. THE MINOR HULL FRACTURE EXPERIENCED AT THAT SAME TIME HAS BEEN COMPENSATED THROUGH THE USE OF A SEPARATING FIELD, BUT SUCH A FIELD REQUIRES A SUBSTANTIAL AND CONTINUOUS EXPENDITURE OF ENERGY. THAT ENERGY CANNOT BE REPLACED, NOR CAN REPAIRS BE MADE, UNTIL THE SHIP IS NO LONGER IMMERSED IN A DENSE SURROUNDING MEDIUM. TRANSFER OF THE SHIP TO ITS DESIGNED VACUUM ENVIRONMENT MUST OCCUR WITHIN THREE DAYS, OTHERWISE PRESENT LEVELS OF LIFE-SUPPORT SYSTEMS CANNOT BE MAINTAINED.

Bony wondered if "vacuum" really meant vacuum. Would it do to raise the *Finder* to the surface, or beach it? That sort of thing would not be easy, but it was an area suited to his own fix-up skills. Given a day or two and some cooperation he could certainly have raised the *Mood Indigo* using the auxiliary thrustors, and probably taken it to space. The *Finder* was much more of an unknown quantity, but he was willing to give it a shot if they would let him.

The computer was not finished. THE ELECTROMAGNETIC COMMUNICATIONS SYSTEM HAS NOT FUNCTIONED CORRECTLY SINCE IMMERSION. THE NEUTRINO COMMUNICATION SYSTEM WAS RESTORED TO SERVICE ELEVEN HOURS AGO, IN SO FAR AS SUCH A RESTORATION IS POSSIBLE WITHOUT A MAJOR OVERHAUL. CONTACT HAS BEEN MADE WITH TWO VESSELS: FIRST, THE *MINISTER OF GRACE*, WITH A CREW OF ANGELS AND OF SELLORAN REGISTRATION. HOWEVER, THIS CONTACT WAS LOST NINE HOURS AGO AND HAS NOT BEEN REGAINED.

The Angel said gloomily, "The *Minister of Grace*, swept into the abyss by the force of the storm. *'Thou art lost and gone forever, dreadful sorry.'* "

The computer ignored the Angel and went on, SECOND, THE *HERO'S RETURN*, WITH A CREW OF HUMANS AND WITH SOL REGISTRATION, REPORTS THAT IT IS NEWLY ARRIVED IN THIS VICINITY AND LIES ON THE SEABED ROUGHLY THREE KILOMETERS FROM OUR POSITION. WE CONTINUE TO EXCHANGE LOCATION AND IDENTIFICATION SIGNALS WITH THE COMPUTER OF THE *HERO'S RETURN*.

Bony decided that the *Finder*'s onboard computer was not just primitive, it was very dumb. He had never heard of a ship named the *Hero's Return*, but it sounded just like the sort of thing you would call a Class Five cruiser. Any decent computer ought to have that kind of information in its data banks—and it should be able to rank information in probable order of importance. This news should have set off every alarm bell in the ship, announcing that the new vessel had appeared. The computer on the *Hero's Return*, along with its crew, must be going crazy wondering why they had heard nothing in return but a bland I/D signal.

If no one else knew what to do, it was up to him. Bony—with the cursed stammer that came always at the wrong time—blurted out, "Ask the *Hero's Return* to s-send us a *p-picture*. And ask for information on ship type."

Vow-of-Silence reached a claw toward the control board, then hesitated. "Do you already know about this ship?"

"No. But if it's the same one that flew overhead when we were sitting on the seabed—and I think it must be—it could be a Class Five cruiser."

"A *warship*?" Vow-of-Silence said, while a flurry of Tinker components rose and fluttered excitedly all around the cabin. "Such an arrival would be unspeakable."

While Bony wondered how to answer—if he were right, it was certainly a warship—Liddy helped him out. "Lots of the old solar system warships have been converted to civilian use. Right, Bony?"

"They have. All the offensive weapons were taken out, and they don't carry a fighting crew any more. But if it's a Class Five cruiser, it will be superbly equipped and difficult to destroy. We would be far safer there than here. All of us." He thought of the Angel. "They have an onboard sunroom and a garden area, for crew relaxation."

"Hah!" The fronds on the upper part of the Angel waved, and the compact body emitted a rapid series of high-pitched squeaks. Even as Bony realized that this was Gressel's digital audio command to the ship's computer, the reply was coming. OUR INQUIRY HAS BEEN RECEIVED AND WE HAVE THE RESPONSE. THE *HERO'S RETURN* IS CONFIRMED AS A CONVERTED CLASS FIVE CRUISER SERVED BY A HUMAN CREW. THE PASSENGER-CARRYING CAPACITY IS

ONE THOUSAND AND SEVENTY UNDER NON-EMERGENCY CONDITIONS, BUT THE SHIP NOW CARRIES A COMPLEMENT OF ONLY EIGHT HUMANS. IT IS ALSO CONFIRMED THAT THE SURVIVAL PROBABILITY OF ALL BEINGS ON BOARD THIS SHIP WOULD BE GREATLY INCREASED BY TRANSFER TO THE *HERO'S RETURN*. SUCH A TRANSFER HAS ALREADY BEEN PROPOSED. WE RECOMMEND IT, AND THE ABANDONMENT OF THIS VESSEL.

Bony wondered just who was recommending the transfer. From the speed of the transaction, the only parties who could be involved were the ships' computers. Had the idea of the move come from this ship? If so, the *Finder*'s computer was condemning itself to oblivion. The machine existed in distributed form throughout the ship, and there was no possible way to take it to the *Hero's Return*. It would fade and die as the onboard energy supply dwindled.

If anyone shared Bony's thoughts, they did not mention it. Vow-of-Silence said, "It will mean suits again. A nuisance, but the journey will be a short one." She turned to Bony and Liddy. "I have called for a crew-to-crew visual link. Since we are dealing with a human ship, initial contact and the indication of our desire to transfer would come better from two humans. Agreed?"

Did they have a choice? Bony waited for the two-way video link. At last, a picture appeared. The display showed a man and woman sitting side by side and looking right at the occupants of the *Finder*'s cabin. The man had a wary, weary expression, the dark-haired woman was fresh-faced and seemed to glow with health.

The two of them stared and stared without saying a word. The man's mouth hung open, while the woman leaned forward and frowned in disbelief.

Liddy glanced around the cabin and could see

nothing to astonish. When Bony remained silent, she at last said, "Hello, *Hero's Return*. Are you there? Do we have contact?" There was still no reply. She nudged Bony, who sat frozen. "Something's wrong with the communications. I don't think they're seeing or hearing us at all. Bony? Are you listening to me? Bony? Bony!"

Not just Chan Dalton and Deb Bisson, but the whole bunch—Dapper Dan and Chrissie and Tarbush and Tully O'Toole. Bony tried to explain about the team to Liddy on their surrealistic dawn journey across the seafloor, but he was not sure she believed him. He was not sure he believed himself. A hundred lightyears, or two hundred, or however many it was from Earth, and the first humans you run into are old friends.

Liddy reacted calmly. She and Bony kept very close to each other, drifting along the coastal shelf in the faint, filtered light of early morning. It was improbable for him to meet his old friends here? Fine, so it was improbable; but it had happened. "Improbable" was something you could only apply to future events.

The *Hero's Return* stretched its length along the seabed, so big that as they approached the center lock for admission to the ship, the bow and stern were invisible through the cloudy water. The storm was past, but here its after-effects lingered on far below the surface. After the first chaotic minutes of hugs and handshakes, the group settled into the ship's main fire control chamber, and detailed explanations began.

Chan Dalton introduced Dag Korin, and the grizzled General offered a terse description of the *Hero's Return*'s Link transition and surprising underwater arrival. As he finished he glared with distaste at the Pipe-Rilla, the Angel, and the assembled Tinker Composite.

Vow-of-Silence took over, but she could add very little. The Pipe-Rilla, like the Angel and the humans, had expected her ship's Link transition to terminate in vacuum. In fact, it seemed impossible that it would *not* do so, given all the built-in safeguards employed by the Stellar Group.

Bony had not expected that he and Liddy would have much to offer, but after Dag Korin and the Pipe-Rilla had explained how they came to be here, one of the crew of the other ship, a tall, woefully thin blonde named Elke Siry, sat down in front of Bony. She had been introduced as the expedition's scientist, and she wanted to know *everything*. What tests had he done on the water? What had they seen of plants and animals on the seafloor? When they were on the surface, had they seen anything of the night sky of Limbo? What could they tell her about the surface gravity of the planet? About the distance to the horizon? Where was Friday Indigo, and the *Mood Indigo*? What had they learned in their brief visit to the land? What about the aircraft he had seen? What about the object that Bony suspected to be a Link entry point? Was he sure it was a changing feature, sometimes there and sometimes not?

Her questions went on and on. Finally she frowned, chewed at her lower lip, and asked, "What else can you tell me about the bubble people? Why are you so sure they can't go on land, and could not be the makers of the aircraft that you saw?"

Bony was sure, but he didn't know how to prove it. Help came from an odd quarter. The Angel, newly rooted in a large pot of black earth, had so far sat motionless and spoken not a word. Now the upper fronds waved and a mournful synthesized voice said, " '*Bubble, bubble, toil and trouble.*' "

That was enough to draw Elke Siry's attention. She

turned away from Bony as the Angel went on, "The beings whom you term 'bubble people' are knowledgeable in certain forms of biotechnology. They are able to control living undersea organisms so as to construct simple domiciles, and they have a fair command of bioluminescent methods to achieve light during the hours of darkness."

Dag Korin glared and asked Bony's question. "How the devil can you possibly know such things?"

"We talked to them when we left our ship, the *Minister of Grace*."

"You have no translation unit."

"True, but irrelevant. We have no need of translation equipment. We learned and spoke their language." Dag Korin snorted in surprise or disbelief, but the Angel went on calmly, "The bubble people lack knowledge of mechanical engineering, of physics, of mathematics, and of the world above the water. They say that the feature which you suspect to be a Link entry point was not always there. They lack sufficient concept of measured time to say when it arrived. However, to them the 'foam object at the edge of the world which comes and goes' is coupled with other bad changes. They are marine organisms and they have never been able to go on the land, but they used to visit the shallow waters close to the shore. Since the suspected Link point appeared, they cannot do so. If they go too close to the shore now, they say they will die or disappear. All this, together with the information that has been exchanged here, suggests certain tentative conclusions."

Only, by the look of it, to Elke Siry. The Angel's speech had come as no great surprise to Bony. Vow-of-Silence had mentioned that death came to Sea-wanderers who went close to the shore, and everything else fitted with what he already knew. But conclusions? He couldn't deduce any. Nor, from the look of their faces, could Chan and the rest of the humans.

Except, of course, for Elke. She nodded at Gressel and said, "Certain conclusions, which perhaps I can make less tentative." She touched the pad on her wrist, and one of the ship's giant wall displays came alive. "The air-breathing pinnaces seem to be damaged beyond repair"—Chrissie and Tarbush exchanged anguished looks—"but the unmanned orbiters survived intact, and a few hours ago the ship was able to launch a pair of them. They are busy mapping the land and sea surface of this planet, and have provided occasional views of the heavens. Here is the night sky of Limbo, as seen from orbit."

The screen filled, not with stars and veils of dust but with hundreds and thousands of glowing spheres. They could be seen in every direction from Limbo, too numerous to count, of all sizes and pulsing with their own soft light.

Elke Siry waited for the gasps and grunts of surprise to die down before she swiveled away from the display to face the others in the control room. "What we see there is not, I think we can all agree, anywhere in the Geyser Swirl. And that fact, together with everything else we know, is enough. With your permission, I will explain where we are, and what happened to bring us here. Though I suspect that she"— Elke stabbed a thin finger in the Angel's direction—"already knows, because we seem to think in rather the same way."

"We much prefer to be known as *it*. However." The Angel opened wide its lower fronds. *"Let me not to the marriage of true minds admit impediments.* Call us what you will. And pray continue."

22

Negotiations

Friday was not scared. Certainly not. He was Friday Indigo, and bad things didn't happen to members of the Indigo family.

He told himself that the queasy feeling inside him was not fear, but he had to admit that he did feel a certain *uneasiness*. Until he caught sight of those desiccated and dissected bubble-creatures, he'd imagined nothing worse for himself than another shot from a black paralyzing cane.

"I am not from here." He didn't like the wobbly sound of his own voice, and he took a breath and started over. "I am not from *here*—not a native of this planet. I came from a star named Sol, through a device that we call a *Link*. But something went wrong with the Link transfer, and instead of arriving in open space my ship finished up in the sea not far from here."

"Aha!" The little eyestalks twitched. "Then it is verified. Soon after arrival, I reassured the Level Threes and the Level Four untouchables that this world possessed no intelligence of use or danger to Malacostracans. When they brought word of an alien ship, washed into the river by the storm, and told of an alien air-breather on the shore, I was surprised. But I was right."

At last, the translation unit seemed halfway to justifying its price. It was time to get down to business before it went wonky on him again. Friday said, "You're not from here, I'm not from here. This planet probably isn't worth peanuts to either of us. But both our races must have technology that the other one doesn't possess." Friday thought, not without a quiver of unpleasant memory, of the paralyzing black cane. "I'd like to propose a swap."

The double pairs of pincers waved, and the Malacostracan inched forward on the flat table. The translation unit said, "*Swap?*"

So the machine wasn't perfect yet. "A *swap* means a trading agreement. You tell me what I've got that you don't have, and I tell you what I don't have. If we agree that they seem equal, we make an exchange."

Credit for making First Contact was wonderful, but alien technology had the potential to jump Friday financially far ahead of the whole Indigo clan. That would show his bastard cousins, always boasting about their money!

The eyestalks began to wiggle, but no sound came from the translator. Friday was ready to try again using other words when the machine finally said, "There is misunderstanding. You are a prisoner. Everything that you know and everything that you possess belongs to us. That includes your life."

It was a bad start, but Indigo family tradition taught that every threat could be regarded as a step in negotiation.

Friday leaned forward. "It's not just a matter of what I know, and what I own. Members of my species and others, together with their ships and their weapons, have also come to this planet. Even if you believe that you can capture and subdue every one of them, it won't be easy. Now, I'm known and trusted by them. You'd be a lot better off with me as a go-between than as a prisoner."

A simple enough statement, you'd think. But again there was that long pause. Eventually: "An interesting proposal. However, it is not one that I am able to accept or reject. It is necessary that we consult one of a higher level."

"How many levels are there?" Friday had a mental image of a series of Malacostracans, decreasing in body size as they increased in authority, until he found himself addressing a Supreme Potentate the size of a flea.

"We have five levels." The four front pincers turned to point inward. "I am a Level Two. What you suggest is a Level One decision."

"How many Level Ones and Level Twos are there?"

"There are five Level Twos. I am Two-Four, in order of spawning. There is one Level One, and she is The One." The little legs propelled Two-Four off the table and into water that rose to cover the carapace. Eyestalks poked up above the surface, and the translator gurgled, "Come."

The Malacostracan headed toward the far end of the building. It seemed to Friday, following, that there was no exit that way. The alien pointed the black cane at the wall. It became transparent, and Two-Four sidled through. Friday followed, eyeing the cane. His respect for it was rising. It didn't just zap people, it zapped whole buildings. And when you walked through the wall, you weren't where you would expect to be, outside in the gusty night air of Limbo where the patrol guards were waiting. You were in another interior chamber, too big to fit inside any of the buildings that he had seen. This one was also well-lit, throwing gleaming iridescent reflections of green and purple and black off the carapace of the little Malacostracan. Also, a pleasant change, the floor wasn't sloshing with water.

How could that be, when this was on the same level as the other room? Friday looked back, and found the wall opaque again. He turned, to see Two-Four inching forward, its body touching the floor and its multiple legs splayed wide. The translator said urgently, *"Abase, abase!"*

He couldn't imitate that walk, even if he wanted to. Friday stayed at his full height and stared. This room was stranger and yet more familiar than anything he had seen so far. The display screens and holo-volumes suggested a command center, but they sat far up toward the three-meter-high ceiling, where he could view them only by craning his neck backward. On the other hand, the banks of dials and switches that presumably controlled the displays formed part of the floor. He couldn't even read or reach most of the dials and switches without stepping on some of them.

Other than himself and Two-Four he saw no sign of any living thing, Malacostracan or other, in the room. But the floor controls were arranged in concentric circles, and at the center of them stood a large black rock. It was bulky, half as tall again as Friday, and the lower part was riddled with holes big enough to put your hand in.

Two-Four said to Friday, "Stay. And abase, abase." It advanced cautiously to the outer perimeter of the control area. There it produced a long series of squeaks and whistles, totally unlike the clicks and clatters of its previous speech. Friday's translator unit remained silent. He guessed that it was using a different language from any that his unit had met before. Worse than that, his translator didn't even seem to be trying. It wasn't providing even the preliminary hoots and whistles that preceded intelligible words.

The black rock offered its own set of squeaks. The Level Two Malacostracan squeaked and whistled again, presumably in reply. Then it was another long sequence from the rock. The talk, assuming that's what it was, went on and on. Friday's translator remained silent, and finally he stopped listening to nothing and began to take a closer look at the half-dozen ceiling displays.

He might be deep underground at the moment, but the screens provided a view from above the surface. Two of them showed the cloudless night sky of Limbo, with its baffling collection of faint and diffuse spheres. The hints of color were not as he remembered them, but that was probably a function of sensors matched to suit alien eyes.

Other screens showed land views. He recognized one of them, or at least he could guess what it showed. It was the view to the west, seen from the rocky ridge above the inlet where the *Mood Indigo* had been driven by the storm. The image had been photo-intensified to make use of faint levels of light. It showed shades of gray and negligible color, but he fancied he could discern the outline of a ship's hull, jutting above the waters of the inlet. The storm had passed, and the waves that met the *Mood Indigo* were slow and steady. He wondered how well his ship had survived. Would it still be able to make a Link transition, assuming he could somehow find a Link entry point?

He turned his attention to the remaining three screens. Two of them provided nothing of special interest. They were land views, bare jagged rocks and ridges and graveled slopes. The final screen, though, made him forget the ache in his neck.

It was another land view, but in this one the hills and valleys were not bare. They were clothed with vegetation—odd-looking forms, all twists and spikes, but no stranger than many of the plants found on Earth or other worlds of the Stellar Group.

Friday snorted aloud. So much for that fat idiot Rombelle, and what he "knew" as scientific fact! No plants on the land surface of Limbo, because on a planet orbiting a blue-giant star they didn't have enough time to emerge from the sea? Sure. Facts my ass. Those were plants on the display, and he, Friday Indigo, was willing to bet on it.

"Alien air-breather!" The sudden words from the translation unit brought Friday's attention back to ground level. The black rock sat immobile as ever. The words were being translated from sounds emitted by Two-Four. "Pay attention."

"I'm listening." At least it had stopped all the "Abase, abase," nonsense. "I told you my name, you know. It's not alien air-breather, it's Friday Indigo."

"Air-breather." The eyestalks waved, and the Malacostracan continued as though Friday had not spoken. "The One has been made aware of your proposal for cooperation. The One desires to know more, and is willing to discuss it with you. However, there are three problems. First, Level One speech is too advanced for your primitive device." A black pincer reached forward and touched the translation unit. "Communication through this would be as unproductive as an attempt at reasoned speech with a Level Four. Something better is needed.

"Second, The One requires additional evidence that you and your kind have something to offer. We have observed your feeble attempts to spy on our surface activities, and are in the process of neutralizing those orbiters. We anticipate no difficulty in doing so. The One declares the orbiters to be undefended and therefore primitive. If that represents your best level of technology, it is of little or no value. Do you wish to comment?"

"No." Orbiters? That was news to Friday. But it was good news. Somebody or something on one of the ships had found a way off the surface of Limbo and into space. All the riches in the universe were no good if you had no way of taking them home. On the other hand, "undefended" in the eyes of the Malacostracans apparently equated to "primitive." That was a clue to their outlook on life, and not an encouraging one.

Two-Four was continuing, "Third, The One believes that you and your kind are in a poor position for negotiation of any kind. We created and we control the sea-sky portal that you refer to as the *Link*. Without the Link, you will remain here on this world until you and all your spawn are dead. Do you understand?"

Friday nodded, then realized that was no use to the translation unit and said, "Yes, I understand." He wasn't much worried about his spawn at the moment. More on his mind was his own immediate future and the split and dried bodies of the bubble people. "I think you're wrong about our technology, though. It's just not represented in the equipment we brought with us. There's a tremendous amount of information in our ships' data bases, about all sorts of things. Everything from astrophysics to zoology. It's not possible that you already know all of it, and without our help you'd never be able to figure out how to get into the data bases."

That led to another two-way stream of high-pitched whistles and grunts between The One and its Level Two subordinate. It went on for a while. Something in Friday's last speech seemed to be producing excitement, and he wondered what it might be.

"It is possible that you are correct," Two-Four said at last. "Although we could assuredly learn everything that you and your kind know, time is important to us. The One is willing to consider acceptance of your assistance. You will become the intermediary between us and your kind. In return, you will not be harmed. However, there is one additional condition. The One is not satisfied with this slow and possibly inaccurate method of communication, first through me and then through your machine. You must agree to receive Level One compressed speech directly, and be able to speak for the Malacostracans to your own kind. How do you answer?"

Friday thought about it. The deal sounded pretty clean and simple, but he had to be sure that his lousy translator wasn't crapping out on some vital point.

"Let me make sure I understand you. I'm going to play back what I heard you say, and you can tell me if I have it right. I learn to understand The One's speech, right?"

"That is correct."

"How long does that take?"

"Very little time, with our technology. A small fraction of a day. At the same time, The One will learn your speech."

"All right. After that, I become the interface

between your people and my own and any other visitors from outside this world?"

"Again, that is correct."

"The *only* interface?"

"Certainly. Only one is needed."

"Ah, but what about *your* technology?" Friday thought he saw the catch. "Will you be willing to tell me about that?"

There was a pause, followed by another two-way transfer between the Malacostracans. Friday again wondered what he had said. It had sounded pretty straightforward to him. But Two-Four was finally replying, and the tones that came from the translator sounded puzzled: "Of course, all knowledge of our technology will be available to you. That, together with all other facts regarding our origins and our plans."

"And I will not be harmed."

"Why would we harm someone who is serving as our intermediary? We repeat, you will not be harmed. You will be our valuable interface."

"Then—I accept." Friday wondered what would have happened had he declined, and decided he preferred not to speculate.

There was a brief squeak from The One, and the translator said, "Excellent. We will begin at once."

"Wait a minute!"

A pause, and a polite, "Yes? Do you have more questions?"

Did he? Friday couldn't think of any, but things seemed to be going awful fast and easy. He reviewed everything he had been told, and finally shrugged. "I guess I don't."

"Very good. Then we will proceed." Two-Four scuttled suddenly and sharply backward. At the same moment, six black hoses, each as thick as a human thumb, emerged from the holes as the base of The One and snaked in Friday's direction. At their ends they divided into fine bundles of thin filaments.

He tried to jump backwards, the same as Two-Four had done, but he was too slow. Two of the flexible arms curled around his thighs, two around his waist, and they pulled him closer to the black rock. The other two moved to attach to the sides of his head, just above his ears.

Friday cried out, "Hey, you told me I wouldn't be harmed." Before he could complete the sentence, something much worse was happening. He felt the divided ends of the cables sliding down his skull. They were entering his ears. They were *inside* him. He opened his mouth to scream in pain and terror, but he was too late. And suddenly it wasn't necessary. Instead of pain he felt the most intense ecstasy of his life. Nothing else—food, drugs, sex—nothing came even close. It was as much as he could stand.

Then it became more intense. Stronger, better. *More* than he could stand. Friday, safe in the protective embrace of The One, swooned into an ecstasy of unutterable pleasure.

23

Explanations and Problems

Bony had met Elke Siry less than an hour ago, but already he had formed his impressions. The scientist was naturally shy to the point of appearing antisocial—he could relate to that—yet she could not bear to sit by and hear wrong deductions being made from hard data. As a result, she had become the leader of the meeting.

General Dag Korin, who was already a known name to Bony, didn't seem to mind. He acted almost as the blond scientist's protector, encouraging her to speak and give her opinions. As a result the whole group had clustered around her and paid close attention to her words. The Angel sat with its roots deep in a great pot of dark soil dragged in by Chan Dalton and Deb Bisson from the garden of the *Hero's Return*. The Pipe-Rilla hovered high above it, with Tinkers clustered around her lower part. The humans, except for Chan Dalton somewhat uneasy with the recently arrived aliens, sat well away from them.

"Most of us seem to have ideas as to what's happened to us," Elke was saying.

Wrong, thought Bony, *most of us have no idea at all*.

But he did not speak, and Elke Siry went on, "Before we start to speculate, let's look at what we know for sure. Four different ships set out for the Geyser Swirl. Each one expected to emerge in open space—more than that, we saw no way that they could emerge to anything other than open space, because of the safeguards built into a Link transition.

"Each of us arrived in water, on a planetary surface. It should have been impossible but it happened, not once but four times. Beyond the planet, according to the observations of the two unmanned orbiters that we sent out, is a region of space that looks nothing like the Geyser Swirl. Instead of dust clouds and normal stars, we see strange dimly glowing circles. We *assume* that they are spheres of some kind, but note that this is an assumption. So far as real knowledge is concerned, they could be circles painted on the sky."

Dag Korin said, "But—" then paused and shook his head.

"No, General, I don't think they are, either." On anyone else's face the slight relaxation of Elke's tight mouth would have been a smile. "I merely point out the difference between knowledge and assumption. What else do we *know*? Well, we know that the gravity field of this planet is abnormally small for its size. So small, the interior must be made of something less dense than ordinary water. But if that were the case, the heavy-water ocean should have sunk toward the planetary center. So let's call that a paradox, with no explanation.

"Also, we know from observations made by orbiters and by some of our party, that the primary star around which this planet revolves is a blue giant. We also know, again from the experience of some here, that there is life in this ocean. The bubble people are not only alive, they appear to be intelligent.

"These two facts together, the short life span of a blue giant star and the long time needed for living things to develop on a planet around it, give some of us problems. But those problems arise from our trust in our own scientific ideas. According to standard astrophysical theories, blue giant stars must run through their stellar lives very fast, in millions of years rather than billions. So Limbo can't be more than a few tens of millions of years old, at most. But according to our biological theories, the development of life requires a much longer time scale. It needs at least hundreds of millions of years to evolve from its primordial forms, and maybe billions of years to produce multicelled complex beings with intelligence. So we have two of our basic scientific theories, and they seem to be incompatible with each other."

More than anyone else in the fire control room, Tully O'Toole seemed at ease with Elke Siry. He was sitting closest to her, and he rubbed at his stubbled chin and said, "I burned my brains with Paradox, and maybe that's my problem. But I don't get it. Two theories sound like one too many. Why should we believe in any?"

That produced an actual smile on Elke's thin face. "I'm not saying we pick a theory at all at this point. I'm just listing the things we know, and the things we don't know but tend to assume. Let me keep going, and see where it leads. We know, from direct chemical tests, that the liquid of the ocean into which we fell is water. But it's not the form of water we're most familiar with, H_2O, which forms the bulk of the oceans of Earth and the water-ice of much of the rest of the solar system. This ocean is D_2O, deuterium oxide or heavy water. Heavy water occurs naturally in the solar system, but it's only one six-thousandth as common as ordinary water. Does anyone have a problem with that?"

She looked at the circle of faces. Dag Korin shrugged, and the others, taking their lead from Chan Dalton, shook their heads.

Elke said firmly, "Well, I do. And so should you. Deuterium is a stable alternate form of hydrogen, with a neutron in the nucleus as well as a proton. They don't turn into each other. And the relative proportions of the amounts of each were defined in the first few minutes of the universe, soon after the Big Bang started the whole thing going. Now, I know what you're going to say"—no one other than Elke showed signs of saying anything—"the Big Bang is a theory, too, and because it's a theory we don't *know* that the proportions of hydrogen to deuterium have to be fixed at six thousand to one. I can't disagree with that, but I'll say only this: if we're going to throw the idea of the Big Bang overboard, we won't have much left of current astrophysics and cosmology. I'm going to make the case for keeping the Big Bang, but before I do that I want to point out one other thing that we *know*.

"This one concerns times. The Angel pointed this out to me, so I can't take credit for it. Let's examine the dates when each of our four ships made the Link transition that was supposed to carry it to the Geyser Swirl. I don't need to go into detail. It's enough to say that it took time to decide to send another expedition when a previous one failed to come back. Months went by between the Link entry times of the Pipe-Rilla and Tinker expedition, the

Angel expedition, and the first and second human expedition. These are known facts."

Bony caught Liddy's eye. No one was tactless enough to say that the efforts of the *Mood Indigo* had been undertaken without the approval or permission of the aliens of the Stellar Group, and also spectacularly unsuccessful. Friday's failure to return strongly suggested that he and his ship had been destroyed in the storm.

"Now consider our *arrival* times, here on Limbo," Elke said. "Again, we're dealing with facts, and not theories. Our ships arrived in the correct sequence, corresponding to the order in which they made the Link transitions; but they arrived *no more than a day or two after each other*. Link transitions are supposed to be instantaneous. Again, that's a theory, but it's a theory supported by many thousands of cases, with no counterexamples to suggest anything different."

Elke paused. "I think I've covered everything that's relevant. Oh, no, one other thing, and again it's a fact. The Link in the Geyser Swirl isn't one that we knew was there before. In fact, until recently every member of the Stellar Group would have sworn that there was no Link transition point anywhere in the Swirl. We didn't make it, and we know of no one else who might have done so. Add that fact in to everything else, and what have you got?"

She glanced from one member of the group to the next. Everyone remained silent, although the Angel was waving its upper fronds.

"I don't think we have anything," Tully said at last. "Unless you count a bunch of contradictions and impossibilities as something."

"I think we do." Elke turned to the Angel. "Would you like to explain, or shall I?"

The fronds dipped in her direction, and the

synthesized voice from deep within the Angel said, "*Too many cooks spoil the broth.* Please, continue."

"All right. I'm going to throw an assumption at you. Better take a deep breath, because it's a big one. On the other hand, it seems to explain everything else. Here it is: the Link entry point in the Geyser Swirl is different from any that we know, and it doesn't perform the usual type of transition. A ship that transfers to it does not emerge in the Swirl. Instead, the ship undergoes a second transition to somewhere else.

"*And*"—she continued before anyone could object or comment—"that *somewhere else* is not anywhere in our own universe. It is in a different cosmos, call it a parallel universe if you like. That's why the safeguards against emerging where there is matter didn't work. And that's where we are now."

Someone, it sounded to Bony like Danny Casement, muttered, "A *long* way from home," and Chrissie Winger said softly, "I don't *like* this. Come on, somebody, give me a nicer explanation."

"If you can think of a better explanation," Elke said, "I'd be more than happy to hear it. But see what my one assumption explains. First, a different universe is likely to have different basic physical constants. Not too different from what we know; in fact things in both universes have to be very close or we wouldn't be able to survive here at all. The very fact that we're sitting talking means that any changes have to be small. But small changes are enough. Minor differences in the physical constants during the first minutes of the universe give big differences in the relative amounts of hydrogen and deuterium. I speculate that almost all water in this entire universe will be heavy water, in order to have a planet with heavy-water oceans. The same differences, later on, affect the rate of stellar evolution. A blue giant star doesn't burn up so fast, and planets around it have time enough to develop life, and even intelligent life. The strange globes in the night sky are alternate forms of stars, things which can form here but which can't form in our own universe. That would suggest a difference in the basic gravitational constant, which would also help explain Limbo's low gravity but large size.

"Now, we might be able to talk away everything I've said, but there's one fact above all else that convinces me that we're in a different universe. That's the *times*. The intervals between the times when our ships entered the Link transition points in our universe, and the interval between our emergence into the ocean here, don't match. We're in a universe where not only the physical laws are different. The *time rates* in the two universes are not the same. A couple of months pass back home, while only a day passes here." Elke turned to the Angel. "You did the calculations. What did the relative rate come out to be?"

The Angel had sunk lower and seemed to be luxuriating in the presence of the rich soil at its base. It roused itself and mumbled, "*Gather ye rosebuds while ye may, old time is still a-flying*. To be more specific, and to three-figure accuracy, time is passing on this world 61.2 times as fast as standard time on Earth, Sellora, or other worlds of the Stellar Group."

Elke had seen the scowl on Dag Korin's face, and added, "In practical terms, General, the Angel is saying that two months will pass on Earth for every standard day that we remain here on Limbo. Our friends back home will already be worried about us. They'll be wondering why we haven't returned from the Geyser Swirl."

"Well, dammit, I'm ahead of them." The General was still scowling. "I want to know more than that. Maybe I'm simpleminded, Dr. Siry, and certainly I'm old, but I don't give a tinker's cuss about deuterium and time rates and all that science crap. The way I see it, we were sent here with a job to do. We had to find out what happened to the other expeditions that came before us. Well, we've done that, and more. Except for Friday Indigo, who it sounds like went off and killed himself in the storm, we have everybody from all the expeditions accounted for and here on this ship. So my question is this: How and when can we go home?"

"I'd like to know that, too, but you're asking the wrong person." Elke turned to Chan Dalton. "What's the condition of the ship?"

"I'm not sure, but I suspect that it stinks." Chan didn't really want the attention on him. He had listened to Elke Siry with mixed feelings. On the one hand, what she said cleared up an awful lot of mysteries. On the other hand, the news that you'd been thrown into some different universe had all sorts of other implications. What else might be different here? Would a ship's drive work, even if you could get it out of the water?

But first things first. He went on, "When we arrived we had to shed our external shielding to slow our descent. That worked and we were able to make a soft landing on the seabed, though apparently it smashed the pinnaces beyond repair. The whole ship isn't in good shape, and I doubt it can ever make a Link transition. Many of our displays report abnormal status." He nodded toward Bony. "The Bun's the one to tell us what condition we're in, and make the fix-ups if they can be made. Unless one of the other ships might be a better choice?"

"Forget it." Bony didn't know the condition of the *Hero's Return*, but Chan's question was still one that he could answer. "The *Finder*, the ship that Vow-of-Silence and Eager Seeker used to come here, was on its last legs when we left it. By now it's a dead hulk. The Angel's ship, the *Minister of Grace*, was swept into deep water by the storm, and we haven't been able to contact it. And although we don't know where Friday Indigo took the *Mood Indigo*, he hasn't responded to any of our ships' signals. His own ship is well made but it doesn't have the structural strength of this one. If he went too deep, the hull would implode. Up near the surface, the storm might have smashed it to pieces."

Chan nodded. "So it's this ship, or nothing. How long will it be, Bun, before you can tell us where we stand?"

"Give me half a day and I'll give you a first guess." Bony hesitated. "Look, is it really this ship or nothing?"

"What other options do we have?"

"I'm not sure. But somebody made the Link entry point, here on Limbo. It's a Link like none we've ever seen before, located at a sea-air interface instead of out in space. We know it wasn't the bubble people who built it, they lack the technology. We know it wasn't any member of the Stellar Group, because the whole design is different. But there *is* someone else on this planet, and they are land dwellers. Also, they have technology. When we were ashore, Liddy and I saw one of their flying machines."

"Did you meet them?" Dag Korin asked.

"No. The aircraft flew over us, and gave no sign that it knew we were there. But if we can contact whoever made it, and if we can communicate with them, and if they are friendly and they will cooperate by lending us one of their machines and let us use it to travel through the Link entry point, then we won't have to rely on this ship at all."

Dag Korin raised shaggy white eyebrows. "Young man, do you realize how many conditions you just hung together in one sentence? But you're quite right. We need more than one string to our bow, and if the only answer is to find and strong-arm another bunch of aliens to get ourselves home, that's what we'll do. You concentrate on the condition of the *Hero's Return*, and the rest of us will think about ways to go ashore and meet the other aliens. One question, though. Do you have any idea whereabouts on land the other aliens might be?"

"No. But if they're users of the Link, you'd expect them to have a base of operations not too far away from it. That means within maybe a hundred kilometers of where we are now." Bony turned to Elke Siry. "You said something about orbiters that look down at the planet, as well as looking up at the sky."

"Quite right. Two of them, launched as soon as storm conditions permitted. They've been returning images ever since, surveying the surface of the planet."

"How good are their instruments? Would they see enough detail to pick out a town or a spaceport?"

"Easily. At their survey altitude they can observe something as small as twenty meters across."

Dag Korin interrupted. "But they haven't done it, have they? Doesn't that suggest there's no spaceport or settlement to be found on the surface?"

Elke Siry gave him a withering look. "Please, General. You should know better." While the others waited for Dag Korin to explode, she calmly continued, "The orbiters are making survey observations and returning billions of bits of data a second to be stored in this ship's data banks. But *data* are not the same as *information*. Before you can get the answers you want, you have to ask the right question."

Dag Korin nodded meekly—confirming everyone's view that the old General had a soft spot for Elke Siry. "And what, my dear, would the right question be?"

"We have to specify a description of what we mean by a settlement or a spaceport, and how it would look to the instruments on board the orbiters. And then we have to instruct the ship's computer to go through all the data received from the orbiters, searching for matches to our description."

"I wouldn't know where to start."

"But I would." Elke leaned over the control panel in front of her. "To begin with, may I bring the ship's computer in as a participant to the meeting? I need to specify a recognition template for settlements and spaceports, but I notice that the computer has not been present so far."

"That's my doing. I locked it out of control room activities, with instructions to interrupt only if there was immediate danger to the ship. Wait just a minute, though." Dag Korin held up a hand and addressed the whole group. "I hate today's womb-to-tomb style, in which every word you ever say can be dragged back and thrown in your face. Does anyone want to say something off the record? Remember, once the computer is in the loop, everything you say will go into the data banks."

"I wish to speak." Vow-of-Silence held up a thin forelimb. The Pipe-Rilla had so far been remarkably quiet. She stretched her long body forward, toward Dag Korin. "Sir, I am concerned about two things. First, the term 'General.' It was used several times by Dr. Siry in addressing you. Is that merely an honorific, or are you a 'general' in the military sense?"

Korin bristled. "Is there any other sense? What do you think I am, a general store? I'm a military general, and I'm proud of it."

"Indeed. Then my second question has added weight. In discussing what should be done to make it possible for us to return home, you used the phrase, 'strong-arm another bunch of aliens.' Were you advocating the use of violence?"

"Hmm. Well, not exactly. I just meant—"

"Because if you had any such intention, I wish to make it clear that neither I, nor any other member of the Stellar Group, will sanction such action. There must be no violence. There are always better alternatives to violence."

"I'm sure there are." But Dag Korin's frown and jutted jaw added a silent, *Like hell*.

"With that understanding, I have no further comments and I suggest that the ship's computer should join this meeting."

"Everyone else agree?"

"Ready to roll." The Angel waved sedately.

"All right. Elke?"

She nodded and touched a pad sequence on the console in front of her. "Gamma-D, prepare to receive recognition templates prior to a search of the data banks received as orbiter survey data. I'm going to draw them."

UNDERSTOOD, WE ARE READY.

"Just one second." This time it was Chan Dalton. "I'm as keen to get home as anyone, and I don't want to hold this up. But before you start describing what the computer should look for, can't we have a quick status report? Even if it's not an emergency, I'd like to know if there's been any significant change in the ship's condition."

"That makes good sense." Dag Korin ignored Elke's

impatient gesture. "Find out where you are before you decide where you're going, always a sound policy. All right, Gamma-D. Let's hear how things stand."

MANY ONBOARD FUNCTIONS ARE SUFFERING A SLOW ALTHOUGH AS YET NON-DANGEROUS DEGRADATION. IT WOULD BE ADVISABLE TO MOVE TO A MORE TYPICAL AMBIENT ENVIRONMENT.

"In other words," Liddy whispered to Bony, "don't stay underwater longer that you have to. For this we need a computer?"

"Shh!"

THE DEFENSIVE SHIELDS ARE LOST, AND THEY REMAIN IRREPLACEABLE WITHOUT A VISIT TO A MAJOR FLEET REFURBISHING CENTER. THERE IS MINOR HULL DAMAGE THAT DECREASES THE LEVEL OF TOLERABLE STRESSES UNDER ACCELERATED FLIGHT. A LIMIT OF TWO GEES SHOULD BE OBSERVED IN OPEN SPACE IN THE VICINITY OF A LINK TRANSITION POINT.

"Two gees in open space, near a Link point," Dag Korin growled. "Don't you wish!"

THERE IS NO OTHER DAMAGE TO THE SHIP ITSELF. HOWEVER, SOME COLLATERAL EQUIPMENT HAS SUFFERED FAILURE.

"What do you mean, collateral equipment?" Chan Dalton had been studying a new schematic of the *Hero's Return* that highlighted any problem area. "Everything here looks fine to me."

THE SCHEMATIC THAT YOU HAVE IS OF THE SHIP ITSELF, WHERE THERE ARE NO MAJOR FAILURES. WE REFER TO COLLATERAL EQUIPMENT IN THE FORM OF THE TWO OBSERVATION SATELLITES THAT WE LAUNCHED.

"Oh, no," Elke groaned. "We didn't get data from them? Gamma-D, I was relying on them to allow a ground search."

THAT WILL STILL BE POSSIBLE. MANY DATA WERE RETURNED, ENOUGH TO PROVIDE A COMPLETE SCAN OF THE

WHOLE PLANET. HOWEVER, APPROXIMATELY TWO HOURS AGO THE SATELLITES FAILED.

"Both of them?" Elke's thin eyebrows rose. "Are you sure that it's not a problem with our onboard receiving equipment?"

THAT WAS OF COURSE CHECKED, AND IT IS IN PERFECT WORKING ORDER. ALSO, THE TWO OBSERVING SATELLITES DID NOT FAIL SIMULTANEOUSLY. THE FIRST FAILED TWO AND A QUARTER HOURS AGO, THE SECOND TWENTY MINUTES LATER.

"Radiation belts?" Elke said, more to herself than the computer. "Solar flare?"

WE RULE OUT BOTH THOSE POSSIBILITIES. COMPUTING THE TRAJECTORIES OF THE SATELLITES WITH RESPECT TO THE ROTATING PLANET, WE DISCOVERED THAT BOTH FAILED WHEN THEY WERE OVER THE SAME POINT OF THE PLANETARY SURFACE. THE PROBABILITY OF SUCH A FAILURE OCCURRING AS A RESULT OF NATURAL CAUSES IS NEGLIGIBLY SMALL. WE CONCLUDE THAT THE TWO OBSERVING SATELLITES FAILED AS A RESULT OF DELIBERATE DESTRUCTIVE ACTION UNDERTAKEN FROM THE SURFACE OF THE PLANET.

"Shot down, by God! Blown apart by bloody aliens." Dag Korin glared at Vow-of-Silence, as though daring the Pipe-Rilla to challenge his statement, but when he spoke again it was accusingly to the computer. "Gamma-D, why the devil didn't you tell us about this as soon as it happened?"

WE WERE INSTRUCTED TO INTERRUPT YOUR MEETING ONLY IF THERE WAS IMMEDIATE DANGER TO THE SHIP. WE JUDGED THAT WAS NOT THE CASE.

"Not immediate, maybe. But soon. Well, it was my fault more than yours." Korin slouched down in his seat. "Gamma-D, do you know the point on the surface where the whatever-it-is that destroyed our observing satellites came from?"

YES. TO REFINE THAT ANSWER, WE HAVE COMPUTED A LOCATION OF MAXIMUM PROBABILITY FOR THE ORIGIN OF THE DESTRUCTIVE ACTION. IT LIES FORTY-SIX KILOMETERS FROM THE SHIP'S PRESENT LOCATION. SHOULD WE DISPLAY IT?

"Damn right you should." Korin watched as an image of Limbo's whole hemisphere appeared on the screen, then zoomed in until one point of the surface showed highlighted by a flashing spark of light. "Well, I think we've answered one question and saved Elke some work. The job of finding an alien spaceport, settlement, military base or whatever has been done for us. We know where they are. And we know what they do. They shoot first, and later they ask questions. The question is, what do *we* do now?"

24

Limbo Plans

"What do we do now?"

Dag Korin had asked the question, but he acted as though he expected no answers. A couple of seconds later he stood up and said, "Well, we'll all think better when we've had some rest. It's been a long day, and I don't know about you but I'm bushed."

As he left the fire control chamber he unobtrusively gestured to Chan Dalton to follow. They walked through the dark interior of the *Hero's Return*, listening to the wheeze of air pumps and the groans and creaks of the stressed hull.

"The computer says we're in fair shape," Korin said gruffly, "but it doesn't sound that way to me. I want a more detailed analysis of the ship's condition. Hear that, Gamma-D?"

WE WILL PROVIDE A COMPLETE REPORT TO YOU.

"Soon as you can. You see, Dalton, the *Hero's*

Return is a space cruiser, she was never built to sit at the bottom of some stinking ocean. My guess is that in a few days we'll have to get this hulk off the seabed and out into vacuum, or we'll be forced to abandon ship. And that raises some pretty interesting questions that I don't want to talk about yet."

The two men walked on in silence, past empty weapons chambers and massive drive engines, past the room housing the ship's master computer, past deserted crew quarters. It was like a ghost ship. Neither spoke until they reached a door of bilious green and passed through into Dag Korin's private quarters.

"Now we can really talk freely." Korin glanced at Chan. "Know why we're in here?"

"Computer?"

"Good man. I checked when I first came aboard. It's the main reason I chose this for my quarters—the only place on the ship that to my certain knowledge has no computer sensor feeds. Safer than asking the computer not to listen, which I've never had any faith in. This place goes back to the time when the *Hero's Return* was on active duty. You'd find one room like this on most military vessels, because in any army and any navy, there's a few things better left off the record. Sit down. And instead of me telling you, you tell me. Where do we stand?"

The general loosened his collar, which Chan took to mean that the conversation would be informal.

"We're in deep shit," he said. "Bad trouble. Right?"

Dag Korin nodded. "I think so. Trouble how?"

"Well, we seem to be in some 'parallel universe,' whatever that means, with different physics. It's a big shock, but that sort of thing doesn't interest me nearly as much as it interests Elke Siry. I have more practical worries. Even if the ship were in good shape, we can't live on the bottom of the sea forever."

"If we could, we sure as hell wouldn't want to."

"So we have to get to the surface. But if we do, I can't see the *Hero's Return* being in any condition to stand a Link transfer back home."

"That's what my gut feeling tells me. We're matching tracks so far. Go on."

"So we have to find some other ship. But all the vessels that our different groups came in are either lost or worse off than this one."

"Do you believe that?"

"I wouldn't believe a computer. But I've known Bony Rombelle for a long time, and he's the best gadget man I ever met. If he tells us the other ships are lost, or pieces of junk that can't be fixed up, I believe him."

"Then I'll do the same—though when I was young I wouldn't have let a man who dressed as sloppy as that out of the ship's galley. What else?"

"The Link point. General, we didn't build it, and it's nothing like the ones we know. Throw in the different physical laws, and not even Bony can be expected to figure the transition protocol out from scratch."

"Understood. So?"

"So if we're going home, we have to locate and learn to talk to whoever built the Link."

"Exactly my conclusion." Korin glanced at Chan from under lowered brows. "And what we know about them already—unless there's two different technological alien groups on Limbo, which is pretty unlikely—isn't promising. In the only contact so far, they put two of our orbiters out of action for no reason except that we were making observations. So they have weapons. We don't. And they're either very nasty or very paranoid."

"Or both. But it's not completely true that we have

no weapons. Deb Bisson always has a hundred personal killing tricks somewhere on her or in her."

"All very well if she can get near enough. Not good if the enemy has real firepower and can blow you away at a thousand kilometers. But we're getting close to what's really on my mind. We have to find out more about the land-based aliens, and we can't do it sitting here. This is where you earn your pay, Dalton. I want you to organize a shore party ASAP, and give us a land base ourselves." Korin stared at Chan's smile. "Suits your taste, doesn't it?"

"It sure does. I don't like to sit around in a metal can at the bottom of the sea. I didn't come here for that. I'm used to *doing* things."

"Good. So am I. So now let's get down to the reason I wanted to come in here before we started to talk. You know the biggest obstacle in our way? No, it's not the hostile aliens—though they'll be bad enough. It's the *friendly* aliens who worry me. The Tinkers and the Pipe-Rilla and that damned oversized vegetable Angel, they're the ones who may make our job impossible. They say, no violence. But they don't tell us how to manage *without* violence. What do you do when somebody tries to shoot your ass off? In my book, you shoot right back, and if they have an ass at all you blow it away. And we're not allowed to. So here's what we have to do." In spite of his insistence that they could not be overheard, Korin leaned forward and dropped his voice to a whisper. "The aliens are worried about me already, because I'm a General. I'm going to talk and act so they'll worry about me a whole lot more. You and your team do the exact opposite. All sweetness and light and talk of peaceful tactics. That way, the Stellar Group aliens are going to keep a close eye on me, here in the ship, and you'll be free to go and do whatever you have to ashore. Do you agree? Remember, once we're outside this room we won't be able to talk without being recorded."

"I agree with most of it. But I have a couple of worries. First, what happens if the aliens insist on coming ashore?"

"Are they likely to?"

"They are if they think we're going to meet other aliens. The Angel is supposed to be an unbelievable talent when it comes to languages. We have one of those talents ourselves, Tully O'Toole, unless his brain has been fried by Paradox. If it has, there's still Tarbush Hanson. He can talk to animals, and our aliens may be close to that. But the Angel may say it wants to go with us, anyway. I don't see how we can stop it."

"I have an idea on that. I think the Angel is the only possible one to work with Elke on a high-priority project I have for her. If some other alien wants to go ashore, don't try to stop it. Your people go, and when they're ashore they split into two groups. What other problems?"

"It's not so much a problem as a delay. I'm sure we can get ashore safely, because the Bun and Liddy Morse already did it. But we'll need maps, at least local ones, of the coastline and land areas. You said we should leave as soon as possible, but I'd like to wait until the computer produces the maps that Elke Siry asked for."

"Of course you'll need maps. An army should never travel blind."

"Not much of an army. Six of us—seven, if Liddy Morse comes along."

"No. Not seven, and not six. I'm sorry, Dalton, I don't mind Morse going, if you want her; but Rombelle stays here."

"I need him ashore."

"You're not going ashore, either—at least, you're not going with the first party."

Chan stood up. "Don't give me that bullshit. I have to lead the shore party. Don't forget that I'm in charge now."

"No. You would have been in charge if we had reached the Geyser Swirl, but we never did. Look, Dalton, I'm not making a power play. I'm minimizing risks. No one in his right mind sends half the total strength of an expedition on a first scouting party, and I'm agreeing on close to that. Four people go. Maybe an alien, too—we can't control them. Pick who you like of your team, provided that it's not you and not Rombelle. You both stay here. I'm taking your word for it that Rombelle is something special when it comes to equipment fix-up."

"He is. That's why the shore party needs him."

"It's also the reason he can't go. Suppose there's mechanical trouble with this ship? It looks and sounds worse every hour. How would you like the shore party to be stranded, with no *Hero's Return* to come back to or to rely on for supplies?" Korin waited for Chan's slow nod. "Then that's the way it has to be. You'll think we're sending an army anyway, when you hear me talking to our crazy alien companions. I'm going to sound like rage and destruction for them. They'll shit bricks—I mean, if any of them shits anything at all."

After Dag Korin and Chan Dalton had left for the general's private quarters, the remaining party broke into two groups.

Most of the members of the old team, plus Liddy, drifted off toward the rear of the ship in the direction that Dag Korin and Chan Dalton had taken. The

Stellar Group aliens followed the slow-moving Angel toward the ship's sunroom and garden. Remaining in the fire control room were only Tully O'Toole and Elke Siry.

"D'you mind if I stay? Or am I in your way?" Tully was hanging around, watching Elke and looking shaky and dejected.

"You're not in my way unless you interfere with my work." Elke was studying images taken by the two orbiters, selecting a few for display with increased detail. "You people really love Chan Dalton, don't you?"

"I can't speak for the rest, but he saved me from worse than death." When Elke gave him a skeptical glance from the corner of one eye, he went on. "I'm talking about Paradox addiction. Do you know what that is?"

She lost interest in the displays and turned to face him.

"Not exactly. But I know something that can match it." She pulled her high-necked white blouse all the way down to her right collarbone, to reveal ugly scar tissue in the shape of a fiery star.

"Slither!" In his astonishment Tully reached out to touch the blemish on her white skin, but she stiffened and jerked away. He sat back and shook his tousled head. "I can't believe this. You and Slither. It's so disgusting, and you're so—so—"

"Pure and spotless and absolutely perfect?" Elke gave him a grim smile, revealing the prominent canines. "I suppose you've been reading about me in the ship's files. You shouldn't believe most of that. I wrote it myself. I decided what to put in—and what to leave out."

"But *Slither*. How did you get hooked?"

"I was seventeen. That's when I knew I was more

intelligent than anyone in the universe. I confused that with understanding about life. I'd heard of the Slithers—we all had—but I knew they could never snare me. I was too smart for that. But I let one sit on my shoulder, and it felt wonderful . . ."

"And it had you. Where did it lodge?"

"Right above my liver. I guess I was lucky, in three cases out of ten it heads for the brain."

"What saved you?"

"You mean *who*. General Korin served with my grandfather, out on the Perimeter. When my grandpa was dying, the General promised that when he came back to Sol he would look me up. I should have been easy to find, because I was a star researcher at the Trieste Institute for Advanced Study. And I was there—almost. General Korin tracked me down a kilometer or two away, in a Slither mating cellar. He confirmed who I was—I could still tell him my name—and he went away. He didn't try to talk to me, didn't ask what had happened. He came back the next day with three of his officers, bundled me up in a sheet, and shanghaied me away into space."

Elke studied Tully's gaunt features, then turned back to her work at the displays. "I didn't think so at the time, but I guess I had things easy. I had the operation for Slither removal and the chemotherapy to end Slither sexual addiction. But I was on Helene, with round-the-clock nursing, not in another universe wondering if I was ever going home. But you're improving, Tully. I see it every day. The worst is over."

"I'd like to think you're right, but I still dream each night. In my dream I'm sitting there with the little purple sphere in my fist, and I'm all set to touch it to my wrist. Deep inside I know that I mustn't, that if I do it will start all over again. But I can't stop my hand. It brings the Paradox globe closer and closer to my skin."

"Ah, I have a dream like that." Elke's face took on an odd wistfulness. "I'm sitting alone, and the Slither is still inside me. It begins calling, 'Go and bring me a mate. Bring us both ecstasy.' It isn't lying. When you and somebody else with a Slither have sex it's too good to be true. So I start to stand up, and I'm on the way to the rendezvous point, and I have the promise of ecstasy squared. But I know it will soon lead to death."

"That's it! That's it exactly. You mustn't touch, but you want it so much. You've felt it, too." Again Tully reached out toward Elke, again he pulled back when he saw her flinch.

He cursed his own lack of sensitivity. No wonder, after being a Slither slave—*say something, anything*. "So it was Dag Korin saved you. I'd never have guessed that."

"Why else would I be here, on a ship lost at the end of the universe?" She would not look at him. She had focused her attention on the displays. "No, not lost in the universe. Lost in the multiverse, an infinite set of universes. I'm here for the same reason as you. You came because Chan Dalton wanted you to, I came because Dag Korin wanted me to. This turns out to be the most exciting thing that could happen to a scientist, but I didn't know that when I agreed to come. Couldn't you tell I was doing it for the General?"

Tully said nothing, and she looked away from the screens to stare at him. "What is it? What's wrong now?"

"Nothing."

"That's a lie, Tully O'Toole. Your face usually looks white as something dredged from the seabed, and now it's all pink. What did I say?"

"You said not a word. It's what I thought."

"So tell me what."

"It's so absurd. I thought that you were here because you were Dag Korin's"—Tully screwed up his face—"well, this only proves what an ass I am. I thought you were Dag Korin's *mistress*."

"A woman could do worse than General Korin, a lot worse. But me, his mistress? That's a laugh." Elke gave a snort that sounded nothing like a laugh. "I couldn't let him—or any man—"

Elke turned away and bent her blond head over the control board.

"I understand," Tully said quickly. "After the Slither, any touch would be too much. But it's all right now I know. Do you want me to go?"

"No, I'd rather that you stay. Two untouchables together. But I must keep on working."

"Of course you must. Can I help? I once had a working brain, and a good pair of eyes." Tully moved so that he could study the screen, being careful to keep well clear of Elke. "Do you know what you're looking at?"

"I'm learning. This is the view from one of the orbiters, just before it stopped recording. The smooth dark area is the sea, and the *Hero's Return* is about here." She stabbed at the screen with a long, tapering index finger. "You can't see us, of course, since we're down deep. But the little blob you see beside the inlet is the *Mood Indigo*."

"It's not in the water. It's on the shore."

"I know. The storm might have carried it there."

"Is it a wreck?"

"I don't know. But the most interesting part of this picture isn't in the sea area, except maybe for this one spot." Her finger moved left, to indicate a small white circle. "According to the inertial guidance system on this ship—which I'm going to assume still works correctly, even if the laws of physics are all a bit different here—according to the guidance system, that's where we first emerged into the Limbo ocean. So my thought is that the little disk is all that's left of the Link transition point. It comes and goes, and it's not there now. And don't ask me how it can be part underwater, instead of in a vacuum or a thin atmosphere, because I have no idea."

"And this thing?" Tully reached carefully over Elke's arm to indicate another part of the scene. "Like part of a great big ring."

"It is. The boundary is an exact circle when you make allowance for the look angle." Elke ran a finger along the smooth arc. "This marks the edge of a zone of destruction. It only shows on the land and not at sea. Inside this region there's nothing but blackened soil and dark gray rocks. Outside the burned part it's a mixture of green and orange. I'm betting that this was originally all growing plants. Somebody sterilized the whole inner region, about seven hundred square kilometers. And guess what's at the exact center of the black circle?"

"Tell me."

"Better than that, I'll show you." Elke tapped at the board in front of her, and the picture on the display expanded, zooming in on one small area. "This is the highest magnification the image can take without losing detail. But it's enough."

Tully counted six drab buildings of muddy yellow, running along each side of a long and narrow stretch of white. At each end of the strip, facing each other, sat two tiny tri-lobed shapes.

"A settlement," he said softly, "and funny-looking aircraft. I told you that the Bun was reliable. He said he saw one in the sky, and now we know he didn't lie."

"We do indeed." Tully and Elke had been so absorbed in the image that the voice from behind made them jump.

"Aircraft, yes," Dag Korin went on. He had entered the chamber silently and alone. "But I wouldn't call that a *settlement*. See the boundary fence, with guard posts all along it? Throw in the scorched-earth perimeter for kilometers in each direction, and you have yourself a classic military camp. Our head-up-their-wazoo Stellar Groupies can preach peace all they like, but whoever made that encampment had war on their minds. This isn't their home territory, either, or they wouldn't blast everything for miles around them. And don't be fooled by thinking this is all defenses. They may have only a few aircraft, but I'll bet they have other weapons."

"More than a few planes." Tully had been leaning close to the screen as the General spoke, studying the enlarged picture. "Look over here, well outside the camp. It's not easy to see them because they match the color of the ground. But isn't that more aircraft?"

"Six, seven, eight." The way that Dag Korin counted made each word sound like a curse. "Aye, and there's another batch of the damned things, farther over. They're camouflaged to match the background, but not very well. I'd have expected these alien buggers to do a better job, they're careful enough about other things. Maybe there's hope for us after all."

Elke was working the keypad in front of her. "Well, if there is hope," she said, "I'd credit our technology more than alien weaknesses. The orbiters had the best sensors that humans know how to build, and they could record signals at wavelengths all the way from ultraviolet to radar. Here's what the ground would look like if the orbiters only sensed the range of wavelengths that human eyes can see."

The picture as a whole remained the same—except that Tully, staring, could now see no details within the burned area. Buildings, boundary fence, airstrips, aircraft were gone. All had been swallowed up within the dark background.

"Well, I'll be damned." Korin squinted at the image. "Bring it back the way it was, Elke. Ah, that's better. We're going to need a couple of printed copies of this, with compass settings marked."

"No problem." Elke did not move, leaving it to the ship's computer to take the necessary action.

"Plus any other information we can deduce about what's down there. For instance, what do you make of that?" Korin was pointing to a pair of oval shapes, close to one cluster of the triple-lobed aircraft but much larger than any. "Can you make those bigger?"

Elke shrugged her thin shoulders. "I can enlarge the picture, but you won't get any more detail. We're at the resolution limit of the orbiter's sensors."

"Pity." Korin rubbed at his jaw. "Well, we'll find out soon enough if I'm right."

Tully didn't think that Dag Korin had a high opinion of him. In fact, he had overheard himself referred to by the General, soon after his arrival on board the *Hero's Return*, as 'that long brain-dead streak of shivering misery.' Well, Tully had improved a lot since then, and Korin's favorite had also once been a Slither slave. He risked what might be a stupid question. "Sir, how do you know what those blobs might be? I can't make out any detail on them at all."

"No more can I, son, no more can I." Korin took a couple of steps away, as though he had said all he was going to, then swung around and added sharply, "I *imagine*, you see. What my eyes won't provide, I imagine with eighty years of war experience to guide me. And the more I look at that picture, the more a little voice inside me says, *military expedition*. Not a full-scale army, mind you, because the scale of operations is wrong for that. This is more like a scouting party, sent out to learn the lie of the land. Maybe sent to find out if Limbo is worth a bigger investment, or decide that the place is a dead loss and not worth another visit.

"Now, there's a logic to a scouting expedition, one that I'd suspect is common to all times and all species. First, you need a base of operations. We see that on the image. You also need the aircraft or ground vehicles to make sorties away from base, and you need to have enough of them to stand some losses from accidents or hostile action. That's what the aircraft are for. And there's one other must-have. You may be able to live off the land to some extent, but you'll need bigger transports—call them mother ships if you like—to bring you to your sphere of operations in the first place. Little scoutships won't be enough for that, and they won't be able to carry everything you need for weeks or months of operations. That's what I think the two ovals are. They brought them here to Limbo, through a Link point of their making and under their control. And in our present situation, those mother ships represent our own best shot at a way to go home."

Korin paused and frowned at the other two. "Now, that's my thinking. It may be wrong, so feel free to poke holes in it. Ask questions."

Elke said softly, "If you don't mind, I'd rather ask about the other part of what you said earlier."

"Other part."

"You told us, 'we'll find out soon enough if I'm right.' What made you say that?"

"No secret there. We can't sit here until this ship rots around us. I'm organizing a shore party to explore the land—"

"That's terrific! I've been analyzing data from the orbiters, and I've been wondering about a thousand other things—"

"—but you won't be part of the shore group, Elke."

"What! I'm not an engineer. I don't know how to keep things running on the ship. But ashore, I can—"

"No. You have other things to do, and they may be a lot more important than going ashore. You were the one who came up with the idea that we're lost, not just somewhere in our own universe but somewhere in an infinity of universes. You're our best shot—I'd say our only shot—at cracking the secrets of the multiverse. I want you focused on that, and the properties of the alien Link. I want to know about other universes that we might be able to reach—are they more or less similar to our own, could humans survive in them. I don't want you distracted by thoughts of Limbo's other life-forms, or war games, or shore parties. Understood?"

It was a few moments before Elke turned away and said softly, "Yes, sir. I'll explore the multiverse, and the Link."

Dag Korin nodded. Only Tully, sitting so that Elke had been forced to face him when she swiveled around, saw the look of secret joy—and wondered if this was exactly what Elke had wanted all along.

25

Shore Plans

Friday Indigo sat on a rock ledge with his legs immersed in water up to the mid-calf. He was inside a long, stone-walled room with a dark pool down the middle. The edge of the pool was marked by a set of tapered columns, conical towers taller than a man. Scores of lumbering Malacostracans, all bigger than Two-Four, scuttled and splashed to and fro at the poolside in what seemed like random motion.

The One stood motionless behind Friday. The thin snaky fingers had withdrawn little by little from his ears, until now they barely touched the skin.

"Once more we will test." The voice that Friday heard did not come from the translation unit. It was inside his head, warm and friendly and infinitely comforting. "Tell us your name."

"I am Friday Indigo."

"That is satisfactory." The tendrils withdrew

completely, slithering back into the body of The One. "We detect no signal loss. We will later confirm the efficiency of operation over greater distances. Now, however, you will answer questions concerning your universe, your world, and your people. You have said that the universe from which you came has 'countless' suns and many habitable worlds. How many suns? How many worlds? How many *habitable* worlds? How does your universe compare with this one?"

Friday struggled to answer. He wanted to do it right, with every nerve, with every brain cell, with every ounce of his strength and concentration. But he could not do it. He lacked information. At last he said, "In our universe, stars are organized into large groups called *galaxies*. Each galaxy contains many billions of stars. One star in every ten of our own galaxy has planets around it. One planet in a thousand is able to support life like our kind and yours. There are theories to explain why planets converge toward common life-supporting properties, but I do not understand them. We have little knowledge of any galaxy except the one that our own sun is in, but we think that they are all similar in their ability to create planetary systems, and that an equal fraction of planetary systems probably supports life. But I cannot compare with *this* universe, because I do not know the properties of this universe."

"You have provided the information that we need." The voice of The One soothed and cheered Friday. "You confirm that your own universe, unlike this one or most of the rest of the accessible levels of the multiverse, is hospitable to life. This one, by contrast, is most inhospitable. Based on the observed properties of the sky-globes, we estimate that the nearest star with a planetary train is more than five thousand lightyears away from here. This universe is a disappointment to us."

Friday felt inside his brain a new touch that could not translate to words. He shivered with shared sorrow and dissatisfaction, until the One continued, "We intend to link ourselves through to your universe. First, however, we need more information. Tell us of your people, and of this 'Stellar Group' that you mention. Talk of your technology, and list your strengths and weaknesses. Warn us of possible dangers. Give every fact that you know. Our powers of absorption are endless, and no amount of detail is too much."

Friday nodded. After a few moments he began to speak. Prompted now and again by The One, he did his best to empty his entire brain.

Minutes became hours. Occasionally The One interrupted to ask a question. Who in humans was the controlling class? Which one was the disposable class? Was there more than one sessile class? Friday had to answer that question in half a dozen different ways, before The One was satisfied that humans had no sessile class and continued: How is human breeding accomplished? How are offspring culled? In the Stellar Group, how can there be many species, without one being dominant?

Friday talked on and on, until all the Malacostracans other than The One were gone, and the long chamber was empty. The water that lapped around his calves gradually became freezing cold. The rock that he sat on was ridged and uneven and cut into his flesh. He had not eaten for almost two days.

He did not mind. He was aware of fatigue and physical discomfort, but they did not matter. He was blissfully happy.

When at last The One said, "That is enough for now," he was disappointed.

The One read his disappointment. "We have proved that your kind can be useful servants," it said soothingly. "Your life will continue. Lie down now, on your back." And, after a brief pause, "Sleep."

It was as well that Friday had received the order to lie down. Otherwise he would have fallen face forward into the water, asleep instantly. He would have died there, too—but he would have died happy.

He did not hear The One, mindful of the needs of the underclasses, add, "And after sleep you will be fed."

Who? Chan struggled with the problem for the rest of the day. Who would go ashore? Who must remain on the ship?

There was no doubt at all that everyone would *want* to go, but that was another matter.

He deliberately avoided Deb during the evening, and he chose a different place to sleep. They had spent the previous night together, but now he dared not allow personal persuasion and closeness to cloud his judgment.

By morning he had made up his mind. The condition of the *Hero's Return* when he awoke helped. The air entering through the ducts smelled stale. It was clammy on the skin, and every exposed metal surface sweated drops of water. The ship's computer insisted that all life-support systems were well within tolerances, but its sensors could not match a human's perception of discomfort or of coming problems.

So Dag Korin was right, and the Bun would have to stay to make whatever fixes he could think of. Chan didn't fool himself into thinking they would be any more than temporary. The bottom of the sea was simply the wrong place for a space-going ship. The *Hero's Return* was slowly dying.

Chan called for a breakfast meeting in the ship's main cafeteria. He made sure he was there first, and he watched their faces as they arrived in ones and twos. He swore to himself. He hadn't said a word to anyone, but they all knew something was about to happen—and it was his guess that they knew what.

He scanned the intent faces as they filled trays with food and carried them to the long table where he sat at the head. Danny Casement took a position next to Chan. He was as neatly groomed and debonair as always—and as inscrutable. Danny was a formidable card player, and no one would read his feelings and inner thoughts. Next to him, Tully O'Toole sat down with a loaded tray that he did no more than pick at. Chan could see the tremor in Tully's hand. He knew that morning feeling, the worst time of day for withdrawal symptoms.

Bony Rombelle arrived next at the table, carrying a big glass of water and a single slice of dry toast. Was this really the Bun? The Bun, whose idea of an adequate breakfast in the old days included eggs and bacon and sausage and pasta, followed by toast covered with enough butter to grease a locomotive?

Was the Bun feeling sick? No, it was something else. Chan saw Liddy Morse sit down next to Bony, and knew what it was. With any luck it wouldn't mess up the Bun's ability to make useful equipment out of any old bits and pieces that were to hand.

When Deb Bisson arrived she moved to sit at the other end of the table, facing Chan. Her eye met his accusingly. It said, *You're a coward, Chan Dalton. You know I won't be going ashore, but you won't tell me in person. You'll go, and leave me behind. That's why you avoided me last night. Don't I deserve better treatment than that?*

Well, Deb might have a surprise coming.

Last to arrive were Tarbush Hanson and Chrissie Winger. Maybe they didn't know after all. As they sat down at the table their faces were puzzled, as if they had no idea what was happening. Maybe they were really wondering; or maybe they were just better actors than the rest. As a magic team, they specialized in misdirection.

"Is there anyone who *doesn't* know why I asked you here this morning?" Chan began. Then he paused. Two others who had certainly *not* been invited were entering the room. The giant form of Vow-of-Silence, crouching low so her head would not hit the ceiling, led the way. Thousands of Tinker components followed the Pipe-Rilla like some long train of purple-black.

Chan waited while Vow-of-Silence folded her limbs awkwardly to perch on a neighboring table. Eager Seeker assembled on the floor next to her as a thick pulsing column about six feet tall.

"Please ignore us," Vow-of-Silence said. "We came only as observers."

Ignore them? When the Pipe-Rilla loomed over everyone? When the Tinker Composite formed a funnel opening in its upper extremity, and was now making the wheezing moans that preceded speech?

Chan said, "How did you learn that there was a meeting?"

"From Dag Korin." The thin head bobbed. "He came to us. He said you were going ashore. He spoke of great violence, of d-death and d-destruction."

"I think you must have misunderstood General Korin," Chan said. "We have no thought of violence ashore." He turned back to the circle of humans. "But there will be a shore party. Tell me, for my own curiosity. Who *didn't* know about this?"

Not a hand was raised.

"So who told you?"

"I heard it from Dag Korin, yesterday," Tully said. "He mentioned it when I was with Elke Siry. I knew what was going on, as soon as he said he would need maps of Limbo made from our satellite images. And he didn't give any impression that it was a secret, so I passed the word on to the others."

Korin again. He had some secret agenda, Chan felt sure of it. But what?

"Well, it's sure no secret now," Chan went on. "So let's talk about who will be going on the first shore party"—everyone at the table sat up straighter—"and who won't."

The tension rose. They all wanted to be on the shore party, of course they did. For that they would be prepared to lie, cheat, steal, even fight. Chan could see them getting ready to argue if they were left out, or defend the wisdom of his decision if they were included.

"For starters," he said, "I'll tell you one person who will not be in the first exploration party." The room crackled with nervous anticipation, until at last he went on, "I won't be going ashore. I will remain here on the ship."

It had the effect Chan wanted. The others sank back with a collective sigh. If he was off the list, no one else was a sure thing—and they knew it.

"Bony," Chan went on, "you can't go, either. This ship's rotting around us, and we need somebody to jury-rig the failing systems. Does anyone argue that the Bun is the only person for that job?"

Nods all round.

"But you can't do everything single-handed, Bony. So Liddy, I want you and the Bun to work together. You seem to do that very well. Tully the Rhymer"—Chan went on without giving either Bony or Liddy a chance for argument or discussion—"you have a job to do here, and it's a tough one. We've been talking to the bubble people using a translator, but they are so alien that we think the mechanical units miss subtleties. I want you to learn the bubble language until you can think like one of them. The Angel will be staying on board, to work with Elke Siry, and already speaks to the bubble people pretty well. Stay close to the Angel, and get all the help you can."

Chan saw Tully perk up a little from his shivering morning misery, and made an inspired guess. "That means you'll be close to Elke Siry, too, so I have one other job for you. I want you to apply your fading charms to Elke. I know she's in Dag Korin's back pocket, and she's doing special work for him. Whatever she learns and tells him, I want to hear about from you."

Chan stared down the length of the table at the people he had not spoken to so far. "Now for the rest of you. It's time either for congratulations or commiseration. Chrissie and Tarbush, I owe you for promising you would go in the pinnace, without bothering to check that the thing could fly. So you'll go, along with Deb and Danny." He held up his hand. "Before you start celebrating, let me assure you it won't be a picnic. We know there's a military camp on land, and we know that whoever runs it blew our orbiters out of the sky without any attempt at contact. Apparently they don't like anyone looking at them. Whatever else you may be when you go ashore, you won't be safe."

Bony said doubtfully, "But Liddy and I went ashore. We were all right."

"I know. That was before we flew our orbiters, and I don't think you got close enough to be noticed. The other possible explanation is that you were damned lucky, and you can't count on more luck." Chan reached down under the table and pulled up the rolled image that he had been holding between his legs. He unfolded it on the tabletop, weighting it down at the edges with mugs and plates.

"We should all look at this. I said at the beginning that some of us wouldn't be going on the *first* shore party, but I expect we'll all be there eventually. The *Hero's Return* brought us here, but I can't see it taking us back. We have to find another way home."

Chan pointed out the black circle on the flattened image. "This is a region of total destruction. The alien encampment is at the center here, and you should expect everything around it to be totally lifeless. When the Bun and Liddy went ashore they found not a sign of either plants or animals. Even the shallow water must have been sterilized. So our shore party won't land anywhere in the destruction zone. You'll go farther north, and sneak ashore in the vegetated area above the inlet that the bubble people call 'Death Fork.' It's actually closer to the location of the *Hero's Return*, so if you head due east along the seabed, like this, you'll arrive on the shore where there ought to be cover. After that"—Chan shrugged—"we won't be able to help. The four of you will be on your own. Do whatever you think is best."

A gentle voice said, "Excuse me if I intrude. But I have something that must be added."

Vow-of-Silence unfurled her body from its tabletop crouch and advanced to loom over the humans.

"I have no wish to interfere with your plans to explore the land area of this planet. I agree that this exploration may be necessary for our long-term survival, something that we all desire. For this reason, I offer my support. I will also go ashore."

The Tinker Composite's speaker funnel whirred for

two seconds like an electric fan, then produced words. "Our presence on land may be essential to your survival. We can send partial versions of ourself, even our individual elements, on rapid scouting missions. We can enter small apertures which would be to you quite inaccessible, or we can serve as inconspicuous observers. We will also go ashore."

Next to Chan, Danny Casement muttered, "It's always the same. Everybody wants to get into the act."

Chan had his own interpretation of what was going on. Dag Korin had been talking blood and thunder, and it had had precisely the wrong effect. Instead of focusing their attention on Korin, which is what the General had anticipated, the aliens now didn't trust any humans.

The rest of the team was looking at Chan, waiting for him to explain to the aliens why their presence ashore would be a bad idea. He decided to save his breath. Vow-of-Silence and Eager Seeker would listen politely to whatever he might choose to say, then do exactly what they wanted. On an issue like this there was no chance that they would change their minds.

Chan nodded to Vow-of-Silence. "The shore party will be pleased to have your assistance. However, you must be prepared to leave the ship in three hours. The party will need plenty of daylight hours ashore."

Deb, Tarbush, Chrissie and Danny were staring at him in disgust and disappointment. He said to them, "I need to work out some practical details with just the four of you. Can we get together right now, in my cabin?"

Giving no time for argument, Chan stood up and led the way out. He headed along the main axis of the ship to his cabin—and past it. Where the corridor widened, Deb Bisson moved to his side.

"I thought you said in your cabin?"

Chan put his finger to his lips. Deb got the message, and did not speak again. Finally they reached the door of bilious green, and passed through into Dag Korin's spartan quarters.

The room was empty. Chan motioned the others inside and closed the door. "We can talk freely here. This is one place—the only place on the ship, according to the General—where we definitely can't be overheard by the ship's computer. Remember that when you leave. Anything the computer hears, the aliens can find out about.

"I want to set a few things straight. You probably guessed why I won't be going with you. It's because Dag Korin won't let me, and he's officially in charge." Chan held up a hand to cut off the protests. "Yes, he is. And you can't have more than one person running things. So unless you want to start a mutiny, Korin has final say. Now I'm going to tell you one order he gave me to pass on to the shore party, something that can't ever be mentioned outside this room. I know you're all pleased to be going, but don't kid yourselves. It will be dangerous. So Korin's order to you—and my order, too—is simple: your first responsibility is to survive. You do whatever it takes to make sure of that. Remember, if you don't survive, you can't report back with whatever you find. If you're attacked, defend yourselves. Don't worry about justifying what you do, just do it. Let the Pipe-Rillas and the Tinkers yell and scream as much as they like about peaceful solutions, we'll worry about that problem when you come back. But make sure you come back. Any questions?"

"Yes." Tarbush Hanson was frowning. "If Korin is in charge, like you say, why are you and he letting the aliens go ashore? They may be useful, but more likely they'll just be a pain in the ass."

"That's probably true, and you'll have to live with

it. I said it wrong before. Dag Korin is in charge of the *humans* on board this ship. Neither he nor I can control what the aliens do—much as we would like to. Anything else?"

"Two and two, like in the old days?" Danny Casement spread his arms wide. "You know, divide and conquer. That way only one group is stuck with the aliens."

"If you can work it. You with Deb, Chrissie with Tarbush. I'd suggest that you have one forward pair and one covering, but that will be up to you. Handle it whatever way seems best when you get there. Anything else that can't be said where it will be overheard?"

The others looked at each other and shook their heads.

"Right, then. Go and get ready. I wasn't kidding when I told the aliens to be ready in three hours. You don't want to arrive ashore when it's almost dark."

Danny, Chrissie, and Tarbush headed for the door and left, but Deb Bisson hung back.

"When I couldn't find you last night," she said, "I thought it was because you had decided that you were going and I wasn't."

"I know."

"I owe you an apology."

"No, you don't. It's nothing compared with the one that I've owed you for all those years. Just promise me one thing."

"What?"

"Promise you won't try to be a hero. And promise you'll come back."

"That's two things." But Deb was smiling. "I'll do my best, Chan. And you, you'd better not hide away again when I do. Otherwise you'll have more trouble on your hands than you'll ever get from any alien."

26

The Best-Laid Plans

The preparations for the shore expedition had gone as smoothly as anyone could wish. Deb Bisson, wading cautiously out of the shallows and across a forty-meter strip of pebbles, was not about to let early success lull her into a feeling of security. Fortune was a fickle god and a random event; good luck could change in a moment to bad.

That didn't mean, though, that you couldn't improve the odds. Deb hurried across a layer of slimy brown plants and into a waist-high thicket of bristly cruciform reeds that snapped as she pushed them aside. She crouched there for five minutes, helmet closed, looking about her in all directions but especially to her right. A hundred yards that way lay the beginning of the "zone of destruction," and if trouble was coming it was most likely to arrive from there.

Finally she raised her arm and waved. The others

had been watching for her signal, their helmets close to the waterline. Chrissie, Danny and Tarbush reacted at once, coming ashore fast and willing to make a lot of splashing to gain a second or two.

The Stellar Group aliens were not in such a hurry. Deb, as unofficial leader of the shore team, cursed Vow-of-Silence's leisurely progress out of the water. The Pipe-Rilla was craning up to her full height, turning from side to side and examining the scene. It was one step short of waving a flag to announce your arrival. Eager Seeker was even worse. Tinker components were vanishing, flying off in all directions. If the land aliens monitored the region beyond the edge of the zone of destruction . . .

Chrissie was the first to reach Deb's side. "Helmets open?" she said.

"Might as well. One at a time, though, just in case."

"Me first, then." Chrissie opened her visor just as Danny and Tarbush, carrying the heaviest supply case between them, flopped down panting at her side. She sniffed the air, cautiously at first and then in bigger breaths. "Ah!"

"All right?"

"You've no idea. Inside the *Hero's Return* I never felt like I was on a planet at all. This is *air*. Try it."

Deb glanced at the beach. Vow-of-Silence was like a four-meter flagpole, making a slow and stately approach. More Tinker components had disappeared, flying into the nearby undergrowth. Now that they were all ashore, they had to see how well they could survive here.

She opened her own helmet, closed her eyes, and sniffed. The air made her nostrils tingle, and it carried an odor that made her feel slightly dizzy.

No, that wasn't the result of the smell in the air. It was the air itself, slightly richer, slightly higher in oxygen content. It was quite safe to breathe, according to the samples that Bony Rombelle and Liddy Morse had brought back. But it was just as well to lie low for a while and let their bodies become used to the changes. The difference in air and gravity between Earth and Limbo was less than the difference between, say, Earth and Europa, and humans made that adaptation easily enough. But they didn't have to do it in a few minutes.

Danny Casement and Tarbush Hanson were following the women's lead, opening their helmets and sniffing the air.

"Put all the supplies down here," Deb said. "This is as good a place as any for our preliminary base. If you take your suits off, fold them neatly. We might have to get into them in a hurry."

Danny, who with Tarbush had laid the massive supply case carefully on a cleared area, paused and turned up his nose at her. "Did you ever know me to do anything that *wasn't* neat? If we do take our suits off, I suggest we make sure we close the helmets, too. How would you like to find one of *these* inside yours when you came to put it on again?"

He reached across to a spindly purple fern and plucked off it a dark red creature as long as his hand. The animal wriggled desperately to escape, scores of legs waving madly.

"Don't be stupid, Danny," Deb said sharply. "Suppose it has a poison bite or sting?"

"If this critter can bite through a suit's gauntlet, we're in bigger trouble than I thought. I vote for keeping suits on all the way. We're going to be *walking* through this stuff, and it's anybody's guess what else is out there."

Danny was right. Deb had been crouched below the level of the plant tops. Now she stood up and made a slow, careful survey of their surroundings. They had come ashore at a site chosen by Elke Siry from the space images. Behind them was the placid sea, moving in slow, lazy billows. Ahead lay a small valley between two ridges of dense vegetation. The plus side was that their landing was less likely to be observed; the minus was that even standing up they could not see over the ridge to the place where the camp of the aliens was supposed to be.

Deb examined the plants in front of her, and she did not like what she saw. Where the satellite images at highest magnification showed only smooth, level ground, the reality was a thicket of dense, spiny vegetation. Also, in places it moved in gentle billows of its own—and there was almost no wind. Something was imposing a rhythmic sway on the tough plants.

Maybe the aliens knew what they were doing. Maybe the region around their camp had been sterilized for good reason.

Deb's worries took more solid form when a small group of Tinkers rose from close by and went winging their way inland. They flew low, just above the tops of the plants. Suddenly they all dipped in unison, at the same time as a wave of purple fronds moved up to meet them. And then every one was gone, absorbed by the wave.

"Eager Seeker! What happened?"

Deb thought she was talking to nothing, but a second later the Tinker Composite was starting to coalesce in front of her. The speaking funnel formed, and at last the words came.

"We no longer have contact with that part of us. We fear that the units are—lost."

"They were destroyed?"

Deb asked the question automatically, and a moment later was cursing herself for doing so. A

Tinker Composite was no better than a Pipe-Rilla at admitting the possibility of physical violence. Eager Seeker produced a muffled stutter, but the Composite was already dissociating into its components. Ten seconds later every element had vanished into the dense bushes.

Vow-of-Silence said in a high, nervous voice, "Perhaps the missing components found something of interest that they wished to investigate."

Tarbush Hanson turned on the Pipe-Rilla. "You think so? So why don't *you* go take a look, an' see what's so fascinatin' out there. Rather you than me."

"All right, Tarb." Chrissie put her hand on his arm. "Take it easy. We work together, or we're all in trouble."

"We do." Danny Casement turned to Deb. "Mind if Vow-of-Silence takes a look with it? Give her something to occupy her mind, and she's supposed to have phenomenal vision."

"Do you think she's tall enough to take a peek over the ridge if she uses it?"

"Worth a try. And if she's not that tall, it's for sure none of the rest of us is. Shall I?"

Deb nodded. Even before that Danny was bending over and rooting in the supply case. He pulled from it a round cylinder half a meter long and about as thick as his upper arm.

"Here, big girl." He handed the cylinder to Vow-of-Silence. "Courtesy of Bony Rombelle, in the bit of time he had before we left when he wasn't fiddling with the ship. See what you can do with that."

"It is a—" the Pipe-Rilla held it in two forelimbs, and turned it over and over "—what is it? Why do you offer it to me?"

"It's a periscope. It works like this." Danny pulled out the extensible tube, foot after foot, until it was as long as the Pipe-Rilla was tall. "You look into one end, the thick end here, and you get a view of what the thin end sees. The question is, if you stand up and raise this as high as you can, are you able to look over the top of the ridge?"

"I do not know. But I will find out." Vow-of-Silence crouched down, then slowly and carefully raised the periscope until it was vertically above her head. "Not from this position. But perhaps if I rise . . ."

The long, thin body slowly unfolded, until it towered far above the watching humans.

"I have a view over the ridge." The Pipe-Rilla's voice came from far above. "And as you say, buildings are visible. Many buildings, around a long cleared strip of land—the airstrip seen in the images. And beings moving, around the buildings. And . . ." The tone of voice changed. "Is there any way to operate this device at higher magnification?"

"Be reasonable!" Danny called up to her. "The Bun cobbled this together from any leftover bits of optics he could find. It's mechanical, not electronic. What you see is what you get. Just what is it you'd like to see in more detail?"

"I am not sure." Vow-of-Silence remained standing for another long minute, then at last crouched down to the same level as the humans. "Perhaps my eyes are deceiving me, but here is what I saw. I saw many creatures moving around the buildings. Some were bigger than others, but all of them had the same overall body plan. Except for one."

The Pipe-Rilla bent yet lower, and placed a pair of forelimbs together in a gesture that seemed apologetic. She stared into Deb Bisson's eyes. "That one—as I said, I cannot be sure, and I do not like to speculate on such an important matter—but that other one had a different shape, a quite different body design." Vow-of-Silence paused, as if not sure that she wanted to say what came next. At last she murmured, almost too low to hear, "That other one seemed like one of you: that other one had the shape of a human."

What Vow-of-Silence had seen, or possibly not seen, led to the shore party's first major disagreement. The Pipe-Rilla was all in favor of walking straight up to the encampment. "They did not harm the one person, who can only be Friday Indigo. So why should they harm us? It is so like humans, to assume the worst of every other living thing. Let me approach the encampment, and announce our presence."

Deb was ready to argue, but she didn't need to. Eager Seeker said, "With respect, it is easy for you to say that. You have not lost a part of you. We urge caution." The mound of the Tinker Composite became taller and thinner. A group of topmost components began a preliminary fluttering of purple-black wings. "We can fly parts of ourself high over the ridge, and make our initial contact with low risk."

"With respect, although as a composite you possess superior reasoning powers, your separate components are not capable of thought or intelligible discourse." Vow-of-Silence began to stand up. "It is far better if I go."

"With respect, we must disagree."

Deb suddenly understood what the argument was really about. "No one should go until we've learned a lot more," she said, "and I'll tell you why. You're both hoping to have first contact with a new species. Well, we humans are just as keen for that. But if it is Friday Indigo inside the encampment, you're too late. And if it isn't Friday Indigo, we have no evidence that whoever lives in that encampment would accept any offer of our friendship."

The Tinker Composite did not speak, but sagged a foot lower. The flutter of component wings ended. Vow-of-Silence crouched low, and stared at Deb. For once the Pipe-Rilla lived up to her name.

"I'm as eager to meet the aliens as any of you," Deb said, "but we'll only do it when we know it's safe. And if it's not Friday Indigo over in the encampment, we all go to meet the aliens together. That way there will be no arguments about first contact. Agreed?"

No one spoke, and Deb went on, "So here's what I propose. I'll snake through the vegetation, keeping low, until I can get a closer look at the encampment. No matter what I see, I won't make any attempt at contact—that's a promise. I'll return here, tell you what I've seen, and we'll decide what we want to do next. Everyone in agreement?"

"No." The objection came not from Vow-of-Silence, or Eager Seeker. It was Chrissie Winger who was shaking her head. "You're the leader of the shore party, even if you don't think so. That means we normally do what you say."

"So do what I say now."

"Wait a minute. The team leader ought not to be an advance scout, because you may have to make tough decisions back here. Suppose you get into trouble, what do the rest of us do? So somebody else ought to go take the look-see. I propose that Tarb and me do it." Chrissie held up a hand, because Deb's mouth was opening. "The two of us have been sitting on our hands for weeks, waiting to find something to do—"

"We all have," said Danny.

"—something that fits in with our special skills. Now, you Danny, you can charm the leg off a chair, but that's not what we need at the moment. You can't charm an alien until you can talk to one. And you,

Deb, you're a weapons master, and your special skill is fighting." That produced a groan from Vow-of-Silence and a hiss from Eager Seeker. Chrissie went on, speaking fast. "We're not allowed to fight. But Tarb, on the other hand, he can read a person or an animal's intentions without them saying a word. And he's stronger than anyone I know. As for me, my specialty is deception. Call it magic if you like, call it trickery, call it sleight of hand—but it works. He and I make a good team."

"Fine. You and Tarb can be the scouts."

"We've been working together for years, in all kinds of situations. Whatever one of us does, the other can back up and support—"

Chrissie broke off as Tarbush Hanson gripped her arm.

"Not another word, Chrissie," he said gently. "Weren't you listening? Deb already agreed."

"She did?"

"I said you could be the advance scouts." Deb spoke fast, before the Stellar Group aliens could question her decision. "But you'll follow certain rules."

"No violence," Vow-of-Silence said immediately. "No m-murder or fighting."

"That's one rule. I have others. You go wearing your suits—including helmets. I know that's a pain, but it's better than bites or stings that could be lethal. If there's any trouble, even a suspicion of trouble, you turn and head back. Don't use your suit radios. That's too dangerous. If whatever is in the camp can detect our frequencies, they'll use the signal to home in on us. We'll be watching as best we can with the periscope, and that will have to do."

"Suits, safety first, no signals." Tarb nodded his bullet head. "Got it. Anything else?"

"Yes. No matter what you see, or what you hear,

or what you think, you don't take risks. I need you here in plenty of time for us to decide where we'll spend the night, ashore or back on the *Hero's Return*."

"No problem. We're on our way."

"You and Chrissie. *Not* that fat ferret." Deb held out a hand. "Give her to me."

"What makes you think I have Scruffy with me?" Tarbush put a fierce scowl on his big black face and tried to stare Deb down. He couldn't meet her eyes. "Oh, be reasonable, Deb, she goes everywhere I do."

"You mean almost everywhere. I'm being more than reasonable. Come on, Tarb. Hand her over."

Tarbush opened a bulky suit pocket and reluctantly extracted the ferret. He placed her on the ground, stroked his modded pet's sleek and bulging head, and bent to whisper something. Scruffy waddled over to Danny Casement and sat down placidly at his side.

"Look after her, Danny," Tarb said, "she's yours if I don't come back. She'll do whatever you and Deb tell her."

"You'll come back. You'd better." Danny picked up the ferret awkwardly and gave the pet a critical inspection. "I sure as hell don't want to be saddled with her. I bet she has fleas and worms. Sterilization—"

Tarbush Hanson was a very tall man. He seemed to grow another six inches. "If you dare—"

"Stop that, Danny," Chrissie said. "You can't make jokes on some subjects, they're sacred." She took Tarb's arm and pulled him toward the spiny bushes. "Come on, animal-man. Let's go—before you two start a testosterone fight."

Chrissie was short and slim and about half the weight of Tarbush Hanson. She was better able to seek out clear patches ahead, and after a few steps he was content to fall in behind her.

For years, both of them had encountered only the plants growing in formal gardens of the Outer System colonies. It had been much longer than that since either of them had walked through a forest or meadow of Earth. Chrissie, pushing ahead, had to keep reminding herself that it was *normal* for plant life to be so vigorous—so *competitive*. It seemed that in every square centimeter where something could grow, something did. No matter how careful you were in placing your feet, a plant or animal down there got squashed. After the first five minutes she accepted that as inevitable, stopped looking down with every step, and kept her head up to find and take the line of least resistance.

There was one exception to that rule: wherever the fronded vegetation tops were in windless waves of motion, she stayed well clear.

Now and again she lifted her head, to stare at the super-bright sky. What she wanted to see was the ghostly spheres that everyone talked about, but the blazing sun made that impossible.

"Careful!" Tarbush said from behind, and grabbed her shoulders. Chrissie brought her attention back to ground level. A body-thick stripe of lurid green crossed her path at waist level. Two more steps, and she would have walked into it.

No problem? Maybe—except that the strip *glistened*, and attached to it she saw the bodies of half a dozen different creatures in various stages of digestion. Not all of them were as small as the dark-red millipede that Danny had picked up. The biggest was long, thick-built and legless, and it probably massed half as much as Chrissie. It was still alive, and wriggling feebly.

"Thanks, Tarb. Looks nasty. For safety's sake we're going to take a bit of a detour."

She headed to the left, to a point where the green

strip merged with a stubby upright cylinder like the bole of a sawn-down tree. The bole gurgled faintly. Chrissie moved another four meters to the left before she felt comfortable enough to edge past.

"Ridge top," Tarbush said, when they had been going for another two minutes. "I'm seeing over."

His height advantage was substantial. Chrissie motioned to him. "You go first. Keep your head down, and tell me what you see."

Tarbush pushed forward for another ten meters, then paused. "Got a good view now. Same as Vow-of-Silence said. We have the beginning of the cleared area, maybe twenty meters in front of us. Bare rock. Fence begins about forty meters beyond that. It's like a network, maybe chain-link, so it's easy to see what's beyond. Other creatures at a few places along the fence. Guards, maybe? Lots of legs, big pincers, stalks that probably carry eyes. Big, dark carapaces. Don't see anything that could possibly be a human. Give me a minute, let me watch what they're doing."

While Tarbush stared in silence, Chrissie came to his side and craned up as tall as she could. She was in the middle of a patch of tall, furry plants that smelled like pungent lavender. "Nothing there looks anything like Friday Indigo," she whispered. "Wonder how sure Vow-of-Silence was of what she saw?"

"No way to ask her now without breaking radio silence. But I'm reading some behavior patterns. See the two different sizes? The small ones are in charge of the big ones, I'll bet money on it. Some level of language, too, maybe not spoken. Maybe chemical, like ants and termites. I'm going to move forward a little farther, get a better look."

"Tarb! Be careful."

Chrissie's warning was too late. He was already edging out to where the bare rock started.

"It's all right. It's business as usual for them, there's no sign they see me. Maybe they don't have good eyes. But I think we've confirmed what Dag Korin suspected when he first looked at the space images. This is a military operation. These critters *move* like a military organization, they're disciplined and in unison when they march. Hold on. They're lining up now. Hold on."

Chrissie, hanging farther back, could see nothing. She waited for what felt like minutes, until Tarbush at last said, "Well, I'll be damned. They're going away. They're filing into one of the buildings—every one of them, including what I thought were the guards for the fence. What's with them? Lunch break? Party time?"

"Keep your head down!"

Tarbush in his curiosity was beyond the cover of the scrub. "It's all right. There's no sign of them any more. Hold on a second, though. I'm wrong, here's one coming out. Lighter-colored, a bit bigger, like . . . Oh my God."

"What?"

"It's a person. A man. Vow-of-Silence was right. There's a human inside the encampment."

"Is anyone with him? Is he a prisoner?"

"Doesn't look like it. He's on his own. He's moving toward the fence—he's coming this way. What do we do?"

Chrissie couldn't stand it any longer. She hurried forward to Tarbush's side and stared at the approaching figure, still about fifty meters away. "It must be Friday Indigo. He's wearing the same style and color of clothing as Bony and Liddy. It was standard issue for the *Mood Indigo*. He's limping."

"Maybe he's hurt. He sure looks like hell. He probably took quite a beating in the storm when his ship was driven ashore. But he's smiling—and he's *waving*. Chrissie, he knows we're here. What do we do now?"

"We ought to turn and run. We were told, no risks."

"Deb said, turn back if there's any sign of trouble. There hasn't been any. Chrissie, we've at least got to wait long enough to say hello to him. He's unarmed, and he seems pleased that we're here—look at that grin, even though he can't possibly know who we are or where we came from."

"I don't know." Chrissie sounded troubled, but she made no move.

"Hello there." The approaching man called the greeting. He had passed through the fence and was still grinning. "Welcome to Limbo. I don't know you, but my name is Friday Indigo."

"I'm Chrissie Winger, and this is Tarbush Hanson. We came here on a ship called the *Hero's Return*. But you're hurt."

Now that he was closer, Chrissie could see streaks of dried blood running down from his temples and ears. His feet and calves were water-soaked, and more blood had run from a jagged hole in the left thigh of his suit.

"Oh, that's nothing." He was still grinning, and he dismissed his wounds with one wave of his hand. "I don't need help, and I feel great. This is a wonderful planet. Wonderful people on it, too."

"You mean the people who made this?" Chrissie waved her hand, to take in the encampment, with its cleared airstrip and the tri-lobed aircraft ready for flight.

"Who else? Come on, I'll introduce you. You need to meet Two-Four, he's a funny little devil and a good friend of mine. Oh, and you definitely have to meet The One—especially The One, he's the greatest."

He had turned and was leading the way toward the fence and the encampment. Chrissie began to follow, but Tarbush said, "Wait a minute. These people you want us to meet. Are they *people*? Or are they aliens?"

"They're the Malacostracans—bit of a mouthful at first, but you'll get used to saying it." Friday was still walking, and they were at the gate to the fence. "They're people, but not exactly like us. I mean, not actual humans. But that's all right, because they're better than humans. Far better."

"Now let's hold it right here." Tarbush had stopped just inside the gate, and he and Chrissie were looking at each other. "I can see I'd think well of anyone who saved my life—but *better* than humans? I don't like the sound of that. Did something else happen to you, messing up your head? Your ears have been bleeding."

"My head is better than it's ever been. I've never thought so well and so clearly." Friday turned back to them. "Come on. If you're lucky, The One will make you feel the same way."

Chrissie took a step backward, away from the buildings. "Who is this 'The One' that you keep talking about?"

"The leader of the Malacostracans. She's beautiful. Oh, don't judge by those specimens. They're lower level and they look nothing like her."

Friday was pointing toward another of the buildings. Three creatures had emerged.

"Those are the ones I saw before." Tarbush grabbed Chrissie's arm. "Let's get out of here. It was stupid to come this far."

"Not stupid at all." Friday called after them. "Hey, it's *running* that's stupid. You're making my friends do something that you won't like—I know, because the same thing happened to me. Did you hear what I said? Stop running!"

Chrissie and Tarbush ran faster than ever. They were almost at the edge of the cleared area when Tarbush risked a quick look back. Friday Indigo was standing where they had left him, still urging them not to run away. The three dark-shelled aliens had advanced to stand by his side. They carried black canes, which they were lifting to point toward the humans.

"Down, Chrissie. I think they're going to fire." Tarbush started to throw himself flat. Two more meters, and they would reach the safety of the scrub.

He heard a faint popping from behind, like the bursting of children's small balloons. Then his brain was boiling, turning to liquid and spouting out of his ears. He heard Chrissie scream, and he began his own matching scream which was never completed.

They were diving forward, seeking cover—and unconscious before they hit the ground.

27

On Board the *Hero's Return*

"Nine, eight, so seven's next. Or did I do seven already?"

Bony was muttering to himself, counting hull partitions as he crawled past them.

He had already seen more than enough partitions. The *Hero's Return* was divided along its entire length into twenty-meter segments, each separated from its neighbors by bulkheads strong enough to allow vacuum on either side. That was all very well for a cruiser in space, where during a battle any section might be breached by enemy weapons; but when you were down on the seabed of an alien planet, with vacuum a longed-for memory, partitions were nothing more than a nuisance with sealed hatches to be negotiated at each one.

Water was seeping into the ship, slowly but steadily, and Bony wanted to know where it came from. The ship's external sensors were no longer working, which meant he had to examine the condition of the outer and inner hulls for himself. That involved crawling the length of the ship and looking for water in the space between the hulls.

He had begun without a suit, and learned by the fourth segment that was a mistake. The *Hero's Return* did not have a bilge like a seagoing vessel, but in a gravity field everything seeped down to pool in the curved space between the inner and outer hulls. As he passed the third bulkhead he had skidded into—and fallen down in—a revolting mixture of oil, water, and slick ooze. He went back and put his suit on, but it was already too late. His face and body were coated with black glop, and sweating inside the suit only made things worse.

"Six—or is it five?" Bony crawled grimly on, oily water covering him to shoulder level and casting rainbow reflections from the light in his suit's helmet. Never before had he realized the true size of a Class Five cruiser. But now he was far past the ship's midpoint, and the curve of the hull was upward. Another couple of sections and he should have ascended until he was above the water level.

That was small comfort. His journey along the lowest level had convinced him that the *Hero's Return* was dying, and far faster than the ship's computer was willing to admit. Jettisoning the defensive shields had been necessary for the ship's immediate survival when they arrived in the ocean of Limbo, but the same act had guaranteed long-term and irreversible failures.

He reached the last two sections, and discovered worse news. On the ship's arrival on Limbo its forward motion had finally been halted by an underwater ledge. Even at a speed of a few meters a second, the impact of the ship's bow with unyielding rock had buckled and twisted the outer and inner hulls and mashed them into each other. Worse than the damage to the hull was the destruction of the vital navigational instruments mounted at the bows. The *Hero's Return* would be ready for another trip to space only after major refurbishing had been performed; which, in practice, meant never.

Bony made his final assessment as he clambered up a tight spiral staircase leading to one of the main corridors, and from there headed for what had once been the fire control room. It was the most likely place to find Chan Dalton and Dag Korin and give them his report. Bony's message would be a grim one: the ship could not be used for a Link transition, and it would become totally uninhabitable in a few days.

Chan and the General were not in the control room. Tully O'Toole and Liddy Morse were; also—a surprise to Bony—the Angel, Gressel, immobile and apparently asleep on a broad-based pot of black earth, while next to it Elke Siry sat at a terminal frowning and grimacing and biting her lips. She was hammering a keypad at a furious rate. Tully O'Toole and Liddy Morse hovered by, apparently urging her on.

Bony opened the visor of his helmet and sank down into a seat next to them. His suit was covered with sticky ooze, but he was too bushed to care. Even though the onboard robots were close to imbecility, a simple cleaning job should not be beyond them.

"Well?" Liddy came closer, but she did not try to touch him. He could hardly blame her. But she knew where he had been, and what he had been doing.

"I give us three days, if we push everything to the limit."

Elke had frowned in irritation when Liddy first spoke, but at Bony's words she spun around in her chair. "Three days for what?"

"Three days until we're forced to abandon the

Hero's Return and try our luck ashore. This ship is dying around us." Bony's wave took in the tilted floor, sweating ceiling, and fading wall lights. "It's on its last legs. Any word from Deb and the others while I've been below? They've been gone nearly ten hours, and it must be getting dark up there."

Tully shook his head. "Nothing. But that's not so strange, because Chan doesn't want radio signals until we know more about whatever destroyed our orbiters. We'll hear from the shore party when they come back and report, not before. Let's hope they make it fast, 'cause this old ship won't last."

"Three days," Elke said. "Damnation. Just when this is getting really interesting." That wasn't the word that Bony would have chosen, but Elke went on, "We're making great progress mapping the multiverse, and we have some guesses about the way the new Link might work; but I can't continue the analysis without a computer."

Liddy looked at Bony. "I suppose we can't take it ashore with us?"

"The computer? Not a chance. It's a distributed system with elements scattered all the way through the ship. It would be easier to take the power plant, and that weighs three hundred tons."

Gressel showed sudden signs of life, rippling its fronds from top to bottom. "Computer," the Angel said in a deep, dreamy voice. "Hmmm, computer. Yes, a computer is indeed useful in defining the Link transition that a homebound ship must make. But that abstract problem, despite Dr. Siry's modesty, is close to being solved, and our own internal computational power should suffice to handle the remainder. Of far more concern, we suggest, is the absence of a *ship* that can *make* the Link transition. Recall the human recipe for making a rabbit pie: *First catch your rabbit*.

Accepting what Mr. Rombelle tells us, we ask: Where is our ship?"

"The aliens on shore have a ship, and more," Tully said.

"But will they make one available to us?"

"Well, if they don't and if they won't, we'll—"

"Do not continue with that thought." The Angel's voice deepened. "Remember, violence is never the answer. There are always peaceful solutions. We will not pursue that subject. Instead, we suggest that a summary of our current state of knowledge is in order. Dr. Siry, would you like to proceed?"

"You could do it better than I."

"How true. But this is to an audience of *humans*, with its own curious cultural referents." Gressel waved a succulent side frond. "*Horses for courses*. Better, we think, if you offer the summary."

"We-e-ll . . ." Elke sighed, but as she turned to face the others she did not seem displeased. "The amazing thing about the multiverse is not that we've discovered its existence. It's that we've been blind to it for so long while it was staring us in the face. We've used the Links to make interstellar jumps for—how long?" No one spoke. "Well, hundreds of years at least. All that time, theorists have argued that the only way you can go somewhere through a Link is by passing through an intermediate space, one that's connected differently from our own spacetime. Points that are widely separated in our universe are close together in the other one."

"But I thought that 'other universe' was just sort of a mental picture," Liddy objected. "Just a way of visualizing things."

"If it were just a picture, how could it work?" Elke's blue eyes were sparkling and she displayed more passion than anyone on the *Hero's Return* had ever seen. "No, this is a real alternate universe—it has to be, because we travel through it. Our mistake was in thinking that there was *one* alternate universe, and it was the *only possible* alternate universe. What Gressel and I have discovered is a large number—possibly an infinite number—of other universes, all just as real as the one we came from, or the one we're in here on Limbo. And we're finding out a lot of things about them. For instance, there are universes in which all the basic physical constants are widely different from what we're used to. A transition to one of them would be fatal, because nothing like us could survive. We were lucky. This universe and ours are very close in properties. We know that, because we're alive. Also, the universe that the land aliens came from, no matter how alien it may be in other ways, must also be close in its physical constants. Otherwise they couldn't survive here, either."

Tully asked, "How do you know they're not from our universe?"

He had moved closer when Elke began to speak, and now to his amazement she reached forward and placed her hand on his arm. "The nature of the Link tells us that! It's completely different from what we're used to, different from anything we've imagined. For one thing, it's on an air-water boundary, which before we came here I would have said was impossible. For another, if the Link had been present in the Geyser Swirl for years, the Stellar Group aliens would have found it. But the Angel and I are beginning to understand it, and how everything works."

She finally realized that she was touching Tully and pulled her hand away. "It's all right," he said, but she turned quickly to the display controls and went on, "See, we're starting to map the *structure* of the multiverse. It contains a whole spectrum of energy levels. Just knowing that those exist is half the battle. I've made a diagram of what I've been calling 'uphill' and 'downhill' universes. Here it is." The screen showed a set of nodes connected by a complicated network of lines. "The yellow arrows are to places that call for a greater energy expenditure to reach them, the blue to ones that you can reach more easily. The aliens who made the Link here on Limbo probably came uphill, because the ships we've seen from orbit don't seem to have huge power units. They'll find it easier to go home than they did to come here. We think the same is true of us. We'll go home"—she ignored Bony's murmured *If we go home*—"easier than we came, because the power drain getting to this place was enormous, much bigger than it usually is for a single transition." She paused in annoyance. A buzzing tone like a giant bee was ringing through the ship, interrupting her final words. "What on earth is that?"

"Main airlock, with an emergency signal that's not working quite right. Like everything else around here." Bony stood up. "It must the shore party, returning to the ship. Come on."

He led the rush out of the control room. After a few seconds of hesitation Elke and Tully followed, leaving the Angel to fend for itself.

"I didn't get to tell them the most interesting part of all," Elke complained to Tully as they went. "Every universe runs at its own individual clock rate. For instance, as the Angel pointed out, time passes in this world more than sixty times as fast as on Earth. If we're here for another two days, four months will elapse for people back home. But it could be a lot worse. Gressel estimates from the structure of the multiverse that some places run a million times as fast. If we stayed in a place like that for just a week, twenty thousand years would pass back on Earth. That's longer than the whole of human recorded history. We're mapping multiverse coordinates so we can be sure to avoid places like that."

Elke paused. Even she, swept away by her enthusiasm for science, realized that Tully was not listening. He was pretending to, but he was staring ahead in anticipation as they came closer to the airlock. Chan Dalton and Dag Korin had appeared from nowhere, and the General was bustling along as fast as anyone and cursing his aged legs. Bony, still muck-splattered and grimy, earned only a raised eyebrow.

"Not too close," Chan snapped when they were at the lock. He spread his arms to keep the others away from the hatch. "I hope I know who's coming out of there, but we can't be sure."

It was a new and disturbing thought. Everyone but Dag Korin took a pace back. The lock seemed to be cycling slower than usual, and the tension was huge until at last the hatch slid open and Danny Casement stepped out.

Stepped was perhaps the wrong word. He staggered forward, sagged against Chan, and allowed himself to be supported. When he saw the waiting group he reached up and wearily opened his suit's visor. "I made it, but I'm on my last legs." He jerked his head back toward the lock's interior. "She's in bad shape."

"Deb!" Chan released his hold on Danny and jumped forward. But there was no sign of Deb Bisson inside the lock. All it held was the giant form of Vow-of-Silence, her pipe-stem body tightly curled and her spindly limbs wrapped tight around it.

"What happened?" Chan was reaching down to lift the Pipe-Rilla, but her body remained rigidly knotted.

"Long story." Danny was sitting on the floor, taking

deep breaths. "I'll tell you everything when I can sit down and have a drink—a strong one. Short version: we saw Chrissie and Tarbush cut down right in front of our eyes."

"Chrissie and the Tarb have been *murdered*?"

"I'm not sure. Either murdered, or they're hostages. They went closer to the alien camp than they were supposed to, and they were spotted. They tried to run, but the land aliens pointed some kind of gun at them and they went down. I'd have said they were dead, except that there was another human in the encampment. It had to be Friday Indigo, from the *Mood Indigo*, and he was walking around free." Danny slowly rose to his feet. "So I'm hoping that Chrissie and the Tarb are alive. But you know how the Stellar Group feels about violence. When it looked like two of our party were killed, Vow-of-Silence went over the edge into some kind of catatonic state. Deb and I couldn't get her out of it." Danny glanced at the Pipe-Rilla, unconscious in Chan Dalton's grip. "Don't ever tell me again that it's easier to move things underwater. I dragged and carried her on land and sea for five hours, and the last part was the hardest."

"But where's Deb?"

"Still ashore. I wanted her to come with me, but she wouldn't. She said that she couldn't desert Chrissie and Tarb, and she was also waiting to see if the Tinker Composite showed up. Eager Seeker scattered all over the place. When I left not a single component had come back."

"Look after Vow-of-Silence." Chan placed the Pipe-Rilla on the floor. "I'm going after Deb."

"The hell you are." Dag Korin moved to block the entrance to the lock. "We've lost two already—maybe three. I know how you feel about Deb Bisson, but common sense trumps emotion. It's night up there.

You stay here until morning. Then we'll review the situation."

"You expect me to sit and do nothing?"

"No. I expect you to listen to what Dan Casement has to say, and then sleep. If you can't sleep, you sit and think. I need brains, not martyrs. Now, the rest of you." Korin turned to the others in the group to emphasize that he was not going to listen to any more argument from Chan. "We'll have a full debriefing on shore party activities in my quarters. Don't worry, Casement, you'll get your drink there—I'll guarantee it." Korin frowned at the group. "We're one missing. Where's the Angel?"

"In the control room," Elke said. "We were in such a hurry to get here, we left Gressel behind."

Korin hesitated. "I'm tempted to say, let's leave Gressel right out of things for the moment. But if we do, Casement will have to do his debriefing all over again later on, and I'm not sure what to do about *her*." He pointed a gnarled finger at Vow-of-Silence, still tight-curled and motionless on the floor. "Oh, all right. Rombelle and Morse, you go get the Angel and bring it to my quarters. Dalton, give me a hand with the Pipe-Rilla. I don't know a thing about alien physiology, but the ship's computer should. We'll drop her off in the med center and hope the unit can give her treatment. Dr. Siry, I'd like a summary of what you and the Angel have found out since last we talked, and you can give me that while we deal with Vow-of-Silence."

"What about me?" Danny said, as Bony and Liddy hurried away to the control room and Chan hoisted Vow-of-Silence to waist level, so Dag Korin could grab the long, curved abdomen.

The General stared at him. "You save your strength and put your thoughts in order. Before any drink goes to your head, I need you to tell us every last thing that happened before you went ashore and after you arrived there. I'd like to know what the land looks like, feels like, and smells like. Describe the plants and animals. Describe the encampment. Describe the aliens. Describe the human you saw, if you saw him. Describe anything and describe everything." Korin took his share of the load of Vow-of-Silence, and grunted at the weight. "You carried her back here all alone? Then you deserve to drink the ship dry if you feel like it. But you won't see a drop until the rest of us know as much about life ashore as you do."

Danny did his best. What he would really have liked was a long, strong drink immediately followed by a long, deep sleep, but he recognized his responsibility and tried to make sure that the others learned everything he had seen, heard, thought, and suspected during his day ashore.

The Angel didn't make his job any easier. Bony Rombelle and Liddy Morse had trundled it in on an improvised trolley, and either its desertion in the control room or the rough journey along the ship's corridors was not to its liking. For the first few minutes, Gressel sat hunched as far down in the pot of earth as possible, fronds folded. And when the Angel finally began to open and take notice and even interrupt, there was a sideways jump to its logic that left Danny blinking.

"At what exact local time of day was it when you emerged from the sea?" the Angel asked, as Danny was busy trying to give every detail of their arrival ashore.

"I'm not sure. Why do you want to know?"

"We wish to develop an exact chronology of all events affecting the shore party."

"Well, I can't tell you to better than an hour."

"His suit will tell us," Bony said. "The thermal balance would change as he came out of the water and into air, and that will be recorded against a time line."

"Look into it later." Chan was impatient to move on to the meeting with the land aliens. "What next, Danny, after the group reached the shelter of the vegetation?"

"We would like to have removed our suits, for comfort, but there were too many unfamiliar critters around. And we didn't want to go crawling through the jungle for the same reason. A few of the Tinker components had already gone winging off over the top of the plants, and they all vanished. So we took the gadget that Bony made, and we gave it to Vow-of-Silence, and—"

Danny wanted to describe what the Pipe-Rilla had seen through the periscope, but Gressel was in first. The Angel clapped top fronds together loudly to gain attention, and interrupted. "Exactly how many Tinker components flew away?"

Another off-the-wall question. Danny was exhausted, he still didn't have his drink, and he found it hard enough to provide a clear version of events without stupid interruptions. "How many components? I'm not sure. There were bits and pieces of Tinker coming and going all the time. What difference does it make?"

"Perhaps none. Perhaps the number will prove of great significance." The Angel sank down into silence.

Danny waited, but apparently no more explanation was forthcoming.

"The periscope," Chan prompted.

"It wasn't long enough for anyone else to see over the ridge," Danny went on. "But Vow-of-Silence was so tall, she could do it. Here's what she saw—or *said* she saw. Remember now, none of the rest of us had anything to go on except what was told to us."

He summarized what he and the others hidden in the scrub had heard about the encampment, and the aliens, and the form wandering around free that looked like a human.

"Looked to a *Pipe-Rilla* like a human," Dag Korin said. "But damn it, do you think some gooky misfit lengths of animated drainpipe could look through a shaky handheld periscope, and be sure she was looking at a person a kilometer or more away?"

The Angel stirred, but Danny could recognize a rhetorical question when he heard one.

"We wanted to confirm what Vow-of-Silence had seen," he said, "so we decided—after a bit of argument—that Chrissie and the Tarb should go take a closer look-see."

"What argument?" Dag Korin said. "I want to hear about that, too. Don't decide for yourself that something isn't important, and leave it out. Let's hear the lot."

Danny sighed. Did they really want to know about the dark-red wriggly thing that he had found on the purple fern? Did they want to hear about Scruffy, and the hassle Deb had given Tarbush about taking the ferret with him? At some point he knew what they were going to say. Other than bugs and plants and soil, he hadn't seen a single blessed thing. *Everything* that he knew about the encampment, about Friday Indigo, and about the mowing down of Chrissie and Tarbush had come to him secondhand as a report from either Deb or the Pipe-Rilla. They had seen and spoken, he had listened. He was a mere conveyor of hearsay.

It was easiest to make no judgment, reorganize no facts, and simply offer a stream-of-consciousness version of events. Let the listener decide what was important.

He described, through Vow-of-Silence's eyes, the appearance of something that looked like a human which had apparently persuaded Chrissie and the Tarb to move forward when they ought to have retreated. The approach as far as the encampment's guarding fence. The emergence of three dark-shelled and fast-moving shapes. The run for cover—the raised black canes—the fall, to lie motionless on the bare ground.

And now, at last, something to which he could personally attest: the high-pitched, eerie moan that had emerged from Vow-of-Silence's narrow head. The final dispersal of Eager Seeker into a great cloud of components, circling Danny and the rigid Pipe-Rilla like a tornado before flying off in all directions. And, five seconds later, Vow-of-Silence's collapse forward at Danny's side, into a fit or trance from which neither he nor Deb had been able to wake her.

"I ask again." the Angel interrupted Danny's reliving of the moment. "How many components had Eager Seeker lost, in total, *prior* to this dispersal? Lost from every cause?"

"Does it matter?" Dag Korin made no attempt to hide his irritation with Gressel. "What difference does it make if a hundred or a thousand Tinker components flew away?"

Danny was glad to see somebody else fencing with the Angel. He no longer had the strength—he was so tired he could barely follow Gressel's questions, never mind answer them.

"It's because of Tinker size and Tinker structure," Chan said suddenly. "I remember it from twenty years ago, when I was working with a Tinker Composite on Travancore. I never saw the effect myself, but isn't there some kind of Tinker stress/stability relation?"

"There is indeed." The Angel produced from its speech synthesizer a sigh very like a human's. "As a Tinker Composite grows in size, it also grows in intelligence. That is well-known. What is less commonly known is that with increased intelligence comes greater sophistication in handling threats to a Tinker's own safety. Unfortunately, the converse holds true. Reduce the number of components and the Composite decreases in stability. Now, as I understand it, Eager Seeker was originally an unusually large Composite. But soon after arrival on Limbo, a substantial fraction was detached to form Blessed Union, and went ashore."

"That's what I was told," Bony said, then felt embarrassed because he had butted in. He muttered, "But it never came back."

"And Eager Seeker went at that point from being a large to a somewhat small Composite. Yet more components were lost when the shore party was exploring. A reduced Composite, subjected to unexpected stresses at such a time, seeks safety using a mechanism ingrained through all of Tinker evolution: *solitation*."

"It flies apart," Chan said softly. "Disperses."

"Worse than that. A Tinker can normally disperse at any time, and then reassemble. But a Tinker who suffers solitation will never come together again as an ensemble without assistance. The components eat, and they can still breed. But they form an uncoupled host of mindless and solitary components." The Angel stirred, as though the sentient crystalline Singer within the vegetable of the Chassel-Rose imagined its own irrevocable separation of parts.

"It's *death* for the Composite," Liddy said. She clutched Bony's hand. "It may not sound like it, but it is."

"Which means that Deb is alone on shore." Chan looked at Dag Korin. "She was waiting for Eager Seeker to come back, but it's not going to happen. And while she waits there she's a sitting target for whatever got Chrissie and Tarbush."

"No." The General shook his head. "I know where you're heading with your thinking, Dalton, but I won't allow it."

"I could go solo. Danny's back, and the ship is safe."

"Not a chance. It would be crazy for you to try, at night and in unexplored terrain. Deb Bisson is a smart woman, too smart to do anything stupid. She won't risk anything at night. She'll lie low until morning. Then like as not she'll decide that she can't wait any longer for Eager Seeker, and head back here."

"I think I ought to go."

"And I'm pulling rank and telling you, for the last time, you're not going. Get a grip, man." Korin stood up, went to the metal bureau in the corner of the room, and opened the doors. "Casement wants a drink, and you should have one, too. We all should. Come on, Dalton, relax. We're all here, and Deb Bisson is safe ashore. Not a damn thing is going to happen, here or there, until morning."

Korin picked up a bottle, opened it, and began to pour Santory single-malt whiskey into a line of small rounded glasses.

As he did so, a loud buzzing drone rang through the whole ship. Once again it signaled for emergency action. Something, it said, was in the main airlock of the *Hero's Return*.

28

Deb's Dilemma

Deb had listened to Chrissie and Tarbush's logic for their being the advance scouts. She had been unable to refute it, but that didn't mean she was happy with the situation.

When they left, crawling cautiously away through the waist-high ground cover, her need to *see*, to know where they were and what was happening to them, grew stronger.

Vow-of-Silence was lucky. She could look through the periscope. Eager Seeker was more fortunate yet. The Tinker could release inconspicuous individual components, each one able to fly high, examine the situation, and return to integrate its findings into the Composite. Deb and Danny alone were information starved. Even if Deb grabbed the periscope she was not tall enough to look over the top of the ridge.

She stood it for about five minutes, during which Vow-of-Silence's remarks were basically one comment repeated over and over: "There is no sign of them. They must be proceeding through the vegetation." Finally she could take it no longer.

She said to Danny, "Stay here and keep your eyes and ears open. I'm going to creep along to the ridge, and just take a peek over."

He raised his eyebrows, and his wrinkled face looked far from happy; but he nodded, and before he could offer any other reaction she was off, snaking into the brush along the line marked by Chrissie and Tarbush. She came to the band of lurid green that spanned the way ahead, with its assortment of dead and dying animals strung along it like beads on a necklace. She followed Chrissie's lead in detouring to pass well clear.

She was keeping her head well down and she sensed rather than saw when she crossed the brow of the ridge. Ahead of her, if Vow-of-Silence's report was correct, the ground sloped down toward the encampment. Thirty yards in front of Deb the vegetation cover would end and be replaced by bare and sterile rock.

That was as far as Chrissie and Tarbush were supposed to go. If Deb peeked out over the top of the plants she should be able to see them.

She parted the ferny top growth as delicately as her suit gloves would permit, wrinkled her nose at the smell of lavender gone rotten, and slowly raised her head.

And gasped.

What were those two idiots playing at? They were far beyond the cover of the plants, walking toward the fenced encampment. Hadn't they listened to one word of her orders?

Then she saw the third one, way in front of them. It was a human male, and he was wearing the same kind of suit as Bony Rombelle. Friday Indigo, it had to be—there was no other candidate in this whole universe. Indigo was waving, and now Deb could tell that he was speaking though she couldn't make out any words. Chrissie was talking back to him—and she and Tarbush were still walking, nearer and nearer to the fence around the alien camp.

Deb wanted to shout a warning, but if she did that her own position would be revealed. She watched, gloved hand over her mouth, as Chrissie and Tarbush and Friday Indigo went on, to the gate in the fence and through it. At that point Tarbush and Chrissie stopped. Chrissie took a step backward. Friday Indigo raised his arm and pointed, toward the encampment and the buildings that bordered the airstrip.

Deb saw three creatures, each as big as Tarbush—and he was a very big man. They had broad, blue-black carapaces, held almost level, and lots of legs. Deb didn't have time to count them, because one pair of the aliens' formidable front claws were lifting high. They held thick black sticks whose highly polished curved surfaces gleamed in the bright sunlight.

Tarbush and Chrissie were moving, racing away from the fence and back across the bare rocky plain. They were almost at the edge of the dense plant cover when the air between them and the crouching aliens shimmered like a heat haze.

Chrissie went down. Tarbush was already diving forward into the plants, but he fell a few feet short. Neither one moved as the armed aliens cautiously approached and bent over them. Friday Indigo stood as still as a statue, back by the fence. Deb did the same, hidden by the covering fringe of ferns. She heard a strange wailing cry from behind her. Danny, or Vow-of-Silence? Fortunately, the aliens took no notice. Two of them squatted down by folding their supporting legs—ten each, Deb counted—and easily lifted the unconscious humans.

They headed for the encampment. The third alien lagged behind with its black cane still raised. As they passed through the fence, Friday Indigo moved at last. He followed them into one of the buildings, a windowless half-cylinder of dull yellow that seemed to crouch and merge into the black rock.

Deb was desperate to do something. Vow-of-Silence and Eager Seeker did not know it, but she was far from weaponless. She had enough firepower concealed inside her suit to handle a dozen unfriendly aliens. But she was rational enough to know that attacking the building with Chrissie and Tarbush inside would be the worst possible thing to do. If they were dead, delay could not further harm them. If they were unconscious and had been taken as prisoners, an attack by Deb would be a sure way to put all their lives in greater danger.

Even so, it took enormous self-control for Deb to retreat slowly and quietly through the thick scrub, over the line of the ridge and back to their own primitive camp. She did not like what she found there. Danny was bending over the knotted body of the Pipe-Rilla, and there was no sign of the Tinker Composite.

He shrugged when she asked him. "Nowhere, everywhere. When Vow-of-Silence screamed, Eager Seeker came apart. It was like being in the middle of a hailstorm. I felt components banging into me and rattling off my suit just like they had no idea where they were or where they were going. Then Vow-of-Silence keeled over. She almost knocked me flat and landed just the way you see her now. I can't wake her. And I've not seen a Tinker component since they all flew away."

Deb bent down at Danny's side. The Pipe-Rilla's long, gangly body had contorted until her head touched the end of her abdomen, and her slender jointed legs were tight-wrapped around the narrow body. Deb tugged at one, and it did not move a millimeter.

"What happened over the other side of the ridge?" asked Danny. "What made Vow-of-Silence scream, and where are Chrissie and Tarbush?"

"Captured. Unconscious. Maybe dead."

Deb gave a summary of what she had seen, making it as unemotional as possible. At the end, Danny simply nodded and said, "What do we do now?"

It was a relief to have a team member able to understand the implications of a disaster without going hysterical. Deb glanced up at the sky.

"Good question. We have maybe four more hours of light. I would say we ought to settle down here for the night, but we daren't do that. I don't think the aliens know where we are, but if they think at all like us they'll assume that Chrissie and Tarbush didn't come here alone. If they head our way, we'll have to run. But this"—she pointed to Vow-of-Silence's unconscious body—"will make a quiet escape impossible. And then there's the Tinker. Eager Seeker's components could come back any time. So we ought to stay here, but I think that's too risky."

Deb looked at Danny. He was small, but he was wiry. "Can you lift Vow-of-Silence?"

"Lift her?" His face wrinkled in perplexity.

"Can you pick her up? Can you carry her?"

"Of course I can. In this low gravity, it's dead easy." To prove his point, Danny placed his arms around the tight ball of the Pipe-Rilla and lifted her to waist height. "See? No problem picking her up. Trouble is, if I have to run with her through the scrub I'm going to make a devil of a noise."

"I know. That's why we have to do it now, and slowly, when nobody's around to hear us. Come on." Deb started to retrace their original path, back toward the sea. "If you get tired I'll give you a hand."

"Where are we going?"

"First, we're going to the shore. Then you're going back to the *Hero's Return* with Vow-of-Silence, and you'll tell the others what's happening. I'm going to stay ashore for the night and wait for Eager Seeker."

Danny stopped dead. "Now wait a minute. You may be the shore team leader, but after what's happened—"

"Danny, ask yourself this. If it comes to a fight who's better equipped for self-defense, Deb Bisson or Danny Casement?"

"Well, you are. You're a weapons master."

"I am. And at the moment there are no Stellar Group aliens around to tell me that violence is totally unacceptable. I'm telling you, if they've killed Chrissie and Tarbush . . ."

The look on Deb's face worried Danny, but he said, "Leaving you alone—"

"—Is the only rational thing to do." Deb moved forward, heading again for the shore and the sea. Danny followed. When they were at the water's edge, Deb took Vow-of-Silence's body from him and closed the Pipe-Rilla's suit visor.

"Sure you can manage both of you underwater?" she asked. "Do you know where you're going?"

"I've got muscles you don't even know about." Danny smiled. "Don't worry, I'll find the way." He started to close his own suit, but paused. "There's one other thing. They're going to ask me what comes next. What should *they* be doing?"

"Tell them that tomorrow morning, if nothing has

happened here, I propose to take another look at the alien encampment. Tell Chan to give me a full day. If I'm not back then—well, then it will be up to him."

Danny nodded. "Good luck." He closed his helmet, took Vow-of-Silence's body from Deb, and headed without another word into the water.

She watched until he was waist deep, then shoulder deep, until at last his small figure with its outsized burden vanished below the surface. Then she turned and faced inland.

The sun was moving behind a line of clouds to the west, and the evening light suddenly dimmed. The dark vegetation ahead seemed gloomy and impenetrable. As she retraced her steps to where they had left their supplies, Deb told herself that she was being foolish. Danny Casement's talents included cunning and a certain devious charm, but he would be absolutely useless in any sort of fight. So why did she feel so much less sure of things now that he was gone?

Maybe because she had no one to boss around now. When you were organizing what other people did, there was less time to worry about yourself.

Deb came to the big supply case in the clearing that marked their original base. It was exactly as she and Danny had left it, with no sign of Eager Seeker. As she pulled out a folding chair and sat down, she could hear unnerving rustles and see small movements in the plants around her. In the growing dusk the native animal life became more active.

It suddenly occurred to Deb, much to her surprise, that she was very hungry. No one had thought to eat since they left the *Hero's Return* over twelve hours ago.

She opened the supply case, pulled out four sealed containers, and examined them. A solar system culinary selection: shellfish from the nurseries of

Marslake; Europan sea-kale, not her favorite but a highly nutritious vegetable; *korlia*, the richly flavored protein that started life as a warm-blooded engineered plant in Earth's polar regions; and finally, beer made from the synthetic grains of the Oort Harvesters. On second thought, Deb reached into the supply case and pulled out another container of that.

She ate and drank slowly and thoughtfully. Now and again she looked up at some faint sound in the scrub, thinking that maybe it signaled the return of some of Eager Seeker's components. It never was.

The sun was on the horizon now, and full night could be no more than an hour away. Before dark she would need to pull out a sleeping bag and a light in case she needed it before morning. There were no weapons in the supply case—the Stellar Group aliens would have vetoed those—but Deb had all she needed hidden away inside her suit.

She leaned her head back to drain the second container of beer. As she did so, something rushed out of the plants around the clearing and jumped into her lap.

She gasped, dropped the beer, and flicked a needle gun from the wrist of her suit. She had it aimed and was triggering the release when she saw her assailant.

"Scruffy! Where have you been?" She picked up the animal and held it to her chest. "You fat furball, I never dreamed I'd be so glad to see you." The ferret snuggled close and whined. "I know, I know. I'm not your human of choice. But Tarbush isn't here."

Deb glanced in the direction of the alien encampment. "I hope that your lord and master is all right, but we can't find out about that until tomorrow. Now I think it's time for you and me to settle down for the night."

She placed Scruffy on the floor, removed the flat

package of a sleeping bag from the supply case, and waited as it inflated. The expanding bag gave a hiss like a striking snake, making the ferret leap for cover.

"Coward." Deb laughed. It was good to have someone around you more nervous than you were. "Come on, Scruffy. Let's see if we can get some sleep."

She didn't have high hopes. There was too much strangeness around her, too many frightening issues waiting for morning before they could be resolved. She lay on her back, the ferret a warm oval curled on her belly.

The light faded. As night moved on, the mysterious spheres filled the night sky of Limbo. It was Deb's first view of them except on a display screen. She studied the globes. They were far less bright than a star or a planet, but far bigger and far more diffuse. She stretched out a hand at arm's length, and found that she could barely span the biggest one. The spheres were so pale, they seemed to hover at the very edge of color.

Deb closed her eyes. This was what she and Chan and the other team members had hoped to find, back in the happy days before the quarantine. All they had dreamed of, and more. This was not just an alien star or planet, it was an alien *universe*.

She had intended to open her eyes again, to study in more detail the intriguing spheres of Limbo's heavens. Somehow it did not happen. Instead she drifted away to other thoughts. What were they doing now, back on the *Hero's Return*? Had Danny arrived, to deliver Vow-of-Silence for treatment and make his report? How was Chan taking it? He was sure to be beside himself, cursing Dag Korin for letting her go without him. He took every responsibility personally, as if he had to solve it by himself without assistance. He didn't realize that a partner was someone to share problems, and triumphs, and defeats. Maybe defeats most of all.

Deb drifted into sleep. The spheres of heaven glowed pale above her, wheeling their stately course across the night sky.

She became conscious all at once, rolling instinctively to her right and already holding a weapon without knowing what had wakened her. It was deep night. Clouds must have moved in, because the glimmer of the sky spheres had gone and when she opened her eyes she could see nothing at all. Off past her feet she heard Scruffy give a warning hiss.

"Now then, no need for all the excitement," a cheerful voice said. "Here, I'll put a light on if it makes you feel better."

A bright yellow-green glow lit up the night. Deb, shielding her eyes against it, saw a male human standing about six feet away from her holding a luminous cylinder. As her eyes adjusted she realized that it was the same person as she had seen the previous day, waving and talking to Chrissie and Tarbush.

"Friday Indigo?" she said tentatively.

"The one and only." He aimed a casual kick at Scruffy, who darted away into the low-growing plants. "Get rid of the vermin, and we can talk. I'm Friday Indigo. Who are you?"

"My name is Deb Bisson." Deb was reluctant to say much until she knew what was going on. Better to ask questions. "I think I saw you earlier. Weren't you down in the encampment?"

"You got it." Indigo took a step forward into the clearing, so that he could crouch next to Deb. "I was there to greet your friends on behalf of The One. Pity you weren't with them."

That was a matter of opinion.

"I saw them shot. Are they alive?"

"Sure they are. Mind you, they're not in as good shape as I am, because they haven't had a chance to meet with The One yet."

That too might be a matter of opinion. Deb was at last getting a close-up of Friday Indigo. He claimed to be in good shape, but he certainly didn't look it. Someone who had been drinking three nights in a row and then lost a major fight might appear the way he did, but chances are they would be in better condition. His eyes were bloodshot, his face was pale. Trickles of dried blood ran from his ears down to his neck. His hair straggled dirty over his forehead, his clothes were full of rips and tears, and he trailed his left leg as he walked.

He didn't appear dangerous, but Deb had quietly been preparing her weapons. If he tried to put a move on her he wouldn't know what hit him. On the other hand, she had no idea what else might be lurking out there in the dark.

"Who is this *The One* that you keep mentioning?"

"The leader."

"Leader of what?"

"Why, leader of the Malacostracans." He spoke as though that was glaringly self-evident.

"The Marla—costrans?"

"Malacostracans. The people who built the encampment on the other side of the hill. The people who live there. If you saw your two friends shot—their own fault, I told them not to run—then you must have seen the Malacostracans for yourself. Only Level Threes and Level Fours, of course. Nothing like Two-four or The One."

Deb had no idea what he was talking about, but she didn't like his tone of voice. It was too self-satisfied, too admiring of the shell-backed aliens.

She said, "Did you come here because you want me to meet with them?"

He laughed. "Good heavens, no. They hardly need the ones they've got. I'm here because The One wants more information about humans and our universe than I can provide."

"I can't give you information."

"I'm not asking you to."

"Then why are you here?"

"To find out if you might have a suit I could borrow. You see, mine was damaged and I can't use it anymore to travel underwater. I have to do that tonight. Do you have one?"

"Maybe." Deb knew quite well that the supply case contained a couple of spare suits. "Why would you want such a thing?"

"Because without it, I can't possibly go to your ship and talk to the leaders of your party. You are the people, aren't you, who launched the orbiters?"

"What if we are? Why would you want to talk to us?"

Friday stared at her pityingly. "To negotiate, of course. It's my job to obtain access to your ship's data bank. I would have used the one on the *Mood Indigo*, but the poor old thing's a bit beat up and I can't get the information systems to work. Don't worry, I have things to offer you people in return."

He snapped his fingers briskly, as though his proposal to negotiate on behalf of aliens was the most natural thing in the world, and went on, "Now, Deb Bisson, do you have a suit for me or don't you? If you do, let's get me into it and I'll be on my way. I can't afford to waste time—The One needs results."

She had to make a decision, and in zero time. "I have a suit for you. It's in the supply case. But I should come with you to point out the quickest way to the ship. And I have to go to the bathroom before we leave."

"I don't mind waiting while you do that."

"Well, I mind. Take the suit and put it on when you get to the beach. I'll see you there in two minutes."

"Two minutes. All right. No longer."

He rummaged in the supply case, pulled out a lightweight suit, and limped away. He held his yellow lamp high, and he was humming to himself.

Deb looked around her. As she became used to the darkness she was able to make out the line of the ridge against the sky and the top fronds of nearby bushes, but everything at ground level was invisible.

"Scruffy?" she whispered. "I can't see you, but can you hear me? Come on, girl. I don't have much time."

There was a rustle close to her feet, and a small form brushed against her leg. She bent down and slipped a flat metal ring onto the ferret's collar.

"I can't understand you, the way that Tarbush can. But I think you understand me. You're on your own now. Go find him. Follow his trail." Dark intelligent eyes gazed up at Deb. "You heard me. Find your idol. Go sniff out Chrissie and the Tarb. This isn't much I'm giving them, but it's the best I can do. I'll be back for all of you as soon as I can."

29

Alien

The ear-splitting drone rang through the whole ship, blocking out speech until it finally ended.

Dag Korin had paused in the act of filling the last of half a dozen glasses with whiskey. "So I'm wrong again," he said, in the dead silence that followed the drone. "Seems we're not done for tonight after all. It's the main airlock again. Dalton, would you?"

Chan was already on the way, racing back the way he had come an hour earlier. When he reached the lock it was still cycling. As the hatch opened and he saw Deb's face behind the suit's visor he let out an explosive gasp of relief. He was reaching to grab her in a bear hug, ignoring the fact that her suit streamed water, when he saw the second figure standing behind her in the lock.

It was a man, much too short to be Tarbush Hanson.

"Who the hell—"

"Friday Indigo," Deb said loudly. Then, opening her helmet, she put a finger to her lips and mouthed, "Chrissie and Tarb alive. Don't talk, take cues from me."

The man limped forward and snapped open his visor, to reveal a tired face whose smiling mouth was stained and crusted with a sticky purple residue. "Friday Indigo, captain and owner of the *Mood Indigo*. I need to talk to whoever is in charge of this ship. Is that you?"

"No. I'm the second in command." Chan glanced at Deb and saw her nod. "But I can take you to General Korin."

"Let's go, then." Indigo glanced about him with pale, intense eyes, as though drinking in every detail of the *Hero's Return*. "I don't have much time."

Deb urged him to go ahead of her and said, "Before anyone will talk to you, Mr. Indigo, you're going to have to explain what happened to the crew members who were captured on shore."

"I told you, they're alive."

"And safe?"

"Safer than they would be here. This dump looks like it's falling apart."

Deb, walking slightly behind Chan and Friday Indigo, could not argue with that. In the time she had been away, less than twenty-four hours, the air had become more clammy, the corridor smelled stale and rancid, and water dripped from every overhead feature.

Chan, leading the way, took his cue from Deb and did not speak until they reached Dag Korin's quarters. When he entered the room everyone sat in exactly the same position as when he had left. Their attention was rigidly focused on the door, and all the whiskey glasses were empty.

"General Korin." Chan had decided as they walked that the less he said, the better. Everyone could see for themselves that Deb was with him, while Chrissie and Tarbush were not. "This is Captain Indigo, of the *Mood Indigo*. He needs to talk with you."

"General. Pleased to meet you." Friday nodded. His eyes scanned the others in the group. He frowned and seemed slightly puzzled when he saw Bony Rombelle and Liddy Morse, but Gressel, squat and dark green, drew most of his attention. He stared at the Angel for a few moments, then abruptly sat down without being invited. His eyes blinked.

"General Korin," he said, in a different tone. "It is my understanding that you are the leader of this force. I wish to speak with you on behalf of the Malacostracans."

"Of the *what*?" Dag Korin bristled.

"Malacostracans. Whom we call the People."

"Never heard of 'em."

Bony Rombelle, unexpectedly, said, "I have."

He and Liddy had been sitting inconspicuously against one wall. Now everyone stared, and he blushed and went on, "Well, not actually *heard* about them, but read about them. And not these particular things, just the name. I think the word must have come out of a translation unit, because *Malacostraca* is the official descriptor for a class of Earth crustaceans. It includes animals like, you know, crabs and lobsters."

Dag Korin scowled at him, and he subsided. Liddy nudged him in the side and whispered, "I was right. You *do* know every useless piece of information in the universe."

"Captain Indigo," Korin said, "you can call your Mala-what-nots anything you damn well please, and it won't cut any ice with me. First, let me say that I'm sorry you lost your own ship."

"Where did you get that idea?" Friday looked puzzled.

"Our computer tried to communicate with it, without success."

"The com antennas were smashed in the storm. But the Malacostracans lifted the whole ship onto land, and the *Mood Indigo* is in pretty fair shape." Friday stared around him. "I don't have any use for it now, of course, but last time I looked at my ship it was in much better condition than this heap of junk."

Korin's jaw muscles tightened. "Captain Indigo, I was merely being polite when I mentioned your ship. To be honest, I don't give a rat's ass what the creatures on shore did for it or to it. What concerns me is that they disabled two of our orbiters, without provocation and without warning. And they captured two of our people. True, or false?"

"I would prefer to say, they have temporarily detained them. Your crew members are alive and well. Upon the completion of satisfactory arrangements, they will be returned."

"I don't know what you're talking about. What's a 'satisfactory arrangement'?"

"I will explain." Friday Indigo's voice changed again, becoming more formal and precise. "To demonstrate good intention, this information is provided in advance of any agreement between us. I will now make certain statements, to any of which you may if you choose offer objections or countersuggestions.

"First, neither you nor the People are native to this planet, or even to this universe.

"Second, this planet is itself an anomaly, in that it is able to support life. The overall structure of this universe is unfavorable for both the occurrence and the persistence of life. This universe is not therefore a suitable site for widespread colonization.

"Third, the People realize that the universe from which humans came is highly suited for the support of living creatures, including the People; more so, in fact, than any other of their expeditions have reported to date in the exploration of other universes."

Korin's head lifted. "Where did they get information about where we came from?"

"I provided it to them," Friday said calmly. "However, even with all the help that I could give, the People lack enough knowledge of how you came here to perform a Link transition. Let me continue. Fourth, if you do not obtain help from somebody, you'll never be able to go home."

"And how the hell do they know *that*?" The veins in the sides of Korin's neck were bulging.

"I suggested it to them, and confirmed the fact when I came here. Although you may have the data needed to return to your own universe, you lack a suitable vehicle in which to do so. This was my suspicion before I came aboard this ship, and it is evident by observation. Space vessels do not take kindly to a sea environment.

"Fifth, this planet itself, while supporting life, is an unsuitable long-term base for operations. Its principal defects are as follows . . ."

As Friday spoke, Liddy was watching him closely. Finally she leaned close to Bony and breathed in his ear, "He's changed. He speaks differently, and there's something peculiar about him."

"There sure as hell is," Bony hissed back. "He's a t-traitor to his own species. He s-sold us out—to a bunch of smart lobsters!"

"I don't mean that. I mean the way he looks."

"He looks like shit!"

"I don't mean that, either. I mean the way he looks at *me*. When we hadn't been around each other for a couple of days, he always had that—well, you know, that *leer*, like he'd bought me and he owned me. But now he looks—"

"Don't tell me how he looks! He's a lecherous bastard. If he touches you—"

"Bony! Not now." Others in the room were looking their way. Only Friday Indigo, smiling serenely, seemed not to notice.

"So there is ample basis for cooperation," he was saying. "If you do as The One suggests, and guide the People—safely—through the Link to your own universe, you will be granted your lives and your freedom. Those of your party who are now held captive will be released and returned to you. However, if you refuse to cooperate, The One will be forced to regard you as an enemy of the People. Your survival, on this world or elsewhere, will then be highly improbable. The technology of the People is far in advance of anything known to humans, or to any others of the Stellar Group. For example, the People possess full control of gravity. That permits their Links to be placed on the surface of planets, and their interstellar ships to land on or leave from there. They also possess weapons far beyond any that you have ever seen. The device which annihilated your orbiters could with equal ease destroy this ship. It is impossible not to admire and bow down to the superior powers of the People."

He stood up, apparently unaware of the expressions of disbelief and disgust on the faces of his audience, and continued, "Even when you agree to become allies of the People, many details will still remain to be worked out. It was my task tonight only to come here and propose a way in which you might serve the People to your and their advantage. I will leave now."

"Now wait a minute." Chan had been watching Dag Korin. The General was red in the face and seemed beyond speech. Chan went on, "You can't just say your piece and run away. We have to talk more about this. I have questions—we all have questions."

"There will be an opportunity for you to ask questions through your chosen representative. But not now. I have been here for too long, and The One awaits my return. I must go."

"It's night on the surface. An hour or two more won't make any difference."

"I must go." Friday limped toward the door. "Have your talks. I can find my own way to the airlock and back to the shore without assistance. Tomorrow, you will send two people with your answer. One will be your representative, who will be privileged to meet with The One. The Malacostracans would prefer that you, General Korin, as group leader, be that representative, but they do not insist on it since you must enforce discipline here." He pointed to Deb Bisson. "She will be the other, to serve only as guide. She will lead you to the place on the shore where we left, and we will meet at midday exactly. Now I must go."

"This is ridiculous," Chan said. "At the very least—"

His words were drowned out by the powerful voice of the Angel's synthesizer. "Let Friday Indigo go. Do not seek to delay his departure."

"That is right. *I must go*," said Friday, and left the chamber.

"Do not try to accompany him." Gressel was at maximum extension, fronds unfolded and wildly waving. Chan, all set to chase after Friday Indigo, jerked to a halt.

"Why not? What's going on?"

"We just had a meeting with a low-down, treacherous swine," Dag Korin said. "That's what's going on. He sold out the whole human race." Korin stood up and walked across to bang his fist on the wall. "The bag of slime, in my day he'd have been put up against a wall and shot."

He glared at the Angel. "Yes, he damned well would, and should, and good riddance to him, and I don't care what you and the rest of the Stellar Group think. There's nothing worse than somebody who betrays his own people. Surely even you can see that."

"We can." Gressel spoke at normal volume. "Angels and humans may be very different, but we are alike in this: We find it difficult to abide one who turns loyalty away from its own kind, and offers that loyalty toward another."

"Well, that's exactly what Friday Indigo is doing."

"No. Friday Indigo did not betray humans—"

"Of course he did!"

"—because the being who came here tonight was not human."

"Of course he's human! He wasn't on an *official* human expedition, but he came here from Earth with Bony Rombelle and Liddy Morse, on the *Mood Indigo*. Ask them."

"We see no reason to doubt that. But Friday Indigo is not human. He is alien."

"You're mistaken. He's as human as I am."

"No. We are completely sure. *It takes one to know one*. The being who spoke to us tonight is as different from humankind as any Angel. We say again, *Friday Indigo has become alien*."

Liddy gasped and said, "I told you so!" Dag Korin stood frozen against the wall. Elke Siry clutched convulsively at Tully O'Toole, her fingernails cutting into his arm. The rest of the room sat like statues.

"How is that possible?" Korin said at last.

"We are less sure of this. However, we suspect that a scan of Friday Indigo's brain would reveal the presence of something which is found in no other human. A type of Malacostracan, perhaps an embryonic form, resides there." The Angel turned slowly and clumsily on its base, so that the speech unit faced the wall where Bony Rombelle and Liddy Morse were sitting. "You spent many Earth weeks with Friday Indigo. Did he display any special talent for alien languages?"

"None at all," Bony said. Liddy added, "He *despises* aliens. To him, aliens are bugs or vegetables—I'm sorry, but that's what he said. I can't imagine him learning *any* alien language."

"And yet, the being who spoke to us understands the needs and desires of the Malacostracans, well enough to be trusted to negotiate on their behalf. In evaluating what was said tonight, do not think of the Malacostracan proposal as presented by a human. Call him Friday Indigo if you wish, but recognize that he is now no more than a communications device. We believe that literal truth was spoken, with the words, *I must go*. The creature in this room was obeying an overriding imperative which could not be denied."

"Orders from The One—whatever that is." Chan had learned something long ago in his dealings with the Angels. When an Angel said it was sure of something, that implied a level of certainty beyond anything offered by a human. "And The One wants our answer tomorrow. By that time, we'd better have a plan of our own."

30

In the Dark

"Not very smart." Tarbush Hanson squatted on the floor, holding his head. "Deb tells us not to go near the camp, so what do we do?"

"I think she might have done the same." Chrissie was feeling her right shoulder, which had taken most of the impact when she pitched forward unconscious onto rocky ground. "I mean, when you see a man grinning and waving to you, and you are pretty sure that you know who he is . . ."

They were speaking in whispers. The room was half dark, shaped like a long teardrop with a keyhole opening, eight feet tall and half as wide, at the far end. In the chamber beyond, crab-like figures clicked across the floor and seemed to take no notice of Chrissie and Tarbush; but two of them carried black canes, and neither human was keen to risk another jolt. Muscle spasms from the last time still resonated in every limb.

They had awakened at almost the same moment and spent the first few mindless minutes staring up at a ceiling spangled with flecks of light. It was just as well that they were faceup, because shallow water lapped at the back of their heads. Tarbush's groan, when first he tried to move, told Chrissie that he was just a few feet away with his head down near her feet. They sat up slowly, shivering, moving closer together and leaning against each other for support.

"Thank God for the suits," Chrissie said. "Otherwise we'd be soaked and freezing. It's *cold* in here. Any idea where we are? The last thing I remember, we were outdoors and it was bright daylight."

"It's night, unless my helmet readout is on the blink. And we're inside a building. But not too far inside, because there's fresh air coming from somewhere. I can smell those plants. Do you still have your stuff on you?"

Chrissie felt inside her suit to her pockets and the hidden pouches. "Yeah. Either they didn't know I had it, or more likely they don't care. I'm not sure a few magic tricks would be much use against those zapper canes. Even if they are, this is the wrong time to try anything. It's going to be up to you, Tarb. Are you getting anything?"

"Nothing that we can use so far." He was staring intently through the keyhole-shaped doorway at the creatures beyond. "Three different sizes, but all with the same body type. I was right about the definite pecking order. Postures give it away. There's an inferior/superior relation among them, with the smallest ones at the top of the heap."

"You're getting that out of their behavior pattern?"

"Yeah. Not too difficult, though. The black sticks must have more than one mode of use. The little ones touch the middle-sized ones on the underside, and they jump like they've been jabbed with an electric prod. Then they go off and take it out on the big ones, and *they* jump. Looks like the big ones do all the actual work. But you know what?"

"Only if you tell me."

"The little ones aren't the king of the hill, either. They're scuttling around like they've got the fidgets, waiting for something."

"Will you be able to talk to them?"

"They won't understand me if I do. I can read general behavior, but they're too alien for anything more than that. For talking you'd need Tully the Rhymer. Hold on. They're getting real excited. Hear them chittering away there? I'm going to sneak a bit closer."

Tarbush eased forward on hands and knees. Chrissie followed without a word. A ledge formed a step up from the chamber that they were in, leading to a drier level beyond, and Tarbush stopped just short of it.

"Don't go any farther." Chrissie was right behind, whispering in his ear. "The light's a lot brighter in there."

"It is. But I don't think it matters. I could do a song-and-dance act right now, and nobody would notice. Look out. Here comes whatever they've been waiting for. Everybody grovel."

At the far side of the well-lit center chamber was another keyhole aperture and yet another room. What lay beyond was in darkness, but the crab creatures were lining up to face the opening and bending their many legs until their flat undersides touched the floor.

"Sweet Lucy!" Tarbush shuffled backward, bumping into Chrissie on the way. "Get a load of that."

An object like a bulky black rock was creeping through the far doorway and into the central room.

It was taller than Tarbush and was supported on a writhing nest of thick tentacles that protruded from holes in its lower part. As it moved forward all the animals in the chamber lowered themselves in attitudes of obeisance.

"See what it's carrying." Chrissie was right next to Tarbush, her lips to his ear. "Am I seeing things?"

"You're not. And it's going to—"

A thinner black hose hung down from the rock's right-hand side. It curled around an oblong green box. As the hulking rock crossed the chamber toward Chrissie and Tarbush, the box uttered a preliminary series of coughs and sighs.

"*This is not the most efficient means of communication.*" The voice coming from the translation unit was harsh and slow, but each word was clear. "*However, I am presently too busy to take the time necessary for your conversion. Do you understand me?*"

There was a pause, until Chrissie whispered, "We have to answer." And then, more loudly, "Yes, we understand you."

"*Listen closely. Your future is uncertain. If your kind agrees to serve the People, you will become part of that service. You will be released, but before that happens you will be modified to provide additional translators. Also, if the translator we are currently using dies, or ceases to function, one of you will become a translator. If your kind refuses to serve the People, they and you will die. Until then, you are prisoners and will not leave these chambers. You will be fed, but should you seek to escape, the Level Threes and Level Fours are instructed to kill you without hesitation. Is all this clear?*"

Chrissie nodded. "Yes. It is clear."

"*Good. If you are hungry, this may be used to ask for food.*" The tentacle laid the translation unit on the floor, next to the ledge. The lumpy rock did not turn, but drifted away backwards across the central chamber. As it vanished through the far opening and the prostrate creatures rose with an outburst of clicks and whistles, Tarbush looked at Chrissie.

"All *clear*. Not clear to me, it weren't. What was all that gab about being translators, and serving the People?"

"I don't know." Chrissie's face was pale, and her nostrils flared. "I just wanted it to go away. I'm not a coward, Tarb, you know that. But I'd have said anything, I was so afraid it would reach out one of those snaky arms and *grab* me. What *is* that thing?"

"Judging from the way the rest of them behave, it's the big boss. I didn't care for it, either. Did you hear the options it gave us? If this happens, you die. If that happens, you die. If you do this, you get killed. If you're real lucky and things work out all right, you get converted into a translator. I'm not sure what a translator is, but I have the feeling I wouldn't enjoy being one."

"What are we going to do, Tarb?"

"I don't know. But I'll tell you this. If you don't want somebody to escape, saying that you'll kill them if they try to escape may stop them trying. But telling them you'll also kill 'em if they *don't* try to escape strikes me as dumb."

"We try to escape?"

"That's my thought. But how?" He stared around the poorly lit room. "No windows. No exit, except the one that leads through to the chamber of horrors there. Floor's solid, so's the ceiling. Come on, Chrissie, we need a bit of your magic."

"You were the one who said you can feel fresh air. That's not possible unless there's some sort of through draft."

"That's it, lady. Now you're thinking. Let's see what we can find."

They walked slowly toward the dimly lit rear of the room, splashing through water that deepened to their knees. Close-up, the wall showed a definite grain.

"Like wood," Chrissie murmured. "But I don't see any joins. It's like it *grew*, all in one piece."

"Seamless." Tarbush extruded the cutting tool of the emergency repair kit from his suit's forearm and dug at the wall. "And tough. This will pierce most things, and I'm not making a dent."

"What about this?" Chrissie was bending down to inspect a circular hole in the wall covered by a coarse-woven mesh. "I think this is a ventilator. I can feel a draft."

"Let me have a go." Tarbush applied the point of the knife. "This cuts easily. I can remove the whole thing if I want to. Not that it will do us much good. The hole's only about four inches across."

"How deep?"

"Hold on." Tarbush removed the little spotlight from his suit's helmet, shone it into the hole, and peered after it. "At least a foot. The wall's a lot thicker than I expected."

"Let me try something." Chrissie reached in, until her arm was buried to the shoulder. "I think I'm at the end, and it's not covered with a mesh. My hand feels as though it's out in the open, there's a breeze on it."

"So your hand can escape. Not too useful for the rest of us. Let's see if there's another one somewhere else that's bigger."

Working in silence, they went in opposite directions around the perimeter of the room until they came to the keyhole doorway that led to the other chamber.

"Anything?" Tarbush whispered.

"One more ventilation tube, same size as before. You?"

"Nothing. Unless you want to take a look in there." Tarbush nodded his head toward the central room. With the rocky monster gone, the crab creatures were once more upright and busily moving a set of nested vertical tables to horizontal positions.

"I don't want to, but we have to." Chrissie stepped forward. "Stay where you are. No point in both of us taking a chance."

"Chrissie!" But Tarbush stayed close to the wall as she moved into the central chamber, adding only a hissed, "Stop if they point the sticks."

"Trust me. But I'm going to try to talk to them." Chrissie stepped up onto the ledge and advanced to where the translation unit lay on the floor. As she picked it up, three of the biggest of the creatures stopped work and moved in her direction.

"Food," she said loudly. "The big boss says we can have food."

The translator produced a sequence of whistles and clicks. Chrissie waited. Eyestalks wiggled. Finally one of the creatures chittered, and the translation unit said, *"Us not can. Not move."*

It retreated across the floor, to the far doorway of the chamber and beyond. Its two fellows had raised black canes and were pointing them directly at Chrissie.

"What now?" But it was hardly a question, and she did not expect Tarbush to answer. She did not dare to move, and waited frozen in position until at last the creature reappeared. It was accompanied by another half its size.

The small one advanced to stand in front of Chrissie. It waited. Finally it chittered into the translator unit, which said in one rush of words, "*Why is this used— What is the problem— Was there no meeting with The One?*"

Chrissie could answer the last question. "If Big Rocky is the same as The One, we had a meeting."

"*But there was no transfer?*" The eyestalks of the little animal swiveled and seemed to be staring at Chrissie's ears. "*Ah, I see it is true. There was in your case not yet a transfer. What do you want?*"

"We would like food." Chrissie did not feel in the least like eating, but it was the only thing that she could think of.

"*The rest period is here. It is not food time.*"

"The One told us we could have food."

Apparently she had said the magic words. The creature in front of her clacked and whistled, and the translation unit said abruptly, "*You will be given food, the same food as the converted one. Then you will remain quiet until day comes, or you will be punished. Go back into your room.*"

Chrissie retreated. As soon as she was beyond the ledge, a curtain of mist seemed to close across the keyhole opening. It gradually solidified, until in half a minute it looked exactly like a brighter version of the rest of the wall.

"I guess *that* didn't work," Tarbush said softly. He went across and rapped on the new wall. "Quite a trick. Perfectly solid. I thought you were promised food?"

"Maybe it changed its mind." But a few moments later, the part of the wall nearest the floor rippled. An object shaped like a small sled came floating through into the room and stood six inches from the floor unsupported. Tarbush bent down to lift the lid of the oblong container that sat on top of the sled, and recoiled.

"Sweet Lucy! If that's what they call food . . ."

He clapped the lid back on the box, but not before Chrissie had seen dozens of purple tentacles reaching and wriggling out over the edges.

"I wasn't hungry anyway," she said. As she watched, the new wall slowly began to darken. It was the only source of light, and within a minute she could not make out Tarbush's outline. "That little effort didn't help at all, did it? We're worse off than we were before."

"Not really." Tarbush again turned on the little spotlight in the helmet of his suit. "They're not watching us any more. We're free to fiddle around any way we like so long as we don't make a lot of noise."

"So what do we fiddle around *with* all night long?" Chrissie advanced, until she stood in front of him and could tilt her head back to look at his frowning face, shadowed by the lamp above it. "Do we take that sled apart and try to understand how it floats in the air with no support? Or do we sit in the corner and play with ourselves? I don't have any ideas. Do you?"

The scowl that he gave her was its own answer.

31

The Nature of the Multiverse

After the Angel's pronouncement on the nature of the changed Friday Indigo, Dag Korin couldn't wait to get everyone away from his private quarters.

"Go on," he said. "Get out of here. It's far too late for an old man like me, and you must be tired, too. Go get a good night's sleep." And to Gressel, "A good night's transpiration for you, or whatever you do in the dark."

And then, one by one, Dag Korin contacted every human and told them to come back.

"I had to do it this way," he explained, when the bewildered group was reassembled. "You know how the Angel would react if I told him I planned to take Friday Indigo and use his guts for suspenders. We need a private planning session without any aliens. What's the status on the Pipe-Rilla?"

"Still curled tight," Tully O'Toole said. "She's in the

cool medical unit near me, and every time I go past I sneak a peek. How long can a Pipe-Rilla stay frigid rigid?"

"Months." Elke was the only one in the room who didn't look the least bit tired. "It's not a big deal, they always curl themselves that way when they estivate. In fact, I suspect that stress may simply induce an unplanned estivation. If so, Vow-of-Silence will be hyperactive when she wakes."

"Then the longer she sleeps, the better. Let's leave her that way." With every seat taken, Korin perched on the liquor cabinet. "All right, first question. How much of that guff about the superior science of the Malacosties do we believe?"

"All of it." Elke replied at once. "I've studied our space images a lot more since last time we talked. The buildings around the airstrip morph every few hours, in their numbers and their sizes. An area of seven hundred square kilometers was cleared and sterilized, with no sign of radioactivity. And their aircraft and ships, from everything I've seen of them, ought not to be able to fly. They possess technology we've never dreamed of."

"I was afraid you'd say that. Anyone disagree?" Korin glanced around at the circle of gloomy faces. "All right, so I have to believe it. The Mallies have science and weapons different from and maybe superior to ours. What they did to Friday Indigo shows that they regard us as expendable. That tells me there's no way we can allow them into our universe. The Angels and the Pipe-Rillas may think those bastards can be nice guys, but even a nice guy who can do anything he likes tends to do things *you* won't like. If we want to live—and I assume we do—we'd better find a plan of action that lets us."

"Easier said than done." Elke was biting her

fingernails, already chewed down to the quick. "The Angel and I have a good idea of the structure of the multiverse, and we think we know how to set coordinates to go to any universe—including the one we came from. But we've beaten our brains out for a way to get there. Our only chance would be to talk the Malacostracans into lending us one of their ships, and it's pretty clear they aren't about to do that."

"I never said it would be easy, Elke. But any plan, even a terrible one, is a lot better than no plan at all. So I'm going to throw out ideas. You can all chip in or disagree any time you want.

"First, and this one's a no-brainer: somebody has to go ashore tomorrow morning with Deb Bisson. We have to talk to the Mallies, no matter how much we hate 'em. We've been told that they can blow this ship up any time they feel like it, and if we don't cooperate with them we'll automatically be considered an enemy. We need to leave here soon—we'd better, because this hulk is dying around us—but right now we're a sitting duck.

"So who goes with Deb Bisson? Well, I'm not inviting discussion, because this one I've already decided." Korin turned to Chan. "You've been itching to go and look for trouble ashore for days—"

"I accept."

"—so here's your chance. You and Bisson seem to work well as a team."

"We do. Any other instructions?"

"Not without breaking one of my own golden rules. In an unpredictable situation, the man or woman on the spot should make the decisions, not the general sitting on his ass a million miles away from the action. But I'll tell you what I expect from you. I need *time*. Time to organize ourselves to leave this ship and establish a base on shore. And time for Elke and the

Angel to nail a way to get us through the Link and off this dump of a planet." Korin waved his hand at Elke. "I know, I know. We don't have a ship, and I don't see any half-rational hope of getting us one. We need time for that, too. Yes?"

His question was addressed to Tully O'Toole, who was holding up his hand.

Tully glanced at Danny Casement sitting next to him, who nodded and said, "Friday Indigo didn't say we could only send two people ashore. He said they only wanted two people to take our answer to them."

"What are you proposing?"

"We have two of our team members in the hands of the Mallies. Tully and I talked about this even before you called us back here. We'd like to go ashore and take a shot at rescuing Chrissie and the Tarb."

Instead of replying, Dag Korin leaned back and put his hand over his eyes. Finally he said, "Damn me, that's a hard one. I don't know what your friends are going through up there, but I can't imagine it's pleasant." He tilted his head forward and stared at Danny. "Worse than anything, I hate to lose people. Ninety-nine percent of me is on your side, cheering you on to give it a shot. But I can't let you do it. We have a proposal from the Mallies sitting in front of us. We don't understand all its implications, but we have to explore it farther. Now, if you make a rescue attempt, whether you succeed or whether you fail, you'll drop a mine on what Chan Dalton is doing. So it has to be no—though I wish there was some way I could say yes."

Danny protested, "So we just sit around, waiting?"

"Did I say that? We're going to be busy, every one of us. Soon we're going to leave the *Hero's Return* and set up camp on shore. We have to pick a site a comfortable distance from the Mallies, preferably in an inconspicuous place that can easily be hidden from overhead inspection. Elke Siry, that's your job. We must also decide what we need to take from this ship and what we *can* take—Bony Rombelle, Liddy Morse, and Tully O'Toole, you make the list and assemble everything by the main airlock. Keep it practical and assume we're never coming back. Food and shelter should be tops, but remember we can't make many trips and we can't carry too much. Danny Casement, you and I are going to float. We'll help out anywhere we're needed. Any questions?"

"How long do we have?" That was Elke, already on her feet.

"Before Chan Dalton and Deb Bisson leave, I want to know where we're going and what we're taking with us. Tomorrow I want us ashore. Anything else? Otherwise, let's get going."

Elke nodded. "One other thing, and it's not good. Before I returned here I checked the condition of our external sensors. Air pressure at the surface has been dropping and wind speeds are picking up. We don't have metsats to provide confirming images so I can't be absolutely sure, but I think another big storm is on the way—worse than when we first arrived. The first front will hit this area sometime tonight, with high winds and rain. Then we'll have a lull, low winds and clear skies, maybe lasting all day tomorrow. But two days from now the *real* hurricane hits. Either we're out of here and somewhere safe before that, or we won't be going anywhere at all."

Everyone gave up all thoughts of sleep. When the meeting broke up, Elke Siry at once headed aft. Chan Dalton followed her.

She turned as they came to the entrance of the

control room. "What do you want? Your assignment may not begin until tomorrow, but mine already started. I don't have time to talk."

"This will take only five minutes." Chan followed her in. "Let me start with a question. You understand more about the multiverse than anyone on board. Suppose we could capture a Malacostracan vessel—don't ask me how. What would our chances be of performing a Link transition in that ship, without help from them?"

"How long would we have to study their controls and operating systems?"

"Let's say, an hour or two."

"Forget it. Without their help our chances would be one in a billion. For starters, we have no idea how to open the Link itself. It turns on and off in a way that we don't understand, and it's been off almost all the time since we arrived."

"It was open whenever one of our ships came here."

"I suspect that it opens whenever something wants to come through this way, but for ships that are leaving it's controlled locally by the Mallies. I realize that General Korin believes the use of an alien ship is our only hope for finding our way home, but I can't imagine it being possible. They won't loan us a ship, and they won't open the Link for us."

"All right, a different question. Back in General Korin's quarters, you said that you and the Angel know how to set coordinates for a Link transfer to any universe. True?"

"Quite true. Of course, I meant we know how to do it using a ship that we understand. Not an alien ship. But with our own vessel, I think we'd be able to Link to any exit point in any universe."

"Can you describe how?" Chan could see that she was becoming impatient.

"Certainly. Once you've made a structural map of the multiverse, navigation across the different energy levels isn't difficult. But you have to be extremely careful what you're doing."

"Because of the different time rates in different universes?"

"There's that. But the Link coordinates give a good idea whether a universe will run faster or slower than the one you're in. In retrospect, knowing what we know now, we could have *predicted* that the coordinates we had for a transit to the Geyser Swirl wouldn't take us there. They showed a transition from one universe—ours—to one like this where time runs slower."

"If you can estimate the time rates, why do you say you have to be very careful with transitions?"

"Because of variability even within the same energy level. It seems as though almost any imaginable combination of physical constants is going to be found in *some* universe. Suppose you Link to a universe where those basic constants are grossly different? And in most universes, they will be. There might be no stars or planets. There might even be no *matter*, just pure radiation. Then the time rate wouldn't matter, because our kind of life, and maybe any kind of life, would be impossible."

"Can you show me how to avoid that problem?"

"In five minutes? Not so you'll understand what you're doing."

"I don't have to understand, not in your sense of the word. I just want to know how to Link."

"In our own ship—or an alien one?"

"Our own ship. Let's forget the idea of doing it with one of their ships."

"The *Hero's Return* will never fly again. But I can show you how to pick a subset of universes that should be safe to visit. That's as far as I can go."

"And will I know the time rate in each one, before I Link there?"

"I think so."

Chan sat down beside Elke at the console. "Show me."

"You have a plan?"

"Maybe. But I don't want to talk about it yet."

"In case it's no good?"

"In case it is. But I still don't want to talk." *Not to you. Not to General Korin, not to Deb—not even to myself. Maybe* especially *not to me.*

Chan stretched his five minutes to ten, and then to twenty, before Elke decided that he understood as much about the structure of the multiverse as he ever would, given his ignorance of macroscopic quantum fields. She threw him out.

"And close the door behind you," she called as Chan was leaving. But she had barely summoned onto the display the satellite image that she needed when the door of the control room was sliding open again.

"No!" she said. "Not another millisecond. I have work to do. Oh! I'm sorry, sir. I thought it was somebody else."

"It is somebody else." Dag Korin hovered on the threshold. "I came to check on your progress. Liddy Morse and the others are making a first list of what we need, and they hit me with some very reasonable questions. Which of course I couldn't answer. Where will we land? How far will we have to carry the things that we pick out? How much of the journey will be underwater? How long will we have to live on whatever we take with us? You're the only one who can answer *any* of those. How's it coming?"

"It's not coming at all. I haven't started yet. Chan Dalton was in here until two minutes ago, asking questions of his own."

"Was he now?" Korin frowned and sat down uninvited next to Elke. "What sort of questions?"

"About whether we could fly an alien ship through a Link on the surface of the planet, and about the structure of the multiverse. He asked me for the transition sequences to different levels, especially to an extreme case that I've been calling the Omega level. He said he needed to know how to initiate the transfers before his meeting with the Malacostracans."

"Did he now. You gave the information to him?"

"Of course. I assumed he was doing it with your knowledge and approval. Shouldn't I have?"

Dag Korin bent his head forward. He was silent for a long time, the only sound in the control room the steady drip of condensation. Elke wondered if he had gone to sleep. At last he stirred and said, "Who's in charge here? I thought I was, but maybe I'm fooling myself. Let me see what you gave him."

"It's still on the display. He wanted a selection of levels where a human can survive. And he wanted to know exactly what the protocol would be to make a transition to those universes. He also wanted to know if a Malacostracan would be likely to use the same protocol as one that we would use."

"And what did you tell him?"

"I said, yes, so far as I knew it made no difference who initiated the transition protocol, humans or Angels or Malacostracans. The parameters depend only on universal mathematical constants, like pi and e. But I would expect any alien ship, including all its controls and operating sequences, to be totally unfamiliar."

"But the sequence should work. All right." Korin was still glaring at the display. "Your list doesn't include *our* universe."

"That's right. I have that, but Dalton specifically told me that he didn't want a sequence to our own universe to be on the list he would take away."

"Curiouser and curiouser. Make a copy of what's on that screen, would you?"

"It's coming now. On the output by your right hand. What's going on? I asked Dalton why he wanted that list, and he wouldn't tell me. Wouldn't talk about it, either."

"I don't know. But I suspect that Chan Dalton is considering some kind of end run. No, don't ask me what that means. I don't know myself—not yet."

"Suppose he returns with more questions. Do I answer them?"

"I think so. I hate all conspiracies unless I'm a part of them, and Chan Dalton is certainly sneaky, and he's certainly up to something. But I don't read him as a turncoat and a traitor. If I'm wrong about that, shame on me and him both. But if he comes back and asks questions, give him whatever you can. Just make sure that whatever you tell him, you also tell me." Korin stood up, slowly and creakily, the multiverse transition list in his hand. "I want to think about this. You get to work picking the site for our camp."

He turned away, his ramrod back for once bowed. Elke, leaning again over her console, thought he looked a thousand years old.

She comforted herself with the thought that whatever Chan Dalton was doing or planning, Dag Korin had probably seen it all before.

32

Escape to Nowhere

It was possible to sleep in a space suit; the manufacturers even claimed comfort in repose, asserting that the universal flexible joints and air cushions made their suit as relaxing as any bed.

Perhaps they were right—in free fall, where thermal balance was perfect and contact with walls or floor was gentle and infrequent; but for someone on a planetary surface, on a rock-hard floor sloshing in icy water that seemed every few minutes to become a little deeper and colder . . .

Chrissie switched on the tiny visor display and looked at the time. Half the night was gone, which was good; but also bad, because it meant that dawn still lay half a night away. She activated the shielded spotlight in her helmet and used it to stare enviously at Tarbush. He lay flat on his back, helmet open and snoring softly. Big ugly bruiser. It was tempting to wake him up, just to tell him how lucky he was.

She turned off the light, lay back, and stared into the darkness. Even the glitter of the ceiling had faded to nothing. The creatures beyond the inner wall had ceased their clatter and chatter. That at least was welcome. Except that when morning came they would waken, and the horrors would start all over again. The jungle of Limbo, which only a day ago had been filled with the alarms of a dangerous unknown, now felt like a sanctuary. Given a chance to escape from this building, Chrissie would fly to it in a bare moment. Up, outside, through the open gate of the fence . . .

Pure wishful thinking. She and Tarbush had poked and pried and hammered for three hours. The walls vibrated and boomed like a giant drum, but they remained impenetrable and they gave not a millimeter. They were sounding now, a low hum that rose and fell in pitch like a mournful siren. It was a rising wind, calling aloud as it swirled around the outside of the building. Back on Earth, in a childhood that seemed like a forgotten dream, she had always loved the sound of the surface wind. It soothed and calmed and sustained her.

Not tonight, though. Now she felt as pent and chained and restless as a trapped wild beast. Now the strengthening wind was finding its way into the building's narrow air ducts, where it sobbed and wailed and cried as if it were a trapped animal itself.

She heard another noise, a low mmm—mmm—mmm. This one was closer. She concentrated, and at last realized that it was Tarbush muttering to himself in his sleep. Dreaming. Pleasant dreams, probably. He was far too placid in temperament for nightmares. Damn the man. He would sleep through Armageddon. How come they got along so well? The attraction of opposites? People had a phrase for everything.

The muttering stopped. Chrissie heard movement next to her and opened her eyes. Tarbush was awake. His helmet spotlight was on, and he was sitting up. Chrissie said, "What's wrong?" and sat up herself.

"Listen." He turned his head from side to side. "Where's it coming from? It woke me up."

"It's the wind outside the building. I think another storm is on the way."

"Not that. Higher pitched."

"I don't hear it."

"You're not tuned in the way that I am. Shh." He held his hand up to silence her. "There. *That.*"

Chrissie heard all the same noises as before. "What?"

"It's *Scruffy*. Whining. Can't you hear her? But where is she?"

The high-pitched keening? Was that what he meant? "It's coming from an air duct. I heard it when you were asleep."

"You should have woken me. Which duct?" He was on his feet, moving to peer into the pipe from which they had cut the coarse covering mesh. "She's not in here. It must be the other one."

He went splashing away into the darkness, his progress marked by the bobbing beam of light from his helmet. "Damn." She heard him grumbling to himself. "Covered with a filter. Have to cut it. Hold on, girl." A remark not addressed to Chrissie. The beam of light steadied. A few seconds of silence, then, "Come on, sweetheart. Easy goes. You don't want to be on the floor, you know how you hate getting your feet wet."

Tarbush sloshed his way back toward Chrissie. She shone her own helmet light, and saw the ferret nestled against his chest. "Didn't I tell you Deb and Danny would find us?" he said. "I'm sure they sent Scruffy here. She followed my scent as far as she could, then looked for another way to reach me. Isn't that great?" He sat down, sending a surge of cold water over Chrissie.

She wiped her wet face. "Tarb, my dear, I hate to spoil your fun and your reunion, but we don't really need Scruffy inside with us. We need ourselves *outside* with her. If Friday Indigo or the Malacostracans find her they're more likely to kill her than appreciate her. Tell her to go back the way she came. Then she can lead the others to us."

"All in good time." He was fiddling with Scruffy's collar. "Here we are. I thought there would be one."

"Would be what?"

"A message from Deb and Danny. Hmm." He had removed from the collar a broad silver ring a couple of inches across. He inspected it in the light of his helmet lamp. "Doesn't look like a message. What is it?"

"Let's have a peek. Maybe the ring opens up." Chrissie held it close to her nose. "It's from Deb all right—see the little entwined DB on the side? But I don't think it can be a message. It's a—I think—" There was a soft click. "The outside opens up. Not a message, though. A reel of twine? But this is so thin—you can only see it from really close up when the light is right. Oh!"

"What?" Tarbush craned forward.

"It's a monofilament strand. Deb used one of these once to cut the head off a man who was trying to rape and kill her."

"I remember. But why send this to us? If she knew we were in trouble, a gun or a batch of explosives would be more useful."

"She had to send something small. Something that Scruffy could carry. She tried to give us a weapon, and she has. The problem is, we don't know how to use it the way she would. And there's hordes of Malacostracans, we could never take on all of them." Chrissie was twisting the ring, which suddenly split in two. The thread, almost too fine to see, stretched between two matching circlets of silver. Chrissie took one ring carefully in each gloved hand and spread her arms.

"How long a length do you have?" Tarbush held Scruffy firmly, making sure that the ferret could not get near the danger zone between the two silver rings.

"I don't know. But the thread is ratcheted inside the rings. I can make it longer or shorter, as I want. Hold something out to me—something we don't need."

"I'll have to put Scruffy down. Do we want to keep her here?"

"I told you, we should let her go."

"Then hold on a minute." Tarbush stood and walked over to the air duct. "Go on, Scruff. Find Deb Bisson and Danny Casement." The ferret hesitated, reluctant to enter the dark, narrow passage. "I said, go on. You found us, that was your job. It's not safe here for you."

He held the animal forward again toward the duct. She nuzzled his hand, then vanished in a sudden blur of brown fur.

"Hope she'll be all right," Tarbush said as he splashed back toward Chrissie. "Listen to that wind! It's not nice out there."

"Tarb, it's not nice in *here*." While he had been gone, Chrissie had removed the compass from the sleeve of her suit. The instrument had provided nothing but nonsense readings since their arrival on

Limbo, and now she balanced it on the top of her boot and brought the silver rings carefully down, one held in each hand, so that the thread lay across the compass.

"Careful!" Tarbush said. "Don't ruin your suit, you may need it again."

"I know that." Chrissie bent forward. All her attention was concentrated on the filament, thinner than gossamer, that spanned the distance between the rings. She was exerting hardly any pressure, but the thread was sinking effortlessly through the hardened plastic and metal of the compass. When she paused and delicately lifted the rings, the compass fell into two neat halves.

"Now I've got the feel of it. The question is, will the monofilament do the same thing to the wall?"

"Even if it can, how does that do us any good?" Tarbush picked up the halves of the compass. "To cut something apart, you have to place the rings on both sides of it. We're inside the wall."

"So we have to be tricky." Chrissie stood up and went across to the closer of the ventilators. "Before I waste any time, let's see if there's any point in even trying." She reached far inside the duct, her hand still holding its silver ring. She brought the other hand around in a semicircle, so that the monofilament met and cut into the perimeter of the duct. A crescent slice, carved from around the wall, silently slid free and splashed into the dark water at her feet.

"Principle established," Chrissie said softly. "This will cut anything. Now for the tricky bit. I have to widen the hole more and more, and hope I can get one hand all the way to the outside."

"Chrissie, let me do it." Tarbush held out his hand. "My arm's longer than yours, and stronger. I can reach outside easily."

"You could—if you could get that great ham fist into the duct at all. Which you can't. Stand clear, sweetheart. Keep your light focused on where I'm cutting. I don't want to start slicing pieces off my own arm."

She was moving one hand in a wider arc, excising from the wall a circular cone half a meter across. As it came free, Tarbush lifted it clear. "Hm. This is *warm*," he said. "That thing you have isn't just a monofilament. I wondered how it could cut so easily. There must be nanos inside the thread, freeing molecular bonds."

"Deb specializes in tricky weapons. But now for the hardest part." Chrissie had her arm in the enlarged hole up to the shoulder. "I can reach all the way through, but I have to enlarge the duct at the outside edge because unless I do that we have nothing useful. I'm going to work one hand outside, hold the ring against the outer wall, then slide both hands in unison to slice a cylindrical section. Don't breathe."

"I'm not sure it's necessary to go to all that trouble." Tarbush had been examining the conical wedge removed from the wall, and now he moved forward.

"We want to get out, don't we?" Chrissie, her hands encumbered with the rings, could not easily push at him. She said sharply, "Get your hand out of the way. If you stand like that you'll lose some fingers."

"No. Back off, Chrissie. I need to try something."

"Tarb!" But he was dangerously close to the monofilament, and she was forced to pull her hands clear. "What are you playing at?"

"Just watch. We haven't used my strongman act for years, but let's see how it plays on Limbo." He stood in front of the ventilator pipe, took a deep breath, and punched his fist deep into the expanded hole that she had made. Chrissie heard nothing, but she saw a cloud of powder fly out around his arm.

"What did you do?"

Tarbush was pushing his shoulder and then his head into the hole. "Take a look at the piece you cut out." He was grunting at some great effort, interspersing his words with gasps. "Push your finger in it—you can, it's soft as cream cheese. This whole building must have an—integrated structure. Very strong when it's complete, forms a single unit, but if any part is—destroyed—the rest is ready to crumble. We're lucky that Deb's—monofilament cutter didn't bring—the whole place down on top of us. But we have to move fast—it's self-repairing, and it's starting to adjust. Going to be touch and go. One more push—hah!—I'm through! My arm's outside. Now for the big push. Look out back there."

He emerged from the hole, coated in gray powder and coughing and choking. "Should have closed my suit—up my nose—going to sneeze."

He did, in a vast explosion of air loud enough to hear above the sounds of the storm. Then: "Follow me! Close your suit. It's a mess outside."

A mess inside, too. Chrissie imagined that she could see the room starting to sag and melt around her. She heard sounds—not the storm—from beyond the wall to the inner chamber. She closed her helmet and followed Tarbush. His head and torso had vanished, and his wriggling legs and kicking feet sent back prodigious clouds of disintegrated wall. The hole, barely wide enough for him, should have been easier for her. It wasn't. Already it was starting to seal. She snaked through, fast as she could, and felt the closing wall begin to squeeze tighter. She gave a desperate kick and plunged headfirst forward. Her helmet cracked against a hard, slick surface.

"No time for acrobatics." Tarbush was lifting her easily, setting her on her feet, shouting in her ear. "Can you stand up?"

Chrissie was about to shout back "Of course I can!" when the wind caught her. Inside the building she had never dreamed that it would be so strong. She felt herself sliding away sideways, down a wet and slippery incline. Only Tarbush's invisible grip on her arm saved her from being blown away.

While she stood braced against him, the darkness was suddenly dispelled by strong light. She turned, and saw a green globe of luminescence drifting across the sky. Tarbush shouted, "They've got us," and pulled her close. The globe lengthened to become a tall cylinder, a vortex column that stretched toward earth and sky. When it touched the ground it vanished. Chrissie felt her skin prickle.

"Not the aliens," she screamed at Tarbush. "Some local sort of electrical activity caused by the storm. But the wind!" She could feel her feet slipping. "I can't hold—it's too strong."

"Let yourself go. We can't travel upwind, but if we can reach the forest—"

He released his hold. Chrissie went slithering and skating away into the darkness. She could see nothing. She felt nothing, too, until with a teeth-loosing jolt she hit the boundary fence. A moment later, Tarbush crashed into the mesh wall a few feet to her left.

"Damnation!" His howl of rage carried over the wind. "We have to try to drag ourselves around to the gate—but which way? I have no idea."

"It may be guarded anyway." Chrissie lay spread-eagled on the fence. "Can you shine your helmet light over here? I ought to have turned mine on before I started."

"Wait a second." After a moment's silence, he shouted back. "The damn thing's not working. I hit the fence face first. But if—"

Before he could finish, another ball of light began to form behind them. Tarbush turned, and saw every building of the Malacostracan encampment glowing with its own halo of electrical discharge. The area around the buildings was—thank God—deserted. While the globe was extending toward earth and sky, he turned back to Chrissie and realized what she was doing. Pinned in place by the wind, she had taken a short length of the monofilament thread and was stretching out to slice through the fence wires that she could reach. As she cut further, the section she lay against began to sag under her weight. In half a minute the left-hand side gaped open.

"Go on." She inclined her head. "Through."

"What about you?"

"Go!"

Tarbush obeyed her cry. As he passed through the hole in the fence he grabbed at the cut edge. It opened farther under his weight.

"You now!" he shouted, but she was already through and sailing past him. The bright circlet of the monofilament ring glittered with green light and spun away from her hand. He made an instinctive grab and missed. Good thing, too. The invisible thread could easily have severed his forearm. Forget it. Deb surely had more, and the little ring would be hard to find even in calm conditions.

As the wind caught him from behind and the green light vanished he ducked his head forward and followed Chrissie. He had little choice. Although it was no longer raining, trying to walk on the slick surface was like skating on ice. He managed to keep his feet, but he went wherever the wind pushed him.

Toward the forest, or away across many bare kilometers of rock? He could not tell where he was going, until something grabbed him at knee-level and tipped him over. He sprawled headlong forward into a tangle of tight-knit bushes. His visor was still open, and thorny twigs scratched his nose and mouth.

"Chrissie?" He shouted as loudly as he could.

"Right here."

He could see nothing. He closed his helmet and began to crawl blindly in the direction of her voice. The suit protected his body, but the vegetation resisted his progress like something alive. While he was still struggling forward a faint light shone ahead. The lamp in Chrissie's helmet? She had managed to get it working; but it was moving away from him.

"Stay there! I'm coming."

"I can't. I have to keep going. Follow me."

As he came closer he understood why. Chrissie had been blown into a thin stand of stalky reeds, and they were not close-grown enough to provide shelter from the wind. She was tunneling on, deeper into a denser thicket. He flattened as low to the ground as he could and butted his way along until he was at her heels. He grabbed her legs and inched forward until his head was next to hers.

"What now?" For the first time since they left the building he didn't have to shout.

"We have to find our way back to the camp. I'm sure Deb and Danny are wondering what happened to us."

"We can't go anywhere while this storm lasts. But neither can they. We're all stuck until the wind dies down."

"What about the Malacostracans?"

Tarbush sat up for a moment, felt the thresh of the wind across the top of the plants, and lay back down. "If they can move around and find us on such a bad night, they're entitled to do what they like with us."

Chrissie opened her visor. "At least it's not raining. If we can't go anywhere I'm going to try to sleep. I didn't get any sleep earlier—not like some people."

She was looking for a response, maybe an argument. But he said only, "You do that. You need your rest. I won't talk any more, but I'll stay awake and keep watch."

Tarbush settled in at her side, one arm around Chrissie and his face close to hers. Within ten minutes she knew from his steady breathing that he was asleep. It was tempting to nudge him, but she didn't.

She lay, listening to the wind. Was it her imagination, or had it eased, just a little? The canopy of plants above her head became faintly visible. Another ball of lightning must be drifting through the atmosphere of Limbo. This one was far off, and Chrissie watched and waited until the moment of its sudden extinction.

She closed her eyes. If Tarbush could sleep, why couldn't she? She deliberately turned her mind back two months, to a time when the embargo against stellar travel seemed permanent, with no chance of ever meeting again the members of the old team; to the time when she and Tarbush had toured with her bag of magic tricks and his animal-talking act, to amaze the colonists of the wide-scattered mini-worlds of the Oort Cloud; to the time—God, why didn't a person know when she was well off?—the time when a "bad night" meant only a poor audience for the second performance of your magic act, and not being pursued by malevolent aliens across the scarred surface of a lost world in an alternate universe.

✧ ✧ ✧

Chrissie felt herself being shaken, and tried to curl into a ball.

"Sorry, love, but we can't have that." It was Tarbush, shaking her again. "The early bird catches the worm, and we don't want the early Malacostracan catching us."

Chrissie yawned, stretched, and sat up. Light, pale and yellow, streamed in horizontally through the leafy roof above her head. The broad fronds were moving, but gently. She heard no sound of wind.

"About half an hour after dawn," Tarbush said. "The wind died down about the same time. I would have let you sleep, but I think we have to get moving. So far as I can tell from looking at the layout of the Malacostracan buildings, our camp lies in that direction." He pointed through the undergrowth. "We have to get to it. Question is, do we go back to the edge of the cleared area, where travel is easy, but we risk being seen; or do we try to tunnel straight through the plants? We know from yesterday that we might come across various sorts of nasties."

Chrissie was finally awake. "I don't like either option. Which way is the sea?"

"If I'm right about where our camp is, and I remember correctly what we did yesterday, I'd say it's that way." He swiveled his body through forty-five degrees.

"I think that's the way we ought to go. Once we reach the shore we can follow our own trail inland. I can't imagine any reason why Deb and Danny would move the camp, but if they did they'd surely find a way to tell us where they were going. And if that doesn't work, we can simply close our suits, go into the sea, and walk back to the *Hero's Return* the way we came."

Tarbush started crawling without another word. He

went first and didn't complain, but Chrissie could tell from their miserable rate of progress that he was having problems. It took half an hour to cut and slash and scramble less than thirty meters. She was ready to suggest that they turn around and try a different route when he paused and said, "There's something funny ahead, a sort of long crack in the ground. Stay well back while I take a look at it."

He fought his way slowly forward another few meters, then abruptly vanished. Chrissie waited nervously, until suddenly just his head popped into view.

"Good news." He gestured to her to join him. "It's a streambed, almost dry but with a trickle of water in it. All we have to do is follow the direction of flow and we'll reach the sea."

Chrissie eased herself down the steep bank to join him at the bottom. The bed of the stream was a mixture of mud and gravel, dry enough to provide a firm walking surface. The plants on the stream banks grew right across, so that the channel would be invisible to any overhead surveillance, and they were high enough to allow even Tarbush to stand almost upright.

A slow and arduous crawl became a slightly uneven walk. In just a few minutes they were at the place where the rock fracture along which the stream ran came out onto the shore. Chrissie heard a loud and changing roar ahead of them. Tarbush, walking slightly in front, paused and peered out from the sheltering fringe of plants.

"The wind has died, but I don't think the sea knows it yet. Look at that."

Chrissie, moving to his side, saw the origin of the unknown roar. The surface of the sea was covered in foam and gigantic white-capped breakers that rolled in endless array to batter the shore. The shore itself was diminished, its fifty meters of shingle reduced to a narrow strand between turbulent water and tangled vegetation. Nowhere, on sea or shore, was any sign of animal life.

"Well, with waves like that we can't go back to the *Hero's Return* any time soon," Tarbush said. "We'd be smashed to pieces before we got beyond the line of breakers. What now?"

Chrissie pointed to the left. "That way. I wasn't paying particular attention, but if we had landed farther to the right surely we'd all have noticed that reddish hump."

Tarbush nodded. "I think so. Left it is, then."

They set off along the strip of shore, alert and ready to jump for the cover of the shoreline plants if anything moved. Chrissie glanced out to sea. If she had her sense of direction right, the Link entry point that had brought their ship to Limbo lay in that direction. She could see no sign of it. That seemed to confirm what the Malacostracans had said, that the Link opened and closed under their control. So how could humans or Stellar Group members possibly escape?

She was staring to the east, and the cloudy sky in that direction glowed a lurid and unpleasant yellow. Weather on Limbo was too alien and unfamiliar for her to read its indicators. Was the storm over, or did the present calm represent no more than a lull? It was tempting to use her suit communicator and try to reach Deb, Danny, or the ship, but the rule of radio silence applied more than ever now. The Malacostracans had advanced technology, different from anything Chrissie had ever seen or heard about.

At her side, Tarbush halted. He was on the shoreward side, scanning the plants there while she looked out to sea.

"This looks like the place where we went into the jungle when we first came ashore. If it isn't, somebody else has flattened the plants." He had turned, to walk carefully into the waist-high growth. "Yes, I'm sure of it."

"Should we call to them?" Chrissie was stepping close behind. "You know Deb. If we come out on them unexpectedly she might blow us away."

"What about the Malacostracans?" But it was Tarbush who raised his voice as he moved forward. "Deb? Danny? It's us, Tarb and Chrissie. We're fine, and we're alone."

In the past few minutes the wind had died completely. His voice was swallowed up by the silent sea of vegetation ahead.

"Deb? Danny?" And to Chrissie, in lower tones, "I don't like this. We're not far from where we left our supplies. They'd answer if they could."

"Do you think the Malacostracans have taken over the camp?"

"I don't know. But maybe we should have kept quiet. You stay here."

"While you get caught and leave me on my own? Forget it."

They advanced together through an unnatural morning stillness, following the faint line of the onshore party's advance. When they came to the little cleared area surrounded by waist-high ferns, Chrissie bent to examine the supply cases.

"These look the way we left them. Except that somebody took something out of this one."

"No signs of a struggle, no signs that the Malacostracans have been here." Tarbush was prowling the perimeter of the camp site. "It looks as though Deb and Danny just upped and left us behind. Not very nice of them."

"Where would they go?"

"Back to the ship. Look, suppose they made a trip to the *Hero's Return*, to tell the others there what was going on."

"Both of them?"

"You didn't want to be left on your own. They expected to come right back here, but then the storm came up. They wouldn't have been able to come ashore, any more than we could get past the breakers this morning. I bet that's it. If we just settle down and wait here, they'll be back. And if they don't come by the time the sea is calmer, we can take off ourselves for the *Hero's Return*."

"No." Chrissie had been nodding her head to agree when she noticed a familiar shape drifting across her field of view. "Get down, Tarb. Somebody's looking for us."

They left the clearing and crouched together under the mat of ferns. The tri-wing aircraft passed far off to the south, heading out to sea.

Tarbush slowly stood upright as the craft vanished in the distance. "It's certainly one of their planes. But what makes you think it's looking for us?"

"What makes you think it *isn't*?" Chrissie stood up, too, and headed for the supply cases. "I think we made a mistake by coming here. Our plan sounded good when we thought that Deb and Danny would be waiting for us, but they weren't and now we don't know what's going on. The one thing we can be sure of is that the Malacostracans will look for us. When they do, they'll find this campsite. It's the worst possible place for us to stay."

"Maybe. But do you know a better place?"

"I'm looking for one." Chrissie had been rummaging, and she pulled out of a supply case one of the maps that Elke Siry had prepared from the orbital images. "Look, here's the Malacostracan encampment. There's where we came ashore. So here"—she placed her finger on the sheet—"is about where we must be now. What I'm suggesting is that we go back to the shore and find the stream channel. It doesn't show on this image, because the plants grow right across and cover it. But from our point of view, that's good. We can head *upstream*, and we'll be hidden from anybody who flies over looking for us."

"Suppose they use radar? That sees right through a canopy of vegetation."

"Then they're too smart for us, and we're cooked. But if we can get far enough into the highlands, way over to the east, we should find all kinds of places to hide. You can see that the ground looks like a great mixed-up jumble of bare screes and rocks and cliffs."

Tarbush was bending over the map and seemed less than enthusiastic. "So we go there—uphill all the way. And then we do what?"

"Wait. We send periodic signals from our suit radios until Deb or Danny calls us back. Until that happens the only danger will be if the Malacostracans triangulate on our signal and it leads them to us." Chrissie was digging into the big supply case. "We need to take enough food and water to last for a few days. And I want something comfortable to sleep on. I'm getting sick of living inside this suit. Medicines, too, just in case. It's going to be quite a load." She glanced over to Tarbush, who was still frowning down at the image. "Come on, don't make me do this all by myself."

Tarbush slowly folded the map, rose, and walked across to where Chrissie was picking out an assortment of boxes and packages. He looked wistfully around him. Not a sign of Scruffy, and they dared not hang around to look for her. He decided to remain silent on one other point. The decision was made, and it wouldn't help Chrissie's peace of mind to point out to her what she had apparently not noticed. That the region of the image where they proposed to go had been marked, in Elke Siry's precise and careful hand, *Badlands*.

33

Ashore Again

By dawn, Chan and Deb were ready and waiting. They would have left, preferring to wait on the beach for Friday Indigo rather than pent up and restless on the seabed. But Dag Korin vetoed any such move.

"Smash on the rocks trying to get ashore, and then how much use would you be to anybody?" Korin was red-eyed and pale. He went on, "You take your marching orders from Dr. Siry. She's been monitoring weather and sea state all night long. When she says the breakers are down to a reasonable size and it's safe to walk through them, you leave. We're all willing to take risks, but I won't lose people if I don't have to."

It was a logical order, though not an easy one to follow. Chan and Deb donned their suits and went to the airlock; and there they stayed, hour after endless hour, listening to Elke Siry's ominous pronouncements on surface weather.

Two hours before noon, Chan placed a call to the ship's main control area. "General Korin," he said, as soon as the General's image appeared, "Friday Indigo was quite specific with us. We have to meet him at midday. He didn't say what would happen if we weren't there, but the Mallies can probably destroy this ship any time they want to."

Korin sniffed and traced with his forefinger the pattern of scattered droplets of water that beaded the desk in front of him. "This place is doing a pretty good job of disintegrating without any help from anybody. What's your point, Dalton?"

"Deb Bisson and I ought not to wait any longer. The wind has dropped and the waves are less. We should risk a landing."

"Dr. Siry?" Korin turned to someone out of the camera's field of view.

"Wind velocity is close to zero," said Elke Siry's voice.

"So why not—"

"But there's still a strong sea-swell. I would estimate that the breakers are well over two meters."

"Everywhere on the shoreline?"

"No. I am referring to the place where our party is to meet Captain Indigo. It's better farther south, on the inlet where the *Mood Indigo* was lifted ashore."

"Very good." Korin turned back to Chan and Deb. "Give it a shot. Try to the south if you have to, and if it's too rough—"

"General." Elke Siry's voice broke in. "I recommend against any such attempt. The chance of being caught in an undertow—"

"Thank you, my dear," Korin said mildly. "Not your call, I'm afraid." He spoke again to Chan and Deb. "I don't need to tell you what to do. You're no use to anyone dead. If it's too rough, wait in deeper water, head more to the south, or come back. I'm not going to second-guess you."

"Yes, sir." Chan cut the connection at once. Deb was already heading for the lock. She said, "Once we're in the water, if he changes his mind he won't be able to tell us about it. Come on."

They waited impatiently while the lock filled, then opened the outer hatch and dropped together to the seabed. Their landing stirred the fine bottom silt into an opaque cloud.

Deb's voice carried faintly to Chan's helmet. "Set your suit's inertial guidance unit for fifty meters due east. The sediment will die down by then. We'll be able to see each other, and I'll take us from there."

Chan paced steadily forward into darkness, keeping the yellow arrow in his helmet display exactly in line with the green one. When the guidance unit had reduced to zero distance, he halted. He turned on his helmet lamp, and saw only gray opacity.

"Deb?" His voice vanished to nothing, as though he stood alone in an empty universe. "Deb, I can't see a thing."

"Nor can I." She sounded close by. "Visibility was fine when I brought Friday Indigo to the *Hero's Return*."

"It must be the storm. The wind has died down, but the water here is shallow enough for the swell to disturb the bottom mud. How far are we from the shore?"

"Three to four kilometers. We're on the coastal shelf so it will be shallow all the way in. We can't be far apart now, but if we keep moving independently we'll get separated. Stand still. I'm going to walk in a spiral pattern until we meet."

Chan waited. It seemed a long time, standing rigid

and hearing only the sound of his own breath, until Deb's hand was grasping his arm. His helmet display told him that it had been less than three minutes.

Deb said, "So far so good," and without releasing her grip she moved until they were visor to visor. "We hang on to each other and use just my suit's inertial navigator. I'm going to angle us south of east. That will bring us ashore too far to the right, but Elke says the waves will be less there. Once we're on land we can walk back north to meet Indigo."

"Let's go." Almost before he spoke, Deb was moving away across the sea floor. She didn't need Chan to tell her that Friday Indigo's deadline was less than an hour and a half away.

It was difficult to walk fast across the silty seabed. Chan had reset his own helmet distance indicator, and before they had moved half a kilometer he knew they were in trouble. He held Deb's arm and forced her to halt.

"This won't do. We'll never make it in time."

"I know. But there's nothing we can do about it. We have to keep going and hope that Indigo won't mind that we're late."

"There's another answer. I talked to Liddy Morse, and when they first went ashore they rose up to the surface and used their suit jets from there."

"That was in a calm sea. If we try that close to shore we'll be smashed to pieces."

"Not if we wait for the right wave, and ride in on it."

"We're lost in the multiverse, and you want to go *surfing*? All right. Tell me what to do first—and don't let go of me."

"Increase your suit's internal pressure by ten percent. That will inflate you enough to carry you up."

Chan followed his own advice. His ears popped as

the pressure increased, and a few seconds later he felt his feet lift clear of the bottom ooze. As he rose the water became clearer. Faint green light bled in from above. He could see Deb at his side, her suit bulging larger than usual. Their heads broke the surface at the same time.

It was full daylight under a yellow-green overcast of cloud. In Limbo's low gravity the heavy-water sea heaved slow and sluggish, like thick, dark oil. Chan and Deb had emerged in the trough of a long, smooth wave which slowly lifted them until they could see across the whole expanse of rolling water. Before they started the descent into another trough they saw, a few kilometers to the east, the white breakers that marked the presence of an invisible shore.

"Low thrust at first," Chan said. "Otherwise you'll tend to drive yourself under. Bony told me that it's better to push too soft than too hard."

He released his hold on Deb and they began to experiment. It took a few tries to reach a setting of suit jets that carried them up and down the watery slopes rather than plunging straight into and through them. Then the time for experiment was over. Life became a roller-coaster ride across the heaving surface, with one eye on the clock and the other on the approaching shore.

Just outside the line of breakers they halted in unison and stared at the beach. Chan said, "Elke was an optimist. Three-meter waves or more. I'll give it a try first."

"Did you ever do this before?"

"No."

"Well, I did. Legacy of a wasted youth. And Indigo wants to talk to you, not me. My job was to bring you ashore. If I get hurt it's no big deal to him. Watch closely."

Before Chan could argue she was away, driving her hard-inflated suit across the water like a giant surfboard. Beyond the line of the first breaking wave, she paused. Five waves passed. As the sixth wave began to arch and build, she turned and flew laterally across the weft, riding along and into the curl for what seemed like minutes. At the last moment she vanished into the foam. She must have deflated her suit in that same instant, because after a hair-raising delay Chan saw her rise from the spray and walk forward to the dry shingle.

It looked easy. Chan did his best to imitate her. He jetted to a point close to where the waves began to swell, and waited. For what? He wasn't sure, but Deb must have seen something different in each one. Five waves swelled, reared, and broke. Finally he became impatient and drove into and along the curl of the sixth one.

At first it was smooth and simple. He was skimming along sideways and forwards at a vast speed, under the curving crest of the advancing wave. Then suddenly the breaker arched right over his head, and he was speeding down a dark, narrowing tunnel. He felt himself turn until he was upside down. Before he could use the suit jets to right himself, a mountain of water dropped on his back and drove him onto the unyielding shingle. Even with his padded suit, the impact *hurt*. He rolled over and over as surf erupted around him. Then another force was dragging at his body, pulling him back toward the sea. He grabbed at the shore with his gloved hands and scrabbled desperately forward. As the wave's suction lessened he managed to heave himself a few yards farther toward the shore. He was still in the water, but clear of the danger zone.

Deb was sitting on the beach in front of him, beyond the reach of the waves. She said, "Well, that was really elegant. Any bones broken?"

Chan had just enough strength to shake his head.

She reached out a helping hand to lift him to his feet. "Come on, then. According to my suit's inertial guidance we're a bit too far south and it's only ten minutes to midday. Don't want to keep Captain Indigo waiting."

She led Chan away along the beach. As he recovered his breath and equilibrium he was able to take notice of their surroundings. The strip of pebbles along which they walked was much narrower than on the satellite images. Because of either storm or tides, the dark, surging water and sterile black rock were now no more than twenty meters away from each other. The thin strip of gray beach dwindled into the distance. Where it vanished and rock and sea appeared to merge, a suited figure stood like a crooked statue. It was facing seaward, the face hidden by the open helmet.

The statue remained motionless until they were only a few paces away. Then it turned, and Chan saw Friday Indigo's dead eyes and fish-white countenance.

"Very foolish." Indigo ignored Chan's gesture of greeting. "A very unwise move. Did you know of it?"

"Know of what?"

"The escape. That was The One's conclusion, that you could not know of it. Lucky for you. If it had been otherwise, there would have been no point in meeting. The One believes that there is still a purpose to be served in speaking with you, but had she thought that you knew of the escape, you and your ship would have been destroyed. However, The One makes it clear that this is your final chance."

"Who escaped?" Chan wondered what effect this might have. The trouble with all desperate plans was that they were at the mercy of chance events.

"The two humans who were captured yesterday. They escaped during the night. Do not concern yourself, they can do no harm and for the moment The One is ignoring them. They'll be recaptured, of course, as soon as it's convenient. But evidence that humans cannot be trusted leads to changes in our procedure. You." He turned to face Deb. "Since we know nothing of your loyalty, you cannot be allowed to remain ashore. You will return to your ship."

"In seas like that?" Chan pointed to the breaking waves.

Indigo turned to him, slowly and painfully. "She came ashore. She can also leave. Now."

Chan tried again. "Be reasonable. She'll be killed."

"I do not think so. The sea is becoming steadily more calm. And this is not subject to negotiation. She must go."

"Don't worry about me," Deb said. "I'll manage." She sealed her helmet at once and waded into the sea until she was up to her mid-thighs. As the next wave broke she dived forward into it. Chan watched and waited for many seconds, but she did not reappear.

"And you." Indigo showed no interest in Deb from the moment when she vanished into the wave. "Are you the chosen negotiator for your party?"

"Obviously. Is there anything wrong with that?"

"You will probably be acceptable, but you are not The One's preferred choice. The senior member of the party, the General, would have been better."

"I have General Korin's full authority to negotiate."

"We will have to hope so. For all your sakes. Come on." Friday Indigo limped away inland. Chan, following, thought that the man looked in worse condition than on the day before. How much longer would Friday Indigo be able to operate without medical treatment—and who would the replacement "translation unit" be when Indigo became too decrepit to serve that purpose?

✧ ✧ ✧

Ten kilometers to the west, Chrissie and Tarbush were doing their best to make nonsense of Friday Indigo's confident prediction. As Chrissie put it, "Anybody who catches us will have to work at it."

The first hour offered few choices. The dry gully they followed led steadily upward, first turning north and west, then curving back southward. Either they followed it, or they must hack their way through the tough scrub on either side.

Tarbush insisted on carrying the big supply case by himself, along with every container of water they could find. Even in Limbo's weak gravity that was a heavy load. As the sun rose, fierce blue light penetrated the canopy of leaves. The air became intolerably hot. As they ascended farther the floor of the gully gradually turned from dry gravel to black, glutinous mud. Tarbush trudged on in silence, back bowed and face dripping sweat.

Twice he refused an offer of help from Chrissie. She was ready to repeat it for a third time when she noticed the way that he responded to every rustle in the bushes around them. His expression was hopeful, not wary. She did not volunteer assistance again. Carrying the awkward load was Tarbush's chosen penance, an expression of guilt for abandoning Scruffy. Chrissie knew it was no use trying to tell him that they'd had no choice.

She fell back a few steps to the rear, making her own survey of the dense vegetation on either side. She thought she glimpsed the purple-black wings of a Tinker, just one component, but before she could be sure it vanished into the shadows. When she turned her eyes again to the way ahead, Tarbush seemed to have shrunk. She heard him say, "Damn mud." Then, "Chrissie, stay back!" He suddenly lost another foot of height.

They had been plowing through the black mud for ten minutes, and what Tarbush was standing on now looked no different; but he was sinking into it, slowly and steadily. Already it was above his knees.

Chrissie ignored his cry, jumped forward, and grabbed at the bulky supply case he carried on his back. She shouted, "Tarb, let go the straps—the weight is pushing you down."

She heaved at the pack, falling over backwards as it came loose. When she was on her feet again, Tarbush had sunk farther. The mud was already to his mid-thighs. He had done the right thing, leaning far backward to spread his weight. Chrissie flattened herself and crawled forward until she felt herself beginning to sink. The mud was more liquid than solid. She reached as far as she could and gripped his outstretched hands.

"I've got you, Tarb. Can you ease yourself out?"

"Dunno. Let me give it a try."

Chrissie braced herself. Tarb gripped her hands and began to pull. He was enormously strong, and he seemed to move a few inches toward her. But then she was slipping forward.

"Not so hard, Tarb, or I'll be in with you."

The pressure eased. They lay still, he on his back and she facedown in the mud.

"Seems like we got us a little problem," he said after a few moments. "If I don't pull hard on you, I don't come out. If I do pull hard, you come in. Maybe we're worrying too much about nothing. Maybe this quicksand stuff isn't all that deep, and if I let myself go I'll stop at my waist."

"And suppose you don't stop? You're not going to try anything like that. Are you sinking now?"

"Don't seem to be. I'd say I'm right about where I started. Question is, where do we go from here?"

"Tarb, can you let go with one hand without sinking?"

"Only one way to find out." He released his left-hand grip, increasing the force on Chrissie's other arm until she could feel her shoulder socket creak. "Seems all right. Don't seem to be moving."

"Good. Can you work your suit controls one-handed?"

"I can." He lay in silence for a few seconds, his actions invisible to Chrissie as she sprawled at full length. "There we are. I've got the gauntlet pad working. Now what?"

"Use the controls to seal your suit at the waist, so the top and bottom halves can be independently pressurized. Then inflate below the waist—hard."

"Will do." After a few seconds of silence he said, "Ouch. That *hurts*. How hard?"

"As hard as you can stand. We want the lower half to inflate like a balloon. Then its natural buoyancy might help lift you out."

"I know what you're trying to do. But I'm *inside* that balloon, and there's things down there below my waist that I'm very fond of."

"I'm fond of them, too. But I value what's in the upper half of your suit a whole lot more. Increase the pressure, Tarb. The suit can take it, so can you."

"The suit doesn't feel it like I do." He gave a series of grunts, then a final, "I'm going to pull now. If that isn't enough, I'm stuck here forever."

Chrissie flattened her face into the mud for extra traction, gritted her teeth, and hung on. Tarbush had her hands in his. He gave a monstrous heave that had her skidding forward, and then suddenly the force on her arms was less.

She raised her head. In front of her she could see Tarbush, flat on his back. Beyond him, rising up beyond his waist, was a great misshapen hemisphere of mud. It was his suit, grossly inflated below the waist.

"I'm half out," he said. "But what now? I can't move my legs, and I can't look any way but up."

"Hang on." Chrissie wriggled backwards a few inches. She pulled, as hard as she could. After a moment when nothing happened, Tarbush's inflated figure slid a few inches toward her. She did the same thing over and over, until she could see from her own boot marks that they were past the danger point.

"You're all right," she said. "You can deflate the suit if you want to."

"If I want to!" There was a huge hiss of escaping air. After a few seconds Tarbush gave a matching sigh and sat up. Chrissie crawled to his side. Together they stared at the innocent-looking stretch of mud in front of them.

"I guess that we won't be using the gully any more," Chrissie said. She stood up and stretched high, trying to peer over the edge of the bank. "So what's our alternative?"

Tarbush remained seated. He stretched over to the pack and pulled out Elke Siry's map. "We do it the hard way. We go due east. It won't be fun. The land is all ups and downs, a mixture of steep cliffs and deep valleys, plus some things that Elke couldn't identify at all from the space images. Hmm."

"What's wrong?"

"Nothing we can do anything about. But I notice that according to Elke's notes on the map, we're still a kilometer short of the area that she marked as *Badlands*."

34

Negotiation and Betrayal

Chan had been itching to get ashore since the ship's arrival in the ocean of Limbo. Now, following Friday Indigo across an open wilderness of seared rock, he had too much on his mind to take much notice of his surroundings.

Back on the *Hero's Return* he had decided, quite deliberately, that he must act completely alone. If others of the crew knew what he had in mind they might have offered useful ideas; but with the Malacostracans clearly able to turn any human into a robotic slave who would tell everything, more people in the know meant more risk.

Unfortunately, the person most likely to become such a slave was now Chan himself. Chrissie and Tarbush had escaped, so if Friday Indigo collapsed Chan was the logical next in line.

They were passing a line of strangely shaped

aircraft, familiar from Bony Rombelle's description and the images taken from orbit. Chan forced himself to concentrate on them, and even more on the two huge and ungainly oval shapes that floated beyond them. According to Dag Korin those must be the mother ships, the vehicles used to bring everything else through the Link from the Mallies' home world and home universe.

Chan studied the alien outlines, hovering above the ground with no sign of support. His conviction strengthened that no human or Stellar Group member would be able to fly one of those without either a Malacostracan pilot or a few weeks of trial-and-error experimentation. The ships were simply too different from anything he had ever seen. According to Friday Indigo, the Malacostracans held precisely the same view: a human might direct the Mallies in making a Link transition, but stealing their ship and flying it home to the human universe was out of the question.

Friday Indigo led him past the line of ships and aircraft, toward a jumble of low buildings. Half a dozen dark figures stood guard outside the nearest one. Indigo walked confidently to and past them. Chan hesitated for half a second, then did the same. He stared at them as he walked by. The crustacean shapes were familiar from Deb and Danny's description, but nothing could prepare you for the strange forward hunch of the flat carapace, or the click of pincers and whistle of breathing tubes.

They find you every bit as strange as you find them. Chan stared straight ahead and followed Friday Indigo into the long dark archway, almost like a tunnel, that led into the building. But he remained very aware of the short black canes carried by two of the Malacostracan guards. According to Deb, those innocent-looking sticks were the weapons that had felled and paralyzed Chrissie Winger and Tarbush Hanson.

The floor of the tunnel descended. Daylight faded. Chan kept his gaze on Friday Indigo, but he felt and heard the splash of dark liquid. They were walking in water—if it was water—that rose steadily to the level of his knees. A right turn, another archway, and he saw light ahead. They emerged into a domed chamber illuminated by the diffuse gleam of melon-sized globes in the ceiling. More water, still knee-deep. In the center of the room, on a flat surface like a low table, sprawled a miniature version of the Malacostracan guards with its many jointed legs spread over the edges.

Friday Indigo paused.

"The One?" Chan said hesitantly.

Indigo gave him a scornful look. "Of course not. This is just Two-Four." To the creature, "Here is the negotiator. Permission to enter?"

The little Malacostracan raised its black cane and emitted a series of clicks and clatters.

"Permission is granted by The One. She is within." The words came from a translation unit—a human-built translation unit, from the look of it—on the front part of the table.

Friday was walking forward. Chan said, "That translator. Won't we need it?"

"Unnecessary." Friday did not break stride. "All we need with The One is present in me."

Chan's tension increased. Here was direct proof of the Angel's assertion: Friday Indigo could say anything that The One wanted said, and in gaining that capability he had ceased to be human. To the Malacostracans, humans were *expendable*.

He followed Friday Indigo, up a gently inclined

ramp to still another room. This one was smaller, dry, and apparently deserted. A huge lumpy rock sat at its center. Its lower part was riddled with fist-sized holes. It looked like an ugly and primitive sculpture.

"We have permission to advance," Indigo said. "Walk forward. Follow me."

Chan approached the silent rock. As he did so, two black hoses emerged from the upper ring of holes and snaked through the air toward him. He started to take a step back, but halted at Friday's urgent, "Stand still! There is nothing to be afraid of."

Chan froze. The ends of the hoses were divided into fine bundles of thin filaments. They had reached his body and were feeling their way up it.

Friday Indigo said, as casually as if he was suggesting that Chan take a seat, "Unseal your helmet all the way. This is part of your negotiation."

Chan took a deep breath. He opened his visor. The thin bundles of filaments moved up, to rest one below each of his ears.

"Now," Indigo said. "You will be permitted the privilege of free speech. Tell how you and your party can be of service to The One and to the People."

"We understand your wish to explore our universe. We can lead you to it." Chan did his best to remain calm and organize his thoughts. He suspected that he was talking for his life—more than his life. It would be worse than death to become a zombie like Friday Indigo, a walking dead who existed only to serve the object sitting in front of him. He went on, "I do not know how to fly your ship, that would require long training. But I am able to work with your pilots, to generate a transition sequence that will carry you through the Link."

"Ah." Indigo was frowning. "First you say *we*, as though speaking for all your party. Then you say, *I*, as though speaking only for yourself. The One asks, does that change have meaning?"

"It does." Chan was very aware of the thin tentacles touching below his ears. He had seen the dried blood on Friday Indigo's neck, and heard the Angel's assertion that some form of Malacostracan life existed inside Friday's brain. "I say that *I*, and I alone, will do this thing for you, because I do not trust others in my party to act in my interests. Which is to say, I do not trust others to do the thing which is best for me."

"And what is best for you?"

"To provide service to you, and so avoid my own destruction."

"And that service is?"

"To lead you to another universe, the human universe, that is hospitable to life."

"And your reward for doing this?"

"My life. My freedom. Perhaps, power as a servant of the Malacostracans."

"And for the others of your party?"

"That is of little interest to me. I care only about my own life and future."

"You are willing to do anything to save that life?"

"I am. I understand self-interest, as perhaps you also understand self-interest." Chan felt the first touch of delicate tendrils, moving into the openings of his ears. He had to talk fast. He said, "My job in leading you through to my universe will be a difficult one, even with help from your pilots. It requires that I have full possession of all my faculties. My brain cannot be drugged, or exhausted. It cannot be changed in any way."

The tendrils stopped moving. Friday Indigo said, "We understand self-interest. It is our impression that most humans comprehend such a thing only weakly. Give proof that you are different from them."

"How?"

A third hose emerged from the rock. Its prehensile end held one of the black canes. The hose swayed forward until it was a foot from Chan's chest.

Indigo said, "Do you know what this does?"

"I think so. It is a weapon."

"Correct. At one setting, it stuns. At another, it kills. This one is now set at a level fatal to humans."

Chan looked down at the cane, pointed straight at his heart. He could think of nothing else to say or do. Had he made some fatal mistake, missed some vital cue?

Friday Indigo said, "Take it."

Chan reached out and grasped the cane. It was smooth, and slightly sticky to the touch.

Friday said, "It is activated by pointing at the target, and squeezing anywhere along its length. Do you understand?"

"I understand."

"Now prove that you are different from others of your party. Give the evidence of your own self-interest." Indigo's voice was calm and relaxed. "Point the weapon at the being standing next to you. Activate it. Kill the human you know as Friday Indigo."

Chan raised the cane. A dozen jumbled thoughts seemed to race through his head at once. *If I kill Friday, The One will have nobody to serve as a translation unit. Maybe Chrissie and Tarbush were intended for that fate, but they've escaped. But I'm here, and available for conversion. So if I kill Friday, I'm probably dooming myself. Suppose I don't kill Friday? Then I'm still doomed. Anyway, I can't kill a human in cold blood. But Friday isn't a human, so I can kill Friday. No? Very well, then admit the truth. I can't kill Friday, human or not. So my whole plan fails, unless The One accepts that I'll need all my faculties intact to guide a Malacostracan pilot through the Link to a human universe. If so, then The One will want to keep my brain intact, and she will still have a use for Friday Indigo as translator. So The One won't want Friday Indigo dead.*

Chan thought, *Forgive me if I'm wrong*, aimed the cane right at Friday, and squeezed.

Nothing happened. Indigo did not fall paralyzed or dead. He continued to stare with calm interest at the black cane pointed at his heart.

"That is adequate proof," he said. "And it was accomplished without the waste of still-valuable material. The cane was of course deactivated. Answer one more question correctly, and we will be ready to proceed. If The One were to call you directly into her service, as I was called, you would gladly tell everything including the correct invocation sequence for Link transfer to the human universe. Prove to The One that it would be a mistake for her to follow such a course of action."

Again the tendrils were poised at the entrance to Chan's ears. He had to swallow before he could speak. "I cannot offer such a proof. All I can say is that conversion of me to The One's direct service might interfere with my ability to assist in the Link transition, should unforeseen circumstances arise. And there is absolutely no risk to The One in leaving me unconverted."

"That is true." To Chan's relief, the black tentacles lifted free of his body and slowly withdrew into the body of The One. Once again he was facing a dull black rock.

Friday Indigo continued, "The Malacostracans will prepare a ship for Link transfer and a first exploration of the human universe. Soon after daybreak tomorrow, you will be taken aboard that ship with The

One, and by midday you will assist in initiating that Link transfer. Until morning you are free to stay here and eat, drink, and rest."

"Very good. But one other thing is necessary." Chan cursed his own stupidity. He had not realized that the Malacostracans would want to move so fast.

"What is that?"

"Not knowing how this meeting would turn out, I did not bring with me the full protocol needed for Link transition to the human universe. I request that I be allowed to go to the *Hero's Return*, prepare that protocol, and return here."

"When?"

"I will be back by morning."

"General Korin is by your own admission senior to you. How can you be sure that he will allow you to return?"

"I will tell him that our discussions here remain unfinished. He will not try to prevent my departure."

After a long, agonizing silence, Friday Indigo nodded. "It is approved. Be sure that you return by daybreak. To encourage you to do so, I will mention that we plan to destroy the *Hero's Return* soon after first light. Do you have any problem with this?"

"No problem." *Just the death of Deb and Danny and everyone else.*

"Then you have permission to leave the presence of The One. It is The One's introspection time."

Leaving was easier said than done. The lights in the chamber suddenly turned off, leaving Chan unable to see The One or anything else. He heard the uneven sound of Friday Indigo's boots, one foot dragging across the hard floor, and turned in that direction. He saw, very faintly, the outline of the chamber entrance. There were no lights in the next room, but a faint trace of daylight bled in from the tunnel at its far end.

Chan hurried along after Friday, through the archway, past the little Malacostracan seated on its flat dais, finally out into open air. The overcast had cleared, the sun was blazing. He caught the sulfurous odor of black rock baking in early afternoon heat, and felt that he had never smelled anything so good. Half an hour ago he would have taken odds against his smelling anything ever again of his own free will. He could still feel those questing tentacles at his ears.

Friday Indigo, a few feet in front of Chan, paused by the group of big Malacostracans guarding the entrance to the building. He rattled off an outlandish sequence of whistles and clicks. Two of the creatures reared up on their back legs, so that their waving eyestalks and purple-black carapaces loomed over Chan.

"I told them to escort you to the shore," Friday said. "You must go directly to the beach, and straight into the water. If you seek to do anything other than that, they will stun you and drag you back here for their further instructions. After you leave, they will remain on the shore until you emerge from the water in your suit at dawn tomorrow morning. They will then escort you here. If you seek to linger on the beach tomorrow, they will stun you and drag you back for further instructions. Do you have any questions before I hand you over to them?"

"Suppose that the waves are too rough for me to go into the sea?"

"That will be your misfortune. It is useless for you to try to communicate with them, because they are Level Fours and of limited intelligence. Your failure to enter the water will be considered a deviation from instructions, and they will stun you—"

"—and drag me back here for further instructions. I get it. I'll see you tomorrow—right on time."

The two Malacostracan guards placed themselves one ahead of and one behind Chan and moved away across the burned rock. They took a different path from the one that Friday Indigo had used, angling away to the right. Soon they were at the edge of the bare area and moving into waist-high scrub. They went forward confidently along a trail marked by flattened plants. They passed through a small clearing. Chan wanted to pause there, but he was too aware of the black canes. He kept walking, taking a quick glance at the open supply cases and the cans and boxes scattered on the ground next to them. The earth was scuffled and marked by the imprint of many clawed feet.

This was where Deb and the others had made their camp. If Chrissie and Tarb came here when they escaped, they had been too smart to linger. But where had they gone? Not back into the water. The breakers during the night would have been enormous.

Chan moved his hand up to close his helmet. The Malacostracan guards took no notice. To them, a human without a suit probably looked naked and unnatural, a shell-less version of a proper animal.

He flicked a switch on his gauntlet controls. Again the guards ignored him. Provided that he kept moving, that seemed to be all that they cared about. He adjusted the radio to the general communication frequency and increased the reception volume. He heard a background hiss and that was all. If Chrissie and Tarb were able to broadcast—if they had even escaped with their suits—they were not doing so. But that also made sense. A distress signal or any other form of message was also a beacon, advertising the location of its source.

Chan kept walking and listening, and heard nothing. They were emerging from the shelter of the vegetation. He saw the shore with its line of breakers, smaller and less threatening now, maybe fifty meters ahead.

It was time for him to take a chance. If his signal was picked up, the Malacostracans should think it came from the sea and the sunken *Hero's Return*.

He added a transmission circuit. "Chrissie and Tarb. Can you hear this?"

Still the bland hiss, and the beach was within thirty meters.

"If you are receiving, stay in hiding. The part of the shoreline near your camp is guarded by the Malacostracans. Everyone on the *Hero's Return* is alive and well"—true at the moment, presumably, but not for long unless Chan did something about it—"and we will be in touch with you as soon as we can. Repeat: stay hidden. If you are caught, the Malacostracans will execute you."

Chan saw no reason to add that the deaths would be drawn-out and agonizing. In any case, he was at the edge of the shore and there was no time for more words. Again he tried to do what he had seen Deb do earlier. He marched straight ahead until the water lapped about his waist, then dived forward into the approaching wave.

This time he was more successful. Chan felt his heels briefly break the surface, then he was under and on his way. He swam as fast as he could. In one evening and one night on Limbo, he had to say goodbye to everything and everyone forever.

35

The Only Answer

Chan had thought that the most difficult part of his return would be the first two minutes. He was wrong.

From the moment that Deb had appeared at the *Hero's Return* to tell the others that she had been forced to leave the land, everyone had naturally been desperate to know what was happening ashore. They wanted to hear about Chan's meeting with the Mallies. They wanted *information*, and compared with that his emotions or feelings were a very low priority.

He gave a lengthy but highly edited version of events after Deb had been forced to leave, concentrating on what he had seen of the Malacostracans and confirming their confidence that they could open the Link entry point at will and fly their ships through it. He described his meeting with The One, but said nothing of the deal that he had made.

"Actually, we spent most of the time just trying to

communicate with each other," he said. "The Angel is right about Friday Indigo, he's been taken over totally by the Mallies. But *talking* to them, even with him helping, is hard work. I still don't know if there's any way that we can work with them to get ourselves through the Link and home. I have to go back there first thing in the morning, and try again."

Chan was uncomfortably aware of Gressel. The Angel was sitting in a well-lit corner, fronds unmoving. It was said that an Angel could simulate human thought patterns so well that lying to one of them was impossible. But Gressel remained silent.

"What about Chrissie and Tarbush?" Danny Casement asked. "Deb said they escaped. Are they still free?"

"So far as I know." Chan was glad to switch to something he could talk about freely. "I tried to call them just before I came back here, but they didn't reply. The land surface is a lot more complex and jagged than it looks on the satellite images. They could be hidden away in a thousand places."

"Out of radio contact, perhaps?" Deb said.

She was looking at Chan very strangely. Maybe it was his own feeling of guilt at what he was concealing from her and the others. But if he told anyone his idea, anyone at all, they would find a reason why he shouldn't go through with it.

"More likely Chris and Tarb were away from their suits for a while," he said. "They must know we're looking for them, and they're far too smart to put themselves permanently in a place where signals can't reach. One good thing, they have plenty of supplies. I passed our first camp on the way to the sea, and they'd raided it long before I got there."

He stared around at the little circle of weary faces. Not one had slept the night before, and it was doubtful if they had managed to rest while he was gone. "You all look as tired as I am. I'm also starving. If nobody objects, I'd like a meal and a nap. After that I'll be happy to answer as many new questions as you can dream up."

Tully O'Toole nodded and said, "Go, Chan man, you need to feed." He looked like a human wreck who had not eaten for months, a gray skeleton in tattered clothes leaning over the back of Elke Siry's chair; but he seemed cheerful. "Don't take too long."

"He's right," Dag Korin said. "Go and eat. I'm not so sure about the nap. We have to leave the poor old *Hero's Return* as soon as possible. The place won't be habitable much longer."

The lights flickered, as though emphasizing his point. Chan nodded and left the control room, heading toward the bow of the ship. He had hoped to be left alone, but he should have known better. Deb followed him into the corridor.

"I haven't had anything to eat, either," she said. "If you're going to have a meal, I thought that we might—"

"Actually, I'm not." Chan halted. "Not going to eat, I mean. I'm too rushed. And I need some time alone."

He saw the expression on her face, and went on, "I have to record exactly what the Malacostracans said to me, while it's still fresh in my mind. It's difficult to do that when other people are around."

"I see." She seemed ready to say more, but instead she turned abruptly and hurried back the way that they had come.

Chan resisted the urge to go after her. He *did* need time alone, even if it was not for the reason he had given Deb. He needed time to think, and then to create a crucial document. He ducked away into a side chamber, once used as a small-arms supply room but now empty and deserted. Water had seeped in from some unseen crack, leaving the floor slick and treacherous. Two of the three lights were no longer working, and the remaining one glowed faint and feeble.

Chan leaned against the wall, reviewed what he intended to do, and made a decision. He dared not tell Deb his plan, much as he would like to; and because of that he could not see her again before he left the *Hero's Return*. Which meant that he would not see her again, ever.

The thought froze his soul. He left the little armory and moved along the length of the ship until he came to the forward observation chamber. In another life, the view from here had been of stars and glowing gas clouds and pinwheeling galaxies. It was from here that he and Elke Siry had watched Ceres fall behind, and he knew that their long journey had begun.

Now Chan saw nothing ahead but the murky waters of Limbo. He said loudly, "Is the computer working in here?"

The audio outlet replied, SERVICE IN THIS LOCATION IS GUARANTEED FOR THE NEXT TWENTY-ONE HOURS, BUT NOT BEYOND.

"That will be more than enough. I want you to record what I say, then make a single printed copy. After I review that document and make changes, I want a single final printed output, sealed in an envelope. No copies."

THERE IS NO OUTPUT UNIT AT THIS LOCATION. THE NEAREST IS IN ROOM I-293, THIRTY-EIGHT METERS AFT ON THIS LEVEL.

"That will be fine. I'll pick it up from there. Prepare to record."

READY FOR INPUT.

Chan took a deep breath. "To General Dag Korin,

from Chan Dalton. Some of my actions in the next twenty-four hours will be useless unless they are accompanied by very specific actions on your part. Let me first define my plan. I intend to proceed as follows . . ."

He spoke, calmly but with numerous pauses, for the next hour. The review and revisions took even longer. By the time that Chan finished he was feeling the hunger that he had pretended to earlier. He was light-headed from lack of food. He also had to solve one other problem: how was the document that he had created to be delivered to Dag Korin, after Chan left the ship and not before? The logical answer was Deb Bisson, but maybe that wasn't logical at all. Maybe it only reflected his aching need to see her one last time.

When Chan left the observation chamber the interior of the *Hero's Return* seemed like the dead ghost ship that it was soon to become. The corridors were empty, and Chan felt reluctant to disturb their silence. He was intending to spend most of the night in a suit, alone in the dark waters of Limbo, waiting for the time when he could again go ashore. He knew it would be unpleasant; but he could face that prospect, and what lay beyond, more easily than the next few hours on the dying ship.

He walked quietly back toward the control room, the sealed envelope held close to his chest. He was passing one of the unused passenger suites, in a location where none of the team had living quarters, when he heard someone talking.

" . . . be working. When all the others are so busy . . ."

It was Bony Rombelle's voice. Chan realized that the Bun and Liddy Morse had not been on board the *Hero's Return* when everyone else chose living quarters. They must have settled here, farther forward.

Liddy—easier to hear then Bony—said, "They're not all busy, they're *resting*. Nothing is going to happen until tomorrow morning. We'll be resting, too. Afterwards. Don't you want to?"

"Of course I do! I have, ever since I first met you."

"Well, then."

"But to do it now—it seems such a bad time. The ship is disintegrating, and if we reach the shore the Mallies are more likely to kill us than help us. By tomorrow night we could be dead."

"So this could be our last night. What would you rather be thinking when we go ashore tomorrow: We did what we both wanted to do, and it was absolutely wonderful, and now we can face whatever comes next? Or we passed up our chance last night, and we didn't do anything, and now maybe we never will?"

"Oh, Liddy. You know what I'd rather . . ."

Chan moved on. He felt uncomfortable, an unwitting audience to private words that no one else was intended to hear. And yet, oddly enough, it solved his own problem.

He walked on, past the control room, past dark chambers that once contained monstrous weapons systems, past the engine room, past the supercooled nerve center of the failing computer, until at last he came to the quarters that he and Deb Bisson shared.

The final steps were the hardest. He went in, half hoping that Deb would not be there; but she was, lying facedown on the bed. He walked forward, leaned over, and placed his hand on the small of her back.

That was a dangerous thing to do with a weapons master like Deb, who relied for survival on instinctive reaction. It told Chan something when Deb did not move.

He said quietly, "I'm sorry for what I told you after the meeting. I really did need time to myself, but it was to write a letter. This letter. I want you to hold it for me and give it to Dag Korin after I leave the ship."

Before Chan overheard Bony Rombelle and Liddy Morse's private conversation, he had intended to stop at that. He would see Deb one last time, ask her to deliver his letter, and leave. Instead he went on, "I didn't mean to hurt you, but what I did was horrible and wrong. I want to say I'm sorry. And I'd like to explain why I did it, and what I must do next. And I want to tell you why."

She sat up to face him. Looking into her sad brown eyes he found himself telling her everything, in a tide of words that he could not hold back.

As he spoke her face filled with comprehension, then misery, and finally despair. She shook her head.

Chan put his arms around her. "I know. But it is the only possible answer. And I'm the only one who can do it."

He expected an argument, maybe a denial. Instead she pushed her long dark hair back from her face, lay down again, and said, "Chan, come and hold me."

"I will." He leaned forward and felt the room spin about him. How long was it since he had eaten? "I will lie down. But if I could just have something to eat—anything at all." That would surely be the last straw, the final insult. "Deb, I'm sorry, but if I don't have food—"

"You stay there and take it easy. I'll make something for you. And for me, too. I'm famished. I was hungry when I followed you from the meeting, but after you sent me away I couldn't eat a thing."

Before Chan could reply she sat up and slipped off the bed in one graceful movement. As he watched her preparing food in the little galley, he was possessed by a sense of longing and loss and vanishing reality. The feeling persisted when Deb lifted loaded plates and glasses and came to sit cross-legged opposite him. The food tasted fine. The wine was as pleasant as ever. Was this how a condemned man savored his final meal, pretending that it was no different from a thousand others?

"Now we can lie down and talk," Deb said, when they had finished eating. "Don't bother with your dish, throw it on the floor. Washing-up is over for good on the *Hero's Return*."

Her manner perplexed Chan. He didn't know how he expected her to react to the news that they would never see each other again, but it certainly wasn't with this calm certainty. Didn't she even care? Her earlier words said that she did, but now . . . He lay back on the bed, while she leaned over him and ran her forefinger along the line of his cheek and down onto his neck.

"You said you needed a nap." Her voice came from a great distance. "You've earned one. So relax and take it easy. Close your eyes."

Relax? Take it easy? When in a few hours you had to put on your suit and slip for the last time into the alien waters of Limbo, and then take an action for which the Mallies were likely to kill you? When you had found someone again after so long apart, and you were going to lose her forever? It was enough to make a man weep—smile—laugh aloud at the cruelty of fate. But that was too much work; better to drift away.

Chan lay still, very aware of the gentle fingers running along the side of his neck. He wanted to sit up and hold Deb, but his body carried on it the weight of the whole multiverse. Even his eyelids were too heavy. The last thing he saw was Deb's dark hair, descending on him like the fall of night.

✧ ✧ ✧

Drugs that produce insensibility rather than death must be calibrated as to dosage. Deb, working quickly and unobtrusively, had been given little chance for precision. She waited for five minutes, monitoring Chan's pulse and respiration rate.

When she was sure that he was sleeping naturally and in no danger she picked up the sealed envelope. He had asked her to deliver it to Dag Korin. That was exactly what she proposed to do.

The General was in his own quarters, sitting upright in a chair, fully dressed and alert as though expecting visitors. He was sipping a glass of amber liquid.

"Medicinal purposes, my dear," he said as she entered. "What can I do for you?"

"You said before Chan came back on board that he might write to you when he did, or maybe leave you a message. How did you know?"

"I'm old, Deb Bisson. I've seen lots of heroism, public and private. I knew some of the questions Dalton had been asking Dr. Siry, and I thought I knew where they might be leading. So he did write to me?"

"Yes. It's here." Deb held out the envelope. "He told me to give it to you after he left."

"My God." Korin sat up straighter. "He hasn't gone, has he?"

"No. He's asleep."

"Good. He must have great nerves."

"Great drugs. My drugs. He'll be out for a few hours unless I give him a stimulant." Deb was still holding the envelope out to Korin. "Do you want this, or do you already know what's inside?"

"I may be old and treacherous, Deb Bisson, but I'm not psychic." He took the envelope and eyed her shrewdly. "You know what's in here, don't you?"

"I do, but not because I looked. Chan told me."

"And as a reward for that, you gave him a knock-out drop. Hell hath no fury like a woman informed. Well, let's see what we have here."

He opened the envelope and read in silence for a few minutes, now and then nodding. Once he glanced up at Deb. "Did he say good-bye to you?"

"He was working up to it. I made him fall asleep before he could."

"You did the right thing. It's annoying, you know, when someone who supposedly reports to me takes off with his own plan. In the old days he'd have been clapped in irons. But now I have to think."

"Do you want me to go and wake Chan, and bring him here?"

"Oh, no. Let the man sleep, he's earned it. Damn fine report, this, logical and complete and with things in it that I never would have thought of." The General tapped Chan's letter. "In fact, with just one or two crucial changes . . ."

He fell silent, staring at nothing and nodding his head. At last he said to Deb, "This drug that you gave Dalton. What condition will he be in when he wakes up? Groggy, or dopey, or good as new?"

"He'll wonder where he is for a few minutes. Then he'll be perfectly normal."

"Excellent." Korin gestured to the chair next to him. "Sit down, Deb Bisson, and listen closely. I'll tell you exactly what we are going to do. And then I have to write a letter of my own."

36

Escape

Chan was far away from the surface, drifting among the tinted luminous globes that filled the skies of Limbo. He was close to one of the pearly spheres, ready to dive into its misty depths, when he heard a faint voice. It was calling his name, telling him to come back. He descended slowly. He didn't want to return to a region of chaos and danger. He dropped into darkness, down and down. He could see nothing, but at last he heard someone wheezing, noisily and close by. It took a long time to recognize the unpleasant sound as his own breathing.

He opened his eyes. Deb was still leaning over him.

She said, "I wondered if you would ever wake up. How are you feeling?"

He sat up and put his arms around her. He saw that she was still clutching his letter to Dag Korin. He said, "Don't deliver that until I've left the ship." His voice sounded hoarse and muffled, as though he had developed laryngitis; but his throat felt fine. He went on, "I'd better be going. You shouldn't have let me go to sleep like that. What time is it?"

"An hour to dawn."

"You let me sleep all night! At daybreak I have to—"

She pulled away and placed the letter in his hand. "I didn't just let you sleep. I drugged you. You have to read this."

"You *drugged* me. What for?"

"You have to read this."

"But I know exactly what's in it. I *wrote* it." Chan paused. The envelope that he was holding said, *To Chan Dalton, from Dag Korin. To be opened only after I have left the* Hero's Return.

Bewildered and cotton-brained, Chan opened the envelope. He started to read. *Chan Dalton—The actions that you have taken so far, and those which you propose in your letter to me, are unauthorized. They are also inspired. I am a natural optimist, but in the past few days I had seen no possible way for our party to survive. I believe that what you suggest offers that survival chance, together with a hope of return to our own universe.*

We will therefore carry out your instructions exactly, with one minor change; namely, you and I will change places. I, rather than you, will deal with the Mallies. You will lead our group, and carry out your own detailed instructions. If you doubt that the Mallies will agree to work with me rather than you, allow me to point out that Friday Indigo, in his meeting here, expressed their preference *for working with the leader of the group. That's me. I know the exact Link protocol that you proposed to follow, because at my request Elke gave me the same thing. The Mallies will presumably ask where you are. When they do, I will explain that I was obliged to kill you, and that my degree of self-interest equals or exceeds yours. It is my impression that such an explanation will be readily accepted. If they want me to shoot or kill one or two of them to prove my resolve or goodwill, I'll be more than happy to oblige.*

Deb was reading over Chan's shoulder. He turned to her. "Did you give him my letter while I was asleep?"

"Yes, I did."

"After I specifically told you not to?"

"Yes." Deb backed away a step. "Chan, this may not make any sense to you, but if you hadn't come back, and if you hadn't told me you were sorry, and you hadn't confided in me, I could have let you go. I mean, I would obviously have had no choice, because I wouldn't have known what was happening. But I would have got over you. Somehow. Only when you *did* tell me, and trust me, and rely on me, I just couldn't stand to lose you. Not again. I'd rather die. Once was too many."

"I know that feeling." Chan could not resist putting his arms around her again, but only for a moment. He said abruptly, "Did General Korin tell you what was in his letter?"

"No. But he called a meeting while you were asleep, and told all of us that he had to leave the ship. You would be in charge, he said, and when I woke you just before dawn you would tell everyone what to do next. I didn't understand what was going on, but apparently the Angel did. It waved at him and said, 'Aha. *I am just going outside now, and I may be gone for some time*. Go, General Korin, with the gratitude of the Angels of Sellora. We are a long-lived species. We hope that we will meet you again.' Do *you* understand all that?"

"Yes. Not the thing that sounds like the quote, but what the Angel meant." Chan read on, aloud. *"You are aware of my opinion of generals and admirals who are miles or lightyears away from the battle, and still try to control the action. My best advice to you is, be flexible and do whatever feels right. Tell everyone—especially Elke Siry—not to worry about me. As I've told her many times, Benjamin Franklin is one of my heroes. He said he wished that he could be pickled in a barrel for a couple of hundred years so that he could see what the world was like when he came out. I feel the same way. And who knows—"*

The knock on the outer door was loud enough to make Chan jump and Deb spin around into a fighting attitude. Danny Casement poked his head in.

"I don't want to disturb, but me and Tully need some advice. We dragged together a whole heap of stuff we might need on shore, but it's a lot more than one trip. The General never got back to us to say how many loads we'd take, and he left the ship before we had time to ask him. He says you're in charge, right?"

Chan stared at the letter in his hand. "I guess so."

"Then how much stuff do we want to take?"

Chan stood up. "Nothing. Just ourselves, the Angel, and the Pipe-Rilla. Is she still catatonic?"

"Coming out of it a bit, Angel says. But look, Chan, we can't set up camp with nothing. We'll at least need food and drink."

"We're not going to set up camp." Chan looked at his watch. By now, Dag Korin should be ashore. "We'll need suits, and that's all. Can you be ready in thirty minutes?"

"With nothing to take we can be ready in five. But I don't know where the Bun and Liddy have got to, nobody's seen them since early last night."

"I know where you can find them. Passenger suite I-47, forward. I hope Bony isn't brain-dead this morning. He'll have lots of work to do."

"Why should he be?"

"Go get them, and you'll see. Deb and I will take care of Tully and Elke Siry. They'll give us a hand with the Angel and Vow-of-Silence."

"Tully's not in his own place."

"Where is he?"

"With Elke." Danny shrugged. "Don't ask me, maybe it's the heavy water. I've never believed it was safe to drink. Or maybe it's the thought that we'll all be dead in a few hours."

"Not if I can help it." Chan stuffed Dag Korin's letter into his pocket. He didn't need it at the moment, because everything to be done in the next hour had been detailed in his own letter to the General. "Fifteen minutes, in suits, at the main airlock. Come on, Deb."

Chan walked out. He knew that Danny was itching to ask questions. Everyone would be. They had to wait. Either there would be plenty of time to answer, four hours from now; or all answers would be irrelevant.

Vow-of-Silence was the most difficult. When Danny had carried the Pipe-Rilla back to the *Hero's Return* it had taken half an hour to remove the curled and rigid form from its suit. Putting a suit back on was even harder unless you knew Pipe-Rilla tricks. By the time that Chan and Deb, carrying her between them, reached the airlock, the others were already waiting.

"Elke." Chan was beginning to worry about one aspect of his own plan. The Malacostracans were not obliged to follow the schedule they had offered the previous day. Suppose they decided to go ahead sooner than expected—any time, once Dag Korin met with The One? "You've studied the satellite maps more than anyone else. Can you lead us ashore?"

"I can. But not as well as you could. You and Deb Bisson and Danny Casement have already been there, I have not."

"I don't want to go to that part of the land. When I left it was patrolled by Mallie guards who shoot before they think. In fact, they can't think. I want to go in along the inlet where the *Mood Indigo* is beached."

"That's easy." Like the others, Elke was fully suited but with her helmet open. Her expression was nervous and her face gaunt as ever, but as usual she answered without seeming to take time to think. "The opening to the inlet is fifteen degrees south of east. After that we follow the line of the main channel due east. The *Mood Indigo* will be six hundred meters along, on the left."

"You're in charge of getting us there. The silt should be back on the seabed and the water clear. If not, we go single file and hold on to each other. Bony."

"Right here." Bony at least didn't seem to be worried. The face inside the helmet was as serene as ever, and he was beaming.

Chan felt awkward now with Bony and Liddy. He knew that was ridiculous. They had no idea that he had overheard their private conversation. He wondered if they had asked Danny how he knew where to find them.

Why did your brain throw such irrelevancies at you, when you were trying to organize to save your life?

"Bony, when we reach the *Mood Indigo* you'll have to work faster and harder than you ever worked. We need to know if that ship can fly, and if it can stand a vacuum environment. Friday Indigo said that it could when he was here, but in his condition I'd hate to take his word for anything."

Bony gulped. "How long will I have?"

"Until we're forced to try for a takeoff. Then we'll find out if what you did was enough—one way or another."

Bony gulped again, harder than before. Chan ignored him. He took a quick look around. Bony, Liddy, Deb, Danny, Tully and Elke; the suitless Angel, silent and presumably grumpy, uprooted from its precious soil pot so as to be more easily carried; the Pipe-Rilla, unconscious and coiled around itself like lengths of flexible ductwork: the whole remaining crew of the *Hero's Return*, as ready as it would ever be.

"Close helmets, and let's go. It will be a squeeze, but we can all fit in the lock. Tully and Bony, you take Vow-of-Silence. Elke, you exit first—but wait for the rest of us before you move."

Chan and Danny Casement entered the lock last, carrying the Angel between them. Gressel suddenly came to life and muttered, "Farewell. *Well done, thou good and faithful servant.*"

Chan realized that Gressel must be talking to the ship's computer. It was enormously capable and close to sentience, and maybe from the point of view of the Angel's own sentient inner crystal the computer was *less* alien than humans. But with a computing system spread through the whole ship there was no possible way to take it with them.

The lock closed and flooded. The Angel was suddenly no load at all. They would have to be careful to make sure that it did not float away from them. As the outer hatch opened, Chan saw that his guess was correct. The sediment had settled back to the bottom as the effects of the storm faded, and the ocean of Limbo was clearer than he had ever seen it.

Communication was not possible using the suit radios underwater. It was a silent and slow-moving procession that followed Elke Siry. Chan wished that they could speed up, but he didn't want to risk rising to the surface and using suit jets when Malacostracan guards might be watching the sea.

Elke seemed to know exactly what she was doing. When she had traveled a certain distance she angled to the left. They had reached a drowned valley, and were walking along its center. In another few hundred meters she turned left again, this time more sharply, and began to ascend the valley slope.

In another half minute the helmet of her suit disappeared from view. Chan realized that it must have broken the surface and was now above water. One by one, the rest followed. Helmet vanished, then shoulders, then chest. Finally it was Chan's own turn, and he instinctively blinked as his head emerged.

Elke was already beyond the waterline. He took one quick look at her, at the *Mood Indigo* on the slope right ahead—thank Heaven for Elke's mania for precision—then up and down the shore. It was full day. There was no sign of Malacostracans. If everything could just stay the way it was for five more minutes . . .

Chan heard a commotion in the line ahead. He dropped his side of the Angel and hurried forward. Tully and Bony were having trouble, trying to hold on to a suddenly animated Vow-of-Silence. In spite of its tube-like build, the Pipe-Rilla was incredibly strong. Vow-of-Silence broke free, and before anyone could manage to reach her she went bounding away along the shore of the inlet in ten-meter leaps.

Bony was all set to follow when Chan grabbed his arm. "No. You'd never catch her. Look at her go."

They followed the Pipe-Rilla's direction of travel. "Away from the Malacostracan camp," Elke said. "If she keeps that heading at that speed, she'll reach the line of vegetation in a few minutes. There's a very rough area beyond it, and I'm not sure we can follow her there. But neither can anyone else."

"Vow-of-Silence will have to look after herself for the moment," Chan said. "We have to get inside the *Mood Indigo.* Come on, up the slope."

Easier said than done. Lifting the ship from the sea to its present location would have been impossible if the Malacostracans had not possessed antigravity machines. The side of the inlet was a mess of sharp-edged rock that at first sight could not be climbed. Liddy was the one, ranging away to the left, who found a long cleft that a person could scramble up. Then it was everyone working together, to hoist the unwieldy bulk of the Angel along the narrowing crack in the rock. In any gravity field stronger than Limbo's they could never have done it. As it was, the whole party was panting and strained when at last they levered Gressel over the lip of the rocky bowl where the *Mood Indigo* lay, and could scramble the rest of the way.

Again, Chan was the last one up. He found Bony standing by the side of the stranded ship, shaking his head.

"Looks pretty good," Chan said, as he came up to Bony.

That earned him a skeptical glance. "Appearances don't tell you much," Bony said. "The storm gave her a terrible bashing. All the external communications equipment was stripped off."

"How's the hull? Was it breached?"

"I can't tell from here. Friday Indigo bought the best, so that should help. But there's only one way to know. Once we're inside we'll change internal pressure and see what happens."

Bony sounded upbeat. Chan didn't let that fool him. Rather than being terrified by their situation, the Bun was exhilarated by the chance to try his fix-up skills on a ship that back in the solar system would have been consigned to the junkyard. Even so, repairing the *Mood Indigo* so it could fly might need magic; and the specialist in magic, Chrissie, was not here.

Chan paused to worry about that, too, while the others were opening the lowest hatch on the ship and putting in place the portable ladder. He watched as the Angel was lifted and stuffed unceremoniously inside.

It was all a question of timing and distance. If The One followed her original plan, Chan had about two hours. Chrissie and Tarbush would have less than that to reach the *Mood Indigo*, assuming that he called them now and was able to contact them at once. Every minute he waited decreased their margin. On the other hand, once he made a call the Malacostracans might detect it, trace its point of origin, and either capture the party on the *Mood Indigo* or simply destroy the ship.

Chan went to the ladder and ascended. He did not enter the ship, but simply poked his head inside the hatch. Bony already had everyone except the Angel organized and hard at work. He caught sight of Chan and called, "Come inside. I want to close the hatch and check pressurization."

"I'll be outside for a while longer. Carry on with your test, and I'll be in when it's finished."

In a sense it made Chan's decision for him. The internal pressure change and test of hull integrity would take at least half an hour. Bony had all the help that he needed. Chan was ready to duck away and descend the ladder when he realized that there was still a missing piece. He stuck his head back in and called again.

Bony glared impatiently at Chan. As he came over to him he said, "Look, if you want me to get this thing to fly—"

"I do. We may have to try, even if the ship isn't ready. Have Liddy keep an eye open for any big vessel taking off from the Mallies' field and heading out to sea. If she sees one, you lift off and follow it—whether I'm on board or not."

Bony looked startled. "But if you're not here—"

"Do it. I'll explain later." *If there is a later.* Chan ignored Bony and called to Elke, "Do you have the protocols you developed for moving between levels of the multiverse?"

She was over by the little computer of the *Mood Indigo*, studying it. She gave Chan or the computer—it was hard to tell which—a disdainful glare. "Of course."

"If Bony takes off, feed him the final one of those protocols, and tell him to use it."

"But won't you be at the controls? You were the one—"

Chan was out of the hatch and down the ladder before he could hear the rest of her sentence.

He glanced around him. He needed a location with some specific properties. It had to be high, so that it provided good line-of-sight radio transmission over a wide area. It needed to be in a position from which the *Mood Indigo* was not directly visible; and ideally it should be hidden from the Malacostracan encampment.

The best he could manage was a compromise. He

walked southeast for ten minutes, away from the sea and over the brow of a jutting ridge. On the other side of the hill he stopped. He couldn't see the encampment, and he couldn't see the ship. But would anyone hear him?

He began transmission. "Chrissie and Tarb, are you receiving? Hello. Can you hear me?"

He repeated the message three times at one-minute intervals. He was looking at his watch and beginning to feel that he was wasting his time when the receiver beeped. A breathless voice said, "Are you there?"

"Chrissie?"

"Yes. And Tarb. We've been sending out signals every hour, but we move around all the time because we don't want the Malacostracans to be able to home in on our signal. We're both fine."

"Good. Where are you?"

"We're in the area that Elke Siry marked as 'badlands.' She wasn't kidding. When we heard your call we were only forty meters from our suits, but it took us until now to scramble back to them. This place is more up and down than sideways. It has caves and crevasses and overhangs worse than Miranda. Where are *you*? My suit shows you farther south and closer than I expected."

"How far?"

"About ten kilometers line-of-sight."

"Damn." Chan chose his next words carefully. He had to assume that the Mallies might be listening, and that Friday Indigo would be there to interpret anything that was said. "We left the *Hero's Return*. You have our heading and our distance. Can you get here in two hours?"

He heard Chrissie's snort of amusement. "Are you kidding? Ten kilometers line-of-sight is like fifty on the ground. We picked this place so we'd be hard to get at, and it's just as hard to get out. If we didn't fall over a cliff or down a sink hole—the area is full of them—we might reach you before dark. More likely it would be sometime tomorrow."

"That's what I was afraid you'd say. How's your supply situation?"

"We took care of that. Friday Indigo gets by eating native flora or fauna, but we didn't like the look of the stuff. We raided the camp supply case and brought enough food and drink to last for weeks."

"Good. Now listen closely, because we don't have much more time. The Mallies could be homing in on both of us."

He spoke fast for two minutes.

"Got it," Chrissie said cheerfully when he was finished. "Go do your thing, right now. Tarb and I will cross our fingers."

"So will we. For you. Oh, and keep your eyes open for Vow-of-Silence. I don't have time to tell you what happened to her, but she's running loose along with Eager Seeker."

"We saw a few Tinker components here and there in the bushes, but no sign of a Composite. We'll be on the lookout. Scruffy is still missing, too, and I'll never persuade Tarbush to go without her. Don't worry about us. We'll manage. Ready to close?"

"Closing."

Chan went at once to the top of the ridge and scanned the horizon in the direction of the Malacostracan encampment. The sky was clear. No angry swarm of trifoliate aircraft was heading his way, but that might change any second.

He hurried back to the *Mood Indigo*. The hatch was closed, but Tully opened it at the first knock.

"Saw you hurrying, had us worrying," he said. "Come in."

"How was the pressurization test?"

"The ship's all right, good and tight. We can fly."

The *Mood Indigo* had been designed for a crew of three, and the flight deck was crowded with seven humans and an Angel. Bony had gone a step beyond Chan's order, and posted lookouts at each of the three ports. "You said to watch for anything coming from the Mallies' field," he said, as Chan joined him at the control console. Elke Siry was already in the copilot chair. "But I thought we ought to know about anything that flies, no matter what direction it comes from."

He stood up. "Here. You and Elke can handle the ship better than me. There's a few hundred things I'd like to check before we take off."

"Tully said we are ready to fly."

"I told him that so he wouldn't fiddle with equipment he doesn't understand. I feel sure we can go up if we have to. But I need another hour before I'm convinced that we can stay there."

Bony headed for the lower levels, down to the engine room of the *Mood Indigo*. Chan sat down and reviewed the status panel. It was a mass of red flashing lights. Every external antenna had been swept away. Most of the imaging sensors were out of action, leaving the ship partially blind. One of the seven main engines was clogged, probably with silt, and another contained a hairline crack in its fuel feed. Neither could be used without danger of an explosion. The ship's profile had been deformed by structural changes to one of the airlocks. Two stabilizer fins were bent, and a third had been ripped off. Atmospheric flight, if it happened at all, would be a combination of computer thrust balance and human seat-of-the-pants improvisation.

In summary, the *Mood Indigo* was a mess. Bony

had primed the five undamaged engines, but the whole ship needed a major overhaul. Back in the solar system it would have been declared a total loss.

Chan was calling for a more detailed summary of engine balance problems when Liddy, over to his left, said quietly, "Something took off. A big something."

Chan glanced instinctively to the displays. He cursed to himself as he realized that the ones he needed were all out of action. He stood up and moved quickly to Liddy's side. A Malacostracan vessel—one of the two big ones, labeled by Dag Korin as mother ships—floated in the sky to the northwest.

He asked Liddy, "Is it coming this way?"

"I don't think so." She was tracking the ship closely, using her hand on the glass of the port to measure relative motion. "If it keeps going the way it started, it will pass well north of us. I think it's heading west."

"To sea," Chan said. "Toward the Link." He hurried back to the controls. One of the imaging sensors in the seaward direction was still working. It showed a flickering yellow glow on the horizon. "Bony?"

"Here."

"We don't have an hour. Stop whatever you're doing. We're lifting off. Now."

"Three more minutes—"

"*NOW!* Everybody, brace for takeoff."

Chan applied power to the five working engines. He did it gingerly, aware that they were not balanced, and he flinched at the creak and groan of the flexing hull. The ship had not been designed to fly with lopsided thrust. It was vibrating all over—and they had not left the ground.

All or nothing. "Hold tight!" Chan stopped breathing and went to three-quarter power. The *Mood Indigo* lifted, tilted, and began to swoop sideways. The computer caught the imbalance with its inertial guidance system and applied the correction in milliseconds. The ship wobbled, straightened, and lifted again. Chan applied lateral thrust. He had to take them west, toward the sea. They must parallel the course of the Malacostracan ship, then angle in toward it once it was well away from land.

How close dare he come? Too far, and they might miss the opportunity. Too close, and they would be noticed.

"Another Mallie ship." Danny Casement was stationed at another port, facing east. "One of the smaller ones. It's coming this way."

Another decision had been made for Chan. He increased power again. The *Mood Indigo* groaned, shivered, and went racing west.

"Elke?"

"Ready." She sat poised over the copilot controls. "I've already entered the sequence. Say when."

The big Malacostracan ship showed as a fleck of light in the imaging sensor. It was moving faster, beyond the shoreline now and skimming along just a couple of hundred meters above the glittering surface. Beyond it, maybe five kilometers away, the line that separated sea and sky was starting to blur and deform into a fuzzy-edged disk.

"Link opening," Elke said in a shaky voice. "Sequence complete. Your action."

Chan accelerated, narrowing the distance between the *Mood Indigo* and the Malacostracan ship. Timing was the key. What happened if you tried to pass through a Link that was still forming, or beginning to close? No human or Stellar Group member had ever done such a thing. Or better say, no one had done it and survived to talk about it.

The disk ahead formed an exact semicircle on the

surface of the sea. The Malacostracan ship was racing toward its geometrical center. The *Mood Indigo* was close enough for Chan to make out pincer-like grapples on the tri-lobed hull.

"The ship behind is closing on us," Danny said in a neutral voice. "It's also changing profile. I don't like the look of it. I suggest that this might be a very good time to hurry."

"Completing transfer sequence," Chan said. Too soon? But he had no choice. And the Malacostracan ship ahead was arrowing into the glowing heart of the circle. At the moment of entry the Link flared and dissolved into fringes of multicolored light.

The *Mood Indigo* plunged forward into the swirl of the rainbow. Chan felt the first hint of a familiar but always-unfamiliar moment of nausea and vertigo. His body turned inside out, turned upside down, inverted to become its own mirror image.

The ship was beginning its Link transfer. Chan and his team were escaping their pursuers, departing Limbo, leaving this universe. And they would come out—where?

In the final moment, a new form of energy swept through the *Mood Indigo*. The control board in front of Chan went dark. The lights went out. *Blind and dead*, he thought. *We're dead and blind.* The crippled ship vanished into the multiverse.

37

Unfinished Business

Stars.

There were stars again, glittering hard-edged points of brilliance in a black sky.

They shone in through every port in their thousands. And nothing inside the *Mood Indigo* competed with their remote luminance; because every form of internal power, including lighting, had failed. The inside of a ship should never be silent. Now this one lacked even the purr of air circulators.

"It happened in the final split-second," Bony said. He was over at the main systems panel, flipping switches and examining displays. "Dead, dead, dead. Not a thing's working." He turned on the tiny lamp on his suit helmet. "No wonder, every level is down to zero. But we were lucky. The other ship hit us just as we were going into the Link. It sucked us dry, but it didn't have time to dump in resonant energy. A few seconds more and we'd have been blown apart."

"Can you do anything about it?" Chan was still adjusting to the idea that they were alive—not just alive, but in a universe showing familiar constellations. The Link exit point must be within a lightyear of Sol. Without any form of power, though, they could not signal for help. And without help their survival might not continue for long.

"Oh, I can fix it," Bony said. "We still have generator capacity, and lots of fuel. A few replacement parts here, a little bypass work there. I'll do lights and air first. Everything else will come back on-line in a few hours and we can tell people where we are. One thing about Friday Indigo, he bought only the best."

Bony spoke confidently, but Chan noticed a curious chill in his voice. He glanced around the cabin. It was hard to make out the faces behind the visors, but everyone was unnaturally quiet. They were not babbling like a group which had just escaped death by the narrowest of margins. Deb would not even look in his direction. Only Elke Siry was her usual self—and the Angel, of course, remained unreadable at the best of times.

"Are you feeling all right?" Chan said. "Was anyone hurt during the transition?"

Shaking heads. But still the coldness, and a long perplexing silence, until at last Tully O'Toole said, "*We* may all be feeling fine, but we left Chris and Tarb behind."

Danny Casement added at once, "Not just Chrissie and Tarbush, either. What about Dag Korin, and Vow-of-Silence, and Eager Seeker? I know they weren't members of our original team, but we shouldn't have deserted them to the Malacostracans."

"Not even Friday Indigo," Bony added. "I admit I hated him, because of the way he treated Liddy. And I know that the Angel says there's some sort of Mallie inside him, so he isn't human any more. But we shouldn't have left him with them. It was wrong."

"And if we had saved him from them," Liddy said, "maybe something could have been done to help him."

"That may well be so." Gressel spoke up unexpectedly. Unlike anyone else on board, the Angel sounded positively cheerful. "Most of Friday Indigo's original brain still exists. Possibly it can be restored to permit independent thought. To the extent, of course, that any human is capable of such. *You cannot make a silk purse out of a sow's ear.*"

Chan wished that Dag Korin were on board, to say *Or get sense from an overgrown artichoke*. Suddenly, he felt immensely weary. He leaned back in the control chair. "We didn't desert Chrissie and the Tarb, or Eager Seeker and Vow-of-Silence. We didn't even desert Friday Indigo. I mean, it looked like we did, but we really didn't. As for Dag Korin . . ."

"The General was on the Malacostracan ship," Deb said. "The one that entered the Link ahead of us. I know you wanted to be on it instead of him, Chan. But we *did* desert Tarbush and Chrissie. We left them behind on Limbo. You can't deny that."

"I don't. But I spoke to them before we left, and it's not the way it seems. As for Dag Korin, we didn't have much choice. The Mallies wanted to be taken through to *our* universe, and that was the last place we wanted them." Chan turned to Elke Siry. "You know the multiverse a lot better than I do. Would you explain that part of it, and I'll do the rest?"

"Well." Elke bit her lower lip and looked at Tully for support. He nodded encouragingly. "Well, I guess so. It starts because the multiverse exists on many different levels. We're back in our own original level now, and Limbo is in a different one. The levels differ in the total mass-energy associated with them. The way that I like to think of it, a higher total mass-energy corresponds to a higher *frequency* of that universe's spacetime, exactly the way that a higher frequency implies a higher energy in electromagnetic radiation. Higher frequency means a higher clock rate. So if you know the mass-energy of a level of the multiverse, you can use it to calculate rates for the passage of time."

"Elke," Tully said gently. "Time is passing right here, and you're not at all clear. I can't speak for the others but I have no idea what you're talking about."

"I do," said Bony. "Or I think I do. Elke, are you saying that a clock can run at a different rate in every multiverse?"

"Exactly." Elke nodded toward Chan. "He knew all this, which is why he asked me to do what I did."

"Which was to seek out the most extreme case she could find," Chan added. "I had given Elke a task: look for a level of the multiverse where the clock rate is *slowest*. She found one that she called the Omega level, a place where time runs two thousand times as slow as it does on Limbo. While one day passes in the Omega level of the multiverse, two thousand days—more than six years—go by on Limbo. And time on Limbo runs sixty times as slow again as it does in our own universe. Two months pass here, one day passes there. So when you put those two factors together, if you spend *one day* on the Omega level *three hundred and twenty-eight years* go by in our universe. It was my plan to take the Mallies to the Omega level"—he glanced at Deb—"but Dag Korin had other ideas. He went in my place."

Chan pulled a printed sheet from his pocket and illuminated it with his helmet lamp. "The General seems pretty upbeat about the whole thing. Here's what he wrote to us: *Benjamin Franklin is one of my heroes. He said he wished that he could be pickled in a barrel for a couple of hundred years so that he could see what the world was like when he came out. I feel the same way. And who knows? Maybe that's what I'll do. As soon as the Mallie ship emerges on the Omega level, I'll tell them that I made a minor miscalculation, and we have to go back to Limbo and try again. I don't think The One will kill me at that point—she will be relying on me. If they make the turnaround at once, say four hours Omega-time, and then they find a way to make an immediate jump through to our own universe—which they're not about to learn from me, you can be sure of that—you'll have fifty-plus years to get yourselves ready for their arrival, because time on Limbo runs sixty times as slow as it does on Earth, and the Omega level runs two thousand times slower than Limbo. I reckon that when they get there you should be able to organize a pretty strong welcoming party. But don't damage the Mallie ship too much, because I plan to be on it. Actually, I suspect that long before I get there, you will have—well, you know my philosophy. I'm going to leave the rest of the thought to you.*" Chan folded the letter. "The first time I met Dag Korin, he said that no matter what people tell you about old soldiers fading away, he didn't want to be like that. He'd rather go down in flames. He also explained to us, several times, his philosophy. Generals and admirals who are lightyears—or universes—away from the battle should not try to control the action. So he won't tell us what we have to do next. But he hints at it, with his comment that time on Limbo runs sixty times as slow as it does on Earth."

Deb said suddenly, "You *didn't* desert them. You knew we'd be going back. You *always* intended to go back."

"Of course." Chan could sense the tension lessening around the cabin. "Look at it this way. Chrissie and Tarbush have loads of supplies, enough for weeks. Eager Seeker is already living off the land, and Vow-of-Silence can survive for a long time without any food at all. Even if it takes three months to organize a rescue party, that's only a day and a half on Limbo."

"It will take less than three months," the Angel said. "How long, engineer, before this ship has the power to send a signal?"

It took a second for Bony to realize that the Angel must be talking to him. A real engineer at last! "Just a few more minutes. We're reaching a critical recharge point."

"Very good. When that happens, we will send our signal. And we will exert our authority, as an Angel of Sellora, to requisition at once another ship; a ship, this time, equipped for a submarine environment and with defenses against Malacostracan attack."

"Do you want to get back so quickly because you're worried about Eager Seeker and Vow-of-Silence?" Elke asked. More than anyone else in the cabin she seemed at ease with the Angel.

"Not at all. They are more than able to look after themselves. What interests us—and them—is the further exploration of the multiverse and the potential of anti-gravity; plus, of course, the vast excitement of adding another species to the roster of known intelligences."

"The bubble people?" Bony said.

"We were thinking more of the Malacostracans."

"But they're *monsters*," Bony protested. "Look what they did to Friday Indigo. And they blew our orbiters out of the sky without even waiting to find out what they were. And if we hadn't escaped into the Link, they'd have destroyed us, too."

"We see your point, of course, and we find it difficult to dispute." The Angel's synthesized voice managed a hint of sly satisfaction. "No such aggressive race should be allowed to mingle with civilized peoples. No one with a history of violence should be part of the community of intelligent beings. No race which has attacked another is worthy of consideration. Such a race should be kept in indefinite quarantine."

Chan cleared his throat. "Well, actually, speaking on behalf of all of us . . ."

"The issue of quarantine will be the subject of discussion on a different occasion. We will say, however, that your actions on Limbo prove to us that humans are acceptable and even necessary participants in many Stellar Group affairs. The question to be resolved now is the composition of the group returning to Limbo."

"Why, it will be *us*," Deb said. She glanced around at the others. "Won't it? We started as a team, we'll return as a team."

"There are those present who may question that assumption." The Angel turned, clumsily, so that its speech center pointed toward Chan Dalton. "We sense that you wish to offer thoughts on the subject."

Chan shook his head and did not speak.

"Chan?" Deb said.

Danny Casement added, "You're the one who brought us here. You organized the whole thing."

"I did." Chan looked not at Danny, but at Deb. "I dragged you here, but I think that was my mistake. I know we haven't deserted Chrissie and the others. Someone will go back for them. But I don't think we're qualified to do it."

"Of course we're qualified!" Danny looked shell-shocked. "We're the team, the original can-do kids. You always told us that."

"I know what I said. We're the team, the best there is. We're up to anything that the starways can throw at us." Chan stared around at the bewildered faces. "I believed all that myself. But just look at my miserable performance since we started. I brought you through the Link entry point without knowing where we were going. When we arrived, I didn't know where we were. We escaped to our own universe—but only because this ship happened to be available. We left our own ship and half of our party behind. We've been like a bunch of children, meddling in affairs too complex for us. And all the special skills, the ones that I thought made us a perfect mix, what did we do with them? Deb is a weapons master, and she didn't use any weapons"— Deb seemed ready to speak, then closed her mouth—"Chrissie couldn't find uses for her magic. Tully didn't talk to any aliens, nor did Tarbush. Danny was a wasted talent. The only one who had to do a good job was Bony, and that was because we messed up in every other way. As for me, I didn't do one thing right. So let me ask you, are we qualified to go back to Limbo? Are we qualified to go *anywhere*? Shouldn't we leave it to people who know what they are doing?"

Deb Bisson moved to Chan's side and took his hands in hers. She did not speak, and the reply, when it came, was from an unexpected source.

"Of course you are not qualified." The Angel's tone was chiding. "Faced with unknown dangers, no organism is *qualified*. It cannot assure its own survival, still less can it guarantee the rescue and safety of others. At most, an intelligent being can seek to minimize risks. However, your team is more qualified than anyone else. You performed vastly better than a team of Tinkers and Pipe-Rillas. Better, even, than an Angel of Sellora. And you did all this, *without ever resorting to violence*. We ask you—we implore you—to take your team again to Limbo."

As the Angel paused, a buzzer sounded through the cabin of the *Mood Indigo*.

"Critical recharge point, all systems," Bony said. "Nearly there. Wait for it."

The lights came on, dim at first but brightening. An air circulator gave its preliminary moan. The display screens came alive, and from the control audio a puzzled human voice said, "*Mood Indigo*? This is the Tortugas access node. Is that the *Mood Indigo*? We are receiving your signal and ship ID, but we show you as lost from the system a year ago."

"A year!" Liddy exclaimed. "A whole year?"

"Something we have to get used to," Chan said slowly. "With the multiverse, time is *really* relative." He turned to Gressel. "I hear your request. But there's another human expression I've never heard from any Angel: *Put your money where your mouth is*."

"We have no mouth. However, we are familiar with the saying."

"Then act on it. You beg us to return to Limbo. If we went, would you come with us?"

"Why, no. Certainly not."

"If we accept, *will* you come with us?"

"We? The Angel, Gressel? Why do you even suggest such a thing?"

"Because you are one reason for our survival. We need you. Even without a pooling of minds, a team of Stellar Group members is stronger than any individual species."

"But there is *danger* on Limbo. We avoid danger."

"So do we. For us, you are part of that avoidance. You speak of civilized peoples. Does a civilized being consider its own survival more important than the survival of other intelligent beings?'

"It should not."

"Then if we return to Limbo, will you come with us?"

Gressel gave a very human sigh. "For us to entertain such a suggestion should itself be unthinkable. *Look homeward, Angel*. We ought to return at once to Sellora. However, we suspect that human insanity may be contagious."

The Angel turned to Bony. "Allow us to use your communications system. *Where ignorance is bliss, 'tis folly to be wise*. We are ready to begin."

continued 

DAVID WEBER

<u>The Honor Harrington series:</u> *(cont.)*

Flag in Exile

Hounded into retirement and disgrace by political enemies, Honor Harrington has retreated to planet Grayson, where powerful men plot to reverse the changes she has brought to their world. And for their plans to succeed, Honor Harrington must die!

Honor Among Enemies

Offered a chance to end her exile and again command a ship, Honor Harrington must use a crew drawn from the dregs of the service to stop pirates who are plundering commerce. Her enemies have chosen the mission carefully, thinking that either she will stop the raiders or they will kill her . . . and either way, her enemies will win. . . .

In Enemy Hands

After being ambushed, Honor finds herself aboard an enemy cruiser, bound for her scheduled execution. But one lesson Honor has never learned is how to give up!

Echoes of Honor

"Brilliant! Brilliant! Brilliant!"—***Anne McCaffrey***

Ashes of Victory

Honor has escaped from the prison planet called Hell and returned to the Manticoran Alliance, to the heart of a furnace of new weapons, new strategies, new tactics, spies, diplomacy, and assassination.

continued